The cub looked at Tsia and growled. Tsia hesitated, then, like intensifying a light, she opened her biogate as wide as she could.

The senses of the cat swept into her mind. Immediately, her nostrils flared and her ears seemed to twitch. Her heart pounded far too fast in her chest. The hair on her neck rose up like a brush.

She did not know how long they stood there like that. Her entire being was focused in one place: the cougar's mind. When she finally shifted, the cougar did the same. His fur smoothed down across his back, and Tsia's shoulder muscles relaxed.

"Ruka." She whispered his name. The cougar growled in return. It was not a threat; she could feel his acceptance.

By Tara K. Harper
Published by Ballantine Books:

Tales of the Wolves:
WOLFWALKER
SHADOW LEADER
STORM RUNNER

CAT SCRATCH FEVER
CATARACT

LIGHTWING

CATARACT

Tara K. Harper

A Del Rey® Book

BALLANTINE BOOKS • NEW YORK

A Del Rey® Book
Published by Ballantine Books

Copyright © 1995 by Tara K. Harper

Library of Congress Catalog Card Number: 95-92016

ISBN 0-345-38052-5

Manufactured in the United States of America

First Edition: September 1995

10 9 8 7 6 5 4 3 2 1

This book is for my sister
Colleen Annice Harper
with the hope that she might someday call

Special thanks to Detective Bill Johnston, Portland Police Bureau; Mike Fleming and Special Agent John Colledge, U.S. Customs Service; and Deputy Kevin Harper, Clark County Sheriff's Department. Also, a special thanks to Pam Ore, Stephanie Hirsch, Dr. Jill Mellen, Ph.D., and Dr. Mitch Finnegan, D.V.M., of the Metro Washington Park Zoo; Dr. Darin Collins, D.V.M., of the Woodland Park Zoo; Phillip Peck; and Dr. Ernest V. Curto, Ph.D., University of Birmingham.

Blow, winds, and crack your cheeks! rage! blow!
You cataracts and hurricanoes, spout
Till you have drench'd our steeples, drown'd the cocks!
You sulphurous and thought-executing fires,
Vaunt-couriers to oak-cleaving thunderbolts,
Singe my white head! And thou, all-shaking thunder,
Strike flat the thick rotundity o' the world!
Crack nature's moulds, all germens spill at once
That make ingrateful man!

—SHAKESPEARE, *King Lear*

1

~~~~~~~~~~

Gray, whipping rain tore the skimmer out of the sky. The stabilizers jammed; the sail slats became immobile; the extended wing refused to respond. Savage winds shook the small craft, then batted it aside. In seconds, the skimmer swung about, then down, steeply down—a pale, speeding spearhead in the gloom of the gale.

Tsia forced her lungs to breathe against the acceleration, compelled her heart to pound in even rhythm. Drove her mind to ignore the pressure of her lips against her teeth and register instead the silence of the computer node that should have been sending its images to the tiny transceiver in her temple. As her dark blue eyes flicked forward, they caught the last projected images in the navigation holotank. She formed a mental command and projected it by thought to the node. There was no response. And while she watched, the holographic shapes in the navtank faded to emptiness as the flight commands abruptly halted.

In the pilot's seat, Nitpicker felt the ship go on auto as her own temple link went dead. With a muffled curse, the pilot watched the control screens fade and flash into manual patterns. The navtank had completely cleared; not even a ghost of a cloud remained in the imaging area. The storm vectors that had boiled through the tank were now nothing more than empty sky. The sea had become a nothingness. The shape of her ship was gone. New data—manual data—flickered across the flat piloting screens in patterns of light and color and text. And at the end of the sequence, the emergency-orbit commands flashed twice. Then they began to take control.

Nitpicker caught the warning with a curse; instantly, her fingers wrenched at the overrides. She did not look back at the other mercs in the skimmer's cabin. Her lips tightened; she hoped five of them were enough to control the sixth—the guide, Tsia, who sat among them.

Beside her, the copilot's voice sharpened as he reported the skimmer's status. "Safeties are coming on-line—starting to override my screens."

"What's your control factor?"

"What I've got, I'm losing. We're looking at an orbital vector within four minutes—"

"Stall them!" the woman snapped harshly. "If the safeties kick in completely, we'll be shot up and out like a sneeze." She glared at the screens and punched the controls. Up and out, she thought, and into the supposed safety of a preassigned orbit. She cursed under her breath and watched yet another screen rim itself with the purple shades of automatic control. Her fingers flicked faster, as if she could keep the violet hue from spreading like a virus to the next screen in line. "Zyas, but I hate that color."

"We're going to see a lot more of it," Estine retorted. "Either the node is hit big-time, or there's a pretty powerful someone who doesn't want us to reach that freepick stake down landside—" His voice broke off as the skimmer jerked, shuddered, and slewed as if it spun on ice, not air.

Behind the pilots, pressed back in her seat, Tsia's fingers were spread against the arms of her malleable chair. Her hands were not relaxed: tension kept her fingers so rigid she could not curl them into the fabric. To her left, Wren's weathered skin whitened while his hammerlike hands dug into the flexan soft as if it were mud, rather than the arm of a flexible chair.

Like Nitpicker, Wren did not look at Tsia—the acceleration toward orbit could hit any second, and he had no desire to have his eyeballs flattened against the sides of their sockets. He could see Tsia, the guide, out of the corners of his eyes.

Her face was tight and her hands clenched; her dark blue eyes were almost blank with suppressed fear. Behind her, and out of Wren's peripheral sight, Tucker's pale blue eyes were steady, and that merc's skin, naturally white, did not show tension any more than Doetzier's weathered tones. Both mercs deliberately relaxed in their seats. In the far back, Striker, her black eyes and brows set in a blank expression beneath her auburn hair, murmured to Ames, the brown-haired man beside her, while Ames stared at the ceiling and muttered to himself.

Six mercs; three pairs of softs. The flexible seats took up the center of the skimmer's cabin, so that only narrow aisles were left on either side. The inner walls of the ship were covered with drab webbing that held gear and weapons. To Wren's right, the hatch, its edges glowing with pale green-blue light, hung on the wall like an eye that dragged his gray gaze to it as insistently as a magnet.

Still diving, the skimmer pierced a storm front and slammed into the wind like a bug hitting a wall. Violently, Tsia and Wren jerked forward before the backs of their softs caught up with them.

"Tight ride," Wren said.

His voice was flat, almost expressionless—as usual, Tsia thought—though his narrow jaw clenched like hers against the pull of the dive. She hated his calm demeanor; hated the fear that grew in herself. And she forced her lips to stretch in the semblance of a smile. The motion drew the claw marks on her tanned cheek into white-taut, jagged scars; her short, brown hair swept back against her forehead. In her temple, the node's metal socket remained cold and blank, as dead as the com, which should have been receiving flight commands for the craft. The skimmer almost stalled midair, then fell faster.

Wren took in Tsia's whitened knuckles out of the corner of his eye. "Think they'll ever reseal the walls of this thing with some design other than drab?" he asked deliberately.

Tsia turned her head to stare at him.

He touched her arm, forcing her to swallow her fear with the contact of his skin. "Think they'll ever reseal?"

Unconsciously, she gazed around the small cabin. There

were no decorations, no paint or design to relieve the dull
shades that met her eyes. The gear webbing was made of iridescent cloth in the same bland, earth-tone shades as her trousers. The flexan softs, each one shaped to the merc who sat in
it, were drab and dirt-toned, as if they had been used too long
without cleaning. The flooring was mottled with burn marks
and patch-melts; the walls were pocked and old. The metaplas—all metal tang and plastic stuffiness—flexed and bent
with pressure and change, yet held its strength through impacts
that would have crushed a similar ship made of folded or
braced alloys and blends. There were a dozen stains from old
crash foam, and the slit windows were dark with that faint
opacity that comes from having their crystal lattices hit too
many times with a laze. Tsia's eyes darted from the thicker
chunks of repaired webbing to the two long, thin laser tracks
on the ceiling above her head. The craft was not four years out
of the shipyards, but it looked as old as war.

The laser tracks led her eyes forward to the empty navtank,
and then to the pilots' cubby. The skimmer's angle was still
steep, but the purple-edged screens had made streaked bands of
color across the front of the cabin. Fear, which grew as the
color spread, became a solid chunk in her mouth. She could
not stop herself from building another thought-image to project
to the node. But her temple link was still dead. She glanced at
Wren and forced her voice to steady. "Node's down," she said.

"Felt it," Wren replied shortly.

She shifted her weight, and just as the flexible soft caught
up with the change, the skimmer hesitated, tried to straighten,
bottomed out, then shot up like a searchlight. Tsia's body hung
forward for an instant, then slammed back. Blackness swam in
her eyes. Her slender fingers stretched out along the flight pad-
ding; she could not turn her head. In front, the merc pilot
jerked at dead controls.

Estine reported almost under his breath, "Safeties are on.
We're heading up."

"Time to orbit?" the pilot snapped.

"We'll be rounder in four minutes, fifteen seconds."

"Open the panels." Nitpicker's voice was low but sharp. "Get those safeties off-line."

Estine forced himself from his soft, bracing his feet against the seat while he groped inside the dash for the navigation cubes, which stretched in thin lines beyond his reach. His fingers fumbled along the edge of the honeycomb board in which the cubes were set.

"Can you reach them?" Nitpicker's voice was still low.

"I'm trying for the nav cubes—"

"The safeties," she snapped. "Not the nav cubes."

"There's a gale on," he snarled back. "You need the nav cubes if we're going to head back down—"

Nitpicker's dark hand struck Estine's shoulder and jerked him back. "I could fly this ship blind through a meteor shower. Now, get those goddam safeties out!"

Behind them, Wren glanced at Tsia's face. It was not the force of acceleration that stripped the color from her tanned and weathered skin; it was not the loss of the node that pushed her heartbeat into her temples. Her fear was growing into terror, and he could smell it on the quickness of her breath. He looked at her clawlike fingers, then back to her jawline. "All right?" he asked quietly.

She jerked a nod, but the edges of her face were white. Cabin pressure dropped, and Wren worked his jaw to pop his ears and sinuses. The skimmer was still on atmospheric settings, and full-seal pressurization was not in force. As the pressure sucked on her cheekbones, her fingers clutched the fabric of her soft like a lifeline. There was a crowd sound in the back of her mind that made Wren's voice seem like the buzz of a gnat next to the roar of a tiger.

Cats. Her mind latched on to that feline image. Pumas and watercats, sandcats and tams . . . Cougar voices growled in her head as their impressions leaked through the intangible mental biogate that opened her mind to theirs. She could hear those snarling feline tones as clearly as if the cats surrounded her in the ship, rather than huddled in the rain far below. She could sense their emotions in the mental yowls they returned in response to the fear she instinctively projected. The biogate expanded with that terror and her lack of control, and cat bodies seemed to leap inside her head. Cat nostrils flared; feline breath huffed in her face; fanged mouths hissed till she choked on the sounds.

"Wren?" Her voice was tight and high. "I can't go sky-side—"

The other merc fought the press of their climb with his hand until he eased the distance between their seats. He touched her arm. The muscles in his fingers were taut, and his clublike hand had a brutal look at odds with the lightness of that touch. He pressed her forearm with silent reassurance.

Up in the cockpit, Estine yanked the covers off a second and third panel, ignoring the clatter as the covers fell clumsily to the floor. Burying his arms in the datacube cavities, he groped for the touch-codes on the honeycomb boards. He muttered, cursed himself, then found his target. Instantly, his hands began to dart from spot to spot, disabling links and pulling cubes from their honeycombs. One honeycomb broke, and half a dozen cubes shot back through the cabin, tumbling till they fetched up against Wren's feet. They wedged there like tiny mice huddling into an overhang. Tsia stared at them as if they were a set of parasites. Safety cubes, she thought, huddled together for protection. She felt a hysterical urge to laugh. She clenched her jaw till the sounds began to choke her.

"Still climbing," Estine reported. "We're in the storm tunnel, still heading rounder."

"Zyas damn it!" Nitpicker cursed under her breath.

"We're queued with the *Phoenix* to fall in behind the *Remorse*. I can't find Jandon's craft. Could be hidden in the noise from the *Saabadhanni.*"

"That's the alien ship—"

"Probably took the node down themselves so they could get a techno-trade option on Risthmus," Estine said.

"They're desperate enough to try just about anything," she retorted.

The skimmer hit a violent updraft, and Tsia turned wide eyes toward Wren. His hand tightened on her arm. "Remember," he said quietly, as if he did not notice the tension in the muscles that jerked beneath his hand, "when you didn't know that going rounder meant going into orbit around a planet?"

She swallowed convulsively. "I can't. I can't go rounder—"

Wren increased the pressure of his hand. "Stay calm, Feather. Talk with me."

She choked out an animal sound. Feather. Her name in the mercenary dialect. A joke without humor for a name that had no power. She tried to control the fear that crawled into her head, but it grew like a balloon of gas that bubbled up in her lungs and burst out of her mouth. She clenched her fists so tightly that her fingernails cut into her palm, and a runnel of blood slid across her whitened flesh. Her jaw locked shut. The skimmer lurched. Tsia's heart moved up another inch in her throat. Its pounding choked off her air. The feet of the cats that paced in her mind clawed at the inside of her skull. Her breathing rate doubled. "Wren—"

He cast a warning glance over his shoulder. Behind him, one of the mercs, Doetzier, forced his weight forward until he got his hands on the back handles of Tsia's soft. Tucker glanced at the other merc, then forward at Tsia's trembling frame, then placed his hands in the same ready position as his partner. Fighting the acceleration, Wren leaned farther across to Tsia's seat till he could slide his hand down her arm. His thick fingers crushed hers. She barely noticed.

Up front, the pilot's voice was sharp. "Rounder height?"

"Two-sixteen kilometers at perigee," Estine returned. "Geosynchronous. Cabin will go to skyside conditions at twenty-eight kays. We're at ten kays now."

The craft bucked and tilted as Nitpicker fought the controls to change the angle of the skimmer's sail slats. "I'm going to lose this rise rate any time . . ."

"I've got half the safeties out," he snapped back. "I'm working on the others."

On the floor, the discarded datacubes skidded against Tsia's feet. She jerked. Wren's hand tightened.

"The quarantine scans," Nitpicker bit out. "At what height do we hit Q?"

"Three minutes after we reach skyside conditions. One-eighty-one kays up."

Tsia's breath caught in a partial whimper. A hundred eighty kays, and she would be in quarantine. Medscans and biofilters. The death of the virus in her body—of the biogate that filled her mind with cats . . . Her eyes turned toward the hatch in the side of the ship.

Wren's grip crushed her arm to the soft. "Don't even think about it," he breathed.

She did not see him. There was an animal fear in the depths of her eyes, and the sense of the mercs around her faded as the strength of the mental catspeak grew with the tension that filled her mind. "Wren—" Her voice was so tight it choked her.

"Nitpicker has spun wind for you before."

"I can't go skyside!" she choked out. "The viruses—"

He stared into her eyes. "I know. Van'ei knows. She won't take you rounder." He glanced forward. Half the physical changes that had made Tsia a guide were maintained only by a set of viruses in her body. If the ship went rounder—if it went through the med filters and the Q fields—those viruses would be stripped away like the leaves from a tree in winter. And all ships passed through quarantine before they went on- or offplanet. Every e-orbit, every standard or docking orbit, every trajectory that pointed out of the system—they all went through Q. It was the one thing permanent about any planet setup. No one wanted to risk another Vendetta.

Up front, Nitpicker heard the panic in Tsia's voice. The pilot's face was tense; her hands flashed like lightning on the controls as she tried to steal the conn back from the automatic settings.

Outside, the storm tore at the side vents locked in the emergency-rise position. "Status," she snapped at Estine.

He glanced across the screens that stared him in the face. "Sixteen kays," he returned shortly. "Still climbing." He broke the last relay in the links and moved to the next panel. "It's smoothing out—we've cleared the storm."

"I can *feel* that."

"You've got the manual conn?"

"I'm on standby—waiting for you to get those safeties off-line."

"I am *trying* . . ."

Tsia's attention was riveted to the feeling of pressure that filled her face, to the white skin that went whiter with each kilometer they rose.

"Height?" snapped Nitpicker.

"Forty-three kays. We're on auto for e-orbit."

Tsia whimpered. Her eyes were locked on the hatch. Wren glanced meaningfully at the mercs behind her. Tucker looked the question at Doetzier, and the older merc nodded. Both men gripped Tsia's shoulders. She flinched at their touch. Bioenergies seemed to hit her through her gate: one—hot and uncontrolled behind a wall of calculation; one cold and steady, spotted with points of light. Cat feet seemed to jerk across her mind with the interruption. Claws seemed to dig into her thoughts. She twisted her head and snarled at Tucker, then at the merc beside her. "Wren . . ." The sound that escaped from between her teeth was almost unrecognizable. Her air seemed trapped in her lungs.

"Eighty kays," reported the copilot. "Still heading rounder . . ."

"Stay calm," Wren snapped as Tsia began to struggle in earnest. "Stay down."

"I can't. I can't!"

He dug his fingers into her arm to hold her to the soft. With a surge of panic, she wrenched free of Doetzier and hit Wren to loosen his hold. The blow caught the gray-haired merc high on the cheek. His head rocked back, but he didn't flinch. "Feather!" he snapped. With an animal snarl, she kicked out of the seat, writhing and sliding down and away from Tucker's hands. Wren did not let go. "Doetzier!" he ground out. The taller, lean-bodied merc lunged around the soft and grabbed Tsia's arm, yanking her back as she struck out at Tucker. Her wrist and elbow twisted; she cried out. One hundred kays. Out of the biosphere, and queued for quarantine . . .

The cold computer link in her temple was forgotten; the loss of the node was no longer important. Only the biogate filled her head, and the frantic fear with which it blasted her thoughts churned her mind to a bestial mass. Pumas seemed to race through her memories. Golden eyes gleamed with the intensity of the hunt, while claws tore at her mind. Her brain was paralyzed with the crosstalk of cat images that did not translate into human thoughts. Her mouth could not make human sounds; her nostrils flared with the sharpness of the scents that seemed to clog them. Wren's mouth worked as if he were shouting in her face; she heard nothing but the growling in her gate.

Doetzier's hard knees dug into her thighs. Someone else sat on her elbow. A body seemed to crush down on her ribs, and another had her fingers twisted back against her wrist. She screamed, and the sound was still not human. There was a keening that did not stop; and the man's voice that rose above it was distant and thick like a thunderhead on a dark horizon. Cougars and tams, watercats and jaguars snarled and hissed in her head. The distance between the ship and the world drew their voices together like an angry, indistinct crowd, and the cat feet that raced from side to side in her skull felt like stilettos stabbing her thoughts.

The skimmer jerked, bucked, and beat its way up through the thinning atmosphere, and Tsia and the mercs who held her slid forward as a group on the floor, then slammed awkwardly back against the base of the softs. Suddenly, the skimmer shot up faster. Far below, the boiling storm was little more than a rumpled stain on the sky.

"One-forty kays," Nitpicker snapped. Her hands were on the panels, her legs braced against her seat. "We hit Q in ten seconds."

The ship shook violently. Estine staggered back, then lunged forward, almost diving into the cavities. "Almost . . ." he told himself, his chin jammed up against the dash. "Almost . . . Got it." He yanked the last honeycomb of safety cubes and threw the panel behind him. Abruptly, the skimmer straightened out. Manual nav commands kicked in; thrusters and sail slats responded. For an instant, the small craft hung in space. Then its nose pressed sharply down. They dove. Back into a blackened, rain-swollen sky. Screaming through the gale like a long, steel whistle headed for the surface of the sea.

Color-edged red spots darkened Tsia's sight. Her eyes widened. The keening in her ears was still constant, but voices began to cut through, slicing through the wail.

"Feather, for god's sake, stop it!" Was it Wren?

"Be quiet!"

Another voice. Another tone. "It's over. We're going down."

"We're going landside. Landside . . ."

Up front, the two pilots fought the controls, shifting the shape of the skimmer's slats to counter the downward dive. Jammed against the arm of the soft by the force of the dive, Doetzier cursed to himself. Wren, sprawled across Tsia's hip and ribs, felt his knees bruise as his bony joints pressed hard against the floor. Beneath the thick fingers that crushed her arms, Tsia's white flesh turned slowly brown, then blue-black and purple as blood vessels broke with the pressure.

"Status?" Nitpicker's voice cut across the din.

"Ninety kays, and dropping, but the sensor taps went out with the node. I can't pick up a goddam thing."

"Clear the windows. We'll go in on visual till we pick up the merc satellite."

"The mersat went down with the main node—there won't be anything off those lines either."

"Mersats broadcast through different relays," she snapped back. "Unless someone knocked out the repeaters, we'll catch the backup lines in a few seconds." She wrenched at the sail-flap controls. "Get a position in the tank. And shut up that guide!" she yelled over her shoulder.

"Feather," Wren said. "Look at me. Listen. We're going down. Landside. Not skyside." She jerked beneath his grip. "Down," he repeated. His voice was cold and sharp, like the mental tang of his biofield. In the hot fear that filled Tsia's mind, she shivered with the touch of that emotionless energy. But the chill of his voice seemed to freeze and snap off the edges of her tension. "Feel the cabin pressure." Like a scalpel, his words cut through her panic. "The proximity of the sea—feel it. Use your gate, goddam it!"

Slowly, warily like a cat, she subsided, still tense as a wire beneath the weight of the mercs. His eyes narrowed at her wariness, and his voice sharpened. "Ease off, Feather. We're going down. Think through your gate . . . Yes, that's it. Ease off." The ship plunged toward the black sky-tunnel of the storm, and Wren relaxed his grip as he felt her tension lessen. Doetzier began to shift. Instantly, she wrenched free of their strength. Doetzier's lean fingers reclenched; Wren's clublike hand tightened so hard that her nerves screamed. Her eyes went wide, and her head was jerked against the floor. "Feather—" Wren's voice was calm and cold. "Listen to my voice. Ease off now. We're going down."

Tsia stared at him, still wild-eyed with the panic that seemed to sweat from her pores. Doetzier moved a fraction, and she bared her teeth. Wren shook her again, this time with less force: her head rocked only halfheartedly to the side. "Feel your biogate, Feather. We're going down. Down to the sea." His voice washed over her ears like water. "Landside," he repeated. "You aren't going rounder. None of us are going rounder. We're at forty kays and still going down . . ."

Some sense of his words filtered through her panicked mind. Some of the wildness left her eyes. The claws that seemed to tear at her skull merely pierced, then retracted through the biogate. The sense of the cougars that hissed and snarled was dulled by the sound of his voice. The keening in her ears grew faint and turned to a whimper.

Wren nodded. His cold gray eyes bored into hers. "Listen to your gate," he said. "Feel the life in the sea. We're closer now, and you can feel it. Landside . . ."

"Wren?" Her voice was hoarse.

He nodded. "Say it again. My name."

"Get off me."

"Not yet."

She jerked, and the mercs tightened their grip again. "I'm okay," she snarled. "Let me up."

His gaze narrowed. The panic was still there in her eyes, but it was receding, and the fury and shame that replaced it was growing. He loosened his hands. In an instant, she wrenched free and flung herself to her feet against the bulkhead wall. Tucker tensed, but Doetzier snapped in a low voice, "Let her be." Tucker halted midstep.

For a moment, Tsia crouched against the wall like a cornered cat. The pulse in her throat was visible, like a drumbeat on a soft, leather drum. She glared at Tucker. Wren eyed her for a moment, then casually returned to his seat. After an almost imperceptible hesitation, Doetzier, then Tucker followed suit. Tsia stared at them till she shivered with the force of her tension. Then, slowly, she edged back to her chair.

Gingerly, she sat down. She refused to look at Wren: the paleness of her cheeks was offset by a patch of dull color that crept in and made her jaw tighten even more. Wren said nothing. Behind them, Doetzier ran his hand through his black hair and murmured something to Tucker, but Tsia did not hear it—humiliation had deafened her ears to their words. She forced herself to lean back, but could not relax. As the skimmer shuddered again, she shivered. The ship's skin seemed to groan, as if it were racked with pain from the force with which the rain struck its hull.

In the back, Striker leaned forward to Tucker. "So," she said quietly, "what were you saying about the freepicks at the mining site?"

Tucker's blue gaze flicked toward Tsia, then he turned to the auburn-haired woman. He shrugged as if to himself, and gave Striker a wry grin. "You know how obsessed you are with the history of the Fetal Wars? One of the freepicks you took contract for is a descendant of the leader of a lifer gang . . ."

Tsia sat stiffly in her soft. Did her cheeks burn, she asked herself bitterly, or were they just colored with the heat of humiliation? She gritted her teeth, then forced them to relax. She didn't notice that her hands rubbed nervously at her wrists. When Wren touched her arm again, she flinched, but did not shake him off.

"Nitpicker has spun wind for you before," he said, his voice so low that only she could hear.

"I know that," she returned shortly.

"Then you should have known she would do it again."

Wren regarded her silently. Her eyes glinted less, he noted; her pulse, though still visible, throbbed more slowly in her throat. The flesh beneath his fingers was more steady to his touch. As the ship shuddered again, then bumped violently, her gaze darted involuntarily from the holotank to the hatch.

"You would never have made it," he said quietly.

"I've jumped before."

"That was a dare, and you were only a hundred meters from the sea. And," he added, "you didn't have me to go through."

She forced her lips to stretch. "Is that a challenge?"

He didn't smile in return. "Not when the sea's in full bloom. Even if you survived, Van'ei would be sure to kill *me*."

Up front, Nitpicker's hands flicked across the panels in near-instinctive sequences while she felt—rather than saw in the screens—the skimmer respond to the winds. Her green eyes were unfocused with the memories that rose with Wren's words: A merc skimmer that darted between blackjack ships and a Shield. A parbeam cannon that seared its way through the nose and side of her skimmer. And the ship shooting up through the smoking sky while Tsia, trapped in the wreckage with Wren and Sullage and Twit, tore herself free only to see the altitude meter climb toward Q.

"Lucky," Nitpicker muttered darkly. "Too damn lucky for me."

Estine glanced across. The silence of the temple link echoed in his head and drew his forehead into a frown. "Feather?" he asked in a low voice.

She nodded.

"A guide in the merc guild is a guide without a gate," he returned. "She knows the risks."

"Uh-huh." Nitpicker's voice was quiet. "The more she flies with us, the more it's just a matter of time before she loses her gate to Q." Or to the guides who hunted her down. Nitpicker did not say the words, but they were there in the woman's mind. Nitpicker had been a licensed merc for one hundred and thirty-two years. Fifty-one planets she had defended or scouted or abandoned on a last-out run. Over a hundred battles with blackjack—half of them onplanet. And fifty-six guides she had worked with. Of those fifty-six, only a dozen still had their biogates. The others . . . The pilot's thin lips tightened imperceptibly. Twenty-one had lost their gates when the guide guild stripped away their biolinks—it was the punishment for working outside the guide guild, when the guild could come up with a charge that would stick. Only four guides had been killed by blackjack. The other nineteen had lost their gates to quarantine, as Tsia had again almost done.

The skimmer bumped and jerked as it hit the turbulence of the upper clouds, and Nitpicker adjusted the sail slats almost automatically. She glanced back and read the tension that lined Tsia's jaw, then the purple-rimmed screens of the dash. Time, she thought, worked against a guide more than blackjack ever did.

2

Beneath the skimmer, far out in the ocean, thickened, gray-black storm clouds churned. Warm air rose ten thousand meters in bare seconds, and the cold air fell like shock waves, densely, smashing into the water and heightening the swells in the ocean. Beneath the thunderhead, the fallen air flowed out along the sea like water that spills from a bucket and ripples across a table. The wind grabbed and bunched up the ocean, birthing new swells. And as the flowing air gave birth to the waves, the cold, dropping air heightened the waves more with each convective current. Sent them speeding out after the storms. Sent them following the fronts across the sea until the waves reached the coast. Pushed the waves to follow the wind that tore at the ocean's surface. And slammed them up against the legs of Ocean Eight, where they made the station pilings shiver like saplings. There, ten kays from the shore, they became the swells that lifted the bloom of the jellies to the surface, where the white pumping bodies shredded the storm's debris and dragged it back down to the depths.

Above the churning clouds, the skimmer hung in a black, predawn sky. The edge of the horizon was an orange-blue, and the stars were still thick overhead. Inside the ship, Tsia stared forward, toward the gray-black windows where Estine's fingers tapped continuously on the manual com and Nitpicker worked the controls.

"Anything yet on the node?" the gray-haired pilot asked.

16

Estine did not glance over. "Nothing, but I've just about tagged a thread of a node line, so I can throw some kind of co-ordinates in the navtank."

"Position?"

"Guessing two thousand kays NNE of the marine station. We've got two storm systems to move through—not counting the one sitting over the station platform. Thirty, maybe forty minutes of flight."

"What about the emergency-satellites?"

"Nothing. E-sats are still down. But if I remember right, the first storm is an isolated boil: force seven and fading. The other is a storm-force ten and picking up."

Nitpicker nodded. "The one we'll be landing in is almost that, and projected to build to a full force twelve by nightfall."

"Zyas, Van'ei, you're not still thinking of landing on the platform?"

"Why not?"

"The node isn't giving us spit. You'll be taking this ship down in a force-nine wind—"

Her sharp, green eyes glinted. "Force ten by the time we land."

Estine shook his head and tapped faster on the manual comm.

Nitpicker glanced at the screens between them. "Should be picking up an e-broadcast from the main sats any second."

"Catching the e-sat now. I'll shunt it to your conn."

"Locking in and—" her fingers slid across a panel "—hitting cruising alt now."

The skimmer leveled out of its dive, and Tsia became briefly weightless as the flexible seat no longer pressed against her spine. For an instant, she felt light-headed; then her sight cleared. Absently, she rubbed her forearms, then stretched them in a catlike motion. Her teeth bared in a silent hiss at the sudden rebellion of her bruised muscles.

"Sore?" Wren asked.

"I have your fingerprints up and down both arms," she said tightly. "There's a knee print in my ribs."

"Would you rather be a flat spot on the surface of the sea?"

"Better the sea than the sky."

"But the true view of Risthmus can only be had from space," he teased ungently.

"My sister might like looking down on the world"—a haunted shadow flickered in the depths of her eyes—"but I'd rather be on—not above—any planet."

"You shouldn't have worried. Nitpicker can fly patterns tighter than the weave of Kirillian silk." He glanced at the gray-streaked windows. The first storm system had whipped away the slight lightening of the dawn as neatly as if it were dusk. Cloud-water washed the windows in a continuous rain. They could see neither land nor sea, just the gray-black gloom of the gale. "Zyas," he muttered, "this is like flying through a lake." He shifted in his seat and leaned his head back.

Tsia raised her eyebrows. Deliberately, she looked around at the drab inner walls of the cabin. She rolled her neck to release some of her tension, then forced her hands to unclench. "It's still a better view than this." She gestured faintly at the beam-burned inner hull.

Wren's lips stretched. With his thin, hooked nose and sharp face, he looked like a raptor perched uncomfortably in a chair. "Only a guide would think that. These metaplas walls have been between you and a laze more than once, and you think a black sky is a sweeter picture? You haven't seen the world clearly since you got your biogate."

The skimmer lurched as it cut through the front line of the first storm system, and the ship's slender shape seemed to bend like a straw before it steadied again. Tsia's hands tightened on the arm of her soft. Her eyes flicked again toward the hatch.

Wren shot her a warning look. "It's just the wind. We're out of the system already."

"I know that," she returned, too sharply. Convection currents and pressure tunnels . . . Nitpicker knew this wing like she knew the hair on her head—the thought repeated in Tsia's head like a prayer.

As if to challenge that thought, the ship dipped sickeningly until the tension in Tsia's body tightened with a snap. Beside her, Wren reached across and stroked her forearm with hard pressure so that her muscles trembled with the strain of being taut. He glanced at the white line of her jaw. Her eyes were still glinting with the remnants of her fear, and he could see the strength of her biogate in the blankness of her gaze. "Remember two years ago?" he asked quietly, his voice still for her ears only. "Nitpicker took you through a storm in a half-powered stinger. And before that, she did a remote-pilot for you when you rode the hook up for the Timbal Point job, and the skyhook car malfunctioned—didn't break off for its glide when it should have. You were heading rounder that time, too." He stoked his hand down over her fingers so that she was forced to relax her clawlike clutch of the seat. "She's a good pilot, Feather. One of the best. You know that. She once set down for you on a rock half the size of her ship, and even she said that the cliff had been so washed with downdrafts, you should have landed *in* the rocks, not on them."

"It was two-thirds the size of the skimmer." Tsia forced the words out as if they would choke her. "Van'ei exaggerates."

Wren felt the tremble that shivered through her arm and tightened his grip again. This time, Tsia shook him off.

"And there was the time five years back, north of Demon Bay," he added, as if she had not removed his hand. "Safeties kicked in when we were hit by that parbeam cannon. 'Picker tore the dash apart to get the conn back before she sent you rounder. Had to do it alone, too. Copilot was no help at all."

Tsia glanced forward involuntarily. "You blamed him for that? He was dead as a stump in a bog."

Wren shrugged. "Everyone has some sort of excuse."

In spite of herself, she laughed—a short sound that burst from her throat more in tension than humor. "Van'ei took us down all right. She dumped us in the offshore shallows right in the midst of a pod of mating nessies. I smelled like watersnake for a week."

"Forrest did not seem to care," Wren said slyly. "Not when he saw you landside and safe."

The skin around her mouth was still too tight, and she had to force her jaw to work. "Forrest was . . . relieved to see me," she admitted.

The smoothness of the skimmer's flight was interrupted by an abrupt rise, then a fall, then a series of shudders. In Tsia's mind, the whine of the skimmer's motors translated into a soft yowl. Unconsciously, she projected the sound through her biogate. The catspeak in the back of her head sharpened until the hairs on the back of her neck bristled. She forced her pulse to slow until it no longer deafened her thoughts, and the feline din subsided. The sensation of wind in her—their—fur became the stroking of Wren's hand on her arm. Like a lantern that moved to a distance, the mental voices of the cats no longer blinded her; instead, they merely filled the corners of her mind with a dull and rumbling purr.

Forrest heard this same type of noise in his head, she thought—not that of the cats, but the energies of the world, echoed into his mind from his own biogate. Wren, who sat beside her, knew her only through time. But Forrest—he understood the wildness of her heart. Her lips stretched in a faint, bitter smile. What Wren called intimacy, she described as the recognition of each one in the other. What Wren called love, she named their need to touch each other through their biogates. Love? Perhaps. But if it was, it would not be she who admitted it.

Wren followed her gaze to the slender hands that rubbed absently at her wrists. Her fingers were lean and strong and without ornament, except for a thin scar that ran across the back of one hand, and some faint puncture marks on the other. The wrists she rubbed were medium-boned and taut with long-used muscles. Forrest had held those wrists, Wren thought. Forrest had shared not just her biogate but her body, and that for almost ten years. It was an interesting match. Wren had not thought her able, with her wildness, to be *heyita* so long with one man. He smiled to himself. Somehow, the word for "bedmate" in the merc tongue seemed more honest than it did in any other. "Too bad," he said slyly, "that Forrest didn't take the same contract you did. You'll miss him out at Broken Tree."

"You sure it's not you who'll miss me at the Hollows?" she retorted.

Wren merely widened his smile. "You and he touch as if you've been bonded for decades."

She glanced down at her hands, and only then realized that she was rubbing her wrists. Abruptly, she stilled her fingers. Her lips thinned to a stubborn, set line. "We are not making the bond."

"Don't see why not," he returned. "You and he are *ava*, after all. You've shared together your intimacies—perhaps even what you call your love. It is not as if you are merely *avya*— bound by loyalty or need."

"Like us?" she retorted.

He shrugged. "I am your *shok saadaa bhai*—your brother in sadness; your brother in grief."

"Brother? Hah. I took the guide virus ten years ago, Wren. I think differently now—I feel differently from you. And if you look at the guide-guild registers, we're not even the same species anymore. You can hardly call yourself my family."

"You think the mutations from those viruses left you closer to your sister than to me?"

His words struck her like a fist, and her lips tightened to a thin line.

Wren noted her expression and lowered his voice still further. "You love Forrest like an *ava*, but you won't make the bond. And why? Because of a sister you haven't seen in six years. Because of a woman who abandoned you for the docking hammers in space. You throw away the chance of a bond because you waste your love on the ragged ideal of a family that doesn't exist." His gray eyes sparked with cold light. "When will you figure it out, Feather? When will you learn to let go?"

"When I'm dead," she muttered.

"You've been dead before, Feather, and it changed nothing. Of course, that was when you were *heyta*," he admitted softly, using the merc word for "slave." He nodded at the hands that still nervously rubbed at her wrists, as if she could still feel the chains that had once hung from her flesh. "But you weren't dead only to the node, but to your guild. Now you're dead to your sister, too, but this is by her choice." He eyed her closed expression. "Hell, Feather, the guild guides are closer to you than your sister is—and at least the guides give you a feeling of danger. Your sister gives you nothing. You'd do better to keep your eyes open to your present, and forget about your past."

Her lips tightened. The guides were a constant fear, but old; her sister was still sharp in her mind. Every time she smelled a certain flower, she thought of her sister's perfume. Every time she unpacked a crate, she almost sensed Shjams's hands on the customs labels. She swallowed the memories and forced herself to give Wren a deliberate shrug. "The guides are more in my past than my sister is—and I've been dead to the guide guild for ten years. It's not as if they still actively search for me."

"It takes only one sloppy trace, Feather, and you know it." His voice was sharp and harsh in spite of its low tone. "One loose line in the node, one image that isn't crystal-sharp and silk-tight, one public node ID from anyone—including a search trace sent to your sister—and the guides would glom on to your ID like a slug on a Risthmus rhubarb. They'd strip your biogate away as fast as they could get a skimmer skyside—with you strapped inside. You'd be a naught—a guide without a gate. Or worse: a wipe." He stared at her face as if his cold, gray gaze alone could pound the words into her head. "So don't give me that garbage about hanging on to family, Feather. It's family that will kill you dead. Not ghost-dead—not just cut off from the node or controlled by someone else. I mean blood-dead—*ragat ka'eo*. Dead like a corpse in a hundred-year grave."

She glanced warningly toward the other mercs, but Wren did not shift his piercing gaze. The tiny lines that sprayed out from her eyes . . . the scars that reached from temple line to jaw . . . they were cat marks. Claw marks—the sign of her biogate. She reveled in that mental link—she couldn't hide that from him. She talked without fear, as if she rejected the threat of the guide guild, but she could not keep the dread from her eyes. The biogate was her life. Without it, she had no future, no life she wished to live. Even now, the felines were close in her mind, thick with the catspeak that clung to her thoughts like a shroud. As for his own voice, she heard him only as a sharpness among the growling din that seeped in through her biogate. He pressed his fingers against her slender, toughened hands as if he could somehow feel the wildness that pulsed within. As if he could put his fingers on her life force—or as though the stubborn hope she still held for her future was something tangible—so that by reaching for her, he could touch what he himself had mislaid.

Absently, he rubbed at his own thick wrists. The sleeves of his blunter hid the white rings that marked his own flesh, but the thirty-four years he had spent in the mines were still as sharp and clear in his mind as if they were his present. What was that saying she had told him? Once a ghost, never unspirited . . . His eyes flicked to the other mercs in the cabin. He and Feather—they were the lucky ones. Most ghosts were erased from the node so completely that they had no chance again of ever imaging a command, even on an open line. Or they were wiped, so that they had no memories or personality of their own. Some survived on the grayscale—as slaves, or worse. Some became blackjack. And some, like Tsia and himself, killed to regain their freedom and so crossed the border of the law. They lived without the illegal protection of blackjack and outside the sanction of the Shields.

He stared at Tsia's tanned, scarred face. They were much alike, he thought. Caught between the Shields and blackjack by the threat of their pasts. Caught between the law and the lawless . . . They hung like paper shapes on a string, suspended between two fires. They twisted eternally, trying to escape the flames of their histories, while the wind that breathed its hope between them tore at their flimsy holds.

He glanced at his brutal, meaty hands, then at her lean and weathered fingers, still digging through the soft. So similar, he thought. So very much alike. He almost smiled.

Some shift in his biofield caught at Tsia's attention, and she glanced up. For a long moment, their eyes met in silent understanding. Then the skimmer lurched, and the pilot cursed, and Tsia turned away.

The ship pierced the second storm system like a gravdiver in a low-gee tube with a high-gee boost behind him. The short-range view of the skimmer, fed only by the ship's sensors, flared up in the holotank and boiled with ghostly colored streams and coils. Instantly, the skimmer dropped, twisted, and spiked back up before Nitpicker got it under control. Tsia's knuckles whitened against the drab shades of the soft.

"Dammit, Estine," Nitpicker said sharply. "Keep everything under thirty kph out of the tank. I can't read that kind of garbage."

"I'm trying," he returned in a low voice.

"What do you mean, 'trying'?" Nitpicker's voice was as low as his.

The tightness with which they spoke did not escape Tsia, and she leaned forward unconsciously, as if she would be able to see from her seat what they stared at on their panels.

Estine hesitated. "It's as if there's a node line coming in from somewhere else," he said slowly. "A line that's force-feeding us information. I can't keep all of it out of the navtank."

The pilot's voice was suddenly chillingly intense. "You think someone's tapped the ship?"

Tsia's biogate-heightened senses brought the pilot's voice clearly to her ears, and she eyed the holotank more sharply. In front, the copilot's brow furrowed as he tried to image a command through his own silent temple link. "I've got nothing on my link," he returned. "There's no trace of a line in the ship's sensors."

"If blackjack's behind the node going down—or if they're blocking our links, our sensors could be caught up in the same web of traces that's swamping the navtank with garbage."

"You can find nothing, yourself?"

"Nothing." Nitpicker's hands flashed across the panels almost in time to his. Slowly, the holotank cleared until only the major ribbons of wind flowed through. As she tried to match the feel of the ship to her body with the view she saw in the navtank, Nitpicker frowned. "Nothing," she repeated, more to herself than to him. "But if there was a trace line tagging our sensors and feeding us a ghost web of data, it's either gone now, or so deep in the datacubes that it would take a line-runner a week to find it."

Estine glanced over his shoulder. "The guide's a terrain artist, isn't she? Put her to tracing it out."

Nitpicker did not bother to follow his glance. "A terrain artist 'paints' images into the node to hide our movements from the node's sensors. She doesn't have to be good at finding false images. Or at filtering through the false scans of a ghost web." She watched the holotank from the corner of her eye as she adjusted the skimmer's yaw. She hesitated, and Tsia could almost feel the tension that grew in the set of the pilot's shoulders, as if a sudden thought had just bitten at her mind. "No," Nitpicker said quietly. "If there's a ghost web hidden in these trace lines, don't trust it to Feather to find."

The old saying rose in Tsia's head: *Once a guide, twice untrusted* ... As if the virus that made her a guide had stolen half her human self and left her less than a beast.

"I heard she was as good a line-runner as you are."

"Better," the pilot admitted, her voice still low. "She can run a ghost line as tight as a deep-pressure nail. But she's only half as good at tracing and breaking someone else's web as she is at building her own. Better to put Kurvan on it when he joins us on the platform."

"Kurvan—the line-runner from Demyan?"

She nodded.

The skimmer lurched, and Tsia's stomach tightened. "Wren"—she forced his name out from between stiff lips—"I thought Kurvan was working the Noose."

"The Shield ring around the Gwaeth system?" The gray-eyed merc gave her a sharp look. "Not for the last year. He's been signed onto this contract for six months—ever since it came open. Said no line-runner worth his credit passed up a chance to code a set of biochips."

The skimmer slammed sideways, then dropped sickeningly before Nitpicker caught it in the wind. Tsia's lips bared as if she would snarl. "He might as well stay skyside now," she said, forcing the words out. "If the node doesn't come back up, he'll have game days for his entire contract. And as high as his tech rating is, the freepicks won't have to pay a tenth of his bill."

"It's a short contract—only a month to set up the security webs for the freepicks to receive the chips. Node can't stay down the whole time."

"Why not? Blackjack could be behind it, just waiting for the biochips to come within reach."

He shrugged. "Kurvan's one of the best line-runners in the business. If there's a problem from blackjack, he'll find it—no matter who's running the ghosts."

Tsia opened her mouth to respond, but she stilled instead. Her temple link seemed to sputter in her head. "Wren—" she said sharply.

Up front, the ghost images of the navtank thickened, darkened, and expanded rapidly into faint gray clouds; the holographic sky suddenly hung like boiling smoke. The slim, silver shape of the skimmer sharpened until it sped cleanly through the storm fronts. In the lower edge of the tank, gray images of ocean swelled and moved. And in one corner, a yellow glow showed their objective: the marine station ten kays from the coast.

A faint mental image sounded a tone in the back of Tsia's mind. It was a standby tone, created by a biochemical signal. But it triggered a trained memory. She keyed into the line of thought that flowed out of the memory. Instantly, an image spun out from her mind and into the temple link. The node read her signal. In response, a hundred biochemical sequences flashed back. Random memories were triggered in flashes so fast she could not follow them to make sense of their order. "Wren, the node—"

"Felt it." Wren's eyes were already closed in concentration.

From up front, Nitpicker called out, "I've got chatter on the lines."

"Reading it," Doetzier returned from behind Tsia. Tucker had broken off his argument with the woman in the back, and now murmured almost nonstop to Doetzier. She glanced over her shoulder, and the younger man broke off; Doetzier caught her attention instead. "How clean are your images?" he asked her.

"Clean," she said slowly, "but I can't find Jandon's ship. Shouldn't he be skimming in behind us?"

"That's what Nitpicker said when she picked me up on the docking hammer. He left orbit an hour behind us, and we stopped for most of that to pick you up in the north. He should have been on our tail by now."

She turned to Wren. "Can you read anything on your link?"

He shook his head slightly. "Images are too confused. What have you got?"

"The node IDs for the other skimmers are listed skyside. E-orbits are locked. They're folding into Q in standard order." She cursed her shiver silently as she stated the quarantine order. "But I still don't find his skimmer."

Wren shrugged. "If he's not up there, he overrode his safeties, like us. We'll see him down on the platform."

A wave of wind smashed the small craft sideways. The skimmer straightened, dropped again, and leveled out. "If he overrode his safeties," she returned, "he'll be trying to land on manual, like us."

Wren gave her a sly look. "What do you want to bet that he hits the drink first, not the deck?"

"That's not much of a bet, Wren. Nitpicker has four decades' experience on Jandon."

The ship bucked violently as it dove into the second storm front, and Nitpicker cursed in a steady stream of profanities that mixed human and alien speech together. Tsia closed her ears and tried to concentrate. She couldn't quite catch the images from the node. Thin—they were like ghosts blown through a wispy fog—and almost too sharp to remain in her memory. It was as if they had no substance, but were perfectly defined.

"Signals are too damn faint," Wren muttered.

Faint, yes, but clear—he should have been able to see them at least as well as she did. She glanced over her shoulder again. Doetzier caught her look and shrugged, but there was something speculative in his expression, and Tsia felt a shiver

crawl down her spine. She turned back in her seat and absently
tapped the tiny metal socket in her temple. She could almost
feel the heat of the images that passed through its circuitry.
The sensation seemed to wash across her brain, and unconsciously, she opened her biogate to soak it up and project it
onto the distant cats on the shore. Instantly, the force of the feline voices strengthened. It was like a draft that seeped from
under a loose-fitting door, then turned into a blast when the
door suddenly opened. Her lips bared, as if she wanted to hiss,
and her fingers dug into the flexan fabric of her soft. She concentrated. Seconds, minutes passed before the thick shadows of
the mercs' bioenergies obscured the catspeak around her and
the cold tang of Wren's biofield was strong again in her mind.

Now, faintly, she could feel all of the mercs in the skimmer:
Nitpicker, with the tension still set in her shoulders, was a
strong, steady light—a quiet energy—like a deep pond, cold,
but without the glacial chill that Wren projected so clearly.
Estine was a fuzzy brilliance that sharpened and faded like a
pulsar. Doetzier, behind her, seemed speckled with light, while
Tucker radiated a knifelike heat that she thought of as anticipation. And in the back, Striker relaxed in her soft as if she
lounged in a dreambar, so that she felt to Tsia's biogate like a
wide, shallow pool of energy that sat like water on sand. The
last merc, Ames, projected almost nothing. Like Wren, he had
built the walls around himself so thickly that he admitted almost nothing he felt to himself, let alone to anyone else.

From behind, Doetzier spoke up again. "The e-lines—
medlines and the like—are up again."

"Nothing more though," Wren returned. "Node lines are thin
as a Sirian on slimchims."

Tsia said nothing. She had opened her biogate too wide, and
now the roar of the felines grew in the back of her mind so
that it drowned out the sense of the mercs. The closer the ship
flew, the stronger became the sense of the life-forms to which
her biogate was linked. The scent of musk and blood and
earth . . . The feel of fur beneath her fingers . . . She shook herself and looked up to see Wren regarding her with wariness.
She shrugged.

He grinned, and his mouth looked like a beak in his sharp face. He glanced at the stubborn set of her jaw, then down at her slender hands. There was strength in her hands, in the will that drove them to act. But it meant little compared to the strength of the gate. Closer to land, and the sense of the cats became a crawling feeling in her skull. Her nostrils flared as if she could smell more sharply with their influence. Wren pressed against her arm to catch her attention, and she looked at him with difficulty. She forced her eyes to focus so that his image no longer blurred.

Striker opened a packet of black nolo seeds and popped one in her mouth so she could suck on its shell. A moment later, she spat a seed like a bullet into one of the hisser bins and listened with satisfaction to it dissolve. Doetzier glanced at the thin smoke trail that wafted out of the decomposition bin. The deke scent made Tsia's nose wrinkle. She tried to breathe out to force the odor from her lungs as her imaged commands spun out to the node and hung in its emptiness like balloons.

"Still nothing but e-lines," she murmured to Wren. "I've tried all three standard sets: maps, IDs, and library codes, but nothing comes back."

He did not bother to nod. "I'm not reading anything from the standard node. Just partials from the mersat. No overlays. No trace lines. Nothing."

The skimmer lurched its way into the third storm system like a toddler learning to walk, and Tsia asked tightly, "How long before we land?"

"Ten minutes. Maybe more. Relax," he said sharply. "Think about something else. Or start an argument with Striker—that's what Tucker always does."

Tsia glanced over her shoulder. The black-eyed woman in the back had her mouth full of nolo seeds, but was already agitated enough to talk around them. ". . . look at history," she was saying flatly. "The lifers who cried 'murder' over abortion were the same ones who sanctioned genocide and war in the overpopulated countries."

Tucker grinned. "Bet you can't believe you're going to have to defend one here."

She grimaced. "Even this long after the war, it's like agreeing with their policies."

"You should have checked the freepick rosters before you signed your ID dot." Tucker ducked the seed she threw at his head.

Striker gave him a disgusted look. "Did you know that the lifers didn't even adopt out the children that they 'saved'? They wanted the luxury of being moral without the responsibility of their stance." She spat another seed into the hisser bin. "That freepick is probably as rigid-minded as her ancestor."

"There are a few generations between them. She might have learned tolerance somewhere."

"If she did, it wasn't handed down from her great-grandmother. I can't stand people who condemn others to a life they don't themselves have the guts to lead." She almost glared at Tucker. "Ayara's eyes, do you realize that the lifers forced girls as young as twelve years old to have babies, but refused to support those teenage mothers with training, education, or family skills? With clothing or baby food or homes?" She chewed a seed vehemently, and Tsia could smell the sharp scent of it all the way up front. "The sponsors, now," added Striker. "They were the movement the lifers should have been."

"Sponsors didn't last long, Striker."

The other woman shrugged. "It costs money to support and educate another family. It takes time to allow them to change. And it takes tolerance and wisdom to allow them to find their own way. Lifers gave mothers none of those things . . ."

"How long now?" Tsia asked Wren.

"Five minutes," Wren said, then added, "Zyas, Feather, I said go pick on Striker, not me. You can see as well as I where we are in the holotank."

She shrugged an apology and studied the navtank before them. Although its images were sharp, the navtank showed only a bare outline of the ship and the sea that surged below it. Tsia squinted at the platform that was beginning to take shape in the imaging area. It was ghostly gray, and she frowned. It should have been purple-white—thick and sturdy—

and shiny with the rain of the storm. Instead, it looked like a spider squatting on top of the water. The skimmer hung like a gnat above the station, and the sky boiled overhead.

Nitpicker started to image a command to the node link to split the tank's images, then cursed under her breath and repeated the command on the manual controls. One side of the navtank zoomed in to the ship and the station. The other side remained scaled in its primary images. Watching them both, the woman banked the skimmer into the wind till the projected image pointed directly at the marine installation. The sail slats responded; the skimmer's ride smoothed out.

The skimmer lurched its way into the third storm system like a toddler learning to walk. The ship dropped lower; the shuddering became a more constant rhythm. In the holotank, the two shapes of craft and platform converged. The ship swung wide, and the waves of wind through which it moved created a series of groans in its metaplas skin. Tsia tried to close her mind to the sound; her sensitive ears cringed at each whimper of metaplas pain.

On the floor, the loose datacubes rolled awkwardly. First one, then another hit the side of her foot, rattled across to Wren's boot, then skidded back with each shift of the skimmer. At the third tumbling roll, Tsia stretched down and scooped them up, then flipped up the arm of her soft to drop them into the blank slots within. She started at the fingers that dug suddenly into her wrist.

"Don't." Wren's voice was soft, but something in his tone made her freeze. "A safety will override a manual from any location in a ship." He gestured at the open slots. "All ships are still on e-orbits. You put those cubes in there, and they will send us back up like a shot."

Slowly, he released her arm. Tsia turned her hand and opened her palm to stare at the tiny cubes. She looked up at his narrow face, then back down. "I didn't know."

Wren sat back and closed his eyes again. "If you spent more time traveling by skimmer, you would."

She hesitated, glanced forward, then stuffed them in her

pocket. "I'm a guide, Wren. My place is on the land, not above it."

He shrugged. "Not what I would have guessed from the way you hang on to your past. You spend more time thinking about those docking hammers than any guide I know."

"Daya, Wren, my sister's up there," she returned in a low voice.

"On Orpheus? Eurydice? You don't even know which hammer she works on now. Customs won't tell you—they keep their inspectors protected. Your sister is your past," he said harshly. "Your future is your freedom from that."

Anger sparked in Tsia's eyes. "Freedom is like a memory," she retorted. "Once lost, twice gone."

"You can't lose what you've never truly had."

"Which? My freedom or my future?"

He turned to face her, and his cold, gray eyes seemed to bore into hers like screws that turned through to her heart. "Does it make a difference?"

She stared at him for a long moment. "No," she said slowly. She sat back, and her mind was chilled and locked in a circle of thought so old and worn that even the bitterness had faded to a faint taste on her tongue. She knew what he meant. She had traded her future for her biogate, then her freedom for her future. Now she had neither freedom nor future, and only the biogate was left. Only the voices of the cats in her skull to remind her of the life she once had. Ten years . . . Ten long and distant years. In her mind, the subtle snarling of the cougars overrode the growling of the feline tams; the distant purr of the sandcats in the dunes was drowned out by the watercats in the sloughs. Only her memories of family were separate from the growling through her gate. It was the only part of her mind still untouched by the sound of the cats. The only part where she still had hope. Stupid hope, she told herself harshly. Hope that had no place in the crime of her existence.

"No," she said softly, but Wren heard all the same. "It makes no difference at all."

From the pilot's seat, Nitpicker steadied the skimmer into

the storm. "Get soft," she called sharply. "We're starting the first pass."

"First?" queried Tucker.

"We're on manual," the pilot snapped back. "With the wind shear, there's no way I can drop us on the deck the first time across."

The skimmer bumped up in a sickening rise, then dove like a stone in a well; it tilted, then surged forward hard. Tsia's fingers dug into the arm of her soft.

Wren glanced at the tightness of her jaw. He opened his mouth to speak, but Tucker leaned forward and asked, "Feather, can you feel the bloom from here? The jellies in the sea?"

Tsia made an irritated noise as the skimmer banked sharply left. "Daya, Tucker, I thought you were bugging Striker, not me."

Wren grinned coldly at her expression. "You've got nothing better to do."

She snorted.

"*And* you're on contract."

She gave him a dark look. "Give me a minute," she said shortly to Tucker. She stretched her thoughts through her biogate. Instantly, catspeak filled her mind. Soft clawed feet seemed to pad across her brain; the murmur of the mental growls was like an orchestra tuning itself in the background. She concentrated until she found, behind the din—like a low swamp fog—the energies of the other beasts. Large shadows became distinct in her mind—those were the schools of fish that clouded the surge of the ocean below. A flicker of light was a nessie who writhed through the sea. But the weight of the pumping, surging hunger that hung like stirred-up silt in the sea—that was the bloom of jellies that rose to and dove from the storm-tossed surface. "I can feel them," she returned shortly.

Tucker watched her curiously, ignoring the lurch of the skimmer and gripping the back of her soft to keep his balance against the turbulence. "I once flew with a guide who couldn't feel anything that wasn't right under his fingers. We're a hundred meters above the sea. How can you"—his voice hiccupped as the skimmer rose again abruptly—"feel a bloom of jellies this far up?"

She shrugged. "They're strong. Just past peak, but heavy—very heavy—in the water."

Wren did not glance back. "A guide whose virus resonates to a tree species can feel an entire forest through the leaves and roots. Why shouldn't she feel the jellies from here?" The ship jerked to the side and swept in a hard turn up against the wind. The skin on Wren's sharp face almost sagged back from his chin with the acceleration.

Tucker fought the pressure to lean forward. His sweet-bitter breath over her shoulder made Tsia flinch. "I meant," he persisted, "how can you tell the jellies from anything else in the water?"

"Practice," she returned shortly. "I've been at it for a while."

"At your age, I would hope so," he retorted ungently. "What I'm asking is—"

"You know what they say about guides, Tucker?" she interrupted. She twisted in her seat until she could stretch her fingers out to his arm like a set of claws. "You can't trust a guide—we're too bestial—too caught up in our links with the world."

His skin seemed to crawl with the chill touch.

"When a guide is threatened—or irritated," she said softly, "she can strike like an animal. Tear the flesh from the bones like a cat gutting a mouse to get at its liver." She stroked her fingernails down the younger merc's forearm, and her eyes glinted at the goose bumps that rose in their wake. Beside Tsia, Wren choked a sound into a cough as she kicked him under their softs. "I've been known to do that myself, Tucker," she said absently. "Tear the flesh from the bones . . ." When she abruptly clenched the merc's arm, the young man jumped. She hissed like a cat. He jerked his arm away. With her teeth bared, she gave him a caricature of a smile.

"Quit the horseplay," Nitpicker called sharply over her

shoulder. "And get soft with the rest of us. We're hitting the deck in ten seconds."

Tsia barely had time to set her weight back in the seat before the faint image of the ship in the navtank struggled above the tiny platform. It shuddered violently, hung for an instant, then slammed down with a gust of wind. Nitpicker jerked the small craft back up before it crumpled against the decks. The wind sheared off, then beat back brutally. Tsia's jaws smacked together; her hands clenched the arm of her soft. The craft smashed down and skidded across the surface as the wind grabbed on to its hull. Crash pads snapped out from the seats. The scent of metaplas filled Tsia's nostrils. She gagged at the smell and flinched from the soft support that encircled her legs and torso. Acceleration pressed her forward while the small ship shuddered and scraped across the deck. Someone was cursing—she could feel the anger echoing in her mind and almost hear the words through the foam that enclosed her head. The ship turned broadside to the wind, then spun in reverse. Landing gear shrieked. Then they slammed against the brake bars of the station like a brick.

3

Metaplas molecules clogged Tsia's breath as if she were suffocating in the porous foam. Stretched forward to the apex of its safety curve, the crash foam began to condense until it pressed her back into the soft. Seconds later, she jerked her limbs free almost before the pads released her, and the sound that escaped her throat was more snarl than curse.

"Cabin coupling," Estine reported from the front.

"Storm locks descending," Nitpicker said, her voice overlapping his.

"We've got some stability against the brake bars, but I can't get a linkup."

"You won't—platform power is off. We'll have to secure the ship manually."

"Manually?"

"You've got a better idea?" she retorted.

He didn't answer, but he set his screens and unstrapped himself from his soft while the shuddering of the skimmer subsided and the motor fields began to fade.

"Wait for Feather's scan," Nitpicker ordered sharply. Estine merely grunted in reply as he moved to the hatch.

While Wren pushed his own way through the suddenly crowded cabin, Tsia snagged her blunter jacket from its webbing, slid it on, grabbed her handscanner, and jammed it into her harness. Then she slipped through the shifting bodies like a cat untouched by the grass through which it moved.

Estine had both hands on the skimmer walls, to feel for skimmer movement, when Tsia and Wren joined him. The co-pilot glanced at her uncovered head. She shrugged. She didn't need her hood to protect her from the storm—she sought the violence of that contact willingly. The bioshield she wore in her blunter and the stealth fabric from which the jacket was made would hide her heartbeat and body temperature from any standard scannet.

She glanced at Estine and received his go-ahead. She nodded shortly and expanded her biogate to feel for the energy that might be waiting outside. Humans had technology to fool the searching beams of a scannet, but they still couldn't keep their energies from the biogate of a guide.

Without hesitation, she swung back the door and let the wind in like a shout. With it came a thin blast of rain like needles. Wren staggered with the force of it and clutched the hood of his own blunter. Behind him, Striker cursed at the cold. Tsia grinned. She turned her face to the storm before jumping out and licked the rain that stung her lips. When she struck the deck, her boots hit and slid on the slick surface, but her body landed solidly in a half-crouch, while Wren skidded to one knee behind her.

"Show-off," he shouted in the din created by the crash of storm and ocean. His words were stripped away in the wind.

"You'd balance, too," she returned over the wind, leaning close to his ear, "if you had ten years' experience in this."

He glanced back. "Your ID makes them think you've got thirty, so make this scan look good." He pointed toward the line of construction huts that lined one edge of the decks. "We've got five minutes for the initial sweep. As soon as we're done, you're on your own for the detail scan. And don't forget the generators. Nitpicker wants to get the skimmer's power charged off the station as soon as possible."

She nodded and judged the wind that stung her skin; it whipped her eyes till they burned with silent tears. The drab shades of her blunter were almost lost in the false dark that the storm gave grudgingly to the dawn, and the dark iridescent shades of her thin, earth-tone trousers flattened and rippled against her skin like silk. The blunt stick-shape of her flexor slapped against her thigh, and the tiny bumps from the safety cubes showed like rocks in her pocket. She took her hand scanner from her harness and eyed the skimmer's position, but the ship was held securely against the brake bars by the wind that had only moments before forced it to the deck. Estine could wait: the ship would not slide farther before her scans were done.

The primary deck, like that on all platforms, was flat and fairly square, with one half set aside for a landing pad. Along the south side were clusters of construction huts and biochemical vats. Eight thick platform legs supported the outside edges of the structure. Four center legs supported the deck's middle. Beneath the deck, around those center legs, and growing out toward the edge of the marine station, masses of sponge were being trained and shaped into rooms and halls and labs.

The construction huts squatted next to the chemical vats like a line of bloated toads. After a quick look, Tsia turned in to the wind to examine them. With each breath, her teeth tingled from the air that screamed across and scoured her mouth. Like an animal, she bared her canines to its force, then bent her body against the gusts that beat her down. This was what she loved best. Being the first one out. The first to feel the wildness of the atmosphere—to judge the strength of the storm. Blind mercs, she thought with wild abandonment. Sightless as birds in a cave. Never feeling the strength of the world around them. Never seeing the energies that filled each creature on Risthmus. She tilted her face back to the rushing, gray-black sky. This was the purpose of her gate, she thought—to give her the life she no longer had herself.

She ran in a staggering crouch to the middle of the deck. Slick, the platform's surface stole her footing. Violently, the wind tore at her clothes. The thin weathercloth of her trousers repelled the rain, but the thicker blunter did nothing to stop the chill moisture from sliding down her neck. She dropped to balance herself with her hands against the deck and squinted against the sheets of gray.

Wren huddled beside her, tucking his wiry body into her

wind shadow. He waited without speaking, his eyes on his own handscanner while Tsia opened her biogate and sought life through her mind. Something about Tucker's last questions bothered her, and she stretched till she could feel the bloom in the sea. Had he really wanted to know about the jellies? Or had he wanted to know about her? He'd felt almost hungry to her biogate—like the bloom in the sea, she acknowledged. She glanced toward the rim where the energies of the jellies were strong compared to the sponges that colored the edges of her mind. Beside her, Wren was the only merc she could feel without stretching: a cold, steady tang, heavy with hidden power. His basic human resonance matched the others in the skimmer, but nothing else on the deck.

The rain subsided to a lighter, stinging wash until it became a series of sheets that slanted across the deck. Placing her lips next to Wren's ear, she said, "It's clear. Nothing but biologicals."

And the cats that clog your brain. She almost felt his thought ring in her head. She stared at him for a moment, while the wind rattled her body like tin. His cold gray eyes seemed to see right through her. Deep in her head, as if they were beside her, the distant tamcats rumbled. Along the storm-slapped beaches, sandcats crouched beneath the stones and waited to fish with the tides. But there were cougars closer, on the sea, and she shuddered with the surge of catspeak that dulled the back of her brain.

"You're reading something," Wren said flatly.

She nodded slowly. "There are cats on the kelp rafts—the floating islands—the brash close by in the currents. They're migrating to the mainland for winter."

"Cats?"

"Sargies—sea cougars."

He followed her gaze to the sea. "They close enough to cloud your gate?"

"There's nothing here but us, Wren."

He motioned sharply for her to go on, and she jerked a nod, closing herself off from the sharp mental snarling that came from the sargies. Ahead, she eyed the line of construction huts along one edge of the deck. There was no sense of movement within the huts—no sense of life—and she forced herself past them in a staggering run toward the edge of the purple-white platform.

The mass of marine sponges that formed the station's base were still soft with mucus and new growth at the edge. She could smell the turpentinic scent of the mucus as clearly as if she stood on its mushy flooring. She did not look behind her; she knew that Wren would follow.

The wind blasted, then gusted so suddenly that she was blown against a deck bar before she caught her balance. Wren shouted something, and she turned, but the wind stripped away his words.

She stared at him through the rain. He radiated power, yet no matter how close he came, his biofield remained dim compared to the sharpness of the cats'. The sargies, the sandcats on the shore—they engulfed her thoughts. They—not just the shame of her crime—were why she had not gone back to the guides. She had given away her past, she thought, and had taken Wren and the mercs as her future. There was only one reality left in her existence: the biogate that seethed in her mind. The link with the cats that pushed and pulled and filled her skull with pawprints. She raised her fists to her head and clenched them at her temples. She could not squeeze the cats from her mind—no more than she could squeeze meaning from her past. To lose this . . . Her fingers tightened into a fist. Wren thought it was her biogate that ate at her brain like a hungry demon, but he was wrong. It was fear—the terror of losing this link.

Wren moved closer beside her, and instinctively she moved away to let her senses stretch out to the sea. She could feel the seabirds huddled beneath the station in the unfinished chambers of sponge. She could feel the flaccid, blue-white jellies rising and diving below. The main deck was almost forty meters above the ocean's surface, but the sea, which moved with hidden hunger, stormed up along the outside legs and sprayed itself over the deck until the salt crystallized along the eaves of the huts and vats like winter icicles.

"Anything?" Wren shouted.

"Nothing," she returned.

"Sure?"

"Eight years ago, I wouldn't have been able to tell the jellies from the birds. Give me enough time now, and I can stand forty meters from the platform edge and feel the jellies bloom. You're even more distinct." She gestured with her arms. "There's nothing here but you and me, and the rest of them back in the ship."

" 'A guide's gate grows with every lick of flame,' " he quoted. "Or in this case—rain." He wiped the water from his brows in a futile gesture.

She grinned at him. "I can taste you like this ocean," she shouted. "Like seaweed on my lips."

"Then be thankful I don't sweat like Kurvan."

Tsia half turned to look back at the skimmer, and the wind twisted her violently. Wren fell back a step as she hit him, steadied her with his huge, clublike hands, then bent forward again to brace himself.

"Check the edge," he shouted, "just to make sure." He squinted toward the water, then stiffened. Tsia felt it, too. Her temple link went active. Not just the e-lines, but the full set of node traces were up. Automatically, she sent a mental request for map overlay, and it flashed back in her head in an instant. The coastline, the platform, the color codes used by the guides for the waterways and sloughs . . . Instantly, she checked the node by locking into one of her standby webs—having been locked out of the node before, she was not about to limit herself to a single set of trace lines.

The false images of her extra trace held. Within seconds, she used those extra, unregistered lines to move farther out in the node. Like tracking a line of references, she followed the command images from one set to another. She called in other lines of ghosts she had created long ago. The false ID of a man on a city pedpath . . . An economist in a red-brown office . . . She checked the overlay for the marine station through the IDs of the ghosts, rather than her own licensed merc line, and it took her a moment to realize what was wrong with the web of images she saw. The deck was clearly shown in her mind, but the ship and the mercs were not. In fact, when she looked for the mercs through the false-eyes of the node ghosts, she couldn't find the skimmer anywhere near the platform. She started to touch Wren's arm for his attention, but the lines went blank, flickered back, and went down again like the dark.

Wren shrugged. "If this is anything like the problems we had on Chaos, it'll be hours before it's steady." He took the handscanner from her weapons harness. "I'll scan," he said over the wind. "You stay on your biogate."

She hesitated, then nodded. Ever since they started building the second docking hammer, the node had been unstable. The construction guilds had not yet melded the two systems together.

Wren pointed to the platform edge, and she acknowledged his gesture. As soon as the wind lapsed, she sprinted across the deck until the flooring beneath her feet became purple-white and spongy. To the right, a narrow catwalk—a thin layer of dark metaplas over the lighter airsponge growth—led out to the edge of the deck. The hardener that made up the deck's surface was still thin and resilient here. It bent and sprang back from her weight and the gusting of the wind like a sheet of thin wood. Rocking back and forth, she tested her weight on the sponge. The platform shuddered beneath her feet.

Wren glanced down. He could swear he saw the sea surge in the holes between the sponges. "Bet you won't go all the way to the edge," he shouted.

The glints in her eyes were sharp. "Is that a dare?"

His thin lips stretched in a ghostly grin. In the gloom, his beaked nose gave him the look of a buzzard. He didn't answer, and her own grin widened. She hadn't needed the challenge. She would have run like a cat on a branch just to see what was floating below.

She pushed out into the wind till she poised on the end of the catwalk, one hand gripping the narrow pipe that served as a guide for materials lifted to the deck. She stared down in fascination, aware only at an unconscious level that Wren was moving back to the ship. Below, the brutal surge slammed against the thin lift until it trembled in her hand. The intertidal sponges grew like violet shadows, crowding together and absorbing the light with their pigments, the same way they absorbed the hardeners they were fed. Like the trunk of a laceleaf maple, they grew thicker the more stress from the waves they received.

She tested the deck with the tip of her boot. The metaplas solution was not yet fully incorporated into the sponge and algae skeletons, and the marine animals had not yet anchored themselves together like solid rock instead of sticky pasta. Under the main platform and above the waterline, there would be chambers and shafts—rooms for labs and halls. Each would be sealed first with a layer of coralline algae, and then sputtered with thin metaplas.

In the intertidal growth, there would be sturdier shafts for the pipe lifts that carried workers and materials up and down. There would be flood chambers where the ocean would be allowed to filter through and create aquariums and drain rooms for research and aquafarming. There would be windows, where some gaps would be filled with filter fields, and others with clear, solid sheets of flexan. And the whole structure would be alive. A platform that breathed the sea and expelled it, that rinsed itself in the ocean's nutrients, gathering strength and growing out and up. Tsia wrinkled her nose. She could taste in the air the thick mucus that coated the sponge skins. Like black turpentine or oil, it did not wash off, but oozed down the sides of the structure. It muted the force of the wind and the sharp nutrient particles that were shot into the porous growth by the waves. Gingerly, Tsia knelt and ran her fingers across the tacky substance on the edge of the catwalk.

"What is that?"

It was not Wren's voice that struck her ears. Startled, she half spun, the wind carrying her the rest of the way around to a half-kneeling stance. Doetzier's tall, lean frame swayed like a reed as the gust hit him, and Tsia, hiding a surge of irritation, looked up at him and opened her gate to taste the strength of his biofield. The sense of him was subtle, with specks of energy at odds with the sense of his general field.

Doetzier pointed at the flooring where Tsia was still crouched, then motioned again at her splotch-stained hands. "What is that stuff?"

"Mucus," she returned shortly. Rain ran down her chin, and she gestured at the flooring before wiping her face. "Touch it."

He stooped and slid one finger gingerly across the soft floor, then twisted his finger to examine the thick, oily splotch. "Natural or engineered?"

"Natural—or it was on old Earth," she corrected. "The sponge platforms here are Gea projects—genetic engineering and analysis. This mucus is enhanced through microbiology."

The lean man gestured back at the massive, battened-down vats. "Those vats—are they for the hardeners?"

"One or two contain metaplas," she explained. "The others are mixers and growth containers."

"Nutrients?"

She shook her head. "More like a three-in-one protection."

"Explain," he ordered.

His voice was curt and commanding, and Tsia hid her expression before Doetzier looked up again. When he did, only the glint in her eyes betrayed her flash of anger. If he wanted to take the time later, he could link up to the library and image down the data for himself. He had a high enough tech rating to access what he wanted. Why distract her with his questions instead? She fingered the mucus on her skin. Her sister had always done that—asked for information instead of getting it herself. Shjams had hated the manual links to the node. Once she was old enough to have her own temple link, Shjams had refused to use anything else, even when the node was down.

Tsia studied the hollows in the other merc's cheeks, made darker by his wet, black hair. The dark circles under his steady brown eyes were smudges in the predawn gloom. She could smell the tension in his body, even though he seemed relaxed to her gaze. He had not been this abrupt the last time they had worked together.

"Do you not know?" he queried sharply.

A slow smile crossed her face. "Tell me your full name," she challenged, "and I'll tell you about the mucus."

"What kind of deal is that?" he asked, startled.

"I heard someone call you 'Ghobhoza' once. I want to know more."

"Why?"

"What's the harm in a name?"

"Maybe none, maybe some. It's not your business to know." He eyed her with a glint in his eyes. "Besides, who are you to bargain? It's in your contract to explain about the mucus—or any other life-form."

"Coward," she teased.

He grinned slowly. "Give me your name, and I'll give you mine."

She eyed him for a moment, then shrugged deliberately and pointed to a lighter splotch on the deck. "The sponges exude a special type of diffusible molecule," she explained flatly. "The mucus doesn't bind—it doesn't form a skin, like the way molecules of pudding make starch on their surface. Instead, each of the diffusible molecules spreads out in solution—like salt dissolving in water. Enough chemicals spread across the surface of a sponge to allow it to recognize another of the same species when they touch."

"Like an ID dot?"

"Sort of. Once a sponge realizes that the animal next to it is another, similar sponge, the two animals bond. Their membranes merge. Their collagen fibrils and spongin fibers mix. That's when the algae grows into the holes between them. The algae, like the sponge, makes a calcite bond that can be hardened further with metaplas. The result is like welding two pieces of metal. But it's a living bond—one that can repair itself if broken and strengthen itself if stressed or fatigued."

He nodded. "Go on."

"You understand that sponges breathe? That they take in nutrients through the water as we take oxygen in from the air?" He nodded, and she pointed to a thin spot in the deck. Tiny spines stuck out like corkscrews where the mineral skeleton was still growing. "The tubes by which they breathe in and out form along the spine. They're helixes. Very flexible. When the sponges grow together, the entire structure is almost eighty times stronger than each would be by itself."

He looked surprised, and she pointed back at the flight deck. In this stage of construction, the lower and upper decks of the platform were the most fragile. Where the skimmer sat, anchored now to the platform, the deck actually seemed to bend. "A sponge by itself is strong—depending on the species— compared to a coral, but it would never carry the stress of a structure this big. And we have to use more than thirty varieties of sponge and twenty-two algaes to build above the tide line. This deck has another two years to go before it is completely strengthened. Then it will have to be sealed."

The rain slashed in a sheet across the deck, and Doetzier waited till it passed before he asked, "The recognition molecules, they are the protection you spoke of?"

"Part of it. The mucus kills surrounding sea growth on contact. There's hardly a single type of coral, worm, barnacle, or weed that can live in the ring around the platform."

"A death ring," he said, more to himself than to her.

She fingered the deck slowly so that the sticky fluid rubbed into her soft skin, leaving it darkly stained. "It took six decades to develop," she explained. "Two more to adapt the process to the other colony worlds. As of last year, we've sold the biocodes for this sponge to forty-one colony worlds and six alien races."

"How do you know so much about the development history?"

She gave him a wry look. "My father worked those contracts. By the time I was six, I could identify the sponge mucus from ten different worlds, model the spicule structures from two dozen colonies, and build three-meter beach castles out of the leftovers he brought home. By the time I was eight, I'd been poisoned twice by fumes—once by taste-testing the mucus on a dare, and once from smoke, when my sister and I burned one of our castles in a siege against our brothers." Her lips twisted bitterly as she mentioned her sister, and as Doetzier looked back up, she turned away.

Doetzier carefully wiped his finger off on his trousers and

glanced down at the roiling sea. "For all its toxicity," he said over the wind, "it seems to do a lot better repelling the fish than the jellies."

Tsia pointed, took a slash of wind right in the face, and shook her head to clear her sight. "Look a little closer. The jellies bloom up and are carried toward the platform by the currents, but they never quite touch."

He peered as she pointed. "Don't expect me to see that kind of resolution in this gloom. I don't have cat eyes like you."

She grinned, not knowing what she looked like. Doetzier had not been out in the storm for long, and his head was protected by his blunter. Tsia's short brown hair, exposed to the wind and spray, was whitened and flaring like a mane about her head. With each blast of seawater, more salt crusted in the strands and formed tiny, thickening crystals as the splashed water evaporated in the fierce wind. Her short hair, stiffened and standing up, gave her the look of an albino lion. Her eyebrows were solid crystals that dragged down to her eyes. Her eyelashes themselves were white. When she grinned, her white teeth looked like fangs in her face. "You could always put in your darkeyes. The rain is dying down."

"And the wind is rising up." The lean man got to his feet, letting a strong gust help him. "Salt-scratched eyes are not my idea of a good time. Those contacts start degrading as soon as the seamites eat into their filters, and you can bet this wind is full of creatures like that. I'll use my darkeyes when we reach the land. Not before." He nodded to her, then retreated to the shelter of the huts. A brief flash of light marked his entrance to one of the structures; then the decks were dark again.

Absently, Tsia raised her mucus-stained hand to her nose and sniffed the solventlike scent. She wished she could touch Doetzier's flesh and draw his scent into her lungs, as well. His tension was something she wanted to taste. His biofield, with those points of light, was something she wanted to suck into her brain and examine. It was like an addiction—her need to touch and smell each thing around her. Odors, heightened by her gate, became exquisite perfumes, which she had to rub on her face or hands. It was a hedonistic compensation, she thought, for the shame that came with her link to the cats. Some sort of primitive reward for the political obligation of her gate.

Spray burst over the deck and coursed across her face. The grit in the water felt like ash from a fire, and Tsia rubbed it on her skin. The virus that sustained her biogate caused the oils of a guide's skin to alter. Only heat—the firepit, the burning of free wood, or an open flame—would trigger the chemical changes that cleansed her body and promoted new oils to her skin. There would be no fire here, she knew. The mucus she touched was flammable, and the chemical heat from a fire with that substance was more than any guide could survive. Low-heat wood fires, cloth, and coals—those were the fire foods in which a guide could dance.

She ignored the cold kiss of the sky and stared down at the sea. In spite of the power with which it smashed the platform walls, the sea was not cresting with wind-stripped cascades of water. Instead, it was swollen with massive, foam-streaked waves. The jellies were like oil on the water, subduing the sea and sating the hunger of the wind. Only where the water crashed against the platform and found the wind shadow against its walls did it blast up and off the storm-flattened surface.

Like worms in the sand, the jellies seemed called to the surface by the thin, slashing rain. The jellies—some a hand-span, some two meters across—dragged their thin, yellow-white, blue-white tendrils beneath their nebulous, pumping bodies. They surfaced where their rippling edges could flare at the air; then they dove back to the depths, dragging their steel-strong tendrils with them. They churned. They drove the undersea to a boil. Rising, rolling, diving . . . The loose debris of the storm was caught in the twining tendrils and sucked down as they submerged.

Wren touched her arm, and she looked up absently, some part of her having felt his approach. He pointed. She followed his arm with a frown, then nodded. High up, barely visible in the drowned sky, a second slim craft shuddered through the falling, rippling rain. A burst of wind blinded her, and she lost sight of the tiny shape.

Wren gestured for them to retreat to the huts. Reluctantly, she followed, but she turned back to the wind with each gust, as if the twenty meters they withdrew was too far from the edge of the sea for her to be comfortable.

"Is that Jandon's ship?" she asked as they reached the windward side of the hut.

"Uh-huh. He picked up the rest of our team down south." Wren had to raise his voice to be heard. "Once he drops off Kurvan and the others, gives me my prototype breaker, and unloads the rest of the gear, he'll take you out to Broken Tree. You know the canyons there. Should be an easy scout for you." He grinned without humor. "And it's cat country."

The hum in the back of Tsia's mind seemed to surge. She raised one hand to her temple, as if to rub out the cat claws that padded across the inside of her skull. "Bunch of new breakers coming in?" she forced herself to ask.

"Breaker, singular," Wren corrected. "Widenet and portable—completely new technology. They say it'll recognize any bioconfiguration from human to Drayne. We'll even have Ixia codes if we need them."

She gave him a sharp look, her attention finally on his words. "Rumor had things hotting up skyside. Didn't know it had gotten so bad we were reconfiguring for aliens."

He shrugged. "By the time the biochips come in, even the Ixia could be actively looking for weapons. Bacts, biocodes—they'll take anything."

"Bacts?" She raised her eyebrows. "No guild has ever sold bacterial codes to an alien race."

"The guilds, no. At least, not overtly. But blackjack has been active, and if they're selling, they're doing it through the guilds in some way. All the Shields need is a single link between the guilds and the Ixia—anything to prove their involvement—and the Shields could move in in force."

She watched the second skimmer with a frown. "You think

an alien is going to be so sloppy that a Shield could track it down?"

"No, but they don't trust humans any more than we trust *them*. You can bet there'll be at least one rep wherever they're buying from blackjack. If the node was up, you could image down the Ixia specs for yourself. Their jamming technology is prime, and they have some other interesting . . . features. I'd like to see you next to one. See how you reacted." He grinned at Tsia's expression and shrugged. "Call it curiosity that I refuse to spoil with an explanation. Did you ever get the details of your contract?" He changed the subject abruptly.

"Not yet. I signed with the job details on hold penalty." He grinned at the mention of penalty credit, and she nodded with a twisted smile. "Jandon said they'd let me know when I got there, but since he's contracted to Nitpicker, he said she—and therefore you—might know now what I'm to do. So what's the deal? Same as yours?"

"No—we're receiving biochips in a month. Freepicks where you're going have a new bacteria—developed it for reclamation. It's hot. The Ixia skyside, at the docking hammers, have been bargaining for two months for a sample."

"I'll be verifying the bact holds?"

"They've got a guide on that already—Hirsch. You know her?"

"Huh-uh, but she's got a good reputation. Why, if they have her, do they need me?"

"She's a full guild guide, not a merc. She can run a scanner like a century-vet, but she doesn't know spit about ghost lines. You do. The freepicks—they want a clean scan of the canyons for their defensive webs. You know them: they don't trust the guilders a meter away. So, they want you to tell them if the guilders have gotten a ghost web into their data banks. You'll spend your time verifying the terrain. When you're done, they'll compare a closed image of your manual scans to the data they read from the node. If the guilders—or anyone else—tries to move in, there will be differences in the scans."

She watched the slim shape of the second skimmer drop

closer to the deck. "So who gives me my contacts? Jandon or Nitpicker?"

"Nitpicker. She'll want to make sure you know the routine before she sends you out."

Tsia felt her lips tighten in spite of herself. If Tsia had linked with the tealer fish or the herons instead of with the cats, would the pilot have trusted her more? She knew what Nitpicker saw when they worked together, but it still hurt to be watched like a zek—as if she were blackjack herself.

Wren watched her expression. "She's always careful, Feather. You know that."

"She never did learn to trust me."

Wren gave her an odd look. "Do you blame her? You're a guide."

"Yes, a guide. Not an animal, for god's sake."

Wren eyed her for a moment, then raised his hand to her cheek. She forced herself to remain still. But she could not help the curl of her lip as his fingers traced the scars. His gaze fell to her bared teeth. "Sometimes," he said quietly, "it's hard to tell."

She shrugged away sharply. "The virus no more mutated me into a half cat than it mutates a heron-linked guide into a bird, or a tealer-linked guide to a fish. The virus just changes the brain chemistry so I'm sensitive to biofields. That's all."

Wren raised his eyebrows against the rain. "Heard you started camping out on the Sinking Plains when you worked that route with Kurvan last year."

"I was tending to a wounded tam," she retorted. "Its head knob was cracked, and it couldn't hunt till it regained its equilibrium."

"Right," he said mock seriously. "The Landing Pact. I forgot. Protect the species and all—"

"I did full-spectrum scans and bacterial breakdowns the entire time I was there," she protested coldly. "The sensor poles in that area had not gotten in two years a tenth of what I brought back in a month—" She broke off at Wren's expression. "All right," she acknowledged. "The tam wasn't hurt that badly, and I didn't need to help the species. I just didn't like Kurvan."

His gray eyes glinted. "Just as well you're going out to Broken Tree. You're like a cat in a cage when he's around."

"I'm better on the scans anyway. I wouldn't know a biochip if it bit me." She watched the second ship drop lower. "You'll be off-contract in a month?"

"It's scheduled, but you never know. Shippers never set a date for transporting biochips—security reasons."

"There have got to be some buyers chomping at the bit to get their hands on that load."

"Buyers including guilders," he said, with a glance toward the shore.

Tsia laughed shortly. "Guilders want everything. I'd rather work for a freepick."

Wren shrugged. "You're guild yourself, Feather. You belong with the mercs, but you take contract as it comes, whether you work for the miners or the freepicks. Look at Striker. She hates the lifers, but she signed her ID on the node. That freepick at the Hollows who's descended from one of the lifer gang leaders—Striker will have to defend that woman as if she were the head of the mercs. Like you'll have to—"

"—defend the guild guide at Broken Tree," she finished for him.

"At least you once liked that guild."

Tsia's lips pressed together. She looked away from him, and her nose wrinkled at the sweet-bitter scent of the sea. She knew this smell as a baker knew bread. She fingered the scars across her cheek, ignoring the rain that washed the whitened skin. The guides had been more willing to admit her death than verify the untruth of it in the node; she owed them nothing now. No moral stance would convince her of an obligation other than the one she signed. The mercs were the ones to whom she owed allegiance now. Ten years she had worked for the guild of fighters—seen for them, scanned for them, hid them in the terrain they crossed. A decade now they'd carried her link ID. It wasn't as if she held some kind of temporary job. The guides—they were no longer her life; the mercs had become her future.

The heat of Wren's hand on her shoulder was a shock to her rain-chilled skin. When she reached up to touch his thick fingers, their eyes met: one cold, gray gaze; one dark blue. They stood for a moment till Wren dropped his hand. Tsia turned back to the sea.

4

Waves swept by, their foam streaking the sea. The platform shuddered with their rhythm. Around it, the jellies methodically rose and tore the underside of the floating rafts, dragging their spoils down. Down, lower, to bury the seedpods where they would feed the jellies' offspring. Caught in the rubbery, feathery bodies, the dim light of dawn faded to a gray-black gloom long before it reached the dark and rocky bottom of the sea. Tsia let her biogate expand so that she could feel far below the sea's surface. She turned slowly in a circle so that she could use her eyes like her gate to sense movement. But there was no threat in the jellies or the platform sponges, no sense of a predator that waited for the mercs. Other than the storm and the growing sonic hum of the descending skimmer, there were no sounds from the ocean but the sea itself.

Beside her, Wren's presence was a constant shadow in her senses. His body, thickened with the age of 148 years, had a heavy feel. His short stature, his wide, wiry shoulders, and his long, lean arms gave him the look of a wrestler who had gone too long without food. His clublike hands were brutally built and far too big for his frame. His whole body radiated a cold power that gave his biofield a menace she could almost taste.

Her eyes drifted toward a growing shadow on the crest of a far swell. A moment later, the front end of a weedis bent over the moving hill of water and slid down the other side. The mental hum of the four sargasso cats—the sea cougars—

crouched on the raft was sharp, and Tsia licked her lips. Louder and sharper, the sense of them grew till it clogged her mind with its low-hum growling. It was her only real talent, she thought without emotion—this sensitivity to the cats. Her biology degrees were worth nothing without the gate—without the one thing for which the merc guild kept her safe. The rights-conditioning that let her use a weapon—they could have trained her for that, though it would not have been pleasant or easy. Guides did not take well to rights-conditioning unless they were trained before they took the guide virus.

Wren peered at the sky from beneath his hands, watching the ship drop out of a streak of gray. He gestured toward one of the huts. Tsia shook her head. "I like the wind," she shouted. "It tastes like freedom."

His lips stretched in a slow smile, and in the murky light of midmorning, the expression somehow flattened his eyes even further. "Freedom? Yes, you would call it that."

"But not you?"

"No." The thick scar rings of white on his wrists stood out starkly in the gloom. " 'Freedom' is a word that's often confused with 'hope.' "

"And that's something you don't have."

"No. Do you?"

She studied him silently while the wind lashed the color from their cheeks and the rain beat the deck around them.

He eyed her back. "Look at yourself closely, Feather. You're not one who's made of hope either, but rather will—or determination. You delude yourself if you think otherwise."

"Everyone has some kind of hope," she returned slowly. "They may not know it, but they do."

"Everyone? What about your sister? She's got no hope at all."

"That's different," she said quietly. "Her hope was stolen from her like credit from the node-blind."

"I don't believe that." He shrugged at her expression. "No one can take anything from you that you don't willingly give. You make choices, not sacrifices. You take action or you decide to remain still. Only victims blame others for their lives."

His gesture took in her braced stance and the gusting wind that whipped her. "You are what you make of yourself. Nothing less. Nothing more."

She licked the spray from her lips and smiled in a twisted expression. "I said that myself a long time ago. It's odd to hear my words on someone else's lips." She watched the spray puddle like tide pools in the mucus on the decks. "Ten years ago, I gave up everything, and I gave up nothing. And look where I am now: in a day that is night, in a sea that is solid"—she stomped her foot on the spongy marine deck—"in a life that does not really exist."

Wren watched the skimmer begin its long sweep to come around. "The merc guild isn't perfect," he said. "But it does protect its members to Vendetta, to death, and beyond. And the freepicks—or any of the people we work for—would not exist without us. They would be crushed by the fanatics, just like the lifers crushed old Earth. The people you protect . . . You defend your world now as much as any guide protects her assigned plot of land. You just do it on a different scale. With shorter contracts."

With death instead of life. Tsia did not voice the words, but Wren gave her a sharp look. She wondered suddenly if he was esper. Or did he just know her so well that he could read her like a dreamer channel?

Wren rocked back with the force of the wind. Doggedly, he shoved his way off again. "It's getting worse by the minute. Let's go in."

She shook her head, her teeth bared to the sky. Wren raised his hand to take hold of her blunter, but her eyes glinted with challenge. He shrugged and stepped back.

She could feel the sea cougars from here—almost see them on the weedis. Flung up and down by the island's motion, the four shapes crouched in miserable huddles. As with the mind-shadows of the fish, Tsia did not see the cats visually; she felt them. The rough ride made their discomfort acute, and it was harder now to ignore them than to acknowledge their misery in her own guts. Up, down, and back across the crests. Whipped down into a trough and flung back up again . . . Like a sickness in her belly, or a rottenness in her nose, her body reacted as if it rode the weedis with them. Her lips twisted at the yowling of the cubs.

Wren's eyes watched the second skimmer hover above the flight deck. Tsia felt for his biofield in her gate. The contrast between him and the cougars was unsettling. Where Wren was a solidity that she smelled and heard more with her bodily senses, the cougars growled in a thick hum that filled the corners of her mind like fog. Where Wren spoke only to her ears, the cats snarled constantly in her head. Humans were dull and acrid compared to cats. With distance, they did not even leave an echo in her mind. Yet she could feel the weight of the sandcats on the beaches ten kilometers away. Could almost touch the grit that clung to their paws and taste the water they drank.

Wren eyed Tsia, then the drop to the surface of the sea. "So what's your range in all this now?" he asked over the wind.

"Human?" She shrugged. "Fifty meters, if it's a focused biofield."

"If it's quiet? Silent? Whatever you call it?"

"Fifteen. Maybe twenty."

"What if it's feline?" he asked slyly.

She raised her eyebrow. "There's a female with three cubs five hundred meters out."

The sky was still dark with clouds, but the sea was now light gray. The float platform shivered, and Wren staggered with the slam of the wind. "A storm like this is worth a month of energy to a marine station," he shouted. "We passed gale force hours ago."

Tsia nodded. Storm force building. She could feel it in the tingling of her skin, in the eager pound of her heart. "Front will hit in the night," she shouted back. "Bet my bonus on it."

He grinned. "That's no bet. I read the weatherscan from the node before it went down. It hits by dusk today."

"You're wrong. I can taste it in the spray. Front is changing. It'll hit between midnight and dawn. We'll get the heaviest rains behind it."

"You never could resist a dare; I never could resist a bet. You're on. Ten credits?"

She nodded. The glint in her ice-blue eyes was echoed deep in her mind by the growling of a cougar. Her lips curved in a slight smile as she picked up the sea cougar's irritation with its stomach-churning ride. Ten years of growing into the biogate with the cats, and the distance from the platform to the island was no barrier to her gate. Like a thick purr that sat beneath her thoughts, the sounds of the cats kept her company. It had become music—the constant tuning of an orchestra that filled the wilder, darker corners of her mind.

Another gust slammed her off her feet and whipped the blunter off one shoulder. Wren glanced at the feral gleam in her eyes. "You always did get a little crazy in these, Feather." He pointed with his chin at the sea. "It's going to be a hard swim to shore for that litter."

Tsia squinted beneath the shield of her hands and frowned at the floating island. Even though it was closer, the dark hump of the weedis seemed smaller than it had before. "No one swims a bloom. Not even a sargie. They'll stay on that weedis till it rubs the rocks of the mainland."

"Not this time," he returned. "That raft is breaking up. It'll be completely gone before we leave the platform, and I bet it'll be torn in two even before that ship locks down."

Reluctantly, Tsia turned to watch the other ship land. The subsonic hum of its engines caught in her bones like tension. The dim glints from the platform lights caught in rain runnels that streaked the sides of the craft. Lower, it dropped, hovered, then blew off to the side and twisted wildly with the shear. Wren gestured sharply. Reluctantly she nodded and followed him to the lee of the huts.

The ship came in high and dropped with the wind in a sudden, sickening movement. Its nose barely missed the edge of the platform. A second later, it burst up over the side and tried to drop down again. The wind gusted; the ship darted forward, then slammed down and slid with a metaplas scream. Tsia's hands clamped over her ears; Wren's eyes flinched. Tensely they waited while the ship, instead of skidding, bumped back up, then slammed down a second time. It hit the brake bars hard and bounced back like a ball. The landing gear, unable to take the stress, crumpled like accordions back up into their bays. The wind lapsed, and the ship, still trying to fly forward, rammed the brake bars until it stuck finally—like a bee in a spiderweb—with its motors whining and churning on high.

Slowly the ship stopped shuddering, and the sonic sounds began to fade. The landing gear unfolded gingerly from the bays. With a grinding sound, the sectioned legs forced their way down to the deck to brace the hull against the bars. Wren glanced at Tsia's expression. "He landed, didn't he?" he said sharply.

She pointed. "Isn't he going to straighten out?"

Wren peered at the ship. "The cargo hatches are clear of the deck. I don't think he's concerned with much else."

She grimaced. "We'll have to help unload then. Is everything on the antigrav sleds?"

"I wouldn't bet on it."

She gave him a sour look.

He shrugged. "After that landing, he'll be lucky to have the sleds intact, let alone packed and ready to go."

They made their way to the craft in time to meet Doetzier and Tucker beneath the skimmer's belly. There, they struggled with the manual clamps until two of the mercs from the new skimmer jumped stiffly down to help them lock the ship to the deck. The faint smell of the cats mixed with the scents of packing gels, and Tsia paused at the triggered memory. Flowers, she thought, as if she could almost smell them. Shjams . . . Then Doetzier caught her sleeve, and she turned back to the clamps.

Once the other mercs joined them, she left them to finish the cargo and followed the first cargo sled to the hut. Ahead of her, a tall, bowlegged merc guided the pack-laden sled across the deck as if the wind that made the motors whine were merely a breeze, not a storm or gale.

When they reached the hut, Tsia had to fight the door to open it against the wind and allow the sled on through. If the door had been a filter field, she would simply have walked through it and ignored the tingle of its semisolid wall. "Digger-damned primitive construction huts," she muttered. The door came open a handspan; then the wind slammed it back shut. She hissed and wrenched at the handle again. This time, the storm tore it from her hands and slammed the door against the wall so hard the entire building shook. Muttering, she motioned Bowdie on through, then looked for the access panel. Tucker, arriving behind her, beat her to it.

"You guides are all alike," he said in her ear. "Put you outside with your plants, and you're happy as a reaver on a full root dike. Give you a simple mechanical problem and you're lost as a lifer without her gang." He pushed her through the doorway and held the door crank as the rest of the mercs from the other skimmer made their way inside.

"Yaza," she muttered, moving past him. Odors swept in with Doetzier and Kurvan, and Tsia wrinkled her nose. Cats and sea salt mixed with packing foam; the solvent-scent of sponges was sharp. She snorted and breathed in again to discern the difference in the sponge scent from the platform, but the sweat odors of the mercs rose with the heat inside the hut, and the sponge scent faded away. Doetzier, giving her a glance, paused to speak to Wren, and Kurvan made his way over to Jandon, who was rubbing one elbow as if it was bruised. Tsia was left with Tucker, who added in her ear, as she turned to shut the door, "I probably know more about construction huts than you do about your gate."

She turned to retort, but Nitpicker cut in. "Tucker, Feather," she snapped. She shielded her face from the surge of needle-sharp rain. "Get that door closed and leave each other alone."

The gap narrowed, and the wind began to whistle through the space. An instant later, the door clicked shut. The sudden cessation of storm sound was almost deafening in itself. Tsia had to work her jaw to pop her ears. In the quiet, her ears burned from the cold, chapping wind.

Nitpicker ran her hand through her gray-streaked hair. Tsia eyed her automatically, feeling for her biofield. The quiet energy was tight as if the tension the pilot caught on the skimmer was still carried in her shoulders. Tsia regarded the other

woman with a thoughtful expression. She rarely got to see a
merc's true eyes. The darkeyes they wore, which let them see
motion, heat, and contrast rather than color—almost like a cat,
she thought—gave them all black irises. But here, with the salt
spray, none of the mercs had their darkeyes in.

Nitpicker's eyes were a startling green. Set off by her deeply
weathered skin, the brilliance of that color made her gray-and-
white streaked hair seem dingier, and her thin frame bonier
than ever. Yet she moved with grace and balance, her feet almost gliding across a floor or deck, and her hands still, except
when shifting deliberately here or there. It was different from
Tsia's stride: Nitpicker, like Striker, had the walk of a spacer
with fifty years of service.

In contrast, Tucker was on only his tenth contract. Beside
Tsia, the younger merc methodically checked his blunter pockets, then weapons harness and pouches. His youthful frame
still looked gangly, as if he would fill out to a broad-
shouldered man, and his large feet were deceptively quick in
moving his tall, pale figure from one spot to the next. Tsia had
watched him out on the platform. Even when carrying gear
from the skimmers to the hut, he had not slipped once on the
decks. Absently, she listened to him speak.

". . . That set of holos from the war?" Tucker asked Striker
as he picked up his pack from the sled to make a final check
on his gear. "They're something to see."

Doetzier shifted his long legs out of the way. "Can't really
call what the lifers did a war, Tucker. The lifers were terrorists,
not an army. They cut up the country every decade or so to try
to rewrite the constitution, and they always defeated themselves with their own bigotry."

The younger merc dug out a small scanner, examined it
quickly, and put it aside. "Yeah," he returned, "but they did a
hell of a lot of damage with their so-called terrorism."

Doetzier shrugged. "So did the Year of the Yellow Death."

Striker scowled. "You can't compare the lifers to a plague,
Doetzier."

"Why not?" He shrugged. "The population problem was
never a technological issue, but an emotional and religious

one—a problem of education and politics. And you can't cure those things without patience and tolerance any more than you can cure a plague without prevention. Both the lifers and the plague—they're parasites. Both look for a host to support them: the Yellow Death wants a human so it can breed; a lifer wants an ideal so he can feel he has power over someone else. Neither has regard for the law. Both of them kill. And neither one shows mercy."

"You do injustice to the plague," Tsia cut in, getting her pack from the sled in turn. "The Yellow Death at least was ubiquitous. The lifers were violently selective."

Striker nodded. " 'Selective' is kind of understating what the lifers did to the choicers. Once the lifers got onto the infochannels, they tracked down people who'd been involved in pregnancy options half a century before. It didn't matter that their victims had had children and grandchildren since then. They called them blood families, and killed them all. Whole generations. Murdered. Just like that." She snapped her fingers. "What do you want to bet that the freepick at that mining site still brags about her great-great-grandfather?"

"Daya, Striker," Tsia cut in, "but that freepick might not agree with her ancestors any more than you do."

The other woman snorted her skepticism.

"Choicers could have hired the mercs," Tucker added. "That's what we're here for anyway: uphold laws, protect properties, bodyguard the veepees"—he leered—"when they're too scared to go to bed alone at night."

Doetzier, who had found a space against the wall, chuckled, and Tsia glanced at his lazy pose with her frown. She could almost feel the tension in his tall, lean frame, and the contrast of that with his casual pose made her think of a cougar hunting. She switched her gaze to Tucker, comparing the two mercs. They were almost the same height, but they looked nothing alike. Doetzier's shoulders would never broaden further; his was the wiry strength of a man who had honed his body to the quick. His weathered skin was tough and darker than hers by several shades, and its color emphasized, rather than hid, the muscles that rippled in his hands. His light brown eyes were

steady and sharp, as if they somehow listened as much as his
ears did to the movements of the mercs around him; and his
black hair framed his face like a shadow. She watched him for
a moment till his quick gaze turned toward her. Their eyes met
and held. The specks of light in his biofield were like tiny stars
dropped in a bucket. When she touched them with her gate,
they disappeared. She dropped her gaze, but Doetzier continued to watch her. She ignored him. She didn't notice, as she
glanced at Striker, that one of her hands clenched like a claw
in her pocket.

Striker, with her stocky frame and toned muscles, looked
like a gravdancer rather than a runner. She had naturally black
irises and black eyebrows, with short, almost shaved auburn
hair. Her creamy complexion was stretched with the thin lines
of eighty years of living, but she did not have a weathered
look, as Tsia did. She would have been beautiful were it not
for the nose that listed slightly to one side, and the mouth that
stretched just a bit too widely across her face. Her cheekbones
were high and flat; her chin was narrow. The only scars she
bore were a tiny set of lines that crossed her jaw like the teeth
of a comb. The overall effect was as striking as a coral snake
until one noticed her eyes. They were filled with emptiness,
and made her look abandoned. When Tsia stretched to the limit
of her senses, she could just feel the biofield of the other
woman. That energy, which should have grown deeper with
age, seemed shallow and uncertain in Striker.

Four mercs squatted on the floor in front of Wren, and three
more against the walls. Kurvan was next to Nitpicker, and Tsia
eyed him warily. The five months she had worked with him
last year was enough to imprint him indelibly in her mind.
Brown hair, brown eyes, a strong chin, and on top of it all, a
lean face, as if he did not eat enough to keep a smaller man
alive. That gauntness, Tsia admitted with a shiver, lent his face
a rugged handsomeness. And his skin was tanned evenly
brown, not sallow or ruddy like some of the other mercs. His
teeth were even and white as if they had never been chipped,
much less broken as Nitpicker's and Wren's had been. No
scars marred his face or hands. There was only the flat hard-

ness of his eyes to speak of his profession. That, and the eagerness in his biofield.

Nitpicker's voice cut into her thoughts. "All right, listen up. Jandon needs more shooters for the Broken Tree team," the pilot said without preamble.

Jandon nodded, and the wisps of hair that stretched across his balding head fell off to the side. "The rest of my team won't ship in till tomorrow, and with the node down, the mining guilders could move on Broken Tree immediately."

From the floor, Bowdie looked up from fixing a setting on the cargo sled. His dark brown hair was thick and wavy, with an unruly lock that fell across one eyebrow. His nose had been broken three or four times, and one of his cheekbones had been shattered and restructured with coral implants. His skin was weathered and tough, coarse with the pockmarks from some obscure disease. It somehow matched the mottled coloring of his weapons harness, where age had worn away at the fabric. And although some part of her brain registered his coarse complexion, her whole attention was struck by his eyes: beautiful eyes, wide and haunted, as brown as the earth, with long, thick lashes that belonged on a woman's face. Instinctively, she opened her biogate to search for the sense of his biofield. There was a heat there, she discovered. An eagerness like Kurvan's, but steady and strong, with sparks that seemed like challenges, where the other merc's seemed reckless and sharp with disdain. As if, in Bowdie's field, confidence and fatalism had combined in a deep, banked pit of fire. As Bowdie regarded Jandon, his brown eyes narrowed, and he paused in fixing the sled settings. "You have the guide," he said. "Won't that give you the edge?"

Jandon shook his head at Bowdie's question. "A single guide can't check every trail. And yes, we have a second guide"—he forestalled Bowdie's automatic protest—"but she's working the reclamation vats."

Wren shifted almost imperceptibly, and Nitpicker nodded at him to speak. "If you take our shooters," Wren said slowly, "you're crippling our team. Our setup relies on a number of bodies to be effective."

"Yes, but you're going in early, and you're going in for setup, not defense, like us. You won't have any action for three, maybe even four weeks. You don't need all your shooters right now."

From beside Tsia, Tucker paused in his weapons check. "What if the shippers send the biochips in early?"

Kurvan glanced at the younger merc. "No freepick would take shipment an entire month early."

"Why not?"

"The Hollows is a new stake, and the freepicks there won't have finished their preliminary scans, let alone the detailed scans of the biologicals they'll have to work around. They won't know half the biocodes they'll need for coring, processing, *or* reclamation. You program a set of biocodes in a chip, and that chip can be used only in the gear for which it was set—and only for the codes it recognizes. Nothing else." Kurvan tapped the hilt of the laze he carried on his harness. "Like this won't recognize a biological—only humans. Take a corer," he added, "one of those wide-beam, short-range lazes. They're programmed for whatever ground—mineral deposits—the freepicks have at their stake. Without the codes for worms and insects and roots, even the best corer couldn't break through rock that was protected by a layer of those things. Without the right biocodes, the chips in the corer won't acknowledge organic matter as licensed for disintegration. They also won't recognize any bacts—bacteria—over the amount specified by the site license. One pocket of roots over the licensed amount, and the corers automatically halt. You stop the corers, and you stop the mining. No cargo, so no shipping, so no payment. Freepicks almost always work hand-to-mouth as far as credit goes. And with the cost of a set of biochips and the codes that go into them, they can't afford to make mistakes. All it takes is a single missing or misprogrammed code, and they'd lose their entire stake. An early shipment could make those chips as worthless as if they'd been left hissing on the sand."

"You're as bad on nodie stuff as Striker is on the Fetal Wars," Tucker said. "So the chips come in early. There's no reason they have to be programmed right away."

"You want to sit on a shipment of chips for a month, just waiting for blackjack to heist them? Unprogrammed biochips are practically priceless, and they have a subtle but distinct signature. With the right gear, hiding a set of biochips on-site would be about as effective as painting them with neon colors and hoisting them on a scanpole. And until the programmer sets the biocodes, anyone can move in. Blackjack, Draynes, Ixia . . . One blank biocode bank and—"

"—a chip can become a weapon." Tucker resealed the other side of his pack.

"Yes," Kurvan agreed sharply. "Not only could you code for a crop-plant or livestock species, you could code for an alien or human. Unprogrammed, a biochip is as dangerous as an idea in a house of fanatics."

"Maybe not as bad as that," Wren said casually.

Kurvan paused, then grinned in spite of himself. "Maybe not, but it is dangerous. To have them on-site . . . That's just asking for a raid."

Nitpicker glanced at Jandon. "You have two of the new handscanners?" He nodded. "Take the rest of ours. We'll keep the old, shorter-range ones. Take half our config gear, too. We'll replace ours tomorrow after we get a message through to the guild. How many shooters do you want?"

Kurvan glanced at Jandon. "You going to set up a manual scannet?"

Jandon hesitated. "Have to now. So, four, I think."

Tucker paused as he checked the antigrav on his pack. "Four of our shooters? Are you crazy?"

Doetzier straightened from where he leaned on the wall. "Who gets the guide?"

Tucker turned to Nitpicker. "If Jandon gets our shooters, we get the guide. She knows all the ridges and half the scree beds between here and the northern Vulcans."

Nitpicker looked at Doetzier. "What do you think?"

Doetzier tilted his head at Kurvan. "He's the line-runner in this group—ask him, not me. I'm just the configuration grunt. I haven't a clue how long the node will stay down, let alone how it got down in the first place."

Wren popped a slimchim in his mouth. "It's not hard to knock down a node," he put in. "Especially if you have inside help. One crooked tech or nodie, and the traders can slip in and out through a darkened net like rats through a shredded screen. Remember that customs tech four years ago? He went on the grayscale and jammed up the shipping for more than a week. He took his credit and ran to blackjack, and he's so far away now that even the Shields can't touch him."

Shields and shipping, customs and Shjams . . . Tsia stretched her gate unconsciously. To touch her sister . . . Catspeak flooded into her mind and made her lips curl. Cougar heartbeats pulsed with hers. Seasickness rose up in her gut and stabbed her with a twinge of discomfort. She wiped her hands on her trousers. From across the room, Doetzier noticed the movement with sharp eyes. Tsia followed his gaze to her hands and stilled them.

"What do you think, Feather?" Doetzier asked.

"About what?" Tsia regarded him warily.

"Where you go. You're a terrain artist—almost the same thing as a line-runner. You should have as much say as Kurvan."

She shrugged. "If the node is jammed, my skills as a terrain artist are almost moot. Let the guilders get into the terrain before I do, and they can set a hundred prepared ghost webs before I finish a single manual scan. Anything I scanned out would simply pick up their preset signals, not the real terrain in the area. And although I could sense the life-forms fine on the trail, I'd never be able to cover all the ground before the guilders moved in on the stake."

Doetzier seemed to pounce. "You think the node is jammed, not down?"

She looked at him warily. "Daya, how should I know? I was just thinking out loud."

Nitpicker studied her expression. "It takes a lot less do-all to dark a net than to drop a node."

"If you have the technology," Kurvan added.

Nitpicker gave him a hard look. "There are three races in this quadrant alone who have better jamming technology than ours. One of them—the Ixia—is in orbit around Risthmus. You don't think the Ixia would sell a jammer to blackjack— especially if the price was right? If blackjack came up with some of the tech toys the Ixia have been after for the past thirty years? And what about the Draynes or the bug-eyes? They're in the same position as the Ixia, and their space is even closer to ours."

Wren glanced at Tsia and made a subtle sign with his hands, finning a message. She nodded almost imperceptibly. The Draynes, Wren's finger motions told her, were a mammalian life-form—like badgers.

Doetzier's eyes flicked as he caught the last subtle finning from Wren, but he said nothing. Nitpicker added, "Blackjack have slipped through the scannet a dozen times in the last forty years. The word is that the mining guild has standing orders with them for any Risthmus biotechnology. One bad nodie on the orbiting hammers, as Wren said, is all it would take to dark the scannet enough to let a zek down and then back out."

Doetzier glanced at Kurvan. "You're a line-runner. How long would it take you to set a web that could hide a sabotage job well enough to dump the node?"

The other man shrugged. "Six to ten months minimum. Two years at the outside. Maybe more. Depends on how many webs get messed up by the construction."

"That second docking hammer?" Tucker queried. "The one on the elliptical orbit?"

Kurvan nodded. "Things have been unstable on Orpheus ever since they started on Eurydice. Half my webs were shredded or shunted before I could use them at all. Just last week I traced three ghosts for sixteen hours until I found out I'd been accidentally shunted to a dreamer channel. I wasn't tracing a set of ghosts. I was catching the images from a recorded experience." He made a sour expression. "No wonder it seemed real. Basically, it was."

Wren chuckled. "And after that confession, you expect us to take you seriously?"

Kurvan grinned back. "If I'm the only line-runner you have, how can you afford to be choosy?"

"Hell, you might as well go to Broken Tree yourself," Tucker muttered, "than fly with us to the Hollows."

There was a flash of tension in Tsia's gate—like the sense of a sandcat who sees sudden movement. Slowly, she sat up straighter. Her gaze moved slowly around the room. Doetzier studied her fingers, taut against her thighs, but she didn't notice his attention until her narrowed gaze settled on his face. She could almost see the speculation in those brown depths.

Kurvan gave Tucker a flat look. "I work setup—biology's not my field. I'd be as bad as you at locating a false tree on a trail—that's Feather's field, not mine." He glanced deliberately at her.

She shrugged. "The bulk of my training was in fields other than biolinks. I'm not much use without the node. So if having me at Broken Tree was more deterrent than defense, the loss of the scannet makes my presence fairly useless. You'd do just as well canceling contract as taking me with either group."

Doetzier eyed her speculatively. "You'd rather cancel contract?"

She could almost see his attention sharpen, and it took her a moment to realize that she felt his focus through her gate, not through her eyes. "I'm no more likely to turn down credit than I am to turn down a dare," she said; but her smile was forced.

Nitpicker pursed her lips. "If Jandon has our shooters, I'd rather have you at the Hollows." She turned to the bowlegged man. "Bowdie, you stay too—you'll be copilot on this jaunt. Jandon, you can take Estine, Ames, Barker, and . . . Shepherd."

"I'd like five if the guide stays with you," he said flatly.

Nitpicker hesitated, then nodded and glanced over the room. Tsia felt a flash of tension, like a sharp light focused through her biogate. She couldn't help the tightening of her jaw. Bowdie's gaze seemed to snap taut. Kurvan shifted as if he would speak. Then Nitpicker said, "Striker, Tucker, Doetzier, and . . . Kurvan, you four stay with me. Bowdie and Wren also. Miloczek, you go with Jandon. Feather, if you're done checking your pack, get it on our sled with Bowdie's. The rest of you either load your gear on Jandon's ship or get it off and in here with the rest of ours. Questions?" No one spoke. "Then let's roll."

The lessening of tension at Nitpicker's words had been almost as palpable as the shiver that struck Tsia's shoulders with relief. Wren's sharp eyes caught the shudder the same instant that Doetzier's did.

"Cold?" murmured Doetzier.

She glanced at him and shook her head uncertainly. "Just a feeling . . ."

"Of what?"

Mutely, she shrugged. Tucker looked up with a grin. " 'The shadow of the future that hangs above us all.' "

"Yaza," she muttered. "Too bad all your ancestors didn't die in the Fetal Wars."

His eyes narrowed. "If I'd been in that war—"

"The lifers were never justified enough in their murders," Striker broke in deliberately, stepping between them at a look from Nitpicker, "to be given the distinction of starting a war. Not in history, anyway. That was just a popular term—like the Decade of the Technodead."

"The technodead weren't as moral," Tucker retorted, provoking her on purpose, though he moved aside for the woman.

"The lifers loved power, not morality," Striker said sharply as she thumped her pack down on the sled. "They were nothing more than criminals, and history has recorded them as such. Ayara's eyes, Tucker, there were almost more deaths from the riots—when the lifers realized that the creative and educated people were leaving the planet—than when they were just concerned about killing mothers and medicals."

"Daya, Striker." Tsia frowned in spite of herself. "Even you can't say that there were no educated people among the lifers."

"Depends on what you call education." Striker met Tsia's eyes with a steady gaze, and the lost look flickered before she stepped away. "Education opens minds," she said flatly, picking up a scanner. "Indoctrination closes them. Lifers used their bigotry to restrict old Earth to one way of thinking. No tolerance. No diversity. No creativity. Only rhetoric and control— like puppet masters who put their nooses around the neck of the world. Education is not about reducing options but increasing them. That's what the Fetal Wars were really all about."

Tucker sealed his pack and threw it on the sled with a *thwump*. "Sure, but I bet more people died in the Fetal Wars than in any war—including the Stand—since then."

The catspeak was growing louder in Tsia's head as the cougars on the sea swept closer, and she said, more sharply than she intended, "Is the exact number of deaths really so important, Tucker?"

"You're a guide," he retorted. "You feel animals and plants. You aren't expected to understand the finer points of intersolar history."

Wren snorted, and Tsia gave the younger merc a dirty look. "You have an interesting view of a guide's education."

"Oh, come on," he retorted. "Everyone knows that a guide thinks only of her gate. Look at the way you reacted when we were going skyside. What if you had gotten free? Would you really have jumped from the hatch, knowing you were kays above the sea?"

"Of course," she said, as if surprised. "Unlike you, I have antigravs on my harness, not just on my pack. The impact of hitting water would have been painful, but not necessarily fatal. It would have been the pressure changes that killed me, not the impact. And"—her eyes glinted—"I'd have made sure I had company to scream with."

Kurvan made a sound suspiciously like a laugh, and Tucker turned sharply.

"Striker, Feather, step it down," Nitpicker cut in. "Kurvan, you and Tucker get out of here and go check the skimmer. Make sure she's tight and steady. Doetzier, you and Bowdie verify the gear. I want all antigrav units, e-wraps, and scanners checked before we take off. Striker, take the sled to the ship and start loading."

"What about the self-contained med gear?"

"The scames? Give two of the three to Jandon. If the guilders are moving in, he'll have more need of them than we will." She hesitated, and something flickered in her eyes, but she turned to Tsia and said, "As for you, I want another scan of the platform. Take your time. We've got another hour before we lift."

Tsia nodded and turned to the door. Nitpicker caught Wren's eye, and the other merc nodded. Still chewing his slimchim, he hopped down from his perch, shifted his own weapons harness on his hips, and made his way to the portal as Tsia's shadow.

The door slammed back to the wall behind him, and he let Jandon shut it. This time, as he left the hut, he barely staggered in the wind. Tsia was already moving toward the catwalk that led to the platform edge, and he leaned into the wind to follow. His eyes followed her closely. The lithe movements of her hips and thighs; the leanness of her body . . . There was no wasted motion—no gracelessness from youth, but rather a concentrated energy, trapped inside her muscles. It was something—a wildness, perhaps—that he desired to touch and taste.

Reaching forward, as if to grip the wind itself for balance, he watched her with cold and steady eyes. Sometimes, he thought, he wanted to grab her to still her when she twisted and yowled like a cat. Sometimes he wanted to squeeze his massive hands so tightly around her body that he wrung that wildness from her throat and drank it like blood. He chuckled, and the sound was choked to silence by the wind. He knew he could tell her what he thought, and she'd still not be afraid of him. Odd woman. He respected that in her. But then—and he looked toward her figure poised on the edge of the platform, her arms out as if she could fly—she was not really a woman at all to him. She was, instead, a guide.

5

Tsia moved through the wind like a dancer. She had the feel now of the storm, and it no longer stole her feet from under her. Her knees bent instinctively, and her arms twisted away from her body for balance. Behind her, near the ship and hidden by the gloom and blinding wind, something moved. Instantly, her senses sharpened. She turned slowly, half crouched on the narrow walk. She could see Wren, but he was not what she felt. His biofield was not focused like a hunter.

No, she could almost taste a presence—smell the musk scent of a cat in the wet morning air. But there was nothing in her biogate but the mercs. Nothing in her sight but the white wing of the skimmer, the dark bulk of the vats. She hesitated, then went on.

The spray and hollows of the whitecaps hid the shadow of the weedis as they wallowed in the troughs of the swells. One kelplike island swelled up and over a crest; the other end trailed behind. Huddled on the matted raft were four of the sea cougars who rode the currents to shore.

Wren shaded his eyes from the wind and got a noseful of spray. "Hell of a way to travel." He had to raise his voice over the wind. "You'd think a cat would drown on one of those things."

She shrugged. "They're stable as an iceberg."

"Safe as mother's milk, huh?"

"Even if the ride is rough, some of those islands are a hun-

73

dred years old. They're woven as tightly as weathercloth. The only real danger is when a cat picks a weedis that isn't old enough to be fully grown together. If the branch structures are weak, the island can break apart."

"The bloom doesn't help either."

"No," she agreed flatly.

"You think those four are going to make it?"

She was silent. Wren glanced at her and, even in the gloom, caught the worry in her eyes. He followed her gaze. The deepening troughs flung the raft up and down like a bucking horse. Long, dark streamers of green floated behind the island. Jellies hung from the streamers, curling their blue-white tendrils around the flat, slimy vines—stubbornly pumping and pulling away to take their spoils down.

"The weedis is thin on one end," she said reluctantly. "Not many seedpods to keep it floating."

"Bet it'll split before it even hits the platform."

"That would be best," she returned slowly.

He raised his eyebrows. "You want it to break apart? You of all people can't possibly want the cats to drown?"

"Of course not," she said sharply. "But if an island breaks up instead of holding together, the loose debris can go down, and the rest of the raft stays on top—including the cats. If the thin part doesn't break off, the jellies can latch on to that section and drag it under. The whole island—cats and all—will sink. It's like a sleeve on a jacket: You pull the sleeve, you get the jacket, too."

He studied the raft for a moment. "I don't think your sargies will make it."

She felt her stomach tighten. The weedis was beginning to tear into strips even as she watched. Already the mother was leading her cubs away from the thinning end. The urgency of the female's snarling caught at Tsia's mind. Tentatively, then with more focus, Tsia opened her gate to the cat. There was an instant in which the cougar hissed; then the sargie seemed to suck at her strength. Tsia paid her will out like a lifeline. A moment later, the female leaped the growing water chasm easily, then bounded carefully through the growth till she found a solid nest.

Tsia could distinguish the thinner energies of the cubs now, and she fed her strength to them in turn. When the first cub leaped across the chasm, Tsia's own feet tightened in her boots. The second cub jumped while the third one pawed nervously at the thinning edge of the raft. The waves surged. The leaping cub landed in the sea with a clumsy splash. Its mental shout was a frigid shock in Tsia's mind. She leaped forward, and only Wren's startled reflexes kept her from jumping out into the sea.

"Dammit, Feather!" He jerked her away from the edge. He stared at the sea, then her. "Don't do anything stupid—it's not in your contract."

She barely heard him. Her attention was with the cub who clawed his way through the brash, then up and out of the water. A massive, foam-streaked crest of water split the weedis apart. The last cub was left behind.

On the thicker island, the two others plunged across to the inner, safer places, but the mother did not abandon the edge. She paced while the sea-softened raft disintegrated beneath her weight, and yowled to her third cub. Tsia took a step and was brought up short by Wren's thick hands closing tightly on her arms. She blinked and twisted.

"Uh-uh, Feather," Wren said harshly. "Nothing stupid, remember?"

"The sargie—"

"The cats are fine. They made the island."

"No," she protested. "One cub is left behind."

He shrugged, but did not release her arms. "They're a hundred meters away. There's nothing you can do about it."

"There has to be. You know my link. That's a cougar down there, not a fish or rat or bird."

"It's too far away, Feather. Let it go."

"It'll drown in the chop . . ."

Wren shook her so hard her teeth rattled. "The cats aren't your responsibility. They won their independence: the Landing

Pact—remember? They earned their rights and freedoms, and now they have to live with them."

Her hands dug into his blunter. "The Landing Pact also states a guide's obligation to protect them. To help them in return for their service to the world."

"Only if they call you."

"They did!" she snarled. "They called me clearly, and took my strength through the gate. They *want* help."

"They took your strength?"

"I helped them cross the water."

He shook his head. "It doesn't matter. The sargies have been migrating for two centuries between the islands and the shore. Every year, some of them don't make it. If this cub dies, that isn't your fault. That's just life." He stared her down. "And not everyone gets to have one."

The female cougar snarled in Tsia's mind; she ground her teeth together. Wren waited, his hands still gripping her arms. Then the cub cried again, and its sharp mental voice pierced her head. Tsia cried out. "Wren, I can't stand it."

"Then figure out what you can do about it," he said coldly. "As far as I can see, you've got ten minutes before the island goes all the way down with the jellies you described."

"The floating docks at the base of the legs—they're rigged as emergency rafts, aren't they, like the pontoons on a skeeter?"

He pointed at the soft spongy areas to either side of the walk. "The station's not half-finished, Feather, and the docks are no more than hollow casings."

"I've got antigrav on my harness."

"That's useless on a bucking surface."

She pointed toward the edge of the floater. "The island will be close to the platform in ten minutes. If the weedis holds together that long . . . There are solid pockets of growth tangled around the station legs right now. What if I went out on one of them?"

"They wouldn't support you."

"I'm careful with my weight, and the tangles are almost solid seedpods. They have better flotation than a dockboat."

"You still wouldn't be close enough to grab the cub."

"I'd be close enough to coax it to swim to one of the empty chambers just above the waterline. I could get it up to the decks from there."

"No chance," he stated flatly. "No way Nitpicker will authorize that—even to comply with the Landing Pact."

"Dammit, Wren, it's going to die!"

"That, I guess, is its destiny."

"This is not a philosophical discussion—"

"No, it's not. It's reality." He took her by the arm and yanked her toward the hut. "Come on. You're due to repor—"

She shook his hand off. "You're a goddam callous bastard."

"I never claimed otherwise. And you," he said, turning on her coldly, "should know better by now. The Landing Pact is two hundred years away, and you were on contract the moment you stepped in that skimmer. Your first concern should be whether or not this station is secure. Your second concern should be whether or not your senses are clouded or unreliable because of the influence of your gate. Your last concern should be the Landing Pact—and not just because you're a guide, but because you're a rogue guide, who works away from her guild."

"Wren . . ." Her fingers were like claws on the fabric of his blunter. "You know me. The felines are my link, and I can't stand by and do nothing."

"*Think* for a moment, Feather. Nitpicker and I know about your link, but what if the others find out? That's five more people who could potentially betray you to the guide guild—to the node."

"They won't find out," she returned tightly. "All guides—not just those linked with cats—are required to help the felines."

Behind them, Jandon's skimmer took off, blasting forward at an angle, then rising sharply upward. Wren watched it go with a curse. "I should have known better than to ride wing with you," he muttered. "Why didn't I check gear instead of Doetzier? Why did I have to play watchdog?" He motioned toward the construction hut, but Tsia balked, and he snapped,

"You still need Nitpicker's authorization to interfere with the cats. I'm only an M-five. She's M-seven. Or does your brain no longer make sense of that either?"

She gave him a scalding look.

"Good," he snapped. "Your brain's in gear again. Keep it that way."

She shook her head. "You tell Nitpicker about the cat. I'll meet you down at the far leg—"

"Tell her yourself. In the hut."

"Wren, there's not much time . . ."

He gestured sharply. "In the hut."

Cursing, Tsia forced herself through the wind.

In the hut, Nitpicker, Tucker, and Kurvan had not yet finished their gear. Kurvan was checking the contents of the medkits; Tucker ran the powerscans for the stabilizers on the packs. Tsia tried to speak before the door shut, but Nitpicker motioned for her to wait for the noise to subside.

As soon as the wind noise died, Tsia began abruptly. "There's a cougar cub on a weedis that's breaking apart a hundred meters away." She paused at Nitpicker's expression. Her jaw set. "I want to get the cub off that island and onto the platform. We can take it to the mainland with us and drop it off on land." She watched the pilot closely, but the other woman simply regarded her without expression, while the cat feet crawled in her head. Hurry, her mental voice demanded. She could almost see the trains of thought whipping through Nitpicker's mind: Had Tsia gone rogue again? Why did she want to do this? A cougar? Could Tsia handle a wild animal even if it was the same type as her biolink? The Landing Pact required that humans help the felines, but did this one cat need to be saved?

"How are you going to get it off the weedis?" the other woman asked finally.

"It will come to me," Tsia answered.

"You sound confident."

Tsia met her gaze squarely, ignoring the curiosity in Kurvan's. "Do you doubt the strength of my link?"

"No," the other woman said slowly. "No, I don't. But I do

doubt the strength of your arms. The swells are heavy and the waves like broken mountains. How are you going to get to the weedis? And how will you keep from being swept away? You can't swim in this."

"I'll go down on one of the lifts. I can control my height from the waterline by sending the lift up or down."

Kurvan's gaze flicked from Tsia to Nitpicker. "She could use a safety line," he suggested. "There are over three hundred meters of flexan cord right here. Even if she fell off the platform, the line is long enough to stretch to the bottom of the sea and back."

Nitpicker gave him a sharp look. "And she'll tie it to what? The lift? If she's underwater, the lift won't go back up without her. And the underdecks aren't strong enough to take the point-strain of a line—the sponges would simply tear between their spicules."

"She can use the other lift on the leg," he suggested. "There are two at each piling. She can tie onto one and ride the other. If her timing's good enough, she might not even get wet."

Tucker snorted and gestured with his chin at the water that dripped from her blunter. "If she got soaked on the decks, she'll be taking a deep bath in the sea."

Tsia followed his gesture and abruptly shook the water from her jacket as she paced back and forth and fingered the flexor on her hip. In its dormant form, it was shaped like a blunt stick, and she nervously snapped it into a sharp point, then an edged blade. The custom-wrapped hilt was a green and brown pattern broken up by swirls of muted purple—the only object with color that she wore.

Kurvan eyed the weapon with a frown. "Best leave that here. It won't work against a biological—the jellies, not the cat," he added quickly at the flash in her eyes. "And the weapon will be awkward in the water—make it harder to swim or get untangled from the brash. Take your knife instead—your flat knife, not your raser," he said sharply. "You can at least bite back with that."

Tsia nodded slowly and tucked the flexor into the side slot on her pack. Then she checked her flat knife in her boot.

Kurvan moved to the door with the scanners. "Tucker, give me a hand with the nav systems on the skimmer." He glanced at Nitpicker. "I'll send him back with Bowdie."

Nitpicker nodded absently; her attention was on the guide. She did not try to speak until Wren had cranked the door shut after Kurvan and Tucker stepped out into the storm. By then, Tsia was near-dancing with impatience.

"Nitpicker," Tsia urged. "There's not much time to decide—"

"Before the weedis is torn apart," the other woman cut in. "I understand that." She regarded Tsia soberly. "How will you hide this from the guide guild? This isn't a standard use of your gate, and interfering with the cats, even for the Landing Pact, will raise questions."

"I know."

"The combination of a feline and a guide will be obvious to any sensor sweep that's still active. You go after that cub, and your guide gate will be pegged to the felines."

"I know," Tsia repeated.

"It just takes one question, Feather," Nitpicker said sharply. "One question about that feline biological—to start a trace along your ID dot."

A trace to her name. To the past she had hidden behind her. She could hear the words as if Nitpicker had said them aloud. "I set webs to protect my merc ID—"

"Any web can be broken if it is tested long enough. You know that."

"What about the merc guild?" Her hands rubbed unconsciously at her wrists. "They've promised me protection. Everything I've done for the last decade has been because of that promise."

Wren cleared his throat. "The mercs can protect your link as long as it's not challenged beyond the time you joined the guild. There are always traces left in the node by a temple link. You know you can't hide every image—every trace of yourself for your entire life. The only way to get a completely secure link—a completely clean ID—is to make a deal with the Shields."

She stared at him. "I can't do that. The risk . . ."

Wren shrugged. "Every time you use a laze, you run the risk of fire from the beam. Every time you set a grazing limit as a guide, you run the risk of misjudging the land so that it's damaged beyond repair. You could burn a cedar stand, and be wiped for that as easily as for being the guide who broke the Landing Pact. Everything you do is a risk. Everything affects a life somewhere."

Tsia's eyes grew hard. "And everything I *don't* do can be just as important. I know I'm on contract, and that if I help the cougar, you could say that I broke that contract with you. But if I don't help the cougar—especially since I've got a link with the cats—I break the Landing Pact. Which one do you prefer I do?"

Nitpicker cursed under her breath. "You know I hate animals."

"I know."

"I'd rather carry a cargo of digger dung—hand-loaded—than some kind of beast in my ship."

"I know," Tsia said more sharply.

"Why can't you just put him back on the next island that comes along?"

"We could be here for hours before a thick one floated close enough to the platform."

"Goddam guides," the pilot muttered. "You've been running ghosts in the node for a long time, Feather, but you aren't as good as Kurvan. You want him to help set the webs to hide this if the node goes back up?" Tsia shook her head almost before Nitpicker stopped speaking. "Then," the pilot said curtly, "make sure your own traces are goddam tight."

The door burst open, and Bowdie staggered in from the wind. His blunter sprayed water, and the straps of his mottled harness shed water like sealskin. Nitpicker barely glanced at him as he cranked the portal shut. "So let's say you get the cub to the deck," she continued. "Where do you propose I land on the mainland—if you ever get the cub in my ship?"

"The beach. It can find its mother from there."

Nitpicker stared at her, then laughed—a short, sharp sound. Bowdie frowned, and stomped his feet to shake the last water from his boots. "You talking about the beach between Iron Bottom Slough and Bashevnel Bay?" he asked.

The cat feet dug into Tsia's mind, and the skin around her eyes tightened. "You landed on this platform. Even with the winds, the beach at least is flat and clear."

"And surrounded by solid rock and barely thirty meters wide."

"The flight deck here is thirty meters wide."

Bowdie ran his long fingers through his hair so that a single brown lock fell across his eyebrow. "The gale is now storm-force and growing. It's a hundred and fifty kays per hour out there."

Nitpicker nodded. "I'm flattered by your confidence, Feather, but even I'm not the kind of pilot you need. Kissing this platform as I did in a ship as tiny as ours—that was a stunt. Kissing a strip of sand right beside a cliff with the up-drafts and eddies, the shear from the front, and the surf smashing us if we miss . . ." She shook her head. "Give it up, Feather. It's not to be." She added quietly, "And it's safer that way for you."

Tsia's eyes flicked warningly toward Bowdie. He said nothing, but she could see him filing Nitpicker's comment away for thought. "What about landing farther in—a kay or two?" she asked flatly.

"At the Hollows? If the cub can stay calm that long. The freepick stake is forty kays inland—across the first row of hills."

"No, no. Forty kays is too far." Tsia started to pace the room. "It would have to cross dozens of established territor-ies—of other cats, grown cats—to get back to its mother. It would never make it."

Bowdie looked at her curiously. "Even if you do help this cub, how are you going to keep it from going crazy in the ship, surrounded by humans? It might be engineered to bond with a guide, but it's still a wild animal. It's not going to like being caged up with eight of us clumsy humans."

Wren jammed his gear back in his pack. "And unlike you, *we*," he stressed, "don't have the protection of a biogate."

The door whipped open again, and Tucker staggered in. He caught the crank as he entered and slammed the door shut quickly. "Finished checking the systems," he said before the wind whistles rose and died. "We're ready for the rest of the gear."

Nitpicker nodded briefly, but her eyes never left Tsia's face. "You think a cub isn't big enough to shred us like paper if it gets scared?" she went on. "You know our weapons don't work against biologicals—not without a specially licensed biochip, which is illegal outside of the Shields. And with the node down, there's no way to get a vetdarter to take care of the cub for us." She eyed Tsia for a long moment. "Ah, hell." She glared around the small room. "Tucker, Bowdie, you want to look good for the Landing Pact? Help Feather catch this thing?"

Tsia shook her head. "I'll catch it," she asserted. "I need help only in getting down to the weedis, and then in getting back up."

Tucker cocked his head. "I grew up on the Keys," he offered. "I've walked more floating islands than you've ever seen, and swum the distances between them."

"Sea weedis are different from swamp islands," Tsia returned tersely. "You have to have a feel for them, or you could end up dragged down by the jellies and drowned in the tangle and chop."

"So what? We've got nose-breathers."

"And an enbee is made for gaseous atmospheres, not for underwater jobs."

"They work fine in emergencies."

"For maybe ten minutes before their filters clog. And not in deeper waters. If you fall in . . ."

"Take no offense, Feather, but, young as I am"—he shot her a wry grin—"I can probably swim ten times better than you. I was freediving with the dolphins when I was six. I made the skyside team by the time I was fourteen, and competed in the Annual Gravdives for eight years. I still make it out to the sector Fluidshutes every other year—I dive the Dryshutes in the off-seasons. And," he added, "I win."

"I was caught out on Needle Rock once in a storm," she said slowly to Tucker. "Had to be taken off with a gale net. I was in the water no more than four minutes, but it felt as if a wall was slamming me in the back every second, and a dozen vat mixers were tearing at my arms and legs. There's the bloom, too. Jellies are dangerous, Tucker. They can pull an enbee from your face as easily as they pull you from the surface. *My* decision is forced by the Landing Pact. Make sure," she made herself say, "that your decision is clear."

"Do you want help or not?" he asked quietly.

She did not hesitate. "Yes."

"Wren?" prompted Nitpicker. "Bowdie?"

Wren forestalled the other merc. "Need you to work on the gear," he said to Bowdie. "Besides"—he jerked a thumb at Nitpicker—"she expects me to do it anyway. Tucker, you take the middle leg of the platform, I'll take the far leg. Feather and I will try it first. If we miss the cat, the current will push it on toward you." He pulled his flexor from his belt and, with a twist of his wrist and pressure from his fingers, snapped the malleable weapon into a hook-tipped sword. It took only a moment to double-coil the flexan cord. Once he located the middle of the cord, he sliced it in two and tossed one end to Tucker.

The younger merc threw his coil over his shoulder and head so that he wore it like a bandolier, then stuck his knife in his harness. He grinned at Wren. "All dressed up with somewhere to go. And I thought this job would be dull."

Wren shoved his flat knife in his boot as Tsia had done. "Feather," he said, moving toward the door, "you're with me on the far leg."

"Why you?" Tucker interjected. "I'm younger and stronger."

Tsia met the younger merc's gaze with a sardonic expression. "Wren has bigger hands."

The other merc turned at the door and leered in exaggeration. "The better to catch you with, my dear." He opened the door and the wind rushed in, deafening them momentarily. Tsia stepped out after him. Tucker pulled up the collar of his blunter and followed with a grin.

6

The wind gusted brutally, then subsided between blasts to a steady push. For the moment, the rain had stopped almost completely. The only moisture in the air seemed to be whipped off the crests of the sea. Wren touched Tsia's arm and pointed to the gale net packed onto one of the deck columns.

Tsia shook her head. "The bloom's too heavy," she shouted back over the wind.

"It's got antigrav units all along its lines."

"Yes, but without the node to guide their force vectors exactly, they aren't strong enough to fight the jellies."

Wren nodded. He paused to unclip a pair of safety carabiners from the net; Tsia grabbed two more and tossed them to Tucker, angling them into the wind. The younger merc caught them, then made his way along the catwalk to the middle station leg, where he disappeared down the cargo lift.

As Tucker dropped below the deck, Tsia felt the hairs prickle on her neck. Warily, she looked over her shoulder. Wren deliberately did not follow her gaze. "What is it?" he asked in as low a voice as he could.

"I don't know," she said slowly. The only movement she saw was that of the mercs by the skimmer, working on the cargo.

"Nothing?"

"Nothing of which I am sure . . ."

He gave her a sharp look. "Is there something out there or not?"

"If there is," she said sharply, "I can't tell. You know my resolution with humans is only a little better than the link I have with other life-forms."

"I've seen you differentiate between a human and a biological hundreds of times."

"Between a man and a bird, yes, given time. But no guide can read energies accurately in a storm. Everything has too much motion. And the difference between an enemy in a shadow or a friend lounging by a hut? That distinction's beyond me. All I can tell is whether or not someone watches us intently—if there's a predator sense in my gate."

"And?"

"I don't know." For a moment, she eyed the deck, then the spray blasted up and showered them both with salt. She motioned toward the far leg of the station. Wren nodded.

As she opened her gate further, her eyes became wide and sensitive. She seemed to see with double vision. Light grew. Images blurred. Her throat tightened and rumbled with frustration. By the time she reached the far edge, she could see the bulk of the mother's weedis washing around the north leg. The sargie's whiskers twitched constantly at the scent of the jellies, and the female's eyes were slitted against the spray. The cougar paused, turned her head up toward the platform, and hissed.

We're coming. Tsia tried to send words to the cat, but the mental sounds spread out and disappeared in the biogate like water mixing in mud. No message reached the cougar. She tried again, this time by projecting a rumbling purr that she built in her own throat, and the catspeak surged in return. The skittering feet sharpened till they seemed to scratch urgently at her thoughts. The snarl that grew in her gate abruptly drowned out her purr.

By the time she ran out on the catwalk, the thin, ropelike weedis, on which the last cub paced, began to wash against the station's base. Jellies bloomed on both sides of the thin mass; they had shredded the edges till it was no more than three meters across. The abandoned cub huddled in the mat like a drowned rat. Every gust of wind sprayed the sea into the weight-crushed nest. Every wave further shredded its raft. Its ears were flat against its head, and its tail twitched miserably from side to side. Even Wren could hear its yowls.

Tsia did not wait for Wren, but stepped quickly onto the rising bar of the lift, checked for the controls, and, ignoring his shout to wait for the safety line, drove the lift down below the upper decks. Dark cliffs of airsponge flashed past with sickening speed. The frigid spray blinded and scratched at her eyes. Black caverns gaped on two sides where chambers were being shaped, and from their darkness she could feel the watchful eyes of storm birds who sheltered from the wind. The platform leg itself was a dirty white; the sponges that formed its base were almost completely solid with metaplas. She scraped her hand along the rough column as she dropped, then jerked it back as the lavalike sharpness of its hardening sides gashed her skin in a shallow, ragged line.

Far down the platform, along the other leg, the female cougar caught sight of Tucker as her larger island washed on past. The cat's immediate growl was so loud in Tsia's head that the guide almost let go of the lift to grab at her temples.

Wait, she told the cat in her head. *We're here to help.*

Cat feet paced, and claws pricked at her brain. She found her hands clenched around the lift's vertical pipe so that she had to pry her fingers loose to use the controls again.

Just above the reach of the ocean, she stopped the lift abruptly. She searched the waves with her eyes, but she couldn't see the cub. For a moment, her breath caught. The sea slammed against the station leg and blasted back; the waves dropped away in a steep wall of water, then swept up so fast that it seemed as though they would crush her. Frigid water stung her face and skin to a pervasive ache. Her muscles were already stiff with the chill. In her nose, the scent of the jellies was a bitterness that rotted on the ocean's waves; the odor of the larger weedis was sweet. The smaller weedis was gone. Her breath caught.

"Please, Daya . . ." She was unaware of the prayer that escaped her lips.

Then, the thin tendrils of the end of the raft surfaced again in the surge. The cougar cub, its nest now awash with water, scrambled from side to side on the tiny island as first one edge, then another submerged.

"Hurry," Tsia shouted up at Wren. She could see him above, adjusting the safety line on his harness. She could see to the north that Tucker was poised just above the heaviest waves, blasted by spray from his wind shadow. Then Wren's lift dropped even with hers, and the merc's heavy hand thrust the safety line into her grip. Precious seconds passed, but she forced her fingers to thread the end of the line through the harness rings on first one thigh, and then the other, and finally her waist. She did not consider wrapping it around her middle to save time. She had fallen on such a swami belt once. It had felt as if her kidneys had jumped up into her throat, and her stomach had popped out her middle. There were reasons, and not just those of having the weapons straps handy, that the mercs wore full harnesses when they worked.

The instant she tied off, she dropped the line and sent her lift into the top of the surge. Waves swept up, then down, exposing twelve meters of liftpipe and sodden platform sponge. The sea swept back up the floater leg, touched Tsia's foot, and dropped away again. The leading edge of the thin weedis swept past.

"Almost," she muttered to the kitten. "Almost there."

The cub yowled and spat, then turned in a circle as the water washed its paws. Tsia concentrated. She could feel the cold sea in her fingernails; she could taste it on the roughness of her tongue. The mental link between her and the cub mixed their senses so that she seemed at first unstable, as if she rode the brash, then rock solid on the lift.

Water surged. She dropped the lift and leaned out to stab her hand at the weedis. She missed and plunged her hand only in the water. In an instant, the wave swept back up. She was not prepared for its shocking, frigid power and the sucking strength that pulled at her legs. The gasp that tore from her throat was more curse than breath. With her elbows bent around the pipe, she clung to the lift till the wave subsided again, and regained her feet on the bar. The next trough swept close. Tendrils and seedpods streamed out in the water, and the cub backed away on the island.

"No," she said sharply. "Come to me." She knew the cat could hear her. "Come."

The next wave climbed up till the sea washed her feet. Instantly, she drove the lift down, following the surge. Again, the weedis was just out of reach. She yowled in frustration. On the disintegrating island, the cub circled in growing fear. It could taste the jellies in the sea, and it knew the acid of their tendrils. Tsia could taste its fear; could feel the predator sense of . . . what? Of the cub? No—something else. Something duller. Something human. Did someone watch? She glanced up, but there were only platform shadows above her, and the two waves that collided in a sudden point when she took her eyes off the sea smashed her against the lift for her stupidity.

Instantly, foaming grit splashed her face; the blunter became a balloon of water. She was dragged off the lift bar until only one stubbornly hooked elbow kept her near the platform leg. Something cut into her thighs, and something else pressed across her shoulders, and she realized that the safety line held her in place.

Wren . . .

The water changed direction. A jelly sent its stinging tendrils right across her neck. She jerked, and her body twisted as it was swung round the opposite way. The wave subsided; the jelly disappeared. The trough dropped away below her legs. Hanging now in midair by the safety line and her one grip on the pipe, she twisted in the wind. Cursing, breathing hard, she pulled her feet back to the bar just as a thick hand hauled her up.

"I'm okay," she yelled. "Go again."

Wren gave her some slack, and she dropped the lift again, but the end of the weedis swept past like a memory too fleeting to grasp. Only the thinnest trail of debris followed after.

"Tucker," she screamed across the wind. The other merc had

been watching, and he signaled as she pointed. "Do it," she shouted. "It's yours."

Tucker had knotted his safety line on the second lift. Now he paid the slack out into the wind, where it blew away in a huge curve. Tsia frowned at the stretch of rope. She looked up at Wren. He mouthed something, and started to coil her own safety line. She shook her head and pointed at Tucker's line. "I'll go," she shouted. "You get this line." Quickly, she unknotted the line from her body and shoved it in Wren's hands. Then she shot the lift up and away from the waves, leaving Wren, cursing, behind to clean up the line.

Already, Tucker was down in the waves where the sea smashed the leading edge of the raft against his piling. As the island tangled at the base of the leg, the merc grabbed for the growth. Tsia, now at the top of the southern leg, halted her lift to watch with her breath caught in her teeth. The wind shadow of Tucker's body allowed the water to crawl right up his chest, where it sprayed out like a fountain over his head. He disappeared into the sea. A second later, he broke up out of the water empty-handed. Tsia snarled silently. The node—the flickers that spoke of active webs . . . Goddammit, she cursed, there had to be some way to reach him—to tell him about his line. But the node was still down. There was nothing. Nothing but the fading sense of a predator that made Tsia's neck prickle as much as the brutal wind that dried the salt like tiny saws on her skin.

Tucker dropped the lift again, timed it wrong, and caught the surge on its way up. He went under, then broke free of the foam. His eyes were screwed closed against the grit in the water, but even so, when he shot up on the lift, he held a handful of green that slapped his legs in the wind, and a dripping jelly a meter across that wrapped itself on his arm.

Violently, he shook the jelly from his hands and threw the weeds away. A second later, he dropped the lift again. Behind him, the discarded jelly tangled on the trailing rope and submerged. In the water, Tucker tore at the weedis, dragging its mass toward him in a shredded mess. He shouted something at the cougar, but the creature cowered on its sinking brash, away from the platform and the grasping human arm. The trapped fear of the cat clogged Tsia's mind. The water still sprayed up to her face, and she didn't notice; the salt crusted on her cheeks, but she didn't scrape it away. As Tucker went down into the waves a third time, she jumped from the lift and sprinted across the metaplas path. A moment later, Wren reached the deck and followed.

At their backs, the wind first lifted their feet, then staggered them with its violent gusts. Tsia caught her balance like a cat, but Wren slid off the narrow walkway into a patch of sponge. The sticky mucus sucked at his trousers, and he cursed at the turpentinic scent. Tsia did not pause to help him, but ran for the middle leg. "Please, please," she prayed to the wind. *Hold on*, she sent to the cub.

Almost before her feet hit the support pipe, she grabbed the controls to start the lift's descent. Nothing happened. Cursing the loss of the node, she hit the buttons again. In her mind, as clearly as if it were shouted in her ears, she could feel the cub's agitation, see it circling and yowling as the sea smashed its vanishing raft. She could see Tucker below, and the dimness of his shape confused her till she realized that she was seeing him visually as a shadow in the gloom, not sharply as a mental image that she sensed through her gate. Behind him, a dark line ran back, ungently curved between the pull of the wind and the tug of the water through which it now dragged.

"Tucker," she shouted. "Watch your line!"

He did not look up. The wind tore her words out of her mouth, whipping them away before they reached his ears. Suddenly, he was waist-deep, the water smashing him against the pipe. One of his arms splashed through the water to grab more of the weedis and haul it closer. He missed, lost his footing, and barely managed to get back to the lift before the wave swept him past. When the water dropped away, he was gasping for breath, and his safety line was pointing sharply down.

Tsia leaned out. "Tucker," she shouted. "Your line. Get your line out of the water!"

Wren reached her as she punched the buttons again. He grabbed her arm hard. "Not without me—"

She nodded urgently, and as one they punched the controls. Still, nothing happened. The weedis was half past Tucker, and Tsia could see its shockingly thin line. There was almost no body to the island now, and the kitten was almost swimming in the barely woven growth as its paws merely took it from one sinking spot to the next. Far past the platform now, the rest of the mother's island swept toward the coast, while in Tsia's head, the feline claws pierced her thoughts. Like a child, she cried out. Wren grabbed her arm and shook her. Flattened, spray-soaked ears seemed to twitch; her lips curled until she shook her own head to clear it.

I'm coming, she told the cub through her gate. Her mental tone was harsh. "Wren, goddammit, help me! Why won't it go down?"

"His safety line." The small man pointed down with one of his clublike hands. "He locked the lift to hold it. We'll have to slide."

Tsia did not wait. Even so, Wren was faster. His thick hands clasped the vertical lift and, like a monkey, he swung his body down so quickly that Tsia was meters behind by the time he lowered himself to the top reach of the waves. Above, Tsia struggled to control her descent. Her hands could not hold her weight against the slickness of the pipe, and she slid quickly down in choppy drops, heedless of her grip and jamming her hands painfully at each footbar.

Below, she could feel the jellies pumping, rising to Tucker's line, tangling their tendrils in its length and turning over to dive. The stench of the weedis clogged her nose. For a moment, she clung halfway down. "Tucker!" she shouted uselessly. "Wren, free up his line. Get those jellies off."

The ocean surged; the wind sprayed all three of them with gritty, fluid bullets. The safety line plunged like a cable to the sea, cutting through the waves and snapping out of the troughs with each wave. What was left of the weedis was wrapped around one end of the station leg, and the strain of that hold against the current tore the island more.

Clinging to the lift above Tucker and blinded by the spray, Wren groped for the line, but even his thick hands could not pull it out of the water. It was like a shaft of steel. He cursed volubly.

Tucker did not notice. His face was set with determination. He no longer bothered to get out of the waves. He stayed waist-deep on the lift, going completely under when the surge caught him wrong. Time after time, he grabbed at the weedis to pull it closer, but he only shredded the edges as if he were a jelly himself. And the cub, clinging to a small bubble of seedpods, capsized and disappeared.

Tsia cried out. Water seemed to close over her head; slimy tendrils slapped her face. She let go of the lift to tear the weeds away, and almost fell. It was the gale, not her balance, that pressed her to the lift and ground her ribs into the pipe to keep her body upright. An instant later, the cub clawed back to the surface. Tsia's hands, curved and grasping, clung to the lift. She yowled, caught her breath, and stared down. Her eyes were filled with the fear she caught from the cat.

Tucker, swamped by weeds and water, gave up and reached toward Wren, but the other merc, hampered by the coil of flexan, could not get down before the next wave took Tucker under. Again, the older merc hauled at the safety line. It did not budge.

Tsia leaned away from the lift. She could feel the pumping, white-clear cloud that gathered on the line. "The jellies," she yelled down to Wren. "They have hold of it. You've got to get them off or they'll drag him completely under."

Wren tried to use his hand, then the length of his arm as a lever to force the line to bend, but the flexan cord was too taut. Tucker, twenty meters below, went under the water again. There was a dark splotch across his face as he resurfaced, and Tsia felt a flood of relief as she realized he had put his nose-breather in. With the tapers of the enbee plugging his nostrils, Tucker stroked hard for the widening pool of weeds where the cub was paddling, trapped and tangled, in the brash. A wave slammed the shreds of the raft against the platform leg, tangling Tucker in their sodden mass, and the merc disappeared again. His hands, white against the slick, gray water, splashed up two meters away. Instantly, Wren abandoned his footing on the stationary bar and swung to Tucker's lift. His massive hands groped in the water as he slid down to the waves and was covered in spray and foam.

Tucker came up again six meters from the piling. His mouth was open, his face tight. His enbee was gone. He shouted something and tried to swim toward Wren, but he submerged before the wind carried his words off the waves. Tsia lowered herself to Wren's position. "The jellies," she yelled. "They're pulling him down. Hang on to me when I go in. Pull us both back on my line."

Wren whipped a loop of the cord through her harness. She unsealed one of her harness strips and took her enbee out, then jammed the tapers up her nose. The chemflaps glued themselves to her cheeks with a tightening sensation.

"Take my enbee for Tucker," Wren directed as he worked. She fumbled with the seals of his harness until she found and jerked the chemflaps out. It took a moment to seal the extra enbee in her gear; then Wren pressed two fingers against his heart, then against her sternum. "For luck," he shouted. She nodded. When Tucker's dark-haired head broke the surface again, she threw herself against the water in a flopdive to stay on top. The impact was a stinging slap across her front, but her arms and legs were already moving, stretching out for the merc.

She barely made contact with the other merc's fingers, but Tucker was ready for her grip. His fingers clamped down like a steel-jawed trap. She drew her breath deep in her lungs through her mouth, not her nose, and did not fight the sea as it took them both down in the surge. In front of her, Tucker's legs were pumping, kicking to keep him near the surface. As Tsia struggled to bring her body next to his, she unsealed her harness with one hand and pulled Wren's enbee from it. She waited for the water to slam them together again, then, her fingers clenched like a fist, pressed the enbee awkwardly against the other merc's cheek. Instantly, he grabbed it. A moment later, the tension in his biofield lessened.

A crest caught and smashed them together, then tried to tear them apart. Curled against the wrenching force, Tsia slid her

knife from her boot and tried to hold it against her sides. The
wave crest seemed to pass; the current steadied. Tsia brought
the knife up to Tucker's hands. He felt the steel against his
skin and squeezed her fingers to acknowledge it. He had lost
his blade, she realized. Now he guided her hand to his safety
line.

Water pushed them together. Water pulled them apart. It
took precious seconds to slide the knifepoint into the knot in
the safety line, and just as she did, Tucker's knee hit her stomach when he kicked to bring them both up. She lost her air.
Above her, Tucker's head broke the surface, but hers did not.
They were sucked below again.

Their hands clenched each other. Seconds, and the current
steadied out, pushing them both toward the platform, while the
jellies tugged down on Tucker's rope. Their legs continued to
kick. They breathed harshly through their noses, and the
enbees split the oxygen from the sea so that their lungs were
filled with air that they used up far too soon.

Another minute, and in the smash of the surge, Tsia traced
Tucker's safety line to his harness and reset the metal knife. A
jelly traced her hands with its tendrils, and she smashed it
against Tucker's chest with her shoulder, then blasted it
through her biogate. It crumpled and washed away.

How long did she pry at the knots in that stubborn cord?
How many times did the waves smash their limbs and tighten
the knots back up? She cursed the line, but flexan fibers would
not be cut by knife. She needed her flexor or raser to cut that
molecular strength. Nor could she slice his harness off him—
its flexan was thicker than the cord. And the cord was looped
through his harness so he could not separate the straps. He
could not peel it from his body. She could not cut him free.

She clung for an instant and tried to think, but the sting of
a tendril touched her jaw and crawled across her lip. Startled,
she jerked in disgust. The jelly found the edges of her enbee
and latched on to it. The tapers ripped from her nose. She
dropped the knife and grabbed at her face. She barely caught
the chemflap as it was folded into the jelly's rubbery body. She
held her breath while her lungs, expecting air, began to suck at

her closed throat. Tucker tapped a message on her arm, but she could not respond in the surge. Instead, ignoring the acid that burned her hand, she curled her fist around the inner jelly organs and crushed the flaccid tissues. The churn of the surge tore at her limbs like wolves, but the jelly refused to let go. The pumping flesh stung her neck and throat. Her lungs burned, and her chest began to convulse as it sucked at nothing through her clenched jaw. Tucker's body tumbled against hers with the change in current. His knees slammed into her legs. They hit the surface, and Tsia arched up. She choked on air and sea. In the slack that caught them for an instant, Tucker became tangled in his line. It yanked cruelly taut around his leg, but Tsia did not notice. The jelly had gone limp and she tore her enbee from its grip. As they went down again, she jammed the enbee up her nose and barely noticed the touch of the acid that seared the inside of her nostrils.

They sank faster this time, but Tsia clung to Tucker's blunter like a leech. Without his legs to stabilize them, they twisted in the current until Tsia was underneath, then rolling to the side before her own safety line straightened them out. Tucker's fingers dug into her upper arms. Brute strength held her body to his. The surge seemed to tear at her; her lungs began to burn. It was the acid that ate at the filters. Like steam breathed in from a cooking cube, the searing proteins of the jelly's venom washed into her lungs.

She ignored the burning and grabbed for Tucker's hand. A fast-finned message, and he pressed back his understanding. His fingers worked frantically at the knots.

Tsia's ears popped. The cold water ached on her body, and another jelly brushed her arm, then encircled her with its tendrils. She blasted it through her biogate, sending its mental shadow a sharp attack of anger, will, and the thought that she was its predator. The soft body crumpled in on itself and washed away in the surge, and Tsia, blind in the water, did not feel the ones that attached to Tucker's back. The merc jerked against her; soft bodies probed his trousers and sleeves to find the gaps to his flesh.

Now it was Tsia's fingers that dug into his. It was Tsia who

choked on the sea. Through her gate, she could feel the ache
in his lungs. Had he lost the enbee again? Had the filters finally clogged? Between them, pulling cruelly back, her safety
line cut into her breast and neck. Her heart pounded in her
ears. Something was tearing her from the other merc, and it
took a moment to realize what it was. Not his safety line, but
hers. Wren was pulling her back, but the jellies still had Tucker's rope. The younger merc felt the water surge between their
bodies. He made a watery grab for the guide, and his fingers
scratched her neck, catching in her collar. The jacket pressed
against her windpipe and she choked. Instinctively, she bucked
and twisted. Tucker lost his hold. The current tore them apart.
Tsia's safety line held her in place, whipping in the rush of the
water; the jellies dragged him down.

She screamed into the murk and lost the last of her breath.
Tucker's fingers were like white ghosts stretching out. Ghosts
she had seen before. White hands in the water. White hands in
her past. Children drowning in the mud off the slough. In a
tide, drowning and reaching out ... Tsia struggled wildly
against the safety line, against Wren. Water rushed past her
mouth and nose. She did not notice that her enbee was gone.

The sea drove itself into her ears. The force of Tucker's desperation cut into her mind, and she could almost feel the pressure build in his sinuses and ears. She could feel his arms beat
at the jellies till they enclosed him in their tissues. Taste the
stinging poison of their tendrils as they crept across his face
and found his nose and eyes. She did not know, as a massive
hand dragged her up out of the water, that she was still
screaming as he died.

7

Wren shook her like a doll, until her body hung out limply over the surge. She stared at him as if he were a stranger, and he shook her again. Not until the senselessness left her eyes and her feet found the lift bar did he loosen his grip. When she finally clasped the pipe on her own, he let go. "Okay?" he yelled over the wind. "Okay?"

She nodded jerkily. She could not look at him. There was horror in her eyes, and she could not tear her gaze from the sea. Her biogate was closed down tight. She did not even let the cry of the sargie through. Wren stared down at the line still taut in the water. "Is he alive?" he snarled.

She stared at him blankly.

His grip tightened. "Alive?"

"No. God, no . . ."

"Where's your enbee?"

"Gone."

"Mine?"

"Gone."

"Shit!" he cursed. "Well, that was useful, then."

Tsia lifted her head to stare at him. This time, there was a spark of anger in her eyes.

"Good," he snapped. "You can be shocked later. If Tucker's dead, there's nothing you can do about it now. You still want the cat?"

99

She breathed in and out, trying to calm the emotions churning in her throat and head. She nodded jerkily.

"Can you keep the jellies away from yourself?"

She nodded again.

His voice was cold as the ocean, and his gray eyes reflected the waves. "Then do it if you're going to. I'll keep you on the line."

She did not move for a moment, then she turned her face into the wind and met the storm's blast head-on.

The weedis was nearly gone. The cougar cub was meters away and almost fully submerged as it washed against the platform, caught in an eddy that sucked and pulled at its body. Tsia watched for a moment, then pulled some slack on the safety line. "It was the line itself that killed him," she muttered. "It was the safety line which dragged him down." Blindly, she undid the knots on the rings of her harness. Wren, judging the distance between the lift and the island, did not notice. When he looked back, he cursed and made a futile grab for the wind-whipped end of the line.

"Are you crazy?" he yelled.

She looked at him as if she had never seen him before. Then, before he could move, she dove into the water.

Liquid ice closed over her head. It was water, frigid and sharp with salt. She could not see, yet there were shadows in her head. Sharp and clear as if she saw it on land, the cub clawed the sea before her. She struggled against the current. Weeds tangled in her legs, and seedpods wrapped on her arms. A jelly rose and pressed against her stomach before it rolled over and reached for her legs with its tendrils. She blasted it through her biogate as she had the ones before. In a second, its white, pumping body crumpled and sank back through the depths.

The water rose and fell with sickening suddenness. She fought to stay near the surface. Deafened by the cub's misery, her ears did not register the sounds of the waves striking the side of the platform. Instead, blindly, she groped for the cat. An instant later, the cub clawed its way onto her shoulder, driving her down below.

She submerged, and in a panic, the cat tried to let go of her blunter. Its claws caught, and it went down with her, beneath the tumbling crest of the wave. Tsia's lean legs kicked. Her head broke the surface in the trough of the swell that followed. The cub sucked air silently. It no longer struggled in her grasp.

"Easy," she soothed. She had no breath for more.

She could see the platform looming overhead, but it was not until the next crest lifted them that she saw where they were. They had washed out of the eddy and passed the middle leg completely. Wren was behind her now, cursing on the leg. He seemed to shoot the lift up, and Tsia almost cried out in despair. Even in the instant her head was above the water, she could see that there was no time for him to get to the southern leg; she and the cub would be long past the platform by then and smack in the midst of the bloom. A brutal wave dropped her, then sucked her under like a jelly. The cub cried out in her head. *Easy*, she choked through her gate. She tried to force her arm to strike out against the current, but the shape of her jacket was a water sail that pulled her farther away from the platform. Farther away from Wren.

Hang on, damn you, she cursed herself. The wave lifted her. A jelly scraped her back. She blasted it through her gate, but it did not go away. Now it was around her neck, and its rough touch burned her skin and sparked her anger to a flame. "Dammit," she shouted. She submerged, choked on her curse, and rose again. Wirelike tendrils swept again against her neck, and she cursed and grabbed the mass with her free arm. And grasped them like death itself.

They were no part of a jelly. It was the safety line. She pulled on it, going under as her weight and the cub's drove it down. Wren. He had thrown the line to the wind, and the storm had passed it on to her.

She twisted as the line was hauled taut against the current. Water beat her down, and her breath burned in her chest. She had no endurance in her lungs. The burn of the cub's lungs was like her own. When the next crest passed and the surge lessened for an instant, she caught half a breath from the surface. She choked, coughed, and lost the air she had gained. Her body bent in a convulsive heave, but she didn't let go of the line.

Current streamed past her face. The cub was tugged from her body, and she clutched it hard, her hand digging into its scruff, her will ignoring the terror that filled its mind. *Hang on,* she told it in her head. *One moment more. One second more . . .*

Water in her nose, her eyes. Water in her ears. Deafness to match the blindness; and sickness rising in her throat. Salt tongue and sweet, weed teeth. She ate and breathed the sea, and the safety line burned in her fingers. She tightened her grip. The current smashed her face; the next giant crest crushed her body. She tried to twist her hand and wrist so that the safety line coiled around her arm and cut into her flesh through the blunter. She snapped her body like a flexor, and as she jackknifed up, her face was suddenly above the sea. She sucked the air desperately. Trapped against her chest, the cub made no sound except in her head. There it whimpered with shortened breaths and dug its claws in fiercely.

Jellies rose around her, but they no longer touched. Again she broke the surface, and again she caught a breath. Half a second. Barely more, before the water smashed her down again. She could no longer hold her breath at all. She could only clutch the line in her fingers and kick, for Daya's sake, kick to keep them near the top of the waves and keep the line from uncoiling off her arm.

She coughed and spit out the sea. Fur was crushed to her chest, and awkward joints jabbed her ribs. Still, the current grew faster, rushing with more power past her face. It jammed itself in her ears and made her body lie straight out in the water till she flailed like a length of rope herself.

And then they were clear, and a clublike hand hauled them off the sea. Wren clung, one hand on the lift and one hand on Tsia's blunter. He submerged with them, then fought his way free. As the water swept down, he clawed his way up toward the controls. Savagely, he jerked them with him. The surge chased them up. A second later, he hit the controls and sent the lift shooting from the surge while Tsia and cub hung from his hand like a limp and bodiless cargo.

8

Tsia could not see at first. She clutched the cub like the lifeline, and could not make her fingers uncurl. Her eyes were slitted like a cat's. Looking at her bared expression, Wren did not doubt the cub had called her to help it. She breathed so harshly he could hear it over the wind.

As the lift reached the platform deck, he slid one hand around her waist and half propelled her forward while she coughed until she retched. Her arms were still curled around the cub as she went to her knees on the catwalk.

"Daya," she croaked. She could see things other than the purple-white deck now: Wren's hooked nose, his pale gray eyes. His gaze darting from her to the cub as he watched and judged her movements. The dark shades of his blunter, the sea spray beading and running off, while more fell like rain from his eyebrows.

With one hand on her back to balance her in the wind, Wren stripped a seedpod from her blunter and a clump of weeds from her boot. She reached up to him, and through her biogate, she could feel his sudden tension, the wariness that was reflected in his eyes. For a moment, she froze. Then she realized that her hand was stretched out like a cat's paw. She blinked, and the feral light seemed to fade from her eyes.

"Okay?" he shouted over the wind.

She did not try to speak again; she just nodded. Her stomach churned, and she felt disoriented by the smell of the wind. It took a moment to realize that the confusion was not all her own, but half from the cub in her grip. She soothed the creature with her hands, but it did not relax. Its nostrils were filled with her scent and the odor of the man. Even through the weather cloth of her shirt, she could feel the light, quick hammer of its heart. As if the death blow would fall any instant, it trembled against her body.

She sat back on her heels and stared into the cougar's eyes. Like a shock wave through her body, her biogate seemed to expand. The snarling in her head deafened her ears. Startled, she turned her head and broke the link. Then, slowly, she reached up to her neck and grasped the claw that was hooked in her neck to shift it onto her blunter. A second later, the cougar dug it back in. She shifted it again, holding the paw until its claws pierced the fabric of her jacket instead of her skin. The cougar growled.

"Stop it," she said softly.

Clumsy cat feet seemed to tumble through her brain.

"Ruka," she soothed, "take it easy. It's all right now." She halted.

Ruka. The cat had a name.

Startled, she looked up at Wren. "It is Ruka."

His eyes shuttered. "You named it?"

"I did not. It had a name that it spoke."

"Through your gate?"

She nodded. The cub still growled, but fear was no longer the dominant sense in its mind. As if the biogate had changed its view of her from human being to cat, it clung to her like a child to its mother. Tsia could barely hold it in her arms. It had been small compared to the older cat, but it weighed almost as much as herself.

Wren reached down and started to haul her to her feet, but at his movement, the cub twisted and hissed. Tsia wrenched it away and staggered up to her feet.

Wren stepped back and said nothing, but his eyes were flat and hard. He motioned toward the bulk of the construction hut. Tsia nodded. She made to follow Wren, but the cub kicked and raked with his back legs so that his claws tore raggedly across her thighs. Staggering, Tsia cursed. The cub vaulted from her arms. He landed half-on, half-off the catwalk and yowled as his rear legs scraped across the sponge. Mucus spread like a film of saliva on his spiky wet fur. In her head, Tsia felt the mother cougar yowl. Abruptly, she poured her strength through the gate to drown out the mother cat's voice. *Stop. Danger*, she sent urgently.

Startled, the cub froze. Wren stayed motionless, his eyes darting from one figure to the other. Ignoring the ragged throb in her thighs, Tsia edged toward the cougar slowly. The blood smell rising through her clothes mingled with that of the seawater, and the two rotting-sweet odors made her want to gag. Downwind, the kitten's nostrils flared.

"You're safe here, Ruka," she told the cub softly. "It's all right. No one's going to hurt you."

His tail flicked and his shoulders crouched, and belatedly she realized that, between the strange smells and the human sound of her voice, the cougar could not help his reaction. She spread her hands and became still as the cub paced with odd jumps back and forth on the catwalk. The sponge mucus frightened him as much as Tsia did, and his mind was a jumble of terror and immature fury. "All right," she said softly, projecting her voice through her link to the cat, not just through her throat. "You're all right now." As the wind rose and fell, the cub began to hear her voice more as a soothing purr.

She kept her gaze locked on the glowing eyes of the cougar, and the cub's scruff and tail fluffed with his warning. "Easy," she said again. "I won't harm you. I'm no predator to you."

She reached out and put her hand below the kitten's face, and the cub's upper lip curled back, baring perfect white teeth. Behind her, Tsia could feel Wren tense. For a long moment, the cub took her scent into its nose. Then Tsia extended her hand and touched it on the shoulder. The young body trembled.

She built a picture in her head of the location of the construction hut, then projected it through her biogate as if she imaged the node. "I won't pick you up again. You can walk beside me." She did not take her eyes from the cub till it moved, tail down, beside her, while Wren brought up the rear. Half the cougar's steps were sideways so that he could see the man behind him; Tsia could only soothe the feline creature in her mind.

At the edge of the hut, the cat paused to lick the mucus off; the taste of the acidic mixture made the cougar gag. Tsia's own stomach rebelled at the flavor he projected, and she closed her gate abruptly.

The moment her mind receded, the cub backed against the wall of the nearest hut and hissed with instinctive fear.

"It's all right . . ." Tsia flooded the biolink again with her voice. "I didn't leave you. This is me. Right here."

The cub growled low, and Wren moved as gently as he could past the cougar to open the door to the hut. Warily, he glanced back. The wind howled with the cougar's voice, and he grinned for the first time with humor. He wanted to see Nitpicker's face when she caught sight of the cub. Six months old and as big as the guide . . . He shook his head. He barely kept hold of the door as the wind grabbed it. To the side, the cub leaped away at the movement. Tsia was there in an instant.

Nitpicker yelled from inside. "Get in or stay out, but get that door shut."

"Quiet," Tsia snapped back. "And don't move."

She turned to the cub and projected as strongly as she could the sense of safety. With his shoulders hunched, his tail crooked at the tip, and his head low and swaying, Ruka eased through the door. Tsia's voice barely held him from bolting. The scent of the humans filled his nose. The light in the hut shone in his salt-stung eyes. His pupils retracted to small circles, and Tsia felt a dull ache in her own eyes become relieved. She tried to ignore the urge to kick her own legs free of the mucus that stuck to the cat; it was all she could do to hold the cub's mind in place.

Nitpicker, Doetzier, Kurvan, and Striker held their silence. Nitpicker's hands still gripped her dart gun; Kurvan's were full of scanners. The cargo sled obscured Doetzier's lower body, and Striker, beside him, held her tools at awkward angles as she obeyed Tsia's order.

All four stared at the creature that crept through the door. Abruptly, Kurvan set his scanner down. The motion inflamed the stiff-legged cub. He arched till his hair stood straight out from his scruff and hissed at the merc with the scanners. Tsia snarled at him through the gate. For a moment, no one moved. Then, inch by inch, as Tsia's voice coaxed him farther in, the cub stalked to a crate, eyed the room balefully, and sprang on top of the box.

Tsia's mind control was rigid, but she could not help the images that spilled to her own brain from the cub. Each movement seemed sharper to her eyes; every scent was thick in her nose. Something there smelled faintly feline, confusing both cub and guide together, and their two sets of eyes flickered from merc to merc. Wren shut the door, the wind roar whistled and died, and Ruka's ears snapped to point at Kurvan, then Doetzier. His nose swung in a low, slow, continuous movement.

"Tsia," Nitpicker said softly. The cat's eyes swung back to the woman, and his tail tip whipped. "We need to discuss your little project."

Nitpicker's face seemed strangely blurred, and it took a moment for Tsia to realize that she was seeing the merc leader through the cat's eyes at the same time as through her own. She had to blink to clear her vision. "Ruka's nervous," she said in a low voice. She moved toward the crate slowly, the skin around her mouth tight as she refused to favor her clawed left leg. The weather cloth shed blood as if it were water, and the fluid that welled from the wounds made sticky runnels down her calves. Along the top of her boots, where her trousers were tucked in, the thick, drying fluid pulled at her skin. "If I clean the mucus from his fur, he should be less agitated," she added. "He'll be better prepared for the flight."

Nitpicker did not nod, but her eyes flicked to Tsia's legs. "Shallow or deep?"

"Shallow," she said shortly. "I'll get a skin graft on it as soon as the cub calms down."

The other woman turned deliberately back to her work. Beside her, Kurvan picked up his scanner again and reset the fields he had checked. Ruka growled at their slow movements, but Tsia stroked him along his back, soothing the stiff hair that stood up. Wren, his back to the door, regarded Tsia for a moment before clearing his throat. Nitpicker looked back up.

"There's one other thing," he said flatly into the quiet. "Tucker is dead."

Doetzier turned his head too quickly, and Ruka's legs, tucked beneath his tawny body, launched him at the merc. Like lightning, Tsia's hand buried itself in his scruff and pinned him to the crate. His cat feet scrabbled. He bit air, but she ignored his teeth. *Stay down*, she snapped through her gate. *Down!*

Doetzier stood still and stared at her, but she didn't think he saw her. His mind seemed to churn and his biogate—with those tiny points of light—seemed to spark to greater brightness. An anger burst within him into a frigid flame, but all Tsia could see with her eyes was the wariness of his withdrawal.

Wren shook out his blunter, spraying the floor with water. The cub bristled. Nitpicker eyed the cat for a moment, then turned an icy gaze to Tsia. "Drowned?"

Tsia's gaze shuttered. "His safety line—there was too much slack. The line blew into the water and was dragged down by the jellies. If he hadn't tied it to the stationary lift—"

"If he hadn't tried to catch a wild cat," Nitpicker cut in viciously. "Ifs have never brought a man back, Feather." Her glare was cold. "Goddam Landing Pact," she muttered. "He had an enbee. What happened to that?"

Ruka snarled into the silence. It was almost instinctual to soothe the cub, and some back part of Tsia's brain noted that the voice of the mother cat was less obvious in her mind—or the cub's voice more clear and overwhelming—each time she opened herself to the cougar. It was not as it had been with Tucker, she thought with sudden guilt. Even when he drowned beneath her, he had not been as clear in her gate as the cub was now. She stared blankly at the pilot.

It was Wren, not Tsia, who answered Nitpicker. "Tucker lost his enbee in the brash. Feather dove in to get him. Stayed under long enough to half drown herself. It was his stupidity, not hers, that got him killed. She shouted at him three times to get his line out of the surge."

Doetzier looked from one to the other. "Why dive in?" he asked quietly. "How did you think to help him, if he was already dragged down by the bloom?"

Tsia's eyes blazed oddly. Doetzier's gaze sharpened. She felt tension creep into her lean body, and beside her, the cougar cub stiffened. His menace through the biogate was almost palpable. "I tried to loosen the knots with my flat knife," she answered slowly. "I didn't have a flexor to cut the line." Her eyes flicked to Kurvan. "But the knots were too snugged up. He was pulled right out of my hands."

"I hauled her up still screaming," Wren added in the quiet. "Practically hit her to make her stop."

Nitpicker eyed Tsia and the cub. "Doetzier, are you done with that sled?" At his nod, she said, "All right, let's get the rest of the gear to the skimmer and give her some space to clean that thing up." She glanced at Tsia again. "Wren will let you know when we're ready to take off."

Deliberately, Tsia looked at each merc, but their sight seemed to pass right through her. With her jaw set like concrete, she watched them file out to the storm. Her link to the cat had killed a man, and she could not blame their silence.

The air they left behind seemed clogged with distrust. She stared at the cub. "So." Her voice was tight, and she had to force her throat to open. "Tucker's dead." The cub growled low in his throat. "Did you hear me?" she demanded. "He's drowned and dead, and you watch me with those eyes, and I can feel nothing of him in your mind. He doesn't exist to you." Her voice tightened. "To me, he's gone, but that's all I see when I look at you. His absence. Not what he was. Not what he did to save you. Just the fact that you're alive." She clenched her hands. "Oh, Daya," she cried out in a whisper. "What biogate have I got, which brings my demons to me?"

She looked into the golden eyes and saw herself reflected. Saw her jaw tighten to a white line, while her breathing was harsh in her ears. The cub watched with a growl. Tsia hesitated, then opened her biogate wide.

The senses of the cat swept into her mind. Immediately, her nostrils flared, and her ears seemed to twitch. Her heart pounded far too fast in her chest. The hair on her neck rose up like a brush, and as she stared, her eyes saw every tiny shift of Ruka's body—every flick of whisker, every rise and fall of the fur on his chest. When she finally shifted, Ruka did the same. His fur smoothed down across his back, and Tsia's shoulders relaxed. Tension flowed out from their bodies like water from a collapsed balloon.

"Ruka," she whispered brokenly. The cougar growled in return. It was not a threat; she could feel his acceptance.

She got a medkit and pulled out a medwipe, which she stroked across his fur. Little by little, the sponge mucus came off, but its proteins had bonded with his hair and skin, and the scent and slightly tacky feel seemed stuck in the kitten's coat. Following the path of the wipe, his tongue licked him dry. But his lips were curled back at the taste of the mucus, and Tsia's own lips twisted against the flavor he projected.

She paused in her cleaning. Slowly, she reached up to touch his gold-brown head. His fur raised up along his scruff, but beyond that, he moved nothing but his eyes. Tsia touched the hair behind one ear, and the ear twitched irritably. His tail tip flicked. "Easy." He growled low in his throat, but he did not snap at her fingers. She stroked the fur again, this time rubbing it with more pressure. The cub still growled, but now he pushed back against her touch. Never letting his eyes move from Tsia's gaze, he accepted her with a wary watchfulness.

She reveled in the coarse feel of his fur. The stiffer, waterproof pelt was smooth along his back and legs. A black line like dripped mascara circled his eyes and curled down around his nose, delineating the small areas of softer, whiter fur. She looked down with a humorless smile as he pushed against her hand. "Don't think to get me too attached to you." She built an image of the coast in her head. "That's where we are going—where we'll leave you. From there, you can go back to your family."

The cub growled again, but rubbed his cheeks on her hands to mark her. For solitary predators, cougars were affectionate, and Ruka was no exception. In the wild, he might not have left his mother till he was two years old, and still the female would not have rejected him. He would simply have drifted off when the new cubs came along. Tsia tried to feel the mother cat, but she could no longer distinguish the rest of Ruka's family from the background din of catspeak. "Don't worry," she told him softly. "She'll accept you back. Cat mothers do, you know."

Moving slowly, she pulled a generic skin graft from the medkit, then unsealed her boots. The sodden, sea-sweat smell of the liners made the cougar's whiskers twitch. He bared his teeth, and Tsia's lips curled back in response. She stared at him for a moment. A faint scent of Tucker . . . A memory of his pack beside the wall . . . Ruka was here, alive and vibrant, and Tucker was dead. And she could not feel anything about his death. Was it too close for her to acknowledge? Or was she so lost in her gate that she had forgotten how to grieve for a death she herself had caused? Abruptly she put the medkit away and stood with savage swiftness.

Barefoot, she stalked to the molecular scrub in the back room. Ruka leapt down and followed like a dog. Tsia's skin prickled with his proximity. She dropped her blunter over a crate, pulled her shirt over her head without unsealing it, and peeled off her trousers. The blood that welled from the ragged wounds still dribbled down her leg. Her sea-chilled flesh looked much paler beneath her tan than it should; the smeared and crusting blood was stark across the leanness of her limbs.

She examined herself without expression, as if her mind were separate from her body. When she pressed against the flesh, the forming scabs split and forced fresh blood from their edges, and she studied the wound for the depth of its tearing. The sharp throbs that shot across her leg and up her back did not make her flinch. Small pains, she told herself absently. They meant nothing. She had felt much worse in the past.

Quickly, efficiently, she shook her trousers over the scrub block so hard that the safety cubes rattled in their sealed pocket. The caked blood flaked off like dried mud, and the garment shook out almost as clean as if it were new. Still, she held it in the scrub and waited while the full cleansing cloud formed. The molecules bound to the grit that still clung to the fabric, and the heat stole the chill from her arms.

It took only a minute to scrub her boots, her clothes, then herself. When the salt crystals were gone, her skin no longer scratched itself each time she changed expressions. The weather cloth of her trousers and shirt shed water like glass, and the blunter dried in seconds in the hydrophilic blasts. In less than two minutes, Tsia was dried and dressed again in all but her trousers, socks, and boots. She ran her hands over her pockets, checking their contents. She hesitated for a moment at the sharp edges of the safety cubes. She bit her lip, then left them alone. There was plenty of time to return them.

Ruka's eyes were large and curious as they followed Tsia back to the other room. When she dropped to the floor by her pack, he padded over beside her and sniffed the tears on her leg. She shoved him gently away. Ruka growled and settled down beside her, and she murmured her approval.

She unrolled the first skin graft and stretched it out over the scratches. The blood still welled out, but she ignored the flow and pressed the thin, transparent sheet over her flesh. She could feel the instant response. As soon as it was exposed to oxygen, the dormant layer of cells activated. Her biogate seemed tickled with molecules that moved and shifted and touched each other, binding and releasing their chemical signals throughout the graft.

Amino acids coiled back upon themselves. They bent and flattened and screwed themselves into helixes. They collapsed into rough spheres with pits and clefts on their surfaces. They became proteins, and Tsia's body reacted. Her skin and blood and muscle cells sent out cyclins to the graft. Kinases filled the protein pits with tiny ball-like shapes. All across the area, phosphate molecules broke off from or attached themselves to enzymes. She could actually sense the neocell membranes open and close to the chemicals. Goose bumps spread out across her thigh. To feel life at such a tiny level . . .

She found her lips pulled back in a feral snarl. Ruka stared at her with fear in his mind, and she could smell the sweet scent of herself in the cougar's nose. She murmured to the cub, soothing him with her voice until she felt the graft cells differentiate. One moment, the graft seemed to crawl with tiny, chaotic movement—as if it were coated with billions of excited molecules that had no pattern to their dance—and the next, it actually was alive.

Cell membranes strengthened all across the graft. New kinases and cyclins burst into action. Cells became skin that divided and grew into a new, transparent layer, separate from the artificial graft. Skin bound to skin; cells became flesh. Dead blood in the open wound was broken apart, then swept away by her capillaries. Tiny phages acted as vectors for the proteins that spurred her blood vessels to grow. Within the hour, the graft would release its calcium and the other growth factors to the wound. The axons of her nerve cells would turn and grow toward each other, creating new pathways through which they could communicate. Within two days, the thin layer of tissue would develop to its full sensitivity and thickness. Within four days, the graft would die and flake off like a sunburn, killed by one of its own coded proteins.

She stroked the graft across her flesh, ignoring the broad pain that washed her leg while she sealed its edges with pressure. She placed the second graft below the first, covering the lower edge of the gouges. Ruka, his nose twitching, moved forward, and Tsia let him sniff. The cat's tongue licked out. Its roughness finally made Tsia flinch, but she held still so that the cub could taste the graft. "It will become part of me," she told the kitten. "Like new skin. In an hour, its smell will be more like mine."

It took a moment to use the seam-sealer on her trousers; when she was done, the only evidence of the tears was a slight irregularity in the iridescent cloth. She got to her feet and pulled on the rest of her clothes, stretching her toes hedonistically inside the boot liners as she felt the warmth of the dry and grit-clean fabric. When she shrugged her harness back on, she fingered the flat slot where her enbee had been stored, then turned and searched for a replacement in the e-packs along the back wall. Her fingers were steady until she put the new enbee in the slot; then a wave of guilt swamped her guts like nausea.

She eyed the cub without expression, then motioned toward the door and built the image of the outside deck and the skimmer's shape in her head. Ruka's body became very still, as if the threat had returned with the pictures. Coaxing him to the door, she turned out the lights and stepped out of the hut. As the door slammed into the wall with the wind, Ruka bolted straight into the dawn. In her gate, she felt him skid around the corner of the hut as clearly as if he had taken her with him. She hesitated, then shrugged. He couldn't go where she could not now find him.

She shut the door and stood for a moment with only the wind in her ears. She could feel nothing of Tucker at all now. No scent. No visual memory from a room or piece of gear. His biofield did not exist, and his body was buried in jellies. She tilted her head to the sky so that the rain dripped from the eaves of the hut to her lips. Bitter, the taste of the sky, she thought. Bitter as her gate was sweet.

Where one of the flight-deck supports rose from the loose sponge mass, two shadows moved in the gloom, catching her attention. They had their backs to the hut, but Tsia felt them clearly. Nitpicker's shape was obvious from her voice, and the club-fisted Wren, with his overlong arms, could not be mistaken. "Tell me about Tucker," Nitpicker said quietly.

Downwind, Tsia heard her voice clearly.

"He drowned," Wren said simply. "His safety line was loose. It caught in the bloom and pulled him down. He drowned. That's all there is to it."

"That's all? There's nothing else?"

Wren hesitated, and Tsia could almost feel his uneasiness. "Van'ei," he said, using Nitpicker's real name, "you know Feather. You know the way her biogate sits with her. She was a rogue gate ten years ago. Her senses are even stronger now—if more controlled—than they were back then."

"You think Tucker's death had something to do with her link to the cats?"

He shook his head. "No . . ."

"Then what did she do?"

"I'm not sure she did anything," he said slowly, then added, "I don't see how she could have done anything."

Nitpicker's voice was dangerously soft. "Explain."

He hesitated again. "When we missed the weedis at the southern leg, she went up the lift before I could clear the safety line and follow. She reached the middle leg a full minute before I did. But it didn't budge. Wouldn't go up or down."

"You think she locked it?"

"Hell, Nitpicker, she only had a minute. And she might know how to run a tight web in the node, but she's still only a guide. She knows nothing about control codes for lifts."

"She's been a merc for ten years," the pilot returned sharply. "You know the odd information you can pick up just by doing your job."

"Yes, but this . . ." He seemed to shake his head again. "She was really angry when it would not go down. She hit it. Almost hit me when I finally got there and couldn't get it down either."

"It wasn't a cover?"

"No. I'm sure of that."

"And Tucker?"

"He could have locked the lift to hold his line steady."

"You don't sound like you believe that."

"At the time, I thought that was what happened."

"But now?"

"Now, I've had time to think. Why he would lock the extra lift? It would have remained stationary whether he had his safety line tied to it or not. Locking it in place would have been superfluous. But the kid was new to this planet—had never seen a bloom before, or a wild cat. Maybe he just wasn't thinking."

Nitpicker was silent for a moment. "Any chance Feather deliberately let him drown?"

Wren did not hesitate. "No. She was hysterical when I pulled her up."

"That could be faked."

"Not like this." He hesitated. "You ever looked into her eyes

when she's got her gate wide open? She wasn't faking anything. If you ask me, I think she felt his death as he went
through it. There was a blank horror in her eyes that was very
. . . realistic. She could not have helped trying to save him any
more than she could help being caught up by the cats themselves."

"What about the enbees? They're not made for salt water,
but they should have worked for a while—long enough to keep
him alive."

"He lost his enbee the first time he went into the brash. Probably tangled in the weeds and jerked it out himself. Feather took
mine and hers down when she went in after him. Tucker had
one in his nose when he came to the surface after she reached
him. After that, it either clogged, or he lost it in the jellies."

"And Feather's?"

"She had hers for a while, then lost it. She was half-
drowned when I pulled her back up. Did you catch the sting
marks along her cheek? Kind of hidden by the scars, but they
were there. I think she lost it to the jellies that hit on her face
and neck."

They were both silent for a while. Then Nitpicker said, "All
right, Wren. Thanks."

Their shadows were silhouetted in the skimmer hatch for a
moment before they climbed in. Behind them, at the hut, Tsia
touched her cheek. She could still feel the burn of the jellies in
her nose. She could still feel the tearing surge of the sea in the
wrenching ache of her muscles. And she could hear the pilot's
voice, like an echo in her mind, accusing as a judge.

Tsia forgot the burn that ate at her nostrils. Forgot about the
cougar. Ignoring the storm that slashed her face, she stood for
a time in darkness.

9

When Wren came to get her, it took all of Tsia's will to coax the cub to the skimmer. The shadow of the ship frightened the cat even while it caught his curiosity. The smells, the movements in the lighted cabin—they were too much. Between his fear and distrust, there was no way he was going into the ship.

Letting him go for a moment, Tsia stuck her head in the hatch. The other mercs, wet from spray that had blasted in as they waited, stared back coldly. Striker looked from Tsia to the cub that paced out in the gloom. The woman's voice, when she spoke, was derisive. "That the cat you traded Tucker for?"

From beside her, Wren's quick, birdlike eyes flicked to the woman's closed expression. "Tucker did his own trading," he said softly. "And he did it for the Landing Pact, not for her. Feather did no less than you or I could have done to save him."

Striker continued to watch Tsia, her black eyes as unreadable as ever. "Like to hear her speak for herself," she said.

The wind gusted, and Tsia shivered before she could answer. When she caught herself, she gave the other woman a steady gaze. She was unaware of the glints that gave her icy eyes their wildness. In her head, the cub's fright was like small hammers pounding at her brain. "I did my best," she said flatly. "I nearly drowned to save him."

The woman eyed Tsia for a moment, her black gaze unreadable. Finally, she nodded with a curt motion and leaned back in her seat.

Cold, silent waves of blame seemed to flow from each merc, and the line of Tsia's jaw tightened. She knew what she felt could not be real. If they thought she had murdered Tucker through either action or inaction, she would have been left behind on the platform, and no one in the skimmer would have looked back twice. But that knowledge didn't change the guilt she created in herself. Nor did it shift the shadows she saw in the eyes that stared back at her own.

She hesitated, then said tersely, "Don't move for the next few minutes. He'll be frightened and wild. He could lash out at anything that shifts. Should settle down in a few minutes."

Kurvan snorted. "The way a tornado settles down on a hut?"

"Can it, Kurvan," Nitpicker snapped from the pilot's chair.

The merc's eyes flickered, and Tsia shivered in the wind. There was a chill in Kurvan's gaze that she had not seen before—a kernel of ice that seemed to coagulate in the hot eagerness of his field. She closed her senses to the mercs and turned back to the storm.

Ruka was still having no part of it. He growled and paced back and forth as if Tsia's will were a leash that kept him from backing farther away. His back was arched and his tail twitched; his head swayed side to side. He approached the skimmer, then backed away, then approached the ship again. "Easy," Tsia murmured, coaxing and cursing in alternate breaths as she urged the young cat forward. "This is the only way," she breathed, "to get you to the shore."

Still, the cub balked. She shoved at him through her gate, but he refused to budge. She tried to pull him with her will. It was like trying to move a glassy, heavy wall toward her, she thought, using only the friction of her fingers against its smooth, vertical surface. "It is not as if I can just lift you and carry you in," she snarled under her breath at the cub.

Ruka swung his head and stared at her with unblinking, baleful eyes.

"Come," she urged. "Now." She reached out and edged for-

ward until she could, carefully and slowly, touch him behind
the ears. Softly, steadily, she began to press. Lightly, she added
pressure, as if to draw him forward. Ruka's growl grew. She
did not crouch to his level. Neither did she release her pressure
on the cub with her hand or her mind. The minutes grew to
two, then five.

Finally, in her biogate, she felt a lessening of tension—like
a rope that goes slowly slack—and, as if he glided without
moving, the cub began to ease forward. She tried to build a
picture of a den and project that to his mind, and his paws
crept faster across the deck, but still, he moved like a snail in
glue.

"Feather," Wren said in a low voice behind her, "the winds
are growing. We have to take off. Nitpicker's giving you two
minutes more. If you can't get the cat through the door by
then, we're raising anyway." Tsia started to protest, but he cut
her off. "When the node comes back on line, we'll send a
vetdarter down to anesthetize the cat and take it to shore."

"No." Tsia's curt response was immediate and unthinking.
"He's moving on his own. He'll get in by himself."

"You haven't got much time left."

"I don't need more. He's coming in now."

"Not quickly enough to show movement," Striker muttered.

Kurvan nodded. "Why waste your time—and ours? You
can't expect an animal to follow your directions as calmly as
if it were a man."

Her face tightened with the effort of speaking through her
mental projections. "This one, I can." She forced the words
out.

Kurvan's eyes sharpened. "Why? Are you linked with the
felines?"

Though she kept her voice low, Tsia laughed outright at his
question. "Now, that would be a useful gate."

Wren's eyes flickered, but he chuckled as well. "About as
useful as a desert digger in the sea," he added.

Tsia glanced over her shoulder. "If I were linked with the felines, this cub would be in and seated like a merc in a soft, and

I'd be asking him if he wanted a slimchim for a snack while we flew."

Bowdie eyed her warily. "Let's just hope he doesn't snack on us if he joins us."

Tsia forgot that the motion of her nod was more frightening to the cat than her voice, and Ruka spun and leaped away. Instantly, she jammed him to a standstill with a blast of emotion even she could not identify. He froze, crouched to the deck. Tsia felt a backlash of fear and danger turn her bones to stone. She tried to uncurl her hands from her sides—attempted to turn her head and make a sound other than the harsh breathing she choked out through her teeth. Between her mind and the cat's, a cord of emotion stretched. It was as if her brain made a stab at the signals Ruka could understand, and hit for the first time on the combination that worked, like the first time she had imaged the node and it responded. It was as though she somehow understood in a single instant a language she had heard all her life as garbled music.

She became aware of the claws that pierced her mind. No longer did they tear at her thoughts. Instead, the cat paws seemed to pick out pieces from her mind. Like a set of words recognized in a book, those thoughts alone were clear. Ruka clung to those images. In the gloom of the gale, where the light from the cabin flashed in his eyes and blinded him to the mercs, while his nose made him choke with their scents, the cougar sought the only safety he could see: Tsia.

"Come," she commanded. "Now. With me."

Blue shadowed eyes stared into gold. Nostrils flared in and out. Ears flicked in the rain. Ruka crouched more tightly to leap forward. And Nitpicker chose that instant to start the skimmer's motors.

Sail slats flared along the sides of the craft. Tsia cursed. Ruka bolted. Tsia lunged after him, caught one of his hind legs, and as the cat jackknifed, twisted and clawed with his forepaws, she slung him through the hatch. The silent howl that shocked her mind was deafening. She rolled to her feet and skidded across the deck, throwing herself after the cat. Wren slammed shut the hatch.

Ruka hit the door like a madman. Wren jerked out of the way. Ruka yowled. He turned and leaped across the cabin, desperate for escape. The mercs cowered in their seats. Ruka's paws hit the arm of a soft, and the cat recoiled at the strange fabric, striking out so that Doetzier scrambled over the seats to avoid his tearing claws. Caught for a moment against the bulkhead, Wren flinched as the tawny beast hissed and spat at his boots.

"You going to control this thing?" Bowdie yelled, jerked back as the cub's heavy paws landed on his legs and shoved off in a massive leap.

"Feather—should I wait?" Nitpicker shouted over the noise.

"No. Go!" Tsia grabbed Ruka's scruff in passing, and was dragged two meters on her knees before she slowed him down. Snarling and twisting, he fought her as she forced him toward her seat. Doetzier, caught in Wren's soft, shifted as far to the side as he could. Tsia ignored him. She strained with the cougar's wildly writhing weight. If her lean arms had been thicker—if her body had had more mass—if she had been Bowdie or Kurvan or even Doetzier, she would have sat on him to hold him.

"Doetzier," she snarled, "your blunter. Quickly—" Her voice broke off in a hiss as Ruka raked a claw across her thigh. With a wrench, she shoved him back down.

"Can you hold him—"

"Yes—" If Daya gave her strength, she could hold him.

Doetzier pressed himself against the far arm of his soft. "If a man is afraid of the teeth of a cat, he'd better not let go of the tail."

"The guide guild," she gasped, "gives us some protection."

"You're no longer of the guild."

"You noticed?" she snapped back. "Then think of the Landing Pact and pray."

Ruka's face was a blurred and snarling vision. Tsia's hands were full, buried in writhing fur. When Doetzier slipped his jacket across her lap, she wriggled it down her legs only to have Ruka's claws hook the fabric and drag it down around her ankles. "Take this wing out fast," she snapped at the pilot. "I won't last three minutes like this."

"Then we'll make shore in two and a half." Nitpicker set the sequence for manual liftoff. "Bowdie, hit the navtank. Let's spike this ship out like a beam from a laze."

His hands flashed from one set of controls to the next. "Gyros on," he reported as the screens before him displayed the skimmer in prep. "Vents cleared. Shore's in the tank now—"

"Shore?" Kurvan's voice was sharp from the rear of the cabin. "I thought we were getting rid of the cat at the freepick stake."

Tsia barely turned her head over her shoulder to answer. "He'd never find his family from there—" Her voice cut off abruptly as something from the node flickered through her mind. Like a whisper heard in passing, like an image caught with the corner of her eye, she lost the flicker before she recognized it. But Ruka felt her hesitation and jerked against her grip. "Sleem take you," she gasped as she yanked him back against her legs.

Up front, Nitpicker did not seem to have noticed the flicker in the node. No one else said anything; Kurvan's eyes were still narrowed from Tsia's tone. She didn't care. At the moment, with the cub clawing the floor to fight her grip on his scruff, Kurvan was not her concern.

"Launch ring cleared," Bowdie said tersely.

"Locations mapping now," said Nitpicker as the lower half of the holotank flared into a dim display of the platform and sea.

"Thrusters on." Bowdie talked right over the pilot. He knew she would hear him even as she reported her own control status, just as he listened while he talked himself.

"Resetting," she returned.

"Flap configuration verified."

"Sensors coming in now." In seconds, the onboard sensors read the wind power from the skin of the small ship and poured the data into the top half of the navtank. Wind speed and shear became swirls and corkscrews of color. The sea remained calm and gray.

"Cabin decoupled. Stay on manual?"

"Yes. Keep the safeties off. And disable the bodychecks," she added sharply. Each soft was configured to its passenger, so that the stretch pads could shape to each flier and slow his deceleration more. But no one was sitting still enough for a bodycheck. Doetzier and Striker had both crawled twice from one soft to the next. Wren had not yet sat down, and Tsia, with the cub between her legs, was not likely to stay seated at all.

Bowdie stretched his long fingers across his screens. "Bodychecks disabled."

"Flight status cleared."

"Give me a lock on direction?"

Nitpicker flicked her fingers across the panels. Colors shifted, and columns of data flashed, then disappeared. "The plan is in the can."

"Got it. Launch when ready."

The skimmer rose off the deck with a painful shudder. Power flowed along its sail slats, and the flap sets turned and responded to the wind. In Tsia's hands, the cub sensed the vibration and lift. The surge of acceleration that hit them both pressed him into Tsia's legs. He panicked. Her grip was so tight, she almost twisted his skin beneath his fur. "Two minutes," she said desperately. "Just two minutes to shore."

If Ruka understood, he gave no indication. As the skimmer tilted, his paws scrabbled for a hold, and finally hooked into the sides of her boots, snagging the seals and popping them open. She grunted and twisted her feet to keep him from tearing her footgear off. The muscles along her arms were taut. When he writhed up again and got his paws on her thighs, Doetzier reached across to shove the cub back down.

"No!" snapped Tsia.

The other merc jerked back as if bitten. Ruka, wild at the proximity of the unfamiliar hand, broke free and lunged across the cabin. Wren cursed. Kurvan snarled back as the cougar brushed across his boots. Tsia sprang from her seat and staggered as her unsealed boots flopped at her ankles. The skim-

mer angled up like a laze. Falling, Tsia barely caught the edge
of a soft in time to blast out a mental command. To the others,
the expression that tightened her face was shocking: her skin
went rigid; her lips pulled back from her teeth; her upper lip
curled and her nose wrinkled. Even her eyes seemed to flash
with an odd golden light.

She did not see through those eyes. Her mind was locked in
her biogate, and there was a deafening snarl in her mind. Cat
feet in her skull skidded to a halt. Ruka froze as her presence
stretched like a claw, hooked into his mind, and jerked him
back to stand before the webbed-in packs.

He hissed.

She snarled.

He edged back and slunk along the wall.

"Ruka—" Tsia forced the words out between taut lips. The
sound made no sense to her ears, and it took a moment to realize that her throat was tight with the din she heard in her
mind. She was locked to the cub by mental cables of scent and
image and fear. The thread of panic made her already taut
muscles rigid. Instinctively, she tried to pull back from the
biolink—to close it down, like shutting off a light. She tried to
pull the talon of her presence from Ruka's mind so that she
could use her own eyes and ears. But the moment she moved
back, something hit her like a hammer in the head.

She cried out. The biolink went wide. Like a hand on her
throat, the gate choked off her breathing and squeezed hard
around her heart. Fear and wildness—a desperate anger—
tightened their grip when she tried to pull away. It was as if the
cub had in turn anchored himself in her mind. There was only
one thing in this alien, unfamiliar craft and swamp of smells to
which he could cling: Tsia. And he clawed her with all his
strength.

Odors beat at Tsia's senses: metaplas, flexan, weather cloth,
boots . . . The hot points of the rasers on standby. The flat, old-
dirt, salt smell of the harnesses that had been wet by the sea
spray. Black nolo seeds. Acrid sweat. Human scent. Fear.

Tsia tried to image through her gate, but the mental claws
dug into the very bones of her skull. Frozen, torn with wild-

ness, she burst open the biogate so that her mind matched the cougar's, and her emotions reflected his. Air seemed to rush to her lungs. Her tendons stood out like cords. Somewhere in her ears, Striker gasped and a man's voice cursed softly. The cub grew still, huddled in on himself against the cabin webbing; his soft, steady yowl was a constant din in Tsia's mind.

The skimmer shuddered, and Tsia swayed. Slowly, as if her bones dissolved, she crumpled to her knees, then her hands. Striker reached to help her, but she flinched away with a snarl.

Still, she faced the cat. Unfocused blue eyes gazed into unblinking gold. She stretched one hand toward the cub and felt its instant, instinctive withdrawal. Only her will, pushed through the biogate, forced him to remain where he was. Fear and bewilderment remained in his thoughts. He could taste the pain in her mind.

Not your fault, she whispered in her gate. *Just one more minute. Maybe two.*

She didn't know what the other mercs were doing around her; she could see nothing but the cub. The skimmer's vibration settled into a rhythm that hummed in her bones, and she knew in the back of her brain that they flew with the wind. Gradually, as if she hummed herself, she let the resonance of the ship seep through her gate to the cub. Slowly, her eyes began to take in light. Blurred images sharpened; edges became clear. She could see, not just feel through her gate, the cougar that crouched before her. His big paws were tucked and taut beneath his body as if he would launch himself at any time. His tail was crooked and flicking.

I can't hurt you, she breathed through her gate. *It would be like cutting myself.*

Ruka growled.

Nitpicker looked back over her shoulder. She could almost feel the strain in Tsia's hands as the guide kept them from reaching for the cat. "Feather," she said sharply. "We're coming in on the shore. Pick your spot."

Tsia did not seem to hear, and Nitpicker motioned sharply for Doetzier to repeat the command. When he shifted to speak,

Tsia stiffened. She blinked and looked toward the pilot. "Landing spot?" she asked unsteadily.

Doetzier, careful not to move again, indicated the navtank with his eyes. Shivering, then steady, then trembling again, Tsia eased back from the cub so that she could look toward the tank. Although Ruka growled without stopping, he did not move from his crouch.

The node seemed to flash again in Tsia's head. For an instant, the holographic skimmer shape hovered in the blackness of space with sunlight glinting off its sides. The land below seemed deceptively calm, as if it were hidden beneath a thin canvas of ghosts. When the flash faded, she was left with memories, not overlays, which she could not follow clearly. But she had grown up in the sloughs of this coast. She knew the cold-packed sand and flattened dune grass; knew the flooded estuaries that stretched back for kays with their gray brine and their dark shrub tips sticking out of the water. She remembered the rocks and mudflats that clung to the bluffs. Saw, long before the navtank recorded it, the white line of sanded rock that snaked down into the slough and disappeared beneath its waves like the children that had drowned so many years before.

"There's the bluff," she said to the pilot, as she watched the faint images display themselves in the tank. "Demon Bay," she murmured. "Pelican Slough. Halona Slough. The dikelands."

"The dikelands?" Bowdie caught on that. "They're flat, and we're already four kilometers inland."

"In this weather, they'll be flooded like lakes. Keep going. Five . . . maybe six kays. Look for a landlocked lake with a broad bank on the west side and a narrow canyon on the east."

Nitpicker's voice was sharp. "You know this place well enough to verify it for a landing?"

"Yes, but I can't verify it as we come in—we descend too fast. I need time to read a . . . creature's memory of the area. It looks clean in the tank; that's all I can say for sure."

Bowdie's brown eyes narrowed and his face pulled with his frown so that the bumps on his nose were as prominent as his cheekbones. "A lot of good the tank does us when the node it-self is down."

Nitpicker's hands were a flickering blur on the controls. "Check as much as you can, Feather. We're approaching fast."

Again, the node seemed to flash in Tsia's mind. Images from webs she had spun years ago seemed crossed with over-lays that flickered fast away. A woman ghost seemed to walk from one station to another. A shadow skeeter skimmed the surface of a slough—it was a ghost image created ten years ago; it had never been erased. One thread, thin as spider's silk, was so old that she barely remembered creating it: a simple man, an imaginary home . . . She traced it in an instant and re-alized abruptly that it was one of her first successful webs— she'd made it two full decades before she had become a merc. She'd even had a running bet with her sister about how long that web would last . . .

She would have followed the flash further, but the skimmer hit a wind pocket and dropped with a sickening lurch. The node flickered out, the ghost woman faded, and the false skeeter image dimmed; but the man and his home remained in her mind like a physical line that tied her temple link to the node. Up front, Nitpicker's neck tensed and Ruka yowled in her ears. Quickly, Tsia touched him through her gate, forcing a mental purr to soothe him.

With a frown, she looked forward again. The holotank now showed only the skimmer's sensor pictures: the lake with its thin and rocky shore, the dense forest dark and still; while the real trees she saw out the window bent with the force of the storm. "The southwest side," she directed the pilot. "The shore opens up below the hill. There's no trees for fifty meters, and the rocks don't start again till you get underwater." She paused and stared at the images for several seconds before she realized what was different than she remembered. Some years ago, a den of reavers had built a dike across a small ravine. Now, Crashing Creek was no more than a still, gray-water pond. It was not a false scan, she knew. The pond had the depth of real water—the detail that spoke of hundreds of scans and dozens of node affirmations.

Nitpicker caught Tsia's expression. "How long has it been since you've been here?"

"Fifteen years," she returned slowly. "That pond wasn't here before, nor was the shore so wide."

Bowdie glanced over his shoulder. " 'It is memory, not history, which moves backwards.' "

" 'And guilt, not time, which stands still,' " retorted Nitpicker. "Time passes, Feather. It was bound to change."

Tsia pointed curtly toward the images in the tank. The lake, filled in her memory with eels and bottom fish, was murky and cold; gray and flat and chill. "Go on down," she said finally. "I feel nothing . . . wrong."

The skimmer slowed and dropped. As it turned, the storm winds grasped it like a giant's hand and shook it in long and shuddering bursts. Humming and turning, jerking and dropping, balanced only by Nitpicker's hands, the small craft hovered lower until the wet hills rose around it. Tsia watched their familiar shapes: Chameleon Ridge, Tarbar Gully, the Plain of Tears, and the Trial of the Seven Toads . . . The ravine where her sister had broken her leg, and Tsia had held her out of the water till their brothers could arrive . . . The falls where she used to go diving . . .

The peaks grayed with the rain that fell outside the window, while in the holotank, each geologic shape became transparent to keep the ship in view. Down and across the navtank water, the ship shape skimmed the lake. Circling gusts shook them from one side, then the other. The resonance of the skimmer rose as it held its place roughly; then it dropped as the sensors first calculated, then compensated for the chaos of the wind.

Tsia reached for Ruka to calm him, and the cub growled in her mind. She tightened her physical hold. He seemed to give—in her mind—and she realized suddenly that she was almost not speaking with him, but projecting the emotions that reset his mental images, just as he projected senses that triggered her response. There was a softness to this link—a kind of malleable texture to the touch of one on the other's mind. As if something was being woven, or a hardener was being mixed.

Then, abruptly, the skimmer shivered in a long, drawn-out ripple, and dropped to the bank like a brick. Tsia staggered; Ruka jerked at the impact and bolted toward the window. Wren scrambled aside as Tsia dove for the cub and caught him by the scruff. Like lightning, he swiped at her face. For an interminable second, his claws hung over the scars on her cheek. Then the ship smacked into the bank like a fist hitting dough. The two of them skidded across the floor and slammed into the bulkhead.

The skimmer slowed abruptly, then oozed forward in a slow, slick motion till it stuck in the mud. Stunned, Tsia had both hands in Ruka's scruff, pinning him to the floor. Up front, Nitpicker stared at her panels. For a moment, no one moved. Then Ruka snarled and Tsia shoved him so that she held him against the wall. Doetzier's eyes were on the navtank; Wren's were on the hatch.

Bowdie glanced at the holotank, then over at Nitpicker's frown. "Damn, 'Picker," he said in a drawl. "You should've been a pilot."

The woman did not smile back. "We shouldn't have landed this easily," she muttered.

"You touch down in storm winds like a feather kissing the ground—no reference to you, Tsia," he said quickly over his shoulder, "and you complain?"

She shook her head. "Something cut out just before we hit. Shunt the control systems to my panels, will you? I want to see the settings . . ."

Slowly, Tsia got to her knees as Nitpicker fingered the screens. The skimmer shuddered and settled further. Tsia glanced around the cabin. For a second, the node flickered, and ghosts rose again in her head. The auburn hair of Striker and the black hair of Doetzier superimposed on each other like opposites. Striker's black eyes and eyebrows were framed by Doetzier's black, short-cropped hair, and her auburn mass was set off by Doetzier's tanned expression. Tsia blinked and tried to clear her sight. "Nitpicker," she said urgently, "release the hatch."

"Just a minute," the pilot said sharply. "It's not clear here. There's something wrong."

Wren, braced against the side of the cabin, eyed Tsia and the cub and tightened his grip on the hatch panel. The skimmer tilted again, shifting in the sludge. Nitpicker's eyes were on her scans, but her tension had not abated. "No, no, that's all wrong . . ." she muttered.

Beside her, Bowdie seemed lost in his thoughts, but Tsia knew he watched his com as intently as the pilot did. Kurvan seemed almost expectant. Doetzier watched the others as if he waited for one of them to move; and Striker, in the back, was silent. Tsia stilled herself, and almost imperceptibly, Ruka crouched lower against the wall. The cub yanked on her arms, and Tsia staggered before she realized that it was the settling of the skimmer, not the weight of the cat, that unbalanced her.

She glanced out the window. The hills were bare and open to the rain: a mudslide had—perhaps hours before—scoured the slope of brush. The brown-black rocks that were now exposed had just been born to the world. Water ran down the slide in new erosion channels and filled the puddle that spread beneath the skimmer's weight. Tsia leaned closer to the window. The gray expanse had stretched almost to the skimmer's half-folded wing. She squinted at the bank.

The navtank showed the skimmer resting on a pebble-strewn bank about three meters from the lake, but Tsia could not see any rocks that would indicate a more solid base than mud. Around the craft was the narrow, caved-in trough where the skimmer had scored the sludge as it came to a stop. Even as she watched, the trough overfilled with water and began to flood the bank. The skimmer tilted again. "Now why . . ." Her voice trailed off.

Nitpicker heard her. The pilot's hands paused above the control screens. "What do you feel?" she asked sharply, though her voice was low.

Tsia opened her biogate. Ruka's presence was like a blanket that enveloped her in fur and teeth. It was too strong, and she pushed it away, heedless of the snarling that grew in her mind with her rejection. Nitpicker, Wren, and Doetzier . . . The mercs were like moving clouds that grayed her vision. But there was something more ... She stretched, and realized that the senses she felt were familiar. Strong. Marine. The lake. She staggered again. But thick enough to feel without good focus. Closer than it should be ...

"Rise us," she shouted abruptly at the pilot. "Get us off the bank—this isn't solid!"

Nitpicker reacted almost before Tsia finished her first word. "Thrusters on!" she snapped at Bowdie.

"This is mudflat not rock," Tsia snarled.

"Gyros on!" Nitpicker ordered

"I can't," said Bowdie. "There's no power."

"Break it free!"

"It's not the landing gear—"

"Goddam it, where's the boost?"

"Get soft! We're sliding."

"We have to get out!" Tsia was not aware that she had shouted again till Wren jumped toward the door.

"Bowdie," he snapped, "get the hatch open."

Doetzier's voice barked in the background. "Get the gear. Move it! Now!"

Tsia didn't think. She clutched the cub instead of her pack, controlling his panicked claws from attacking the mercs in his fear. Wren had to tear her arm from the cougar and thrust it through the strap of her gear bag. Her training took over, and she stuck her other arm back blindly, while Wren shoved the pack up against her spine. The force of his push made her stagger, and her shoulder hit the wall with a thud. Ruka yowled. His claws bit deep in her arm. The ship lurched again, throwing them against the line of softs. The cat yowled, and the fear in his tone doubled her heartbeat like a drum.

The ship listed like a dunken man, and the mud at its base disappeared beneath the water like a slough when the tide came in. Then, as if the shifting of the ship had given the mountain permission to drop, a portion of the slope slid away from the hill and swept toward the bank of the lake. Both window and navtank showed it clearly. The front edge of the slide hit the ship like a hand slapping the craft across the shore. In a comically precise movement, the mercs fell forward into the walls, then staggered back violently to their seats. Wren landed on the floor; his back struck the arm of the soft behind him before Kurvan could catch his weight.

Tsia hit the holotank hard and fell through the images so that they swam on her face and arms. The cougar yowled, and Tsia did not notice that the sound was in her brain, not her ears. It was all she could do not to cry out in turn as his claws bit into her mind. One side of the ship flipped up; the mud forced the other into the lake. The only thing Tsia could do was twist so that Ruka landed on top as they fell back against the webbed-in packs. Her spine bent across her pack; Ruka fell onto her gut, then broke free and leapt away.

The ship slid along the bank like a crate across a floor. Up front, Nitpicker grabbed for the panels. The skimmer did not respond. In slow motion, the bank collapsed. One instant, the skimmer sat hatch-side-up in a puddle on the shore; the next, the ship lurched with a new wash of mud and moved smoothly, bottom-first, into the lake.

10

Wren used his seat like a trampoline and leaped to the hatch controls. With his narrow legs dangling below him, he triggered the portal open. As a gap appeared, Striker sprang up to hang beside him from the edge. Wind and rain slapped into their faces. Striker, then Wren levered up and onto the rim.

"The gear," Striker shouted, crouched on the edge of the hole. The skimmer jerked and tipped; the woman lost her balance with a splash. Ruka shot up and out of the cabin like a streak of light. His forelegs barely touched the rim of the hatch, and Wren did not even have time to shift as the cougar whipped on by.

Tsia, tangled with Bowdie's legs, struggled wildly to free herself as she screamed at the cougar's back. "The water. Go for the water. Stay away from the shore!"

Doetzier grabbed her arm and yanked her clear of Bowdie's long legs. He grabbed up a pack, only to have Tsia snatch it from his hands and throw it up to Wren. Behind her, Kurvan grabbed another pack and jumped for the hatch. He hauled himself up with one hand until Wren grabbed him and yanked him clear. A second later, he crouched on the edge with the older merc and reached down for the rest of the equipment.

Wren yelled down at the pilot, "Van'ei, get up here. We're going under—"

"We've got nose-breathers—"

"Does no good in mud or silted water. Move it! *Now!*"

133

Tsia glanced toward Nitpicker; Doetzier grabbed one more pack and jumped for the hatch. Bowdie jumped at the same time, and Doetzier hung for an instant as Wren and Kurvan grabbed the larger merc by his collar to help him up through the hatch. Water began to slide in over the edge. Clinging to the rim, Doetzier was blinded by the torrent, while the force of it twisted him violently. Wren had hold of his wrists, but the gray-brown cataract tore Doetzier down by his pack even as Wren yanked him up.

"Drop the pack—" shouted Wren. "Unbend your arm. Get rid of the pack—"

Tsia's biogate seemed to surge, and Doetzier seemed to shout his rejection in her head. Wren cursed. His muscles bulged. Then he dragged Doetzier over the edge like a log hauled up through a waterfall.

As if his body had been a plug, the cascade turned into a deluge. Tsia was pounded into the corner of the cabin. She couldn't see Nitpicker or anyone else. Even with her arm over her face, she could barely breathe in the bone-smashing torrent. In her mind, Ruka snarled and seemed to grow closer. Something snapped taut between them. Some part of her mind melted. She tried to scream, but the sound was not human, and it did no good anyway—the water smashed the shriek against her teeth and jammed it down in her throat. Her claws stretched up. Ruka's hands stretched down. The biogate was torn in two. And in its place, a mental cable of solid will twisted out from the gate and whipped around both minds: the one, in the lake, with furred, pumping legs that pushed his body through the waves; and the other, with her teeth bared and pounded by the water that crushed her against the walls.

Frantically Tsia groped for the pouch that held her nose-breather, but the enbee was not there. Panicked, she tore at every seal in her harness. It took an eternity to realize that her clothes had twisted with the flow of the water; the pocket was not where she thought. With her hands clumsy as paws, her lungs began to burn long before she found the enbee in its pouch. A second later, she shoved its tapers up her nostrils, sealing her nose from the lake.

The water immersed her torso now, and the savage pounding lessened over her chest and legs till it felt like only a hundred rubber hammers banging at her flesh. Now only her head was still smashed with blinding brutality against the skimmer wall. She dragged the collar of her blunter up over the side of her face, then forced herself to wait, pinned against the wall of the cabin while her pack tangled more in the webbing and the enbee's chemflaps glued themselves to her cheeks on either side of her nose. Finally, she drew a breath of air. In her mind, Ruka's lungs expanded. Her skin ruffled like fur in the whirlpool current that circled the cabin area. An arm brushed her body, and she grabbed it; Nitpicker twisted with the flow and squeezed a message back against her hand. *Wait.*

Tsia acknowledged the finger-tapped message with pressure of her own. A moment later, she struggled free of the webbing and followed the pilot to an air pocket at the front end of the cabin. Her head broke the surface with an audible gasp. She looked around quickly, while Nitpicker peered down at the submerged conn. The skimmer lights were still on, but the water was so thick with sludge that neither woman could see her waist, let alone her feet.

Nitpicker groped in her blunter for her enbee. "We have a few seconds—" she managed as she caught her breath. But by the time she plugged her nose and sealed the chemflaps to her cheeks, the water had risen half a meter. The two women were floating with their toes barely brushing the walls. Tsia made to move toward the hatch, but Nitpicker held her back. "Wait—"

Her voice was muffled by the sound of water and the closeness of the flooded cabin. Tsia nodded, but in her mind, the sense of the cat was overwhelming.

Nitpicker caught sight of the feral glints in Tsia's eyes. She dug her fingers into the guide's shoulders. "Not now, Feather. Not yet."

Tsia nodded jerkily. She could feel Ruka swimming, his thick, furred legs like pistons in the water. The water closed up to the hatch; the air pocket shrank to a half-meter's height. Tsia's back arched automatically as the shape of her pack pushed her hips down. Nitpicker kicked her legs in a scissors kick and fought to hold her position. They washed in a tiny circle. Tsia tried to see through her gate—through Ruka's eyes—for the mud that must even now be sliding toward them, but all she could see was the motion from the waves of the lake.

Ruka, she shouted through her gate. *Look toward the mud!*

The cat obeyed, and Tsia's eyes flooded with shapes that flickered and shifted. The trees in her mind bent like berry pickers. There were the tiny figures of mercs who crawled out of the water. Cold water slapped her nose, and her ears twitched with the fluid that filled them. And to the cougar's right, in his mind and in her own, she saw the hill shift down toward the lake.

"The mud's coming now," she gasped. "We have to go—"

But neither woman was prepared for the brutal sloshing that slammed them up against the roof and dropped them again with ankle-jamming force against the backs of the seats. The reaction wave washed them away from the hatch and up into the front of the ship. They hit the roof hard before being sucked viciously back down.

Tsia could not fight the awkward shape of the pack. Her ears popped. Depth, she thought. They had dropped at least five meters. Submerged, she breathed completely through the enbee while her hands grabbed on to rough fabric. She pulled herself along the wall till she found the gear webbing. She could feel Nitpicker nearby.

Black, stirred-up silt blinded her. Lake grit bubbled into her mouth. The enbee stripped oxygen from the murky water, but its silt-plugged filters gave her limited breaths. She gathered her legs beneath her and thrust herself toward the hatch.

Something caught her at her waist. She ignored it and hit the edge of the opening with her shoulder. The pack caught. She twisted, freed it, and grabbed the slick metaplas edge to pull herself out. Nitpicker was right behind her—she could sense the other woman in the water. Sense another merc nearby. Silt swept into her face and urgently she shoved herself away. Behind her, Nitpicker followed suit. And then the mudslide slithered over and buried the skimmer like a fat snake on an egg.

Disoriented, Tsia stroked hard, her body rolling as the pack fought her for buoyancy. A second later, her hands hit mud and struck deep into waterlogged sludge. An eel slid across her wrist; instantly, she recoiled. Beneath her, the mud gathered speed and slid on past. The slick mire caught at her feet like quicksand. With sudden panic, she whipped her body madly, but as she twisted, the pack caught in the slide. She panicked and jerked one arm free of the straps. Cat feet seemed to tear at the surface she stirred up. Then she tore herself away from the gear, leaving it behind, buried in mud, while she clawed her way through the water.

She moved into a long-armed stroke that was instinct as much as training. Her boots felt like bricks on her feet; her blunter trailed and rippled like drags along her sides, and her flexor snapped against her thigh with every kick of her legs. She didn't know if she swam up or sideways; only that she was no longer in mud and that the cub seemed close—too close. The shore—she tried to image the shore to the cub, but Ruka hissed in return.

At the sound in her head, she stopped swimming. For a long moment, while her heart pounded and her cheeks poured their heat into the water, she floated without moving. The cold water began to chill; the silt ground between her teeth. She could not see, but when she put her hand over her face, the bubbles floated out through her fingers, and she knew finally that she was on her back.

She turned over and checked her bubbles, and this time, she followed the air to the surface. Pressure did not allow the enbee to give her full breaths, and her nose sucked in as she pulled only shallow breaths from its filters. She hit a warmer clime in the water, and a cold one as she followed her gate toward the sense of the cat. Then she hit the surface so abruptly that her arms were half out of the water before her eyes registered the lighter, flat-reflecting gray. Something bumped her from behind.

She twisted like a fish. Ruka? She cried out in a sound that was more sob than laugh of relief. Golden eyes stared back. The cub had not swum to shore. He'd stayed behind like a beacon to guide her. She opened her mouth to say his name, and her mouth filled with the slap of the water. She choked, went under, kicked back to the surface, and motioned through her gate toward shore.

The wind slapped water up against their two heads; the rest of the lake was flat. The storm had whipped off the crests that would have formed in calmer air; the spray from the missing crests was a vicious, horizontal rain. Tsia squinted to keep her eyes clear and began to swim toward shore, but her body did not lie flat in the water. Her legs dragged down with the weight of her boots, and like a sail, the blunter billowed around her.

A wave struck her in the head, and she didn't have a chance to struggle before she went under. In her mind, the cougar yowled, but she reassured it instantly. She had her enbee—she could breathe; air was not a problem. And swimming a meter underwater, she realized suddenly, was easier than fighting to stay on top. Even blurred, Ruka's sight through the gate told her where the mercs were on the shore. There were two on the bank already, a third climbing out from the water with the aid of a fourth, and one more in the water ahead.

Tsia paused and kicked and recounted.

Five.

Not six. One of the mercs was missing. With the wind and water blinding her, she could not tell which one. She opened her biogate to feel for the sense of a human, but she had to close herself to the cub; the sense of him swamped her so that she could not feel the other species. The void that she created ached with the faint sense of marine life that was left.

Floating, carried by the wind current on the surface, she forced herself to concentrate. She began to identify distances and the mental shapes of light. Below, there was a growing sense of eels, and a school of slim, blue-green tealers surged to her left. Wedge growths of weeds waved on the bottom. And each second that passed, she felt the mercs more clearly.

Wren was first and easiest—she almost smelled him as much as saw his cold, hard energy. Doetzier and Striker—a cool, wary tension; and a closed, shallow light. Kurvan up ahead, wading out of the water, his field as wary as Doetzier's, but his energy strong and hot. Bowdie with the heat of fear and irritation clear even at that distance, as though he forced himself to do something of which he was afraid. And Nitpicker . . .

She could not quite feel the pilot . . . She opened her biogate wide, and the weight of life in the lake swept in like a shadow that darkened her mind. It took a moment to separate her senses from the one that she sought. And she realized that what she felt was behind her with the eels. Behind, she thought, and down. As if Nitpicker was still with the ship. As if the woman was . . .

Trapped. Abruptly, Tsia kicked hard for the shore, moving partly against the wind current to reach Wren where he waded out to help her. "Your enbee!" She shouted. She staggered on the bottom and sat abruptly down, her neck deep in the lake. "Your enbee—did you replace it on the station?" She yanked her blunter from her arms; it sank just below the surface, but she didn't care. Wren would pick it up. "I need the breather." Quickly, Wren dug his new enbee from his pocket as she ducked under again and struggled to wrench off her boots. A moment later, she surfaced, grabbed the enbee with one hand, shoved the boots and flexor into his arms, and threw herself in a long, twisting dive back into the lake. Wren was left, waist-deep in the water, staring at the flat-calm surface. His eyes narrowed, he stooped, groped in the water for the blunter Tsia had left behind, and hauled it up. He looked back twice. Tsia came up and stroked strongly along the surface, then went down and did not come up again.

Barefoot and free of her blunter, she moved smoothly down through the climes. The fabric of her clothing rippled against her skin. She could feel Nitpicker more closely now, but the biofield was weak. With each meter that she dropped, Tsia found her heart pounding in her temples and her lungs beginning to ache more than her arms. She struggled for her breaths before she realized that she had closed off her own throat. Breathe, she snapped at herself. She had an enbee. She had air to take in. It was Nitpicker she was feeling—Nitpicker who had no air.

Air ... The strength of the biogate brought her memories too close to the surface of her mind, and a vision of white hands seemed to stretch out in the water. She gasped and choked as water came in her mouth. The sense of children drowning ... Tucker at the platform; Monument Rock in the past ... Urgency clutched at her skin. The cougar growled, and the sound amplified the memories until it seemed as if a thousand voices flooded into her mind and deafened her.

"No!" She shouted the word underwater. This was not then—it was an hour since Tucker had died. Twenty years since the children had drowned: tiny hands, cold hands, little mouths begging her to get them out of the mud, out of the cold, out of the slough that choked them with every surge of tide. She tried to close the memories out of her mind and focus only through Ruka, but ghosts from the node flickered in her head and overlaid themselves on the hands. She shoved them away harshly. She stretched—she reached—she tried to feel only Nitpicker, but something interfered.

It was the beginning of unconsciousness.

An iciness struck for the first time through the waters of the lake. Desperate for speed, Tsia reached out to the cub and sucked up the strength he projected, but that was a mistake. In her haste, she shot past the woman below before she felt the change in the biofield's intensity. She twisted, sculled, and flipped around, stroking back along the bottom. This time, she went more slowly, her hands outstretched and searching above the sludge.

She could feel Nitpicker's panic grow as the first drowning blackness faded and the colors began to burst behind her eyes. Exhaustion clung to Tsia's legs, but as the mud churned before her, Tsia realized that she sensed not her own ache but the other woman's body. The weight—the fear ... Nitpicker was pinned in the mud.

Tsia struck out widely, sweeping to reach as far as she could. Weeds, silt, a submerged snag ... Then a hand that hit, then latched on to her arm like a talon, cutting deep in her flesh. She let herself be drawn in, needing to be closer to get Wren's enbee in place.

But Nitpicker's hand tangled in Tsia's shirt, and savagely, with all her desperate strength, she jerked Tsia close and struck unerring at her throat. Cold, steel-like fingers squeezed. Instinctively, Tsia jerked her chin down. The bone of her jaw jammed against the fingers that tried to crush her larynx. Her hands pried frantically at Nitpicker's fingers, palms, thumbs. Her flesh tore. Cat feet clawed with hers against the other woman's arms. Something snarled in her ears, and she could not tell if it was herself or the din in her biogate that deafened her to her pain. Frantically, she groped for the other woman's face. She punched, then clawed to loosen the pilot's grip. Clumsily, again and again she struck out, the extra enbee closed heedlessly in one fist. She twisted and wrenched until, in a panic, she jammed the enbee in Nitpicker's nostrils.

It was not a clean shot; only one of the tapers was up Nitpicker's nose. But the woman's hold froze instantly, then released. Tsia wrenched away, kicking up more silt and mud. Her mouth seemed filled with the grit. She gasped and took in water, gagged and coughed and doubled over, convulsing with the effort of breathing when her throat felt torn and collapsed.

The heightened tension radiated up like steam. The panic in the other woman's field was hot. But now, Tsia's own heartbeat pounded heavily in the water, and her breathing was harsh through nostrils that tried to gasp through the thin breaths of her enbee. The ghosts of the node weren't solid, but the medlines—the only part of the node still active—automatically took over. Electrochemical signals poured into her brain. Proteins that coded for clotting genes. Tissue regeneration ... Nerves. The subconscious part of her brain whirled while Tsia tried to breathe.

Then, cautiously, she swam back down to the bottom. Warily, she reached out among the mud-buried weeds. She touched a shoulder, and the body beneath her jerked. She could feel the sudden spurt of fear, of panic. She was cornered—

Immediately, Tsia withdrew. Then, kicking slowly to keep her position, she forced herself to extend. Mud shifted on the bottom; Nitpicker's biofield surged with controlled terror. Tsia touched the woman's arm and left her hand there so the pilot could feel who it was. The other woman's hand closed over hers and gripped it tightly, then moved up her arm to her face. Tsia allowed her hand to feel. She squeezed the pilot's bicep in pattern, finning quickly.

Her hands found the mudslide that had engulfed the woman's legs, and as Tsia dug her hands into it to see how solidly the pilot was trapped, it shifted like sand, surging forward another quarter meter and flooding up to the woman's waist. Nitpicker's hands dug into Tsia's arms. Tsia felt her heart begin to pound again in her throat. A white line of rock twisted in her sight. A line that sank in the slough in permanent memorial. And Tucker, with that safety line cutting through the surging sea . . . Daya, she whispered in her mind. Not another one, she begged.

How long had they been under? How long would the enbees last? She forced herself to think, then tapped her fingers against the pilot's hand. She repeated the finning, as the other woman did not immediately respond. She could feel the tension rising in the pilot's body with the message. Finally, Nitpicker finned back in agreement, and Tsia opened her gate.

Shadow forms of fish and snails played at the edges of her mind. Freshwater celphs floated past. She could sense the mud worms, benign and hungry, tunneling toward the looser silt. There was a pressure against the inside of her skull—a cacophonous resonance built out of energy itself. And within that din was one she knew well—and hated.

She called it. Found its resonance through her gate and matched it with a projection of her own. Food, she sent. Flesh cold and ripe for eating. Within seconds, a shadow grew around her. Something brushed her arm. Nitpicker's hand clenched suddenly on her own, and she knew the woman had been touched by an eel.

Tsia fed the force of her welcome into her biogate. With all her focus, she called out a cold, dead image and spread it in the water. Spread the sense of it down in the mud. The water stirred around her, and she tried to hold her position as the currents began to swirl. The pilot's grasp hauled her back and tapped out an urgent message. Tsia finned back a steady response, but as she did, a slick body slid along her side. Nitpicker's fingers threatened to dig all the way through Tsia's hand. The eels swirled around Nitpicker's head, and Tsia forced the woman to bend her arms to protect her face and neck.

One eel made a dive for the mud. It could sense the warmth of the woman's legs, and it hesitated. But it was hungry, and Tsia projected food and chilled fish flesh. It made one pass, ignoring the woman's exposed torso and arms; its prey was a bottom fish, flat and streaked with tapered gray-green stripes. It wanted buried meat—cold meat—not the warmth of a human body.

As Nitpicker's grip grew tighter and tighter, Tsia realized that the other woman did not know the eels could sense the movement of her legs in the mud. She finned another message to the pilot, and the woman forced herself to hold still. Like pigment, the shadow of the eels thickened. The pilot's arms, twined around her head to protect her face and neck from the eels, left her only her hands to clutch at Tsia. Each time the eels stroked along the woman's skin, she whimpered into the water. Each time they wrapped around her head, she jerked. Their flickering shadows darted in Tsia's head, back and forth, like faint, malevolent lights. She tightened her grip on the woman. Any minute now, they would begin to tear at the mud. Any second now . . .

Something barreled clumsily into Tsia, and she slammed forward over the pilot. A rough hand grabbed at her arm and yanked her hard away. She struck out wildly to reject the man who dragged her up, then realized that it was Bowdie who had hold of her. Instantly, she dug her fingers into his bicep, finning to stop him with her message. He froze, then pressed close beside her. A quick return fin—he acknowledged her response—and together, their hips brushing as they stroked, and her shoulders clumsily scraping along his ribs, Tsia jackknifed them back through the blackness.

The mud had shifted up another handspan, and Nitpicker was bent and buried to her waist. Her arms were clear, but her shoulders rigid; her gray hair floated from between the flesh of her arms. Tsia projected the image of fish in the mud, and suddenly, as if they understood at last, the eels responded with shocking intensity. A single eel struck down. Like a shot, the second, and then the others drove down. Mud slid and flowed. Nitpicker seemed to cry out in the water. Sludge flowed up into the lake as if huge spoons dug into the slide and cast the mud away. Tsia and Bowdie grabbed Nitpicker by her arms. Bowdie started to kick hard, pulling up with brute strength, but Tsia waited. The eels were striking now like lances. Nitpicker's body jerked with each hit. But she loosened. Tsia felt the give and shouted. Water and silt rushed into her mouth. Hard—she kicked as hard as she could. She split the water with the force of her legs.

A slow release; a sloppy, spucking sound . . . The woman's body slid free while the eels attacked violently the soft hole she left behind. The pilot kept her hands over her head. Her entire body shuddered. Kicking and struggling, the trio rose like gas bubbles toward the surface, and as they hit the first cold clime, Nitpicker began to kick with them. Tsia did not let go of the woman's jacket. The pilot's legs were weak, and the chill in Tsia's bones did not seem to be from herself, but from Van'ei.

Up, up and toward the wind. Up through blackness, through the grime of the storm-torn lake. They hit the surface as suddenly as Tsia had reached it before, and Nitpicker struck free of them, gasping as the air stung and whipped her face. And then they bobbed in the flattened waves and sucked the air that was shoved down their throats with the wind.

11

For a moment, Tsia hung on the surface, ignoring the slap of the lake. Beside her, Bowdie trod water with difficulty. His pocked face was red, and his breathing rough. She could feel an odd tension in his body, and took a moment to realize that it was fear—his discomfort in the water. He hated it, she realized. His brown eyes peered down as if he expected the eels to follow them up, and the emotion that flooded their depths was countered only by his hatred of the lake.

"All right?" she managed, looking at Nitpicker. Her voice was harsh—more like a croak. Her throat still felt crushed.

The pilot nodded. She did not try to speak. Sluggishly, she hauled her arms through the water. She still wore her blunter, and the sleeves slapped heavily with the two strokes she managed before the water pushed her under. Bowdie hauled her up and dunked himself in the doing; the two mercs kicked for a moment to catch their breath.

"Give me your jacket," Tsia said to the pilot. She caught at the collar and held Nitpicker up as the woman struggled out of it. Tsia took a second to roll the fabric up; she sank before she got it in a tight bundle. Then she tucked it in the crook of her arm and followed the other mercs in a stilted sidestroke. She quit almost immediately; as soon as she turned her face to the lake, the water slammed down her throat without stopping. The low growl of the wind was almost as loud as the sounds of the cougars in Tsia's head. "Daya-damned yaza wind," she muttered. She choked on water, and closed her mouth with a snap.

She shoved the blunter bundle ahead of her with her chin, while her arms kept her body afloat. The water's chill seemed to intensify as her adrenaline subsided. The lake tasted flat after the salt of the sea, and the green scent of algae deadened its flavor. She stared doggedly in the direction of the shore. How could it take so long to swim so short a distance? She could barely see Nitpicker and Bowdie; the clouds cut so much light from the sky that the pilot's gray-streaked hair was almost invisible against the surface. The brown hair of the other merc was no more than a glistening shadow. It took Tsia a moment to realize that the wind was circling at the end of the lake, pushing her along the shore instead of directly toward it. She had fought it before; this time she was too tired.

Even though her muscles were moving, and she was sweating as she swam, she seemed to have no warmth in her bones. There was no semblance of color left in her face; the wind that whipped the water over her head stripped even that from her skin. In her head, Ruka growled and curled against her skull. The cat seemed closer than he had a moment before, and Tsia opened her biogate further and searched for the sense of the cat. Wet fur seemed to scrape and catch on her skin; her ears twitched in the water. And then Tsia felt buoyed up by a warmth that spread from her belly along the inside of her arms.

It was energy. Heat through her biogate—sent by the cougar to ease her chill. She almost stopped swimming. *Ruka?* she asked in her mind. The cub's only answer was a growl.

Ahead in the water, Bowdie stopped, and Tsia caught up with difficulty. "Okay?" she asked.

Bowdie tried to nod, opened his mouth to answer, but choked on the lake instead. Tsia nodded toward the bedraggled woods where Ruka hid in the brush. It was a hundred meters past the point where the other mercs waited. "We've been fighting a surface current. Just stay afloat and kick in that direction." She pointed. "Wind will push us ashore."

He didn't bother to nod. Instead, he turned and kicked clumsily with the wind. Nitpicker followed him doggedly in, the thin line of her dart gun waving along the surface like a tiny black scanpole. Tsia trailed behind.

On the bank, three of the mercs began jogging to meet them around the eddy. By the time Bowdie swam in to the shallows, all three were back in the water, wading out waist-deep on the rock ledges that ran beneath the surface. Bowdie stood up before Kurvan could help him, and the lake water ran off his bowed legs like waterfalls. He took a step, slipped, and went under. A second later, he broke the surface again. Painfully, he got to his feet, pulling Nitpicker up onto the rock with him. With Striker supporting Nitpicker on the other side, the four waded out of the water.

Wren waited for Tsia while the others staggered to the shelter of the trees. She swam in until her knee stubbed painfully against rock almost the same moment her fingernails jammed into the rough stone. Wren offered her a clublike hand, and she took it gratefully. "I'm all right," she said hoarsely. She hauled Nitpicker's blunter from the water and gave it to Wren in trade for her own. Quickly, she shrugged into the sleeves and wrapped her arms around her waist. The wind had slapped the cold back into her bones the minute she rose from the surface.

Wren gripped her arm. "Doetzier found an overhang between two lava bombs. We can shelter there till we figure out what we're going to do."

She nodded without speaking and staggered clumsily after him. Her numb feet seemed to hit every ragged bump and crack beneath the water, and she wondered that Wren didn't feel them through his boots. Lake grit dried across her cheek, and she peeled the enbee from her face to seal it in her harness. A few moments later, her feet hit the lake bank, and she trudged, then forced herself to jog behind Wren. As she reached the trees, she stepped on a sharp, hidden stick. She swore quietly, and put her foot down directly on another. "Daya-damned digger dung," she cursed.

Wren glanced back at her mincing run, then pointed toward the bank where he had originally waited. "Your boots are back there. I only brought the blunter."

She nodded and limped after him until the sharpness of the

bruise subsided. The cold mud squelched beneath her toes, but she seemed oddly immune to the storm. Was she so numb she could no longer feel the chill? The wind gusted and drove a thin sheet of rain across the lake, and she felt it ruffle her fur. She stopped midstep. Her lips raised in a silent snarl.

She was still taking her body heat from the cub. Through the gate.

This time, the chill that crawled through her bones was real. When Ruka first gave her heat, she had not thought beyond the gratitude that the chill was no longer a danger. But now—she accepted the heat as if it was instinctual. As if it was all right to take this from the cub.

She stared toward the brush where the cougar crouched. This was not the same as touching an adult cat's mind. No full-grown tam had ever given her an energy that she took in as her own. No watercat had ever quenched her thirst by mental thought. What Ruka was doing—was it normal? Or was it a sign that Tsia had stepped beyond the law of the Landing Pact? Contact when the cats requested it—that was accepted by any guide. But to take from the cats automatically—and to take heat, to take energy itself . . . If the cub responded like this to her unspoken needs, what would he do if she accidentally projected a need for action?

She had to force herself to move forward when Wren glanced back with a frown. But a flash of tawny skin melted into the shrubs beside her. "Go back to the beach," she whispered. "East. Go east. You can find your family if you hurry." Deliberately, she turned her back. *You can't stay with me.* She sent the message through her gate as strongly as she could create the images. *I don't want you here.*

The scent of mud seemed suddenly sharp, and she closed her gate abruptly. "No," she snapped. She was not aware she had spoken out loud until Wren turned back.

"What is it?" he shouted over the wind.

She shrugged, unable to answer.

He came closer and studied her expression with narrowed eyes. "What do you feel?" he repeated.

Her teeth, when she looked up, were clenched. "The cub."

Wren regarded her for a long moment, his flat, gray eyes unreadable. "Following?"

She jerked a nod.

He watched her for a moment. Then he turned and continued thoughtfully toward the shelter.

Ruka slunk through the forest to her right. The cord between them almost choked her when she tried to snap it off at the biogate. Blankly, she stumbled after Wren. How could she have let her gate grow so strong? Only once before had she felt this kind of immersion in the senses of the cats, and that was when she had first become a guide—when she hadn't even known control. What was her excuse this time?

Wren waited while she stopped to pull on her boots in a heavy wash of rain. The rain was not alive except with physical power, but her biogate seethed with the force of life around her. Ruka blinded her; Wren's voice echoed. The Landing Pact . . . The past . . . The law. But she had called the cub for help here—now—and that in itself was a crime. She stared up at the black and waving arms of the Rushing Forest. The trees that had taught her sister how to dance over twenty years ago now reached for the sky like abandoned dreams. Like lives left behind. Like hands. She choked on her guilt and stiffly followed Wren to the cave.

Bowdie waited for them at the edge of an overhang where two lava bombs crushed together and formed a rough cave. Tsia started to duck under the boulder, but Bowdie eyed her strangely. He seemed to see right through her—to the ghosts that lay in her past. For a moment, all she could do was stare back. Then she shivered and pushed her way by him.

Wren paused outside and dug in his pocket for a sealed packet of seeds. He spilled some into Bowdie's large hands and popped a few in his own thin-lipped mouth. He spoke to the other merc in a low voice, and Tsia could not hear him. She wrinkled her nose and wrapped her arms more tightly around her body. Wren knew she hated that odor; he could have stood downwind.

The inside of the hollowed area was wider than it appeared. Striker, who was seated on a crumbled protrusion, moved over to make room for Tsia, but neither woman stretched out her legs. Instead, they huddled for warmth. Striker's thick braid still dripped water, which ran down her back in a skinny, twisted stream. On the far side of the cave, Nitpicker leaned against the rough wall with Doetzier and Kurvan beside her. Her trousers and the lower end of her shirt were torn with a dozen small holes. Her shoulders were bowed, as if she were in pain, but Tsia could almost smell something stronger through the heightened senses of her biogate; and what she smelled was fear.

Tsia watched Nitpicker closely. Wariness she had felt before, and even fear in the pilot—when the dart ships whipped by the Nitpicker's fibergun had been discharged so she couldn't fire back . . . When the nessies had almost crushed the pilot the time she fell in the pod . . . When the woman had faced down that laze, and the weapon misfired instead of burning out her heart . . . But fear—now? In the safety of the cave? In her head, the cougar padded closer, and she felt her hands clench tightly.

East, she muttered in her head, to the cat paws that answered her thought. *Go east*.

Striker glanced at her face. "You okay?" she murmured.

She jerked her head up. "Of course," she returned sharply.

Kurvan caught Striker's expression. "Your neck," he said to Tsia. "What happened?"

Something in Nitpicker's eyes flickered. Tsia stilled. There was no tightening of muscles—nothing she could discern with her eyes . . . No one else reacted; but in her head, the cub snarled, and Tsia's scalp hair prickled. "Got jammed in the cabin," she said slowly. She didn't look at the pilot. "In a torn piece of webbing. Just about jerked my own neck off to get free."

Kurvan studied her for a moment, then dug in Wren's pack for the med gear. Automated for almost any kind of injury, the scame took only a moment to set up. He held up its attachments with a question in his eyes. She nodded slowly.

Tilting back her head, she gave him room to work on her neck. As the scame fields swept over her flesh, the medlines automatically dulled the sensation. When Kurvan sat back, he looked satisfied. "There'll still be some swelling, but that should do it except for a salve." He pulled out a tube and tossed it to Tsia; he left her to rub that on herself while he began to repack the scame.

Tsia unsealed the tube and ·wrinkled her nose. From the damp dirt beneath the rocks she sat on, from Nitpicker's open wounds, from the salve itself—scents seemed to grow in strength. Ruka padded closer; Tsia's nostrils flared. There was an almost acrid odor that reminded her of something like Wren's nolo seeds. The hairs on her neck prickled again. She fingered the tube absently, then tossed it back to Kurvan.

He caught it with a slap. "Could get infected later," he said mildly.

She shrugged.

Striker barely opened her eyes. "No microbe would dare dig into a guide's flesh or bone. You know what they say: You can't kill a guide 'less you get one through his gate."

" 'Sightless without the biogate, and blinded when they use it,' " murmured Doetzier. He pulled his darkeye case from a slot in his weapons harness, gave Tsia a glance, then neatly slid the darkeyes into first one, then the other brown eye. The contacts turned his irises completely black, and he blinked twice to center them. Expressionlessly, he returned Tsia's gaze.

Tsia hid a shiver. The darkeyes the other mercs used, which made motion and contrast so clear, made a guide claustrophobic. Without her link to the cats, which sharpened her vision of movement, she could never have worked as well as she did with the mercs. Her night sight was only half as good as vision through the darkeyes. She eyed the other two packs in the cave. "Did we lose the rest of the gear?" she asked.

Striker grunted affirmation.

Doetzier eyed Nitpicker as she pulled the skin grafts from the medkit beside her. "What happened down there?" he asked quietly. "Wren said Feather came back for his enbee, then he sent Bowdie to help."

Nitpicker shrugged. "I got tangled in the slide. Lost my

enbee. Mud kept coming. Feather called the eels to dig me out." Gingerly she unsealed her trousers from her boots.

Doetzier eyed Tsia speculatively. "I thought eels were carnivorous."

Nitpicker rolled her trousers above the first bite mark. "They are." She glanced over at the other merc. "Toss me that scame, would you? And get me some seam-sealer."

Doetzier complied. Tsia, unable to meet Nitpicker's eyes, got to her feet and pulled her blunter close around her body. When she stepped out from under the overhang, Wren and Bowdie made room for her beneath their rock. Behind her, Doetzier watched her retreat with thoughtful eyes.

"Nice job, getting 'Picker out," Bowdie murmured.

"Thanks."

"Thought she was a goner when I first came down. Those eels were so thick on the scanner that I could hardly tell you were in the midst of them all."

"Thought you were an eel yourself, the way you latched on to my arm."

He shrugged. " 'Picker was in trouble, and I didn't know what you were doing. Good thing you're a fast finner."

"Good thing you read it as fast as I send."

They fell silent, but Tsia regarded Bowdie warily. There was still a tension in his biofield, and it grew when she was near him. Did he think she had shoved the pilot in the mud herself? There had been someone else there—before she went back for the pilot. A presence she had not read in her panic with the mud. And Nitpicker was now as tense as the man . . .

To the north, Ruka picked up her restlessness and reflected it back through the gate. The tautness of the bond between them stretched like the muscles of Nitpicker's shoulders, and Tsia shivered. Then the wind ruffled Ruka's wet fur, and she realized that the knot in her stomach was partly from the ache in the belly of the cougar.

"Go away," she breathed to the cub. "Go hunt if you're hungry. Don't knot up my guts with your need."

Yet he crouched and waited, as if she would bring him his

meat. "East," she said impatiently. "Go toward the coast. The beach. The smell of salt. Your family waits for you there."

Wren glanced up as her lips moved, and she caught his look. Without speaking further, she stepped out from under the rock and tilted her face to the sky. Overhead, the purple-gray clouds streaked across in a boiling, seething mass. Like horses that churned up the sky, they raced from behind the trees to the rain-smashed tops of the hills. With mindless speed, they tore each other apart.

Bowdie gazed out at the lake, his brown eyes shuttered. His thick brown hair dripped onto his eyebrows with rain, and he raised his hand to wipe it across his forehead. "Lot of rain for a single storm." He spat his last seed and glanced again at Tsia. "Thought it was going to get tough down there. Thought Van'ei was a goner." He turned and moved back in the cave.

Tsia glanced at Wren. The rushing sound in the wet leaves made a roar like the cats in the back of her mind. Tiny hot points that rumbled in her head . . . That was what Bowdie felt like—tiny sparks of light that sharpened when she used her biogate like a scan. Tsia drew in a breath and let it out so that the biofields were subdued, and only the sense of Ruka remained strongly in her thoughts.

She hesitated, then said quietly, "The cub isn't leaving me."

Wren chewed for a moment without speaking. Finally, he said, "Saw it in the lake. He swam in, then went right back out again." He spat a seed to the side. "You called him?"

"He came back for me. He's there now, to the right."

"Does he know he's pushing you to work against the Landing Pact?"

She shook her head. "I think he's too young to read that from the minds of the other felines."

"Thought the knowledge was coded into his genes—into his memories."

"It is, but he's also probably too young to trigger that part of his brain. When he goes back, his mother will teach him before they grow apart."

"Even if he doesn't know the Pact yet, seems like he ought to want to get back to his mother, rather than hang around on your human heels, squatting in the mud." He popped another seed in his mouth. "He ought to at least want out of the rain."

She stared back at the trees where Ruka's tawny form flickered briefly between the trunks. "Cougars don't care much about weather," she said slowly. "They'll hunt in rain or sleet—they'll track an elk through a snowstorm. Not much seems to bother them. That's why they made such good scouts for the First Droppers. They can live almost anywhere, eat almost anything. They aren't so small that they become a prey species, and they aren't so big that they can't hunt enough food from among the rats and reavers."

"And he's not hungry now?"

"He's hungry, but he's . . . linked with me. He doesn't want to leave."

"Linked?" Wren's voice was suddenly sharp.

Stiffly, she nodded. "They're more open to it when they're young. It's part of their socialization."

Wren gave her a sober look. "You're playing a dangerous game, Feather."

"It's not as if I have a choice. The Landing Pact—"

"The Landing Pact may be law, but even it has limits. And the guide guild has as long an arm as the lifers, when they were in power. The guides watch the felines as if they themselves were hunters. You're not truly safe, even here with the mercs. Remember that."

"I'm aware of my position, Wren."

"Are you? The guides—they know you have ten years' experience; the merc guild lists you with thirty. A new ID dot; a history that's not yours—so far, the guides have never looked beyond the ratings to find you, but that 'so far' is as much protection as you'll ever have—unless you make a deal with the Shields."

"Sure," she retorted. "And what have I ever had that they want? I'm a guide, not a guilder. I've got nothing but my past and a cougar dogging my heels. I'm not trained to follow a blackjack thread. I don't know any alien zeks. *I'm* the one on the grayscale, Wren. Hell, why don't I just call them myself and show them just how badly I've broken the Pact?"

"You might as well," he snapped back. "Running scared of your demons—that's the fastest way there is to lose your grip."

Her lips tightened. "And you're not afraid of your past? Of your demons?"

"Afraid? No." His voice was flat. "They don't own me. Not like you: you're letting your fear move you without direction."

She smiled bitterly. "The merc guild gives me direction with every contract. And it is they, not my demons, who own me, Wren—as much as I allow it." She stared out at the lake. It looked like a piece of sky, fallen between the hills and trapped by the wind in the valley. She rubbed at her wrists again, chafing the skin on the cuff of her blunter. "The mercs—they own my future, too," she said, more to herself than Wren. "But only because I haven't figured out how to get it back for myself."

His cold eyes flicked to the set of her face. "You tried for twenty years to fit the mold of the guides, and it got you only chains." He motioned with his chin at her wrists. She stilled her hands abruptly. "You try now to fit the mold of a merc, and your inner self fights that as much as you deliberately guide us. Look at you. You hide your wildness in motion— constant motion. You dance in every firepit you see. Hell, Feather, you dance in the wind when there aren't any flames for the oils of your skin. I look at you and all I can see is that your biogate is always open now." He nodded at her automatic denial. "The cats—they move in your mind. I can see it, Feather—in your eyes, in the movements of your body." He spat a seed over the lip of the trail and watched it whipped away by the wind. "You can't always hide in action, Tsia- guide. You run too far forward before your past steadies up, and you fall off the edge of your life." The stillness of his ex- pression seemed somehow brutal on his birdlike face. "If you're not more careful, someday you'll wake up with your demons staring you in the face."

"I wish they would," she whispered. Demons, dreams, and memories . . . There were people in her past. A sister who had fled to the cold depths of space. An old friend, lost to the tradelanes . . . There were the cats around her, forbidden to her by the guides whom she defied with every breath. She clenched her fists inside her blunter and stared up at the sky, ignoring the rain on her face.

Wren followed her gaze. His voice was quiet. "You think about the things you've lost. You hang on to your memories like a tiny spider, tugging on a wind-torn web."

Her eyes were tight with pain. "What else do I have?"

"You have nothing." His voice was flat and abrupt. "Nothing," he repeated harshly, "that you don't make for yourself. You made your past, but no one else's. Take your sister: you hang on to her as though you could fix her life, but you didn't make her problems. Your problems are here—now—in getting us to the freepick stake. In dealing with that cub. Your sister's problems—they're not yours, but hers, to solve—"

"No, Wren—" Tsia cut in. "We're family. Her problems are as much mine as hers. She didn't ask to be caught by whatever or whoever trapped her. And somehow, she was persuaded to give up everything that had ever been important to her." She shook her head. "Every com we had, there was denial in her voice of what she was doing to herself. I could hear it. Feel it in every word she spoke."

"She abandoned you. You owe her nothing."

"You've never spoken of your own family, Wren," she retorted. "What is it you reject in them?"

"I gave them up a long time ago."

"I gave up my past, my guild, and my life," she said softly. "I refuse to do the same with my family."

Wren glanced over his shoulder to see if Nitpicker was finished sealing the holes in her trousers, then spat his last seed. "Seems as if, with your gate and all, you'd be able to tell just how strong your sister's rejection is. Just how futile it is to fight it."

"I can tell," Her voice was low. "Sometimes, I can almost feel her. As if she were close enough to touch. As if, were I to scream her name loudly enough, she would answer through the wind."

Wren glanced at her face. He could almost see her stretch through her gate. See the animal snarl that shaped itself on her lips. " 'O tiger's heart,' " he murmured, " 'wrapped in a woman's hide.' "

Slowly, she turned to face him. One hand rose to his chest, her fingers curled like a claw. She rested it on his sternum till she felt the cold power of his biofield like the rain that slashed her skin. Slowly, her eyes cleared of the glints that sparked in their dark blue depths. She said nothing, but when he turned to go back to the cave, she followed without a word.

12

⚭⚭⚮⚭

"The freepick stake is just over the ridge," Striker said to Kurvan as Tsia stepped back in the cave. "Why not hike it?"

Kurvan frowned. "We lost every scanner but the one Bowdie was carrying on his harness. How do you expect to pick up a trail? The node's still down, so we can't call up a map overlay. And with this storm, it's not as if the paths are clearly marked."

Striker pointed at Tsia with her sharp chin. "We've got a guide. That's part of what we pay her for—pathfinding. You got a guess, Feather? About how far it is to the freepick stake on foot?"

"As the crow flies, about twenty kilometers," Tsia forced herself to respond. "Thirty-eight to fifty by trail."

"It's only midmorning now," Striker said. "We could make the stake by tomorrow's dawn."

Nitpicker got gingerly to her feet, wincing as the movement pulled on the fresh skin grafts. "There's more than one trail?"

"Five," Tsia returned. "Three will be impassable—there's been six solid days of rain—and most of the cable bridges will be under water, if they haven't been torn away by snags."

"You've hiked these trails yourself? You know them in storm conditions?"

She gave the pilot a faint, twisted smile. "Daya has always damned the fools who hike trails like these in storms."

158

Doetzier gave her a speculative look. "Not that you haven't done it yourself?"

Tsia shrugged. "Fifteen, sixteen years ago, I spent a few months out here, working with a friend. I know three of the trails in this area well; one trail somewhat, and the fifth trail I crossed only once."

"Fifteen years is a lot of time for change," he remarked.

"I ran each of those main trails over a dozen times. Mud can't hide my landmarks."

" 'Brush grows and snags burn, but the peaks remain the same,' " quoted Striker.

Doetzier regarded Tsia curiously. "Why run a trail so many times?"

"I had a Gea contract to track the shaper swarms as they came across the ridges."

Bowdie raised his brown eyebrows. "I've been on this world two years now and I've never seen any chameleons, let alone a shaper."

"A merc who sees a shaper is in a world of hurt," Wren commented. "Better to keep your eyes closed and miss them by a mile."

Tsia nodded. "If you're not out in the right weather, it's not likely you'll see them unless they're attacking for food, or you're in the path of a swarm. Remember when SarabCo came out with their new e-wraps—the kind we use now for camo? Power and sensor strips sewn in; configuration threads, blunter fabric . . . Lots of advertisement—new technologies, new materials. People here on Risthmus just shook their heads. An e-wrap that changed shape, not just color, to match your terrain? Shapers have been doing that kind of camouflage for millennia." She glanced outside at the rain. "In this weather, they'll be hungry. You'll probably stumble over a few on the way."

"Just what we like," Striker muttered. "Venomous scenery."

Doetzier studied Tsia carefully. "What do we look for?"

"Nothing." She shrugged at his expression. "Your darkeyes won't help you find them; shapers don't radiate much body heat, and they won't move till they're ready to attack. They have a layer of fatty flesh and muscle across their backs which they can reshape into a hundred positions. Rocks, leaf piles, roots—they can imitate just about anything. And you think your e-wrap is quick to configure? You should see a shaper swarm. You look at the ground and think you're staring at the wind shadows moving in the roots, but you could be watching a mess of shapers slide around the base of a tree."

"They are venomous, aren't they?" Striker persisted.

Tsia nodded. "Like old Earth snakes. The proteins in their venom do some of the digesting for them—break down cell membranes, liquefy your veins, ferment tissues . . . Basically soften up the meat so that they can fit it between their lips and into their gullet sacs." Unconsciously, she rubbed the back of one hand. "There's a neurotoxin, too. One bite and you get tingly in seconds, then numb. Your chest feels compressed. Your heartbeat drops. You can't breathe. Your heart slows some more till you go comatose and the blood-breaker proteins can go to work. It's kind of like a slow suffocation."

"Huh," Bowdie said. "Medlines can image down an antivenom as easily as anything else."

Tsia shook her head. "Antivenoms are complex molecules. It takes time for your body to make them, even with direct chemical instructions to your brain. And once the body's nervous system is slowed, it can't process enough signals fast enough to get itself going again without help."

Doetzier watched the way she rubbed the back of one hand. The hollows under his eyes made him look ghostly in the darkness of the overhang, and Tsia wondered at the surge of focused interest she could feel. The expectancy—the anticipation or eagerness—she was not sure that came from Doetzier at all. His energy—the flecks of light in his biofield—was steady and almost distant, as if he were holding himself behind a wall. She had to stop herself from reaching out to touch him as he asked, "You ever been bit?"

She glanced down and stilled her hands. "By a spiker," she answered slowly, "the shaper's cousin—once. On the hand. Friend of mine dared me to catch one."

"And you just couldn't resist."

She shrugged. "I won the dare."

He grinned in spite of himself, but the expression did not reach his eyes. "Can't have been very old if you did something like that."

"I was eleven," she admitted. "No temple links till you're twenty-one—till you learn to control your imaging patterns, you know—and we had lost our coms in the swamp. Jak had to sprint through mud and then a bristlebrush meadow to bring my parents home to treat me. Saved my life."

Striker snorted. "Jeopardized it first, if he challenged you to catch a shaper."

"Spiker," Tsia corrected.

Nitpicker resealed her trousers to her boots and stomped to check the seals. "Are you done with the lecture, Feather, so we can get back to work?"

Tsia stilled. She eyed the other woman carefully. "What trail do you want to take?"

"What's your recommendation?"

The pilot's tone was curt, not impolite, but Tsia could still see the tension in the woman's shoulders. "The trail south of here is called Derzat," she said slowly. "It's slippery and steep, but flattens out in the middle around the lakes and meadows. Drops off above the freepick stake in a fast, straight-up-and-down trail."

Bowdie groaned.

"It's doable," she said sharply. "Even in this weather. The other trail—Tabletop—runs along the lower, flattop hills and in and out of a dozen box canyons. I ran Tabletop twenty times or more, in all weather conditions, and I can tell you that, in this weather, it will be completely flooded. Derzat's tougher but more direct. Would save us eight kilometers and a heck of a lot of wading."

"Then we'll take Derzat," Nitpicker said.

Kurvan hoisted his pack to his back, and Tsia motioned at his bag. "What kind of weight do we have to port?"

Nitpicker looked at her without expression. Her voice was curiously flat when she answered, "About half what we started with. We lost four packs with the skimmer: Bowdie's, yours,

Striker's, and mine. Bowdie had the antigrav units and half of the scanners. You had the rest of the scanners and the extra stabilizer for the configuration gear. Striker carried half of that config gear—Doetzier still has the other half—and I carried half the source gear for setting up the scannet at the freepick stake." She spat to the side. "Ironically, the two things we didn't lose were the two things that were heaviest—the config gear and the breaker."

Doetzier glanced at the status flap on his own gear. "Why the concern about weight?" he asked. "We've got antigravs and stabilizers. We could load up even more if we had to."

Tsia shook her head. "Antigrav offsets only part of the weight of your gear. You ever hiked in a gale?" she asked Doetzier. "Or a full-fledged storm?"

"I'm a skyside merc, not a slogger. I've swung through over sixty alien ships, but this is only my third landside contract."

She studied him for a moment. A skyside merc with his technical rating usually worked salvage jobs or set up installations with high-profile gear. A defense setup for a freepick stake seemed trivial for a man with his experience. Unless he was going to stay at the stake and program the chips himself. Her gaze sharpened without her awareness, and Doetzier's unreadable eyes hid the cold speculation she felt in his field. She opened her gate more widely. His biofield was still flecked with color, as if he had dots of sharp energy attached to his own well-centered field. They were different somehow, from his other energy—like raindrops in the dust.

"Landside storm winds are gusty and unpredictable," she said finally. "They act like stabilizers on the blink. Jerk your pack around like a strong man learning to swing dance in zero gee." She glanced at the powerflap of his pack. "If your stabilizers and antigravs aren't already on high, you'd better set them there before you leave this overhang. You'll need all the help you can get to stay on the trail in this." She looked at Kurvan. "What gear are you carrying? The breaker?"

He shook his head. "I've got the other half of the source gear—for setting up a scannet into which I can start building webs." He jerked his head at the other merc. "Doetzier has the half of the configuration gear that didn't sink—for rafts, bivouacs, shelters, whatever. Wren bears the breaker."

Tsia turned to Nitpicker. "We should consider leaving some gear behind, cached here in the cave. Maybe not the breaker—prototypes are always expensive—but at least the config gear. The biochips aren't due for a month—there's plenty of time to come back tomorrow in one of the freepick ships and pick it up. Maybe even raise the skimmer out of the mud—"

Her voice cut off. A resurge of tension struck through her biogate like an arrow. Tsia could smell the sweat odors in the cave as if her own sense of smell were heightened. Through her gate, the cub seemed to focus on those odors he could taste, as though he had scented a doe. The feeling flowed back into a flavor for Tsia; her tongue licked against her teeth. She rubbed harder at her wrists.

Unobtrusively, Wren shifted closer to her body; Kurvan edged away. Tsia's brain noted each movement as if it were a leap of muscle, not a subtle shift. Hunger swamped her guts, and left her with glinting eyes and a hand pressed to her belly. Someone breathed behind her. She twisted quickly, startling Bowdie.

"Feather?" Nitpicker asked sharply.

Tsia stared at the pilot.

Deliberately, Nitpicker touched her arm. "Okay?"

She nodded jerkily.

"Okay?" the woman repeated meaningfully.

"I'm fine," she said shortly. "Just . . . hungry."

Wren dug a pouch of slimchims from his harness and tossed them to her so that she caught them with a hard, instinctive slap. Doetzier eyed her thoughtfully. "How long since you've eaten?"

Ruka growled in her head, and she returned without thinking, "Three hours—"

Her voice broke off at the other mercs' expressions. Three hours was not enough time to get a hunger cramp; it sounded like a lie. She pressed her lips together and shrugged. "Using my gate makes me hungry, and slimchims just don't have the body of a real meal." Deliberately, she threw Wren's pouch back at him.

Nitpicker watched her carefully. "About caching the gear—that's a nogo. What's left can be carried as well as cached. Anything we have is too good to leave to the zeks."

Bowdie murmured, "If they've got their own scannet up, they could be watching even now—just waiting for us to leave, so they can take salvage rights under the guise of the law."

Wren gave Bowdie a sideways look. "I'll lay you three-to-one that the Ixia are a bigger threat than any zek or blackjack."

"I'll take those odds," he murmured back. "Those aliens have done nothing harsher than sit up at the orbiting docking hammer and threaten to trade us bad scanners."

Doetzier raised his eyebrows. "They say that the webs of diplomacy can hide more murder than the node, Bowdie. I'd lay odds with Wren, not against him."

The other man shook his head. "I won't worry about the Ixia until they team up with blackjack. Now, that's the combination that could kill."

A chill crawled down Tsia's back. Blackjack. That tension she felt at the aliens' name. The smugness when she made mistakes . . . Ruka's senses had heightened her own so that she almost reflected the mercs around her. And what she felt herself—it was as though someone was almost directing her actions and speech, like a puppet. Using her—for some purpose of his own. As though this person helped her place her feet in mud, then positioned himself like a crooked gambler, waiting to see her fall . . .

"Kurvan," she asked abruptly, "have you gotten anything from the node?" Her gate seemed to swamp with more tension at her words, and Tsia's nostrils flared with the heavy musk scent from Ruka. She looked at Kurvan hard. He looked too relaxed, too friendly—was it he who projected such muscle-taut focus? Was it Bowdie or Striker or Wren? Doetzier, with his careful questions? Nitpicker with her fear?

But Kurvan shook his head. "A flash of a web every now and then. Nothing other than that."

Tsia nodded slowly, her mind churning between her biogate and her thoughts. Though brief, the node flashes she received were strong. It was as if it was she, not the node, who refused to image correctly. She scowled unconsciously. Kurvan's eyes narrowed. Ruka bristled in the gate. The skittering of the cougar's feet pierced her mind, and she realized she was staring. Then she turned away.

"Check your stabilizers and antigravs before we go," she said sharply over her shoulder. "Windmites love organic circuits." She paused at the mouth of the cave. Ruka was there, waiting for her to leave, to join him in the forest. Again, she tried to shut him out and read the sense of the humans, but with the cub so close, the mercs were still just points of light compared to the cats who blinded her.

A flash of lightning cracked across the ridge on the far side of the lake, and Tsia bared her teeth. Bowdie moved up beside her. A rush of wind struck them both, flapping their jackets back. Bowdie eyed the boiling sky, and murmured, " 'Risthmus roars and shakes his fires in the burdened air.' " He grinned faintly at her surprise. *The Marriage of Heaven and Hell,"* he explained. "William Blake."

"Isn't that supposed to be 'Rintrah,' not 'Risthmus'?"

"Seemed more appropriate the other way around." He shrugged at her expression. "Striker likes historians. I like poets."

She stared at his thick-shouldered frame, his pocked face and large hands. "Poets."

"It impresses the hell out of clients."

She shook her head to herself. "With the node down," she said, "you'll have to remember to manually check the status bars on your pack every fifteen minutes." She leaned back to verify his pack herself.

He twisted so she could see. "I hate manual checks," he muttered.

"Might as well get used to them. Half a merc's life is working off the node just to stay out of its webs."

"Not this merc, and not this nodie. And I'll blame blackjack for this one."

"Can't blame blackjack completely. Could be a nodie like you who's gone to the grayscale for credit."

"Not like me," he retorted. "Customs maybe, or a tech on the hammers."

"You'd think the Shields would be watching them," Kurvan muttered, as she caught the end of his words.

Nitpicker glanced over her shoulder as she moved up behind them. "The Shields have a tenth as many line-runners as we do. Why do you think they subcontract to us? You expect them to keep up with everything?"

Striker pulled up her collar as she stepped out of the cave. "They do all right."

There was a faint bitterness to her tone, and Tsia eyed her thoughtfully. Striker's biofield was suddenly hot and sharp, and its shallowness seemed to stretch over a void.

Nitpicker did not glance at the other mercs. She eyed the lake, then the hills. She motioned toward the trailhead with her chin. "Let's do it."

13

The storm was still growing as Tsia led the mercs from the cave. In hours—maybe by dusk—the full force of the gale would hit. The sky would become a dozen hands tearing at the earth. The rain would become thin and lancing. And Ruka would be gone, thought Tsia, and she would stand in the Rushing Forest with the rain in her eyes and scream through her gate for an answer to the snarls she heard in her head.

It took ten minutes to reach the trailhead, and by the time they did, the mercs understood her caution about power settings. Even with the stabilizers, the three men carrying gear lurched like drunkards with every gust.

Tsia kept to the trail with a long, loose stride, ignoring the mercs behind her. She wanted only the cub in her mind. He was like a brother, calling her to follow, to leave the trail and jump from rock to tree and down again across the trail. Not to go straight, but to wind between the trees. Not to stare ahead along the path, but to duck and flick her glance from side to side—to catalogue each movement like a hunter searching for prey. Somehow this cub had bonded to her through the biogate, and she could not shake him free. Her jaw tightened slowly as she realized the strength of that link, and she cast a sideways look back at Wren. She could not help but wonder, if she reached out long enough—far enough—through her gate, if she could just focus enough, like an esper who could stretch to contact a loved one, if she could force her biolink to reach her sister. If she could just stretch that bond so that she heard Shjams's heartbeat as she did the cat's. "If I can just make Shjams feel my presence . . ."

She bit her lip until she tasted blood. "Blood should make up for distance," she muttered. "The blood I sense through my biogate locks a cat to my mind, but there's not enough blood in my body to bring back my sister to me."

A low snarling answered her voice, and she blinked and shook her head to clear her suddenly blurred vision. Ahead, Ruka paused on a stone outcropping and eyed the line of mercs until Tsia felt his attention like an alien prickling on her shoulders. "Go east," she muttered. "You fill my mind like a fog in a valley, but you belong with your mother, not me."

He growled in return.

"Go back," she snarled. "Or hunt to satiate your guts. Don't settle your hunger on me." She stretched her legs until the mercs behind her cursed.

At midmorning, she led the group around a stand of stinging cores closed tightly against the storm. By noon, they crossed a stretch of flooded mud. They climbed and jumped on the arching roots of a massive stand of sinktrees. They circled a sleeping group of shapers, then a herd of bedded-down brown-backs. Near noon, she stepped out from behind a horitree and was blasted to her knees by the force of the wind. She threw her head back and laughed. The storm was a savagery she had come to expect.

Behind her, Striker, who had seen her fall, called out. Slowly, Tsia looked back. Her eyes still glinted and her teeth were bared to the wind. Ruka was too close. She could not feel the trees except as shadows that moved and whipped around her. She could feel the watercat crouched in its den. She could sense five tams on the ridge. But she could feel nothing else. Her gate was too strong. Too focused. She had to shut it down to see the woman who approached.

Striker eyed her warily. "You okay?"

She nodded jerkily.

The other woman was silent for a moment. With her auburn hair hidden beneath the hood of her blunter, and her black eyes and eyebrows the only edges of her expression, her flat-boned face looked like a mask. "Anything we should know about?"

Tsia shook her head slowly.

Striker just looked at her. Tsia knew the woman had dark-eyes in, but they made her look no different from normal. Her biofield, so shallow, struck Tsia suddenly. Shallow. No past. No history . . .

The node flickered, and Tsia stiffened. Automatically, she imaged a quick command to the webs through that one thin ghost line she had found. The trace became, for the first time, tight. Like a jumble of thoughts that suddenly tied together, the traces linked and flowed into a smooth story line. Webs—old webs, not just the one—were active still and strong . . . Images of false people who went about their unreal lives . . .

"You catch something through your gate?"

Tsia stared at the other woman. Had Striker not felt the flash in the node? "I felt a touch from a web," she said slowly.

"Felt that myself," Striker returned noncommittally. "Not enough to figure anything, though." She glanced back along the line. Bowdie was catching up, and his bent legs made it seem as if his blunter was somehow heavier than all three of the packs the other men carried. "Not that I've the experience to follow a trace like you."

Tsia turned slowly and studied Striker's face. "You're a wipe, aren't you?"

Striker's face went still.

"Are you?" Tsia repeated.

Striker stared at her. "How did you know? Through your gate?"

Tsia studied Striker carefully. "You say things," she said slowly, "and then there is the sense of you . . . It's different from the others."

The other woman took a half step forward. "Different—how? What do you feel in me?"

There was urgency in her voice, and Tsia hesitated. Was this part of the tension she had felt from the group of mercs? Did Striker's lack of past haunt the woman as much as Tsia's demons haunted her?

"I feel a thinness," she said after a pause. "A lack of depth. As if you were a child—without history—or an adult without direction."

Striker's face flushed, and she stared out across the hills. Her narrow chin was sharp and taut. "I don't know what I believe in. I don't know now who I am."

Tsia hesitated again. Finally, she motioned at Striker's side where the flexor hung from her belt. "You used to carry a laze," she offered.

The other woman looked back sharply.

"It's the way you hang your right hand," Tsia said quietly. "You stand as if you had a flexor on your back which you wanted to be able to reach, but you carry your weapon at your side. Only thing short enough to ride on your back and require a down position is a laze. You swear like a spacer. And when you're in a skimmer, you move like a spacer. A laze is a better weapon skyside than dirtside—known gas ratios to carry the beam. If you had worked more landside, you'd be more used to carrying a flexor."

Striker stared at her. "Would not have guessed a guide would know so much about spacers."

Tsia shrugged. "I've done as many firedances as any other guide. Spacers always came to watch, even at the trainings."

"How'd you get to be a line-runner anyway? Guides don't usually learn how to set a web. You're supposed to be too wrapped up in that training to care about anything else."

Below them, Doetzier, then Bowdie negotiated the switchback, and Tsia watched him as he climbed. "Learned in the trading classes," she returned.

Striker followed her gaze. "You wanted to be a trader? And ended up a merc?"

"I wanted to be a guide. Only that."

"Guides don't waste their time on the trader's guild—not when they can never go skyside. Why did you bother?"

"Had a friend who needed a study partner."

"The same one with whom you scanned these trails before?" Reluctantly, she nodded.

To her surprise, Striker gave her a sly look. "Good friends

are hard to find. Especially that kind." A slanting sheet of rain
hit them both at the same time, and Striker pulled up her hood.
Her eyes were shuttered again; her voice completely casual.
The moment of connection was over. "If you had to learn," she
said, turning back to the trail, "the trade guild was the best
place outside the mercs from which to take your training.
They've a reputation for detail."

Tsia stared after the other woman. Detail, she thought bitterly, was the one thing she was good at. The ghosts she
sensed—they were made with details that had stayed solid for
three decades. If she could build webs that tight, she could
build anything for the mercs. No longer did they need metric
tons of stealth cloth to hide a camp from the scannet. They
needed only an artist to "paint" the virtual images of shrubs
and shadows that disguised a merc's location. Just one guide
who could create ghosts as detailed and solid as if they were
real people and plants, real creatures in real canyons. And Tsia
could lay a ghost line so tight that a pack of mercs would look
like a patch of sand or a cloud that crossed a hill . . . She could
make a tree seem like a shrub and a shrub seem like a blade
of grass, and hide a merc behind all three. Yet for all the details she could shift, for all the ghosts she could create, she
could not find the one ghost she sought more than any other:
the traceline of her sister. Her eyes followed Striker as she
turned and waited for Tsia to lead on. Lost—like Shjams,
she thought with a chill. Lost without family forever.

The thin imaging line to the node began to shred as she
climbed past the other woman. Instantly, she tightened her focus.
Ruka growled as she drew away, and Tsia stumbled with the
sudden sense of double image he forced into her brain. She
barely stayed on the traces. There was a moment of mental
pushing—the one challenging the other; then the cougar seemed
to meld again with her mind. Without thinking, Tsia added a cat
to the street on which her ghost man walked, then cursed herself
silently as she had to maintain its ghost image as clearly as the
man's. The wrinkling of the man's trousers as he walked; the
light lift of his hair in the wind—she called up a library of

imagery and from it painted with careful strokes the movements of the ghosts.

Ghosts: her mind traced the webs. Wipes: the image of Striker . . . Blackjack was here, she thought with a chill as the rain slid down her back. For what—for the breaker? It was maybe worth enough on the grayscale to justify an attack . . . If they wanted the biochips, they were too early by weeks—Kurvan had pointed that out clearly on the marine platform. She tried to pull back from the biogate to think more clearly, but Ruka growled and tore at her mind. "Go home," she snarled back under her breath. "Go back to the coast. To your family. You don't belong here. You don't belong with me."

Ruka only snarled in return, and Tsia cursed. "I can't do both," she snapped at the cub. "I can't image through the node and stay open to your mind."

The cougar lowered its hips even more, and its head seemed to sway back and forth. Tsia found herself dropping down in a crouch, and she had to shake herself to regain her feet. "Stop it," she snarled. "Either help me or stop hindering me. But don't keep interrupting."

Her biogate went silent. For a moment, she thought Ruka had completely withdrawn, and she could not help the silent cry she projected through the gate. Instantly, the sense of the cat swept back. She found herself crouched again on the rock, her hands clenched to her temples.

A boot scraped stone. Doetzier reached up, and automatically she stretched back her hand, then, as she realized it was a man, not a cat—and maybe blackjack—that she touched, jerked it away just before the other merc grabbed on. He overbalanced and staggered back. The wind whipped his blunter, billowing it out, and his ID disk glinted before he caught his balance and yanked his jacket closed.

"What the hell was that for?" he snapped.

Tsia stared at him. The technical rating on the disk surprised her; the intensity of his biofield was almost a burn through her gate. She forced her hand out again. "Something in my biogate," she said tersely. "It startled me. Like . . . someone walking over my grave."

" 'The chill hand of the killer,' " he retorted, " 'who touches like ice in the night'?" He swung up beside her. "You're getting spooky, Feather."

"Do you blame me?" she asked sourly. "It's noon, and the sky is as dark as night." She looked up. " 'It is a storm for ghosts,' " she quoted, more to herself than him.

" 'Who roam the Plain of Tears.' " He shrugged at her expression. "Just because I come from Alile doesn't mean I know nothing of Risthmus." He gestured to the other side of the ravine. "We're close to it? The Plain?"

"The other side of the peak," she answered shortly.

"You've been there?"

"Yes." Her voice was a rebuff.

"History grips you, doesn't it?" His voice was so soft, she thought it was her own mind that supplied the question. "The fire in the sapgrass that killed your aunts and uncles?"

"Sometimes, I can almost feel the heat—"

She stopped short. Doetzier was gazing at the rain-grayed mountain, as if he didn't notice that she halted, but his eagerness was a hot brand inside her biogate.

"How did you know?" She managed to keep her voice steady.

"Everyone in this area lost family to the fire. If you lived here long enough to memorize the trails—"

"I only know them somewhat."

"—you must have lost someone to the flames." He watched her for a moment.

She studied the ravine as if it was of more interest than his words.

"Where's your family now? Did they stay in this area?" he asked.

She gave him a cold look. "Does it concern you?"

"I meant no insult. You work this area often. Saw it in your files." He got to his feet. "I just wondered, that was all." He glanced back up the ravine. "Even if you didn't have family here, I can understand why you stay."

"Oh?"

He motioned broadly. "This."

She followed his gesture. At their feet, whipping treetops bent away; and beside them, trunks rose up so steeply that there were almost no branches to slap their faces. The cut behind them was deep and dark and led to a ridge that was topped with jagged spires. There, the rain seemed to catch and dim the black rock till it was gray as a dream. Tsia nodded slowly. Perhaps he felt it too—the power in the land, in the wind and rain.

The wind shoved her off balance, and Doetzier caught her, but not before a flicker of some dark emotion flashed through his eyes. Warning? Violence? Tsia stiffened and drew back. The man schooled his face to blankness.

He motioned for her to continue. "Tabletop, the Plain of Tears . . . What does Derzat mean?"

She stepped back to the trail. "Dare. Challenge." Her voice was curt.

"Apt—for you."

"The wind gets stronger up top," she said, walking stiffly on. "Check your stabilizers."

Noon approached like a slow thought. One kay passed and then three more. The brush thickened to an impenetrable mass along the side of the trail so that Tsia's blunter caught on tangling boughs. Once, when she slipped and hit her knees on the rock, the sharp pain of the bruise shafted through her biogate automatically, and Ruka's answering snarl forced her lips to curl. She cursed the gate beneath her breath, and tried to draw back from its link, but he was growing stronger. With every hour that passed, he clawed his way more insidiously into her mind. It showed in her face—she knew it did. This gate with the cats—the snarling of her lips, the feral gleam in her eyes. How could any of them not see it? Did they think all guides were so wild?

She had not noticed that she'd stopped moving forward, and she jumped when Wren caught up to her on the trail. "Van'ei wants a break," he said, raising his voice to repeat his words.

Tsia nodded and didn't even notice that she was looking through Ruka's eyes to find an overhang deep enough for shelter. She pointed to a high cave, its entrance half-hidden by a fallen tree. She climbed up to its ledge and examined it carefully, but there were no scents of larger predators. She stepped out and gestured sharply. One by one, the mercs filtered in.

". . . would not even have temple links," Bowdie's voice went on as he nodded at Tsia, "if it weren't for my family."

Wren shrugged off his pack with a graceless thud. "Your family has about as much claim to fame as Doetzier's. And as for Doetzier, a man who carries only one name doesn't have much of a past. I should know."

" 'A man without a name, is a man who hides from fame,' " quoted Bowdie. He looked over his shoulder at Doetzier. "Someday, you're going to tell us your full name, and we'll have one heck of a laugh, because it'll be something like Cecil Fudmandon Brash."

The tension that surged through Tsia's biogate at Bowdie's words made her stiffen. Quickly, her eyes flicked from merc to merc. Doetzier's gaze seemed open and casual, but Striker had closed up, as if the words had been aimed at her. She studied the two she stared at. Blackjack . . . Doetzier's questions were far too careful, but what would a wipe have left to lose?

"Names are power," Doetzier returned calmly. "And power is not traded away for nothing."

Bowdie snorted. "He probably has a dozen names and needs two temple links just to transfer them from line to line."

"As if you knew enough about temple links to use them if you had more than one." Kurvan dumped his pack on the floor and rolled his shoulders to ease them.

"My family's responsible for the development of the links," Bowdie drawled. "I know more about them than you do."

"The temple links came out of the cyberdad generation," Striker said, "not out of a single family line, no matter what the contribution by the techs in your past."

"I can't believe you know any history but the Fetal Wars," Bowdie teased ungently. "Try this: Yahtra Kalakar Kuhrto."

Striker's black eyebrows raised. Even Doetzier did not bother to hide his flicker of surprise.

"My great-great-et-cetera-grandfather," Bowdie added with satisfaction. "And the Kuhrto Conduit—the biochemical trans-

fer of charge. A molecule shaped like a hollow helix. Ions pass
through its middle, like peas through a boost chute. The node
sends a signal to your temple link. Your temple link sends a
charge through the conduit. The charge triggers your brain. Every image you build and project is translated into an electrical
pattern, which can then be passed on to the node."

"Gawd," drawled Wren in an imitation of Bowdie's speech,
"you're either practicing to be like Striker, or you've inherited
the old man's mouth to patter on like that."

"They say I have his eyes . . ."

Tsia watched him sharply. Bowdie slouched and drawled as
if he belonged more on a trail than a starship, but his tech rating was as high as Doetzier's. She had seen his ID a few years
back, when he'd first come down to Risthmus. He wasn't a
line-runner, but he was as hot on a tech job as Kurvan was on
a ghost. She tried to focus on Bowdie's biofield, but his eagerness was a blurring heat that almost completely hid the other
tiny lights of his emotions.

Silently, she moved to the mouth of the overhang. She
closed eyes, and the sense of her gate swept in. Slick, cold
rock seemed to grip her fingers. Her eyes opened and her pupils shrank with the light. Her lips stretched as if she had
fangs, and her nostrils flared. Striker touched her arm, and she
twisted with a snarl. The other woman backed off, and Tsia,
with a shudder, turned her back on the shallow cave and
stalked out, climbing quickly off the trail.

She tried to unclench her hands from their clawlike posture,
but her fingers did not want to obey. It was not the cold. She
licked her lips with the same movement the cougar made, two
meters away . . .

Two meters. She looked up and met the golden, glowing
eyes in the figure that crouched on the rock, out of sight of the
mercs. Tsia's lips stretched in a humorless grin. Let the node
keep its ghosts, she thought with sudden violence. And to hell
with the guilds—let them keep the Landing Pact for those who
needed its fences. Wren was right; the cats did not reject her.
She broke no law to speak with them—not when it was they
who pressed their voices onto her. It was not she, she thought,

who created this contact; it was the virus in her body, and the cats themselves who forced their way in. Like a mold, they crawled into her skull. Bound themselves to her memories. And with the node near silent, she could taste the cats like sour fruit—strong and sharp and harsh on her lips. She licked her lips again, and then became still.

"Daya," she whispered to the cub. "Six hours with you, and I now justify my crimes as if I did not commit them. No wonder the mercs don't trust the guides—I hardly trust myself." She stared at the golden eyes. "You follow me like a dog, and I don't know if it is you or I on the leash."

Ruka's nose touched her hand. She caught her breath to close off the sense of his mind, so focused on her movements. He fought her withdrawal, keeping the gate open by himself. Tsia struggled for a long moment, then shuddered. Whatever cloth was woven between them by her biogate, it was not something she could tear.

Nitpicker moved to the mouth of the overhang to catch Tsia's eye, and Tsia regarded the woman blankly before shaking herself to respond. The node—those threads of ghost lines . . . She gave Nitpicker a meaningful look, then glanced deliberately downtrail. The other woman nodded.

A moment later, they met under a tree, while Kurvan and Striker watched from the cave. Tsia didn't mind; it would have been strange had not someone kept watch on the trail.

She studied Nitpicker's face carefully, but the woman's irises were hidden by the black contacts of the darkeyes, and her expression was blank and waiting. "There's something wrong with this setup," Tsia said after a moment. "I've got access to the node. It's not full access," she said quickly, "nor is it through anything but a ghost web, but I'm imaging the node right now and have been for almost ten minutes."

The other woman stared out from the trail and let her gaze roam across the steep hill to the lake far below. "Go on," she said softly.

"I've got an entire web that's active. Very tight. Seems normal. Except for one thing." She paused. "It isn't through any trace on my current ID dot."

Nitpicker did not shift her gaze. "I see," she said slowly.

"You understand what that means?"

"I do."

Tsia eyed her for a moment. The tiny lines around her eyes deepened with her uneasiness. "The webs are on my old ID line," she added. "The one I had before I joined the mercs. They're not on my current traces."

"I understand," Nitpicker said more sharply.

"And?"

"That's all."

Tsia stared at her. "No questions?"

"No."

A spark of anger grew in Tsia's gut. "That's it?"

"Yes."

"Just 'Yes'? No discussion? No questions at all?" No trust in what I say? she wanted to snap.

Nitpicker turned finally and met her eyes with a cold look of warning, then turned and walked back along the trail.

Tsia took a half step after her, then halted. Her hand went halfway to her throat. She could almost feel Nitpicker's fingers against the flesh of her neck. Could almost feel the fear in the woman beating against her own ribs. Her jaw set abruptly. The pale scars along her cheek went whiter as she held her tension with fury.

As Nitpicker passed Kurvan, the other merc said something, and the merc leader nodded with a faint smile. Kurvan glanced up and met Tsia's eyes, and she could taste the satisfaction that flushed through her biogate. He hated her, she thought. Had hated her since Tucker's death. He wanted her to fail. She could taste it like dung in her mouth. Kurvan looked once more at her face, then turned away to the cave. Tsia, left like a stick in the rain, merely stood and stared, her eyes unfocused, and her biogate taut as her jaw.

14

She stared at Ruka where he crept down to meet her. Never in the ten years she'd worked with Nitpiker had the pilot provoked her so deliberately. Had that been an act? A test? And if so, who had she been testing?

An old ghost cropped up in a node that was supposedly down. A pilot choked out one of her mercs. A biochip shipment was not expected for weeks, but a group of mercs was so jittery that their tension cut through Tsia's biogate like a laze. She pressed her hands against her temples and climbed off the trail till she could crouch in the shelter of a fissure, far above the cave. She could still hear the mercs, their voices floating up through the crack in the stone, but Ruka was too close to her mind, and she could not focus her thoughts.

The cub rubbed his head on her fingers. Wet hairs stuck to her skin, and she stared at them as if they were tiny lines of the node. Her stomach growled. Or his. Absently, she pulled a slimchim from her pouch and handed it to him. "You're like a fluke on the heart of its host," she told him sourly. He gulped the slimchim quickly, and she let him take another. "You create a hole, through which you suck my thoughts." She watched him chew on the chim and said slowly, "Yet without you, I think I would bleed to death."

She stared at the rock crack from which the other mercs' voices rose. Resolve seemed to settle in her guts. Deliberately, she got up and carefully, silently, followed the fissure down until their voices were clear and sharp.

". . . so why shouldn't she tell us?" Kurvan was demanding. "A guide linked with marine life does us no good out here. Look at what almost happened to Nitpicker. We might as well be trying to follow a broken scanner as her."

Striker's voice returned. "How do you know she's linked with a fish? Why not a reaver or hawk or pipeplant?"

"She called the eels to help 'Picker. A guide linked with a tree or digger couldn't do that."

"Give her a break, Kurvan," Striker said sharply. "It's tough enough to get a guide into the merc guild without making her miserable while she's on contract. Beside, she got 'Picker out of the mud. She's earning her credit as much as any of us."

"I still want to know what her gate is."

"Why?"

"Did you see her expression when Doetzier caught up to her an hour ago? She didn't exactly help him up that rock. How can we expect her even to do her job when she's that uncontrolled? She's just a guide, and not a good one at that."

Nitpicker's voice cut in quietly. "She's a genetic ecologist, Kurvan. A skilled terrain artist. If being a guide makes her a little wild too, that's only to be expected. What guide, so changed by viruses, is ever completely human? Look them up in the stock charts. They're M-three, not M-one. Mutants, twice-removed from our original genetics."

"And just as unpredictable as any alien. For our own safety, we need—"

"To know no more than we do." Nitpicker cut him off in a calm voice. "Hand me that seam-sealer, would you, Wren? I've got another hole to patch."

Thoughtfully, Tsia sat back. She stared at the fissure, as if more words would float out, but only the wind made sounds.

The cub's ears twitched as he regarded Tsia with the patience of a hunter. Against her fingers, his slick, waterproof hair felt almost greasy, not sticky, as the sponge mucus had felt. She sniffed her fingers. She could still smell the turpentinic scent of the sponges on her skin. She rubbed her slim, strong fingers together and felt again those other steel hands at her throat. Unconsciously, she touched the swollen flesh. "Did you feel it?" she asked slowly. "Did your throat choke with her fingers?"

Ruka growled, and Tsia laughed, a short, bitter sound. "I'm so desperate for someone to talk with, I turn to you—an animal, for Daya's sake—as if you were my family—"

Abruptly, she stood and began to stalk back to the mercs. "Damned idiot," she cursed herself. "Talking with an animal. Your brain can't take in my words," she snarled. "You think in catspeak which I barely understand; and I project emotions which you don't even have." She turned and stared at him as he paced her in the brush. "What do you really sense? The hunger in your stomach? The smell of the hare in the grass? Could you sense a biochip? Or tell a freepick from a zek?" She stared at him, letting the sense of his hunger gnaw at her guts. Then she dug out the last of her slimchims and, with a sharp motion, dropped them in the mud. Deftly, he snagged them in his teeth, gulping them as quickly as a wolf takes a piece of meat.

Tsia glanced at the hill where an older cougar watched her move, and wiped her face of expression. Then she made her way back to the trail, where Doetzier could spot her from the cave.

Curtly, she waved for him and others to rejoin her. Doetzier motioned for her to wait for Wren before she took the lead. A moment later, Wren came abreast of her and said quietly, "Bowdie ran some scans on the trail. He found nothing, but we all had the sense we were being watched. Is it you?"

"No." She half snarled the word, and his hand flashed to her arm before she could wrench away. His thick fingers clenched her jacket. "Just the cougar," she forced the words out. "It's not hunting. Only curious. The trail is clear."

"Like your mind?"

She shrugged away. "My mind is clear," she said sharply. Her lips twisted in a bitter smile. "It's only my heart that's clouded."

"The link is getting stronger," he stated, more than questioned.

She nodded.

"Dammit, Feather," he said harshly, his voice almost a whisper. "You have to get rid of him. Push him away. Think of him as alien, as an Ixia, if you must. Or are you so desperate for your sister that you substitute the cub?"

She snapped back. "I see little difference between them, Wren. Ruka is here, now, climbing into my brain, and I can't seem to stop him. Shjams was always there, and I can't cut her out."

"So tell yourself that she's no longer part of your life. If you must, tell yourself that's she's dead."

She stared down the trail. "But I know she's alive. And knowing that—and not being able to see her or talk to her— not being able to connect . . . It's like having a sister with a terminal illness. One which has taken her to the lip of the grave—but refuses to push her in. As long as she still lives, I can never finish grieving, and I can never quite give up. It's like a death that has no resolution. A death that has no proper end."

"You said once that she was searching for herself. Can't you just give her the distance she wants and get on with your life?"

"If that was what she was doing," Tsia returned shortly, "then, yes. But we know it's not. She's lost, Wren. She's up there in space running—sprinting—from her demons, and all she's done is run right into their hands."

Wren gave her a speculative look. "You of all people should be able to understand that."

The catspeak drummed in her head, and Tsia's lips thinned. "You have to face your demons, Wren. You have to destroy them before they annihilate your self. Something happened to Shjams in the past. Something that caught her in a cycle of fear as securely as . . . as I was caught before. But Shjams never moved out of that cycle. She's still running. Like a reaver who can't find its way out of its own dike, she is digging her own grave."

"And you have found your way out of the grave? Away from your nightmare-demons?"

She looked at her wrists. They were tanned and weathered like the rest of her skin, but she always saw them white, marked with the same iron-chafed circles that Wren bore on his. Her face was so still that only those dark blue orbs seemed alive in the toughness of her scarred and weathered skin. She smiled suddenly, and the expression did not seem to touch the muscles of her face.

His sharp eyes noted flecks of bestiality that glinted from her eyes. He dropped her arm and motioned to the trail. She stared at him, then led the others on.

15

By late afternoon, when the gloom pretended to lighten to the shades of a medium gray, they dropped into the steep cut between the Pallas Ridges. The trail there was a meter-wide ledge which ran above Pallas Cat Creek. The rain barely reached into the cut, but the shadows and crashing creek kept the air dark and moist.

It took an hour to build a tiny, two-line rope bridge out of the flexan cord and metaplas pieces they carried. Then Tsia led the first two mercs in a swaying, edging, hand-sliding movement along the flimsy bridge. Behind her, Kurvan slipped in the crossing, and Tsia caught his arm as it flailed out. With a cry, he countergrabbed and crushed her slender fingers. He looked into her eyes and smiled; his hand seemed to sprout claws. Instinctively, she jerked back. A surge of cold energy hit through her gate. Her lips bared in a snarl. Bowdie, behind them, cursed and lunged. He caught Kurvan's hand, and then Tsia grabbed again at the other merc's arm. Her flexor caught for an instant on Kurvan's elbow and almost snapped out from her harness. The weight of Kurvan's pack swung both her and Bowdie down. The bridge whipped wildly in a V toward the rocks. Bowdie's long legs slipped along the line. On the far bank, the others could do nothing but watch. Then the wind gusted and Bowdie yanked hard, and Kurvan's hands scrabbled for a grip on their harnesses. Tsia's straps split; Bowdie's mottled edges unsealed. Dark objects fell away. Tsia's flexor slapped hard against her thigh. The wind, which had helped a moment before, thrust at their bodies. Kurvan looked down and saw the boiling water and ebony rocks. He jackknifed and kicked up. Then his feet regained their purchase, and Tsia and Bowdie hauled him up.

Kurvan gripped the cord of the bridge, glanced down once more, then murmured his thanks to Bowdie. He gave Tsia a dark look. She stared at him, then twisted away along the rope. Her body still shivered, and the power of his grip seemed to cling to her skin. There was a hunter in his body, she thought. A predator as deceptive and eager as the dark puma who watched the group from its den. High up, in caliginous shadow, the adult cat eyed Tsia and reinforced her fear of the man. Encroacher . . . Danger . . . She shuddered again, hiding the motion in the sway of the bridge. Not until she reached the bank on the other side did she relax, and only then because she moved quickly upslope, where she could turn and crouch in the lee of a tree.

She stared at her hands as if they belonged to a stranger. Had she lost all control over her gate? And this wariness—was it hers or the cat's? Her gate widened with the touch of Ruka's mind, and she twisted at his proximity. He had crossed upstream on the boulders, and now he slunk close, visible only as a trick of tawny light in the forest.

"Daya," she whispered. She pressed her palms to her forehead and closed her eyes as tightly as she could, as if she could hold in her biogate by flesh alone. She could smell Kurvan's sweat on her fingers. There was an almost turpentinic musk to the fear in it as it mixed with the rain and sweat, and she shivered and drew her blunter close.

The cougar on the ridge projected more strongly, its eyes flicking from the mercs below to her own predator shape in the woods. She snarled at it through her gate, and her message, even in words, was clear: Do not hunt. Don't attack. The humans here are protected.

Her lips twisted as a warning was returned: Pass through. Pass through, but do not stay. The lines of territory were marked and they would be defended.

Against the mercs. Against her. Instinctive reactions and natural fear . . . Command: response, countered by the faith in the

Landing Pact. That was what she felt. She was like a puppet. She moved, but her movements were choreographed; she acted to another's direction. Kurvan had smiled, and she had jerked back. As though he could have anticipated her response, he had given her a look that seemed so full of menace, she could not help but recoil. She rubbed at her wrists with a shiver. His hands seemed imprinted on her arms. His biofield seemed to feed the anxiety of her gate. If he had fallen—if Bowdie had not been there . . .

She wiped her hands against her trousers. The hard edges of the safety cubes scraped against her palm. "I feel dirty," she whispered to Ruka. "As if I had been used."

Ruka turned his head to stare back, unblinking. His claws extended. Pressing through her blunter, they cut, cold and hard, through her shirt till they began to pierce her chest. She lifted his paws, and shifted her harness, and realized its edges were unsealed. Uneasily, she looked down.

The medkit and her e-wrap—both of them were gone. They had fallen away when Kurvan grabbed for her harness. "Sleem take it," she muttered. All the gear from her front straps was gone, including her antigrav packs. Only the raser, with its short, knifelike laser blade powered down, was still on her hip by her flexor; and her bioshield—but nothing else—was still in the pouch against her chest. She felt the cold in her teeth, and realized her lips were bared as she stared down at her unsealed harness. Kurvan and Bowdie, and her gear falling away . . .

Ruka growled, low in his throat, and Tsia's eyes gleamed. "Had I claws like you," she said softly, "I would have cut, not caught, Kurvan's hand." A chill struck her shoulders.

"Daya," she whispered. "Have I lost my mind?" She stared at her hands. They were clutching her flexor, and she didn't remember drawing it. She flicked her wrist. The weapon flowed into a thin-edged bar, like a sword. She shifted her grip and snapped it into a point with a set of hooks along a long, thin blade. The hooks flowed smoothly back into bumps. Stars in a biofield; bumps on a sword . . . She flicked her wrist and the flexor became a stiff tri-blade. The shadow of the point cast a faint, flamelike ghost on her trousers, and she stared at it for a moment. The windburn from the storm felt like fire to her skin, and she saw in her memories the coal classes in which she first learned to dance. The heat against the pads of her feet; the sweat she had learned to call at will . . . And the other guides whose bodies flashed and leaped as lithely as her own. Faces that had disappeared with time. Like the features of her sister, which had not changed in her memory, but only deepened and aged, as if Tsia had acknowledged the years, but not the distance that had grown between them. Firedancing . . . The guide guild . . . Her family . . .

She wiped her hands on her trousers and stared at Ruka as if she could imprint him even more deeply on her mind. "Do you know," she asked the cat in a harsh voice, "how long I waited to have you in my head? What I have given up to touch you? And how little it takes to strip you away?"

The cougar rumbled. She got slowly to her feet. She felt old inside. Not the forty-nine years that made up her life, but five hundred years or more. What good was her past, she asked herself, if she could not let it go? And what had she become, that she could no longer separate herself from the biogate in her head? The wind's rough hands tore at the bark beside her, as if daring her to do the same. She threw her head back and opened her throat. The sound came out as a bitter laugh that turned into an animal scream.

She did not answer when Wren climbed up and gestured, but she moved out of the gloom like a cat. When her feet hit the trail, she did not bother to look at the mercs. Even when Nitpicker signaled for her to take the lead, she did not acknowledge the woman's motion with a word. She merely bent her head against the wind and hiked on.

Another hour on the trail turned into two; the afternoon passed like a ghost. They forced their way through two waterfalls that blasted across the trail. The medlines of the node were no longer active—they had dropped out halfway through the day. Tsia had barely noticed. Her mind was filled with the sense of the cat and the pulse that beat in her throat, and when they came to a wall of broken rock, she pointed toward the peak. "Shortcut," she shouted. "Straight up." Halfway up across the rocks, she looked back at the mercs, who followed like dolls on a string. Or lifers, she thought, like puppets with guns. She stared at her hands and wondered . . .

Early evening found them at a rise of basalt, where moss and lichen overgrew the stones, and gray-white trunks of a burn as old as Tsia dotted the slopes around them. The ache in the legs of the mercs had turned to a numbness that they bore in silence while they cursed at the mud. When Bowdie, then Tsia took a break behind a boulder, Tsia stumbled, and Bowdie caught her arm. The heat of his biofield seemed suddenly sharp with sparks, and she stared up at his suddenly shuttered face. He tossed her his decomposition spray and returned to the group. Tsia was left by herself.

The scents that clung to the deke tube he'd tossed made her nostrils flare. She hesitated before she sprayed her fecal matter. There was something about the scent of the deke . . . Her brows drew together, and she lowered her head to sniff the tube. To a normal human, a deke had no odor; but to Tsia, with the senses of the cats interpreting the smell as they crawled into her mind, there was a distinct sweetness to the tube. Memory flicked at the back of her brain. Today . . . That morning. Another tube, and a cave . . .

The medkit. The salve—when they had climbed out of the lake, her neck had still been sore, even after the use of the scame. Kurvan had thrown her a salve tube out of Wren's medkit. She had opened the tube, but had not used it, and the odor . . . She sniffed again, then deliberately, she aimed the deke at her stool. The small pile dissolved in seconds, leaving only a darkened place on the soil.

A deke in a salve—in a medkit? "Insane," she whispered. One drop from a deke, and a cut would become a necrotic gash. A gash like that could result in an amputated limb. Her stomach tightened. When the cat feet padded through her head, she started. She was too close to her gate, she thought. It was clouding her mind with suspicion. Abruptly, she made her way back to the group. She tossed the deke to Bowdie without a word, but she could not help the look she shot at Wren as she stalked back to the head of the line.

Shadow turned to blackness, and fir dancers became tree demons. The darkeyes of the mercs allowed them to continue into night as if it were day, but Tsia had to look through Ruka's eyes to see the placement of her feet. At ten, when they took two hours to sleep, Tsia curled up and opened the biogate, and let the cougar's mental hum lull her into dreams. Faces seemed to march through her mind, in time to the cougar's growling. First Ruka, then Wren, then Nitpicker's eyes . . . A hard-chiseled face floated above her, and she kissed the man before he melted into the stone that formed his own biogate . . . He sank into earth that cracked and cried and turned into a stream, where her sister's visage, cloudy as ice, seemed trapped beneath the surface. She reached in for her sister, but the water rippled, and it was her own face that stared out . . .

At midnight, they resumed their ragged march. The dark was now so thick, and the rain so blinding in the violence of the wind, that the night seemed impenetrable and solid. The sky breathed, like a god, in their faces, battering them from one side of the trail to the other while the trees broke and flew through the wind. It was a night of brutal darkness; a night that had no end.

At a switchback, she missed the trail and slipped, lengthwise, like a log down a water track, into a nest of hummers. The rodents squealed as her feet broke through the flimsy roof of the nest. Three sets of teeth snapped at her boots. Cursing beneath her breath, she yanked her legs out and climbed back to the trail, her fingers digging her holds out of the sodden earth while the wind slammed into her back.

"You remember this?" Bowdie shouted over the wind as he helped her back up to the trail.

She shook her head.

"I thought you knew this trail."

She stared at the pale blur of his face. "In the dark?"

He seemed to grin.

"This isn't one of the main trails, and I ran this one only twice up to here." She pointed. "I had to take the long route around the meadows and lakes when I was working this area before."

There was a shriek of wood, a crashing sound from ahead, and Bowdie stared into the darkness. "Too bad your biogate won't tell you what's ahead."

"Like a bird's-eye view of the sky?" She laughed. "Even that wouldn't tell me much in this."

He eyed the darkness of the woods with its black and whipping branches, then nodded shortly. He gestured for her to lead on.

They crossed the yellow-white grass quickly, then went again beneath the trees. At a fork in the trail, Tsia paused, and Wren pointed to the thin, boiling sky with a grin, as if she had lost their morning bet. She jerked her thumb east in return. The heavy blackness promised the rains that she projected. "By dawn," she yelled above the wind, "you'll have your rain, and then some."

She moved on, and the cougar paced her in the brush. With a narrowed gaze, she accepted Ruka's sight to look beyond the fork that split the trail. There was a blurred sense of trees, which bent with ponderous grace. Then she felt the wind that ruffled her fur. The left trail petered out in a box canyon, she realized. The right went on to a meadow.

"I understand," she breathed.

Ruka's growl seemed pleased.

The images faded; the cat feet in her skull became fainter. She rubbed her fingers together. She had been able to read the felines for ten years, each year with greater sensitivity. But Ruka had just pointed out the trail to the freepick stake as clearly as Tsia did for the mercs. As if the cub understood her goal. To partner with that kind of intelligence . . . To move through the mountains with two sets of eyes . . . Daya, but what had the Landing Pact given up for guides like her?

She guided the mercs across a creek, then into another meadow. One creek ran beside the wide clearing; another gray line of water glinted across the expanse of two-meter tallgrass. The grass flowers, tightly closed against the wind, were small gray flags, which would flare yellow after dawn. Soon the flowers would be ripe, and the wind would tear them open so that their seeds blew out like static-charged foam and clogged the branches of the shrubtrees around the meadow.

The meadow itself was like a lake, and Tsia could feel the shadows of movement beneath the puddled ground. To her left now, Ruka slunk into the meadow, but between the gloom and the grass, his body was just another motion of the wind, invisible to her eyes. Behind her, Wren, then Bowdie, then Kurvan filed through the grass. They began to fan out as the ground grew too wet to follow exactly where she stepped.

Her foot sank up to her knee, and she struggled to pull it out. Her biogate distracted her from her path. She stepped for a clump, missed it in the dark, and sank into the puddle beside it. Phosphorescence swirled like tiny sparks. It took full seconds to struggle free.

"Daya," she muttered. The sense of life in the meadow was strong enough to make her frown. Behind her, the other mercs formed a long line in the grass. The steadiness of their bodies looked odd surrounded by the whipping stalks. Wren, the closest, staggered heavily, and she moved back into knee-deep roots to give him a hand and check the settings on his pack. Neither tried to speak in the wind.

Ruka was already across, waiting, hunkered down on a rock. His golden eyes watched the mercs unblinkingly. Only his ears and tail twitched as he crouched; and Tsia judged the distance between them. Where the creek between them flooded out into a small pond, the mercs would have to wade—or swim in the dark, she admitted with unease. She glanced down and scowled at the water pooling between the clumps of grass, then jumped ahead again.

The earth shimmied beneath her and, startled, she jumped ahead to a more solid clump. Even that grass shivered with her weight, buckled. Ahead, the flooded gray creek grew wider, until it seemed as if the sky lay down in the meadow to sleep out the storm on the ground. Tsia grinned at the image. She put her foot down. Into nothing. And toppled forward.

Cat feet leaped abruptly in her head; someone snarled in her ear. "Daya—" She twisted frantically before she hit the water. Her legs and hips slapped the lake with a flat splash. Her arms flung out as she grabbed at the grass. Her torso hit the edge of the mat, and she clung to that flimsy raft like a gale net spread on the sea.

For that was what she lay on, she realized. A weedis on a black sea of water. A raft of grass. There was no meadow beneath her feet—it was actually a lake. And not a temporary lake that had flooded from a simple creek, but the water that had lain, still and dammed, for years behind the ridge of earth that blocked its lower end.

Infinitely slowly, she dragged herself back up on the mat. The thin island trembled; its root system shredded beneath her weight. In her head, the cougar paced and clawed at her skull until she snapped at him to leave her alone. Easing back in a long-body crawl, she shifted her elbows, then hips past her footsteps where the traces of herself were left in phosphorescent, sparkling pools among the grass.

As Wren caught sight of her, he quickened his pace.

"Wait—" she shouted. "Don't come any closer—"

He didn't hear her clearly. Heedless of the swirling lights, he waded knee-deep through to help her. And sank up to his waist in the brash. "What the hell—"

Tsia cursed under her breath. His pack seemed to drag him down in a cloud of phosphorescence. Before she could climb over to help him, he was up to his chest in night-gray weeds that sparkled with greenish lights. He threw out his arms to catch his armpits against the sagging clumps, but she could see the floating mats tear with every thrust of the wind.

His eyes rose slowly to hers. "I think," he said, "I'm going down."

"Your antigrav—"

"Just cut out. This is dead weight, all the way." He sank another handspan, and his blunt fingers tightened on the grass. "I thought you just checked the settings."

"I did."

"There's something moving around my legs."

"Eels. Sucker fish. I don't know."

"Can't you feel them?"

"A shadow. Nothing more. Don't struggle. Do you have an enbee?"

" 'Picker's still got it. You?"

"Lost it on the bridge." Her stomach tightened. She judged the distance between them and eased forward another half meter. Bowdie appeared through the grass, and the brash mat shivered; Wren sank another handspan. "Bowdie!" she shouted. "Stay back!"

The other merc froze. "What—"

"Stand still," she shouted. "Your enbee—quickly. Throw it here."

"What?"

"Your enbee!"

Wren jerked and sank abruptly up to his neck in a new swirl of greenish light. "Don't move," she snapped at him harshly. "You'll tear the brash and tangle like a stick in a pile of yarn."

He didn't nod, but his eyes, black and unreadable, stared back into her own. Behind him, Bowdie moved quickly back to a more solid clump, and his long fingers searched his harness as his own heart began to pound. Tsia could feel the strength of it like the points of light in his field.

"Get the line," she directed.

Bowdie nodded and shouted behind him to Striker. "Get the line up here!"

"Goddam worm-spawned reavers," Tsia cursed under her breath. Kurvan eased up beside Bowdie to a precarious perch on a thick mat of mallow. He dumped his own pack in an awkward tangle, then tore open the flap and yanked out a metaplas form.

"Stay back," Tsia snapped as he tried to approach. The grass mat shimmied. Her knees sank in. The wind roared through, and, with a silent ripple and a cold, steady gaze, Wren disappeared in the lake.

Tsia lunged forward, heedless of the thin, tearing brash. Her arms plunged into the blackness; her face hit the water. She groped wildly. There were swirls of green sparks of light, but they did not lighten the blackness. She grabbed hair, pulled and tore at nothing and realized it was only roots in her hands.

Kurvan scrambled across with a rod pieced together from the config gear and spread himself out on the other side of the sinkhole.

"Hurry," she snapped, her arms deep in the water.

Kurvan gave her a cold look. "For Daya's sake, he's got an enbee. He can breathe as well as you."

"He gave his to me on the platform, and I lost it in the sea—"

"Shit."

"Give me yours here; I'll give it to him when I reach him."

"Haven't got it," he returned, stabbing down with the rod. "Lost it in the lake."

"Where's Bowdie's?"

"Said he lost it back at the bridge." He stared down as if he could see through the water. "Can you feel him?"

"No, but he's right below us."

"Daya," she cursed under her breath. How long had Wren been down? The water swirled and sparked and fought beneath her hands.

"Get an e-wrap," she shouted at Bowdie. "Spread it out— and get an enbee from Nitpicker or Striker."

Striker started searching her harness, while Doetzier and Bowdie yanked the config gear from the packs. The first e-wrap they unfolded ripped itself from their hands and blew away across the meadow like tissue paper. The second one they configured as they sat on it, letting it mold itself to the contours of the grass. In the dark, as it shifted its colors to the meadow, it was invisible to Tsia. Quickly, Doetzier caught the connected lengths of metaplas that Striker slapped into his hands.

Tsia hooked her feet in a tangle and deliberately thrust her head and shoulders beneath the black surface again. The slimy grass clung to her face like seaweed. Her hands stretched down. She could almost feel Wren beneath her. His heartbeat, his cold, steady thoughts. He was there. She knew it. She caught cloth in her hand. A sleeve—the fingers that followed to clamp down on her arm could not be mistaken for roots.

Tsia lifted her head from the water. The grass wallowed beneath her weight. Her lungs ached with tension. How long had

Wren been down? Two minutes? Three? She could feel the time in his lungs.

She writhed and twisted, and her body rolled back a bit on the mat. Her face came free. Wren, feeling her pull, began to kick against the water. Instantly, curls of phosphor sparks whipped around his body. The root mats swirled around his feet. They tangled and tightened until they trapped his free arm in thick and rotting debris. Desperately she finned a message against the back of his hand: *Passa nyey.* Don't fight. Don't struggle. She could barely hold his weight against the pull of his pack.

Kurvan shifted his position, probing down with the pole, and with his movements, Tsia's face slapped water in a flare of green sparks. She jerked her face out. "Stop it. Stop!" she choked. "You're driving him under!"

"I almost had him," Kurvan snarled.

"I do have him," she returned savagely. "Get back. Ease back—let Doetzier through."

Even in the dark, she could feel the other merc by those tiny dots in his field. Lights of hope, she thought as he shoved the configured e-wrap platform forward. Kurvan rolled away to the side. Two of the packs' antigravs were fixed to the corner of the e-wrap, and the flexible platform rested on the water and weeds. She could feel the whine of the power cells on the edges of the wrap. The sound cut through her biogate like a sonic on full, and she could not stop the snarl that stretched across her face.

"Have you got an enbee?" she snapped at Doetzier.

He jerked it from his harness and held it out over the water to Tsia's stretched-out hand. But the wind gusted, and Kurvan lost his balance. The merc fell against Doetzier and the enbee disappeared in the brash.

"Shit!" Kurvan lunged after it, but missed.

"It's gone," snapped Doetzier, hauling at his shoulder. "Let it go. Give Feather a hand."

She glared at Doetzier as if she did not see him. "Hurry," she snarled.

"Do you have him?"

"Barely. Hurry."

"Don't let go."

"Goddam it, then, hurry!"

"Give me the pole," he directed Kurvan. The other merc shoved the metaplas length across the grass. But the grass mat rippled. Kurvan and Doetzier both fought for footing. Kurvan started sinking, and Doetzier fell against him. The tip of the pole caught in the water. Silently, neatly, with a line of green light to show the path of its passage, it slid from Kurvan's hand like glass and sank beneath the surface, just out of Doetzier's reach. Violently, Kurvan cursed.

"I'm slipping." Tsia's voice was matter-of-fact now. The hand clenching hers seemed to tighten. Just before he died. The sense of Wren was no longer sharp in her gate. The chill tang, cold, like old metal, was not as strong on her tongue. She tried to reach his biofield, but she could feel only a cold deliberation not to move. A steady determination that faded with every breath she let out of her lungs. "Do something," she cried out. "I'm losing him!"

Doetzier looked up, met her eyes, saw the bared teeth and the wildness that stretched taut across her face. "The antigrav isn't strong enough. He has to get rid of the pack."

"He's carrying the scame—the med gear, not just the breaker gear."

"It's too heavy. He's got to drop it."

"I told him not to move." And he could not hear her anyway, said some back, callous part of her brain. He was already almost unconscious. The finned messages she pressed against his skin created no response. The only thing left in his brain was a frozen certainty that if he moved, he would make it worse.

"If he stays as he is," Doetzier snapped, "if he keeps the pack, we can't bring him up through the grass. We have no way to cut the growth. My flexor doesn't work against it. Does yours?"

"Of course not."

"We can't tear it or we fall in ourselves—"

"For Daya's sake, don't tear it," she snapped back. "Those roots are the only thing other than my fingers holding him near the surface. If he sinks beneath the mat, he won't come up again. There are eels down there. And sucker fish. He's out of air. He has to come up *now!*"

Doetzier clenched one hand in a half fist as if he could strike some sense into her across the short expanse. "He has"—his voice was cold and clear—"to get rid of the pack. Signal him with your hands."

"Goddam you," she screamed. "He's unconscious."

"You're a guide," he snarled in return. "Reach him through your gate. Force him to think again. To fight."

Tsia glared at him, at Bowdie, at Kurvan. At Nitpicker, who eased up from behind the other three. Her eyes were wild. "Where's the line?"

"Striker's digging it out. We configured the e-wrap first."

"Then give me the sleeve of your blunter."

He did not hesitate. He shrugged out of the jacket and twisted one sleeve around his hand. He threw the other across to her. She barely had time to wrap it once around her hand before she started to sink forward. She twisted her head to stare down into the water. Gray water. Green sparks. The stench of rotting weeds and roots. Her eyes turned to Doetzier's. Her voice, when she spoke, had a curious, pleading sound. "Don't let me go."

He nodded. She hesitated, then lunged forward and down, and into the depths of the swamp.

Swirling, circling sparks . . . Her right arm caught with a wrench as the blunter jerked taut between them. Then she sank down by Wren's body. As her feet hit his chest, she hauled up on his weight and kicked her legs around him. Roots caught on her neck and she flinched at their touch. She could see nothing but glinting, greenish sparks that lit the bubbles of her movements. She could feel only wirelike strands that matted like wet string in the wind.

She tore at Wren's pack. The brash caught in her fingers like old pasta, and in her frustration, she screamed through her biogate. A violent surge answered like a wave that rolled through her mind. Claws seemed to grab at her flesh. And then her hand caught a seal. Instantly, she stripped it open and jerked it from his limp shoulder. Like claws, her fingers raged at the straps. Water and weeds swirled in her face. Fish bumped her legs and back. She could feel the pressure of the water. Or was it that of her heart?

Ruka was tearing at her thoughts. She was swimming—no, she was fighting with Wren's pack. Its weight pulled back, then sank slowly down in the grass, pulling a mass of brash after it like a slow, green-lit whirlpool. The root mat tore.

Rotted grass was in Tsia's nose, weeds across her eyes. Ruka screamed in her head and leaped across the flooded creek to race toward her through the grass. She thought she saw stars in the sky. No—that was phosphor in the water. She was still looking down.

Doetzier hauled her up till her arm flopped over the edge of the e-wrap platform and tilted the raft in the water. He could not lift her further; her legs wrapped stubbornly around Wren's waist.

"Striker," he cursed, "I need help."

It was Nitpicker who crawled out and dug her fingers into Tsia's shirt. Together, they hauled up the guide. As Tsia's shoulders cleared the raft, the top of Wren's head broke the surface in a soft wash of green light.

"Let go," Doetzier snapped at Tsia. "Let go, so we can bring him up."

Can't let go, she snarled back in her head. Won't. She struggled weakly in his grip. The antigravs whined into breakdown, and the energy field pulsed in the water.

"Let go—Feather," he snapped, "give him up."

"You'll drop him!" she cried out as his hands tried to pry off her legs.

"Goddammit!" He shoved her back, and she lost her grip. Then Doetzier got Wren by the shoulders and hauled up so that the other merc's face was clear. Water washed over the raft's edge.

"Pull us back," he shouted. "Hurry!"

Bowdie and Kurvan hauled. Doetzier didn't try to lift Wren's dead weight. He merely held Wren's head and neck above the surface. Wren's body was dragged along it until they were on more solid brash. Tsia, trembling, scrambled off the platform; her mind, still caught up by the cougar, shivered with angry catspeak.

She stared across at Wren. Limp roots clung to his face like leeches. His sharp, birdlike chin hung open; his eyelids were closed, but she could feel a tiny light in her gate. She screamed at the cats in her mind to shut up. Ruka growled audibly to her side. She glared at the cat, and the cub was silent. With the wind, no one else even noticed.

"No pulse," reported Striker, reaching around Doetzier to feel the other merc's neck.

"It's there." Tsia did not recognize her own voice, it was so harsh.

Striker looked up. "I feel nothing."

"It's there."

"He was down for over four minutes, Tsia. Even if the medlines fed his body the codes for oh-two—"

"He's alive," she snarled. "I can feel him in my gate. No thumping," she snapped as Doetzier made to bare Wren's chest.

Striker did not bother to nod. She tilted back his head and, while Doetzier held him, scooped the water from his mouth. A moment later, she began to breathe for him as well as herself.

Tsia hung on that breathing. Ruka crouched in the grass, and unconsciously, Tsia reached back for the reassurance of the cat. She connected with his body, and the cougar shifted closer. "Damn you, Wren," she whispered. "Breathe."

"I've got a pulse," Doetzier said sharply.

Striker automatically turned her face to feel if Wren breathed on his own, and didn't even realize how futile that gesture was in the roar of the wind. A second later, she jerked to the side just as Wren vomited. He coughed, convulsed, retched, and coughed again. The woman sat back on her knees. She looked up and nodded at Tsia. She did not need to speak.

Tsia's hands trembled as she clenched them to her temples. Abruptly Wren curled onto his knees and spat. His hand, when he reached for the water to clean his lips and mouth, held a tiny tremor.

He looked up, and Doetzier steadied him against the wind.

He squinted. The strands of grass that clung to Tsia's weather cloth made her look like a beggar. Wren tried to grin. Doetzier helped him to his feet, and he grasped a clump of tallgrass in his hands as if to steady himself.

Tsia stood slowly. The cub had not left her shadow, and she had to push him away to get him to move back in the grass. Her gate was still wide open. Her heart seemed to beat in two rhythms, and neither was slow. The cat, who flicked his tail, growled constantly in her mind, and his feet seemed to pad across her thoughts so that she could not concentrate.

Doetzier looked at the water. "The frame that Kurvan dropped," he asked Tsia. "Was it close enough to fish out?"

She shook her head.

"And Wren's pack?"

"It sank. It's far below the grass mat now."

She caught Kurvan's dark expression as he watched her from the side. Doetzier eyed her in silence. She could feel the hostility in his gaze, and it made her edge away. "It had antigravs," Doetzier said softly.

"Wren said they cut out just before he went down. I didn't think to try them."

He did not nod.

"I was more concerned with getting Wren," she snapped, "than checking on his gear."

He shrugged and turned away to collapse the makeshift raft.

Tsia stared at him and got to her feet. "Damn you," she breathed. "Damn you all to hell." She did not even know who she cursed.

16

It took them twenty minutes to break down the gear and get back out of the brash. No one mentioned the scame that was lost with Wren's breaker and the pack. His gear . . . The enbees . . . Uneasiness grew with every step Tsia took down the muddy trail. The skimmer crash . . . The antigravs . . . Since the moment the mercs landed on the platform at dawn, they had been pared down, she realized suddenly. Twelve mercs—thirteen, counting Tsia—and now there were seven left. Jandon had taken five shooters; the ocean had taken Tucker. Nitpicker almost went down in the lake. Kurvan would have gone off on the bridge. Of the two packs that were left, one carried only configuration gear, the other Kurvan's scannet. No manual coms were left in the packs. No e-gear or wide-range weapons. Only one handscanner on Bowdie's belt, his parlas, and the flexors on the hips of the other mercs. It was like surgery where, in a predefined pattern, the pieces were cut away, so that all that was left were the bones and the biofields.

She paused and stared at the slick, gray water that still sat like harmless puddles. When she looked back at the other mercs, only Doetzier met her eyes. The tightness of her jaw made her shudder till she welcomed the chill of her skin. It was three hours before dawn.

Kurvan saw her pause, and pushed past the other merc to catch up with her on the trail. He motioned with his chin back at Wren. "I thought you said you couldn't sense a human through your gate."

She didn't answer for a moment. "I've known Wren for a long time," she said finally. "I'm familiar with his energy."

"So you knew he was alive."

"He was a shadow, like any other. Like you."

"And like me," the man retorted sharply, his voice gathering and projecting the fury that his biofield hid, "he almost died because of your inaction."

Tsia stared at him. "What?"

"You may not have meant to push him down when you grabbed for him, but it would have been a hell of a lot better to let me finish bringing him up with the pole." He nodded at her expression. "I had him," he repeated coldly. "You pushed him down. I could have brought him up long before he lost consciousness—if you hadn't made me lose my grip with the pole."

She stared at him in disbelief. "It was you—not I—who pushed him down. I had him. I dug my fingers into his hand as if he was my own brother."

"And you also almost drowned him in place. Just like Tucker. And"—Kurvan's voice was harsh now—"perhaps, Nitpicker, too, before Bowdie swam down to help you—back in the lake?"

She opened her mouth to speak, but nothing came out. A snarl grew in her throat. Ahead, in the forest, Ruka paused and turned back.

Kurvan eyed her as if she were a parasite that had crawled out from a pore in his skin. It had been a long time since anyone had looked at her with such revulsion, and she took an involuntary step back at the vehemence of his expression. "Makes me wonder," he said with a cold, deliberate tone, "why these things occur only when you are there to . . . help. Do you really lead us to the freepick stake? Or do you work to keep us here? Away from the biochips, and away from the manual coms?"

He eyed her for another moment, then brushed past along the trail. She stared after him without moving. There was a snarling in her ears, and she could hear it resonating in her bones: It was her own throat that made those sounds. She shut her lips abruptly, but she could not move from her stance. It was not until Doetzier reached her frozen form that she realized the wind had carried Kurvan's words to the other merc as clearly as if they'd been spoken in his ears. Doetzier shot her a single look, then spat deliberately to the side. She could only glare at him till he passed.

"Goddam digger-spawned worm of a dith carcass," she cursed. At that moment, she didn't know which she hated more: Kurvan for thinking it of her, Doetzier for believing, or herself, for blaming neither one.

She shoved her way up to a thin stand of topoff cedar, while Nitpicker and the others slogged past. She could feel the cub slinking through the brush to meet her, and she welcomed him with a hedonistic rage. The odors of the mercs filled her nose and made her fingers clench. She almost writhed with the focus that Ruka sent to her brain. Then she realized what she was doing.

"Daya," she breathed. The violence of her anger shocked her, and she pressed her hands against the tree and stared at them as if they belonged to someone else. These were the fingers that held such instinct for self-preservation—such desperation when the fear hit her hard. Yet these were the same limbs that carried death inside their bones. And with Ruka there . . . She shook her head against the bark of the tree until the wood ground against her skin. She knew, if she pushed, the cub would track Kurvan down and kill him.

"Ah, Daya," she whispered. "What have I become?"

A thick hand touched her shoulder, and she whirled, spinning into a crouch. One hand stretched before her, and the other hand drew her flexor before her eyes focused and she recognized the stocky shape of Wren.

The other merc held his ground. He met her feral gaze with a look that seemed to bore its way into her center like a screw turning, chewing its way through the walls and layers of shielding she had built around her heart. The shadows of the whipping trees moved over his face like demons.

"Jit paka'ka chi," he said deliberately, in the old tongue of the mercs. "You gave me my tomorrow. My life."

She stared at him for a moment. Then threw her head back and laughed. The sound was harsh; and Ruka, crouched on a spur of rock to the left, snarled in response. Wren's eyes flickered. If he saw the faint outline of the cougar pressed against the stone, he said nothing.

"That's rich, Wren," she said finally, choking on her bitterness as the rain drove itself into her mouth. *"Jit paka'ka chi."*

"Tsia—"

"Tsia?" she cut in. "Feather?" She spat. "You can't say it, can you? You can obligate me with your life, but you can't say you trust me. All these years, and you can't even call me *'avya.'* Not friend, not trusted one. Nothing."

He regarded her coldly from his sharp-chinned mask. "Are those the words you need to hear?"

"Everyone needs words, Wren."

"Those words?"

"Words of importance. Words of . . ."

"Love?" His voice was rich with derision.

Tsia clenched her hands at her sides.

Wren was silent for a moment, but the sense of his biofield was cold and hard. "Do you look for love in me or seek it in yourself?"

Tsia stared at him. "Did you hear Kurvan? He thinks I deliberately pushed you down in the swamp. He thinks I tried to drown you."

"Something pushed me down," he returned. "It wasn't the hand that held me."

Tsia cursed violently. "If it wasn't, you didn't say anything to them to defend me. Doetzier and Kurvan—even Bowdie thinks I'm responsible for the whole thing."

He shrugged.

"The antigrav—is that it? I checked it just before it went out, so you don't trust that I didn't push you down. *Jit paka'ka chi,"* she said bitterly, as if it was a curse.

"Do your actions change what you are?" he asked softly.

"Dammit, Wren—"

"You're a guide, Tsia."

"That doesn't mean I'm not human."

"Doesn't it? You're as alien as an Ixia, and that will always be between us."

"Why?" she cried out.

He studied her for a moment. "You don't even know who you are—what you'll do for yourself—let alone what you can do for others."

She stared at him. "So I can expect no trust. No love or loyalty. Is that what you have to say?"

"Trust, love, loyalty—what are they?" he snapped back harshly. "There's never been any love in this life, Feather. You lose too much to love anything but yourself. Or you love too much to give any one thing meaning. Do you need the words? Then here, I name you *avya*. Friendship, loyalty—you have whatever I can give."

"*Avya*," she snarled. "How many bonds do you mock with that term?"

"I mock nothing but the thing between us which you force me to name."

She shook her head mutely.

"There is no trust, Tsia-guide. No such thing at all. There's only knowledge in this life. And that knowledge is that you'll lose something important when the one you trust has failed. Perhaps it will be your hand or leg. Maybe your credit or control. And maybe it's your life. Knowing that is fatalism, not trust." He stepped forward and gripped her arm, jerking her wrist up to the rain. His scarred, brutal hand looked like a club next to her bruised, slender fingers.

She twisted against his strength, but he gripped her more tightly. His thin lips looked cruel. "Look at me. Look at you. You know this hand—it's yours. Look at it," he snapped as she glared up at him. "Do *I* know how much strength is in your flesh? No," he answered his own question.

Violently, she wrenched her hand away, but he yanked her back and forced it up so that she had to stare at her own clawlike fingers. On the stone behind her, Ruka leaped to the rain-flattened grass and slunk closer, behind a shrub.

"Do I know at which point the hand or will in you will break?" he demanded. "I can't know that. Striker can't. Kurvan can't—not until you do break. And the breakpoint is something only you can know. If you find out where that breakpoint is, it means you've gone to the limit of yourself and found the edge of your fear and determination. You've found the edge of your will. It means you've shattered your illusions and ideals and all your rigid walls, and shot out into the void of Truth. That you've pulled yourself back for the first time in your life to see yourself clearly. And it means that, for that truth, someone else has probably paid the price."

He released her hand. She refused to rub the circulation back in. Instead, with hatred in her eyes, she reveled in the ache that flooded back with her blood. His cold gaze narrowed. The wind whipped her face to a white blur, and the rain dripped from the claw marks on her cheek.

"Is that what you would call trust, Feather? *Avya?*" he said deliberately. "Blind belief in a will you cannot judge? Dumb acceptance of a strength you cannot test?" He snorted. "You can't build trust. You can't earn it, and you can't force it to occur. It doesn't exist where you seek it. Do you understand? Why did you help me? Do you know? What you search for in us, what you sought with the risk you took for me, is something that doesn't even exist outside yourself."

Her fingernails curled into her palms. "I didn't do it for trust, Wren. I didn't dive in just to gain your respect. Nor to fulfill a contract, or because it was expected." Her voice was low, shaking with anger, shaking with emotions that filled her body and trembled against the walls of bone and flesh that held them in.

He raised his thick, scarred hand to her face and touched the claw marks that ran from temple to jaw. "*Avya,* I know."

Hands clenched at her sides, she said harshly, "There was no choice in it for me. I could not let you die."

He looked at her for a long moment, then, deliberately, slapped her so hard that she spun half around and staggered against the tree. Ruka leaped from the brush. Wren threw out his hand and roared. Tsia's gate seemed frozen. It was not her, she thought blindly. It was not her who turned to stone in fear. It was the cat, caught in a moment in which the prey turned and the predator became the game. She could feel Ruka's heartbeat. Hard, fast against her ribs. She could feel the thick fingers of Wren's hand against her cheek—the marks glowed red, then faded to a white more pale than the scars on her chilled skin.

A sound half snarl, half cry escaped her throat. She was still caught like the cat, crouched against the bole of the tree. Wren glared at her. Somewhere in the back of her mind, some odd, objective part of her brain noted that it was the first time she had ever seen him angry.

"You gave me my life," he snarled coldly, "and you expect gratitude—and a trust that does not exist. A loyalty that you mistake. You expect me to be other than I am. Are you blind? Can't you see clearly—feel the violence in my hands? Can't you smell the blood on my skin? You ask me to trust you— when I know your past? I look at you and see myself instead—like mirrors lined up in my skull. In that violence, we are bound, Feather-guide; in that blood, we are lovers. Look at you. Look at your crouch. Your eyes. The way your hands curl like the claws of the cat that even now is afraid to face me. Your mind is filled with the edge of life. With the blood that pounds in your head and clouds your thoughts so that my words are like birds beating against your face. Trust? Bah. It's a heart that you seek. Perhaps the one that you lost." He made a savage gesture. "Don't look for love here, Feather. I bring you no such gifts."

She stared at him. Her throat seemed torn open all the way down to her gut. Her stomach clenched. Her voice, when she spoke, was as harsh as his. "I hear you, Wren." She shoved herself away from the tree. "I believe you." She focused on her gate and forced Ruka to slink back through the shrubs. The unblinking gaze of the cat never wavered, and she had to shake her head to see Wren through her own cold eyes.

He smiled without humor, and the expression pulled his face into lines as sharp as a knife. "Illusions are far more dangerous than hate," he said softly. "The one can be mistaken; the other can only be seen for what it is."

"You trust no one, not even me."

"No"

"You need it, Wren—the love, the trust. Hide it behind whatever words you want; but you need it just as much as me."

"The need to trust is not important to me," he said flatly.

"It is to me." Her voice broke on the last words.

Wren's eyes seemed to flatten—to lose the last vestiges of expression they had held before. It was as if a mask of glass slid down over his gaze. His anger was gone. His rage might never have existed. She stared at him and reached out through her gate. His bioenergy was almost nonexistent; his voice was distant as the gray-black tops of the mountains. "I know you, Feather—Tsia—of Ciordan. Guide of the merc guild. Dance-fighter from the desert where I first saw you walk the flames of your trade. I *know* you," he repeated. "I don't have to trust you."

Wind blasted through the trees and lifted his hair as if it could be torn from his scalp. The scars on Tsia's cheek pulled tightly white against her skin. She dropped her hand to her side. Her voice was cold with a chill that seemed to pierce her teeth. "The one thing you do not know," she said slowly, "is who or what I am."

17

ᏜᏜᎧᏜᏜ

Tsia jogged blindly toward the head of the trail. She did not speak to Striker, or Doetzier. She did not glance at Kurvan. Her brain was filled with catspeak, and she could not get the claws out of her skull. She barely noticed the kilometers they moved. The storm, now steady, gave time no meaning at all. Her neck was greased with rain.

Doetzier and Kurvan traded their packs off to Bowdie and Striker; Nitpicker and Wren took their turn after that. Wren silently gave Tsia his slimchim pouch when they paused for a break on the trail, and she took two chims for herself, then tossed half the rest to Ruka. She didn't speak to the other mercs; she could feel them like death on the trail. The nose of the cub seemed to flare with their scents. His eyes seemed to watch from behind. One of them was blackjack, she told herself with a chill. One of them was death.

Twice, she pointed out places for the mercs to ease around. The first time, the sharp musk scent of the shapers rose from the path just ahead, and she froze. Behind her, the other mercs automatically stilled their steps. This scent was not through Ruka's nose, but had come to her from her own. The shapers were close. Ruka's senses flooded over the faint detail of the heartbeats she sought, and she had to shush him with a snarl.

Faint . . . Sluggish . . . As if they slept. As if they waited. She stared to the side of the pocket of life till the rain rippled across the trail. A flicker of movement caught her eye. One

209

edge shifted; the water dripped across. Had she blinked, she would have missed it. Had she looked straight at it, she would have thought it was her mind, not reality, that slid the rain from the trail.

She soothed Ruka so that he withdrew from his perch in the stones. Then, infinitesimally, she eased her body back. No more vibrations on the trail to kick them out of their hole. No sudden moves to make them eager to follow. She was as careful with her feet as she was with her eyes, refusing to stare at their backs, as if they could feel the heat of her gaze through their dozing watchfulness. A moment later, she led the mercs around the trail where Ruka had already gone, and where the scent of the cat lingered like paint on the rocks.

The second time she smelled the musk, it was through Ruka's nose, not hers. That time, the scent came from a place offtrail, to the right, and Ruka, his gold eyes gleaming, regarded the pocket as if he were a pointer whose line could be followed by Tsia's thoughts. She acknowledged the shapers and eased the mercs on past.

When Ruka joined her again, she could feel the hunger in his belly grow. "Go," she told him then. "Go hunt on your own. Don't wait here with me."

He growled in return. She motioned sharply, as if to scare him away, but he knew her now, and the motion merely made his eyes sharpen, as if she herself might become his meal. She laughed at him and snarled back through the gate, then tossed the pouch with the rest of Wren's slimchims into the rocks. She did not have to see the paw that snagged the bundle before it hit the ground; she could feel him tear it open and gulp the contents so clearly that her own throat convulsed.

An hour before dawn. Doetzier and Kurvan took their packs back; Tsia still stalked at the head of the trail. Ruka, the low hum of his growling ever-present in her mind, climbed and leaped and padded so that Tsia's feet did not seem to feel the trail, but rather jumped from stone to stone and crisscrossed through the forest behind herself. She grew almost used to the feeling of double vision.

They climbed through the last cut and paused where the

trail opened out onto the top of a cliff. This was the part of the trail she knew well, even in the dark. The wind, which curled and eddied along the rock wall, tugged at their balance as much as the mud that had sucked at their feet. Where the cliff dropped away, the rocks shot down like arrows and ended in a tumble of broken columns.

Tsia padded out to the edge of the wall, knowing it had no undercut. From behind, Kurvan yelled a warning, but she waved him off. Instead, she poised on the rim and rolled her shoulders till the tension left her arms. Gingerly, Kurvan stepped up beside her and looked down.

He gestured at their feet. "How did you know the edge was safe?"

She cocked her head to hear his words in the wind. He was like a cougar just before it pounced, his voice low while his biofield crouched to attack. "I know this wall," she said flatly. "It's as solid as it is tall at this point."

His voice sharpened deliberately. "If you know this trail so well, how could you not know there was a lake beneath the grass back in the meadow?"

"It was night, and I can't wear darkeyes."

"Yes, but you're a guide."

She twisted to face him, and her rain-pale face was thin and sharp. The white scars on her cheek seemed to channel the rain to her lips, and she licked them almost unconsciously. "I'm a guide," she agreed with a soft snarl, "not a god. The middle part of this trail—I never hiked it before. Only the beginning and ends. With the node down, I had no way of knowing what was under the grass."

"As a guide," he snapped back, "your responsibility is to feel what *is* there."

"I can't sense things as clearly in a storm—no guide can. There's too much movement. What I sensed in the meadow—lake," she corrected, "was life that made sense for the movement of the wind."

"You said there were eels, sucker fish. If you could feel them, how could you think it was grassland?"

Ruka's fur had bristled with Kurvan's tone, and his hostility became Tsia's aggression. She had to clamp her lips to keep them from snarling. "Just what are you getting at?" she asked slowly, fighting with her throat to make the human sounds.

"Seems like you feel only what you want to feel through your so-called biogate. You come out with barely a scratch each time there is an accident; but Wren and Tucker? Nitpicker? It's always someone else who pays for your mistakes. And with the scame gone down with Wren's pack, how could we fix a more ... *fatal* accident?"

She took a step forward, Kurvan took a step back, and Nitpicker materialized from the wind. The pilot gave Kurvan a meaningful glance, and he withdrew without a word, though he cast a cold look at Tsia's hand, which clenched the hilt of her flexor. Nitpicker did not watch him go. She merely stood in his place and looked out from the cliff as if she did not notice the flash of Tsia's eyes.

Tsia struggled with her breathing. Her eyes seemed blinded by the movement of the woman's clothes in the wind. She was focused like a hunter, she realized. She was taking in Ruka's will as if it was her own. It was like the heat of a fire: all-consuming, all-surrounding. She shuddered visibly, and Nitpicker noted it out of the corner of her eye. The pilot's darkeyes caught movement the same way that Tsia did through her gate, and the shudder that Tsia fought to control was as obvious to Nitpicker as the wind that rippled through Tsia's hair. The pilot had seen the guide like this before—when fire had called Tsia as strongly as her gate. When she had been drawn to the flames as strongly as she was sucked in by the cats who crawled in her mind. How did she really think anymore? How far could Tsia be trusted? Nitpicker shot a glance at Tsia's throat, and tightened her lips at the bruising. The blackness of her finger marks was as dark as the whiteness of the claw marks on Tsia's face. The swollen flesh as thick as the anger that seeped from Tsia's muscles. The pilot balanced like Tsia against the wind and tried to feel the currents as if they were heat instead of chill air.

"I suppose this seems like fire, not rain, to you," she shouted.

Tsia nodded.

"Still crave it?"

She shook her head. She knew what Nitpicker asked, and the pilot seemed intent, but not intent on her. "I'm ten years out of my gate," she answered, expanding her gate to search where Nitpicker focused. "Only new guides have a physical need to dance in the flames."

"You don't need the fire at all?"

"Not need, no," she returned. "But desire, yes. The heat on my flesh . . . The smell of ash in my sweat . . ."

"Then it's the biogate, not the firepit, that calls you now?"

Slowly, Tsia nodded. "I can feel the cats as far away as that mountaintop." She gestured with her chin.

"Strong gate. Too strong, perhaps?"

Tsia turned her head and met Nitpicker's eyes, and her gaze had a wildness beneath the dark blue that was not fury, but eagerness. "You and the others," she said softly, "you're right not to trust me. A tam can call me to it just as easily as I could call that same cat to me."

"Your mutation was not supposed to stay so wild, Feather. You were supposed to become controlled. To be able to control your gate like you do your ghosts in the node."

"I did. I can."

"Yet you say they call you, too?"

Tsia closed her eyes. "As easily and strongly as the node calls you through your temple link." Cat feet skittered across her skull, and she rubbed at her temples, then threw back her head and screamed the cry of the cougar into the wind. Behind the two women, the other mercs leaned against the wall of rock and watched.

Nitpicker eyed her for a moment. "You've lost yourself, Feather. You've given yourself up to your gate."

When Tsia opened her eyes, they glinted. "My hands don't shake; my thoughts are clear. I'm not controlled by this," she said flatly. "There's only myself inside me; and the gate—it's a door, not a void."

"I look at you and see a cat clawing its way out of the human skin which surrounds it."

Tsia's lip curled. "You're the one who doesn't see me clearly, if you see only the gate in my mind."

"I see more than your gate, Tsia. I see a guide so lost she knows only the trail she treads, not the life she wishes for herself. I see a Feather so buffeted by the wind that she has no path of her own. I see you accepting your biogate as if it was your only view of the world."

"I'm a guide. I can't help but see through the gate."

"See through it or live through it?" Nitpicker studied Tsia for a long moment. "If you were threatened—if you were told the gate would be taken away, what would you do to save it? How far would you go to protect yourself at the expense of those around you?"

Tsia's eyes narrowed. "You think I'd betray you to save myself? That I'd trade your life for my gate?" She nodded slowly. "That's what you think has gone on here, isn't it? You think I've been working against you."

"Have you?"

Tsia's jaw tightened. "There's something you're still not saying, Van'ei."

"Look at you," Nitpicker returned harshly. "Your eyes are wild. Your fingers curl like claws. You look like a stormwitch, not a guide. I can see you dancing in this as if it were fire, not wind that whipped your hair. As if your blood burned the same way as your anger. I see death in your footsteps, Tsia-guide. I see it when you're threatened—when you're angry. And I see it when you connect with the cats." She eyed Tsia with a cold look. "You never left the cub behind, did you? You drew him here with us, and all along this trail, he's been clouding your mind so that you can't even remember that you're human."

Tsia could not answer, but the expression in her eyes was enough for Nitpicker to tighten her lips in fury.

"So. I'm right." She stared out into the valley blindly until she saw the points of light that marked the freepick stake. "Zyas dammit," she swore finally. "No cats as scouts; no obligations; no calling by the humans: that's the Landing Pact that the cats themselves negotiated. But here you are, taking advantage of a cub who's been engineered to link with you if you want it. And you want that badly. Don't deny it, Feather. It's in your eyes." She cursed again under her breath. "You disobeyed my orders. The platform stunt was one thing; this is something else. Here, you're deliberately breaking the Landing Pact that you of all people should honor. Sleem take it," she said in disgust. "There's some kind of irony in the fact that we're protecting you from the guides, while the guides protect the cats from you. Neither you nor the cats obey the Pact that everyone else is keeping."

"He wants this link as much as I do—maybe more," Tsia returned harshly. "I can taste it in his field. Every time I send him away, he just refuses to go."

"Do you really expect him to withdraw from what is as strong to his nature as hunting? He's been engineered, Feather, to link with you as a scout. He has no choice in this. You do. And if you let this continue, he could bond with you for life. He could become as much a slave to your gate as you are to the ID dot that protects you from the guides."

"Van'ei," she said softly, "I can't hate him enough to drive him away. He saved my life in the lake. And if he hadn't done so, I wouldn't have known to come back to help you. He—not I—is the reason that you're alive, too."

"Perhaps." Nitpicker turned back to the freepick's valley. "When I was trapped in the mud, there was someone else nearby. Someone who ripped the enbee from my face. You were there. You bear the marks to prove it. You were with Tucker when he died—it was your idea that drowned him. You almost dropped Doetzier on that stretch of rock. You did drop Kurvan on the bridge—it was Bowdie, not you, who caught him and kept him from falling. You led Wren right into the water."

"I didn't know it was a lake—"

Nitpicker cut her off coldly. "I accepted Wren's word about Tucker. I gave you the benefit of the doubt about myself. But Kurvan—we saw it, Feather. It was deliberate—your letting go—as if you just threw him away to the rocks."

"Daya, how can you say this? You know me—"

"Ay, I know you."

Tsia stared at her. "You provoke me, then defend me. You joke with me, then push me. We've never been close, but at least we could work together. Now there's something else in your mind. Something you're not saying."

"I want truth, Feather-guide." Her eyes flicked to the swollen ring of Tsia's neck. "I want to know what you see in your gate—if you obey the cats of this world, or if you follow another voice. Something foreign perhaps? Or alien?" She watched Tsia closely.

"I don't understand."

"I want to feel for myself the truth of what you tell me."

"I don't know how to give you that."

Nitpicker said softly, "But you do know how to choose, don't you? Between an ethic and the desire that floods you through your gate? Striker will fight to the death to defend a lifer's rights, even if she hates what the lifer stands for. What ethics in you are stronger than your desire for the cats?"

Tsia's eyes narrowed. The pilot's questions probed like a scalpel for the rotted tissue of a pressure bruise.

Nitpicker watched her carefully. "How far are you controlled by your gate?" she demanded softly. "How much are you directed by the guide guild you claim to have left? Or directed by something else?"

"I left the guides when the guides left me. I owe them nothing."

"I've heard that a ten-year guide should be able to pinpoint the organic circuit of an antigrav in the clutter of a shiptech's lab."

"You know my link," Tsia returned with vehemence. "And it's to the cats, not to a bacterium. I have no such resolution."

"You don't have to be so linked to feel such detail. All gates should have the potential of that sensitivity. Linked to the felines or linked with the fish, you should be able to feel a biochip within a dozen meters."

Tsia stared at her for a long moment. "I thought you understood," she said slowly. "I thought you knew."

"Knew what?"

She glanced at the other mercs, but they were to the side,

not downwind. "I was taken from the guide guild," she said, "before I was trained to my gate. I never learned how to use it." Her hands clenched with growing frustration. She couldn't blame Nitpicker for her distrust, but she could not help her anger. "Everything I know," she said in a low, vehement voice, "I've learned by myself or through Forrest, and I've got almost no resolution outside the link to the cats."

Nitpicker regarded her strangely for a moment. "When you detected the shapers, what did you feel?"

"I smelled them first—I didn't *feel* them."

"And once you knew they were there?"

"I isolated them through the gate."

The other woman nodded.

"It wasn't easy," Tsia said flatly.

Nitpicker stared out over the black valley till she located the faint lights from the freepick stake in the distance. "Your sister works in customs, doesn't she?"

Tsia stared at her. "What does that have to do with anything?"

"Customs," Nitpicker repeated. "That's a useful trade. Lot of contact with aliens. Lot of credit in the grayscale."

"Not for her. She's as straight as they come."

"No interesting stories? No small slip-bys for a little extra credit?"

Tsia eyed her warily. "Traders tried it, but Shjams—she never bit."

"Lot of inspectors go to the grayscale," she remarked. "They say hooking in with blackjack is a ticket to Paradise. Information about a biochip shipment would pretty much pay your way to Paradise and back."

Tsia felt a coldness spread throughout her middle. "So through Shjams, I could be linked to the Ixia or blackjack. I could be a zek myself."

"You'd do most anything for her, wouldn't you?"

"She's my sister, for Daya's sake—"

Nitpicker glanced at the valley floor. The shadows didn't lengthen; they merely darkened as the sky stretched black fingers where once the clouds had been gray. "It's two hours before dawn. We should be moving on."

Tsia didn't shift. "My gate, my resolution, my sister up at the docking hammers— If everything points to me, every accident, every death, why do you think I'd guide you rightly at all—to the freepick stake or anywhere else?"

"We have seven or eight kays left to go," the pilot said coldly. "If there is one more mishap—even a slip in the mud—between here and the stake, I'll know then what to think of you."

She motioned sharply, and the flesh tightened along Tsia's jaw. Without a word, Tsia turned and gestured to the other mercs. They fell into line behind her. Kurvan, Doetzier, then Wren like a shadow. Nitpicker with that cold, intelligent anger still tightening her field like a knot. Striker with her blunter sealed tight in the rain, and Bowdie at the end. They were a winding snake of suspicion that followed her down the trail. A line of tension that stretched like a trip wire waiting for her misstep.

18

Tsia moved down the trail, her eyes seeing automatically through Ruka's eyes, and her mind lost in the thoughts that circled like loose river wood in an eddy. "I should be able to feel a circuit or feel a biochip . . ." Her voice was sarcastic, and she glanced back at the mercs. "Biochips at thirty paces . . ." A sweep of rain stung her face in points. Her eyes widened abruptly. Points of water. Points of light?

Slowly, then more deliberately, she began to jog through the mud, and behind her, Kurvan cursed and picked up his pace. Doetzier, then the others sped up, till their feet slipped and slid with their speed.

Tsia stretched her gate to feel them. It was easier when their pulses were up—as if the way they expended energy brightened the pattern of each biofield. Wren, in the back, was still the easiest for her to distinguish: cold and distant and quick as ice cracking across a pond. Nitpicker: cool, not cold, and wary and sharp, like chilled needles. Striker like sand, without form or shape, but fluid and moving each minute. Bowdie with his gallows humor riding his eager, light-spotted field, and the haunted gaze so hidden behind his darkeyes. He loved a challenge almost as much as she did, but the heat of his field was nothing compared to the hot sense of Kurvan's. Eager, hunting, watching . . . And then there was the last one: Doetzier, whose cold, watchful eyes were like daggers in her back. Whose field was pricked with points of light. Like tiny stars. Like living things.

Tsia had to force herself to remain facing forward. She let herself be drawn through the biogate into Ruka's mind until the colors she saw seemed to shift, and movement became more acute. The rhythmic pounding of the booted feet matched the pulse she felt in veins that were not her own. She could see them clearly now—the way they kept their distance from each other. She could watch from the corners of her double-vision eyes the way each fighter breathed. She could smell the scents of men and women, and reach out for the points of light.

She came almost blindly to the first of the three rocky drops that led to the freepick stake. She took a deep breath, then stepped out over the edge. When she hit the wide, flat top of the column, her ankles jarred, and shock traveled all the way up to her knees. A second jump, more reckless, shivered up through her thighs and renewed the throb of the claw marks beneath the graft on her leg.

The cougar did not hesitate to follow. His tawny shape flashed by so quickly that Tsia jerked and banged her knee against a protruding stone. She stifled her curse with a taut grimace. Should she not have admired his grace? he seemed to say. Tsia opened her mouth to retort, then stopped herself abruptly. She jumped the rest of the way with her knees tucked and bent for the shock of the ground. And Ruka, his golden eyes glaring at her figure, slunk to the side and disappeared in the brush.

His hunter eyes, which watched the mercs, made her turn and watch them as warily as he. The mercs—one of them was blackjack. And it was Doetzier, she swore to herself, who was the final key.

On the marine platform, there had been that presence—that sense of being watched when she checked the location of the cats. Someone had not wanted her here—or Tucker either.

Doetzier hit the ground while Kurvan made his way awkwardly down. As soon as Striker started her climb, Tsia turned to the trail. There was blackjack here. She would swear it. A killer. Not a merc anymore, but a murderer.

Tentatively, she imaged a command through her temple links and felt it echo away. The one ghost she maintained—she found its trace again. The image of the made-up man who went about his business. A man oblivious to the fact that his false world was no more than the webs of the node. Like tapping into a holo on a dreambar channel, or catching a thread of someone else's conversation, the ghost man was not solid, but he was active. Active on an ID dot that Tsia had given up more than ten years ago. An old ID dot and an image that clung to the node like honey to a spoon . . . She wondered for a moment, as she watched Bowdie descend, what would happen if she made the ghost an active trace. And if she did so, would her old ID become fully active once again? How long would it be before the guide guild caught on that Tsia of Ciordan, not Feather of the mercs, was still on the node and active? The rain thickened as if in answer, and Tsia closed down gently on the traceline and let it settle quietly in her mind.

The dawn did not lighten the sky with color, but only cracked it with a faint gray light at the edge of the black horizon. Tsia quickened her pace and urged Ruka to move faster and ahead where his shape would be less visible to the limited range of the darkeyes.

She reached the second rocky drop and caught sight of the freepick stake, half a kay away. The lights were on and visible in the squat, brown-gray huts that surrounded the skimmer tarmac. Like a diamond with slightly rounded edges, the stake was perhaps two hundred meters across and six hundred meters long. Down the middle, in a long, clear stretch of tarmac, were the landing pad and maintenance deck. The main freepick structure was a clumsy hub with short, stubby arms. To the northwest was a row of construction huts. Farther down were four vehicle cradles and three skimmers that squatted like flies on the deck. On the other side of the hub, three rows of cylindrical storage units looked like rows of checkers. The northwest end of the landing pad was bare and flooded with puddles.

Across the tarmac were two more rows of huts and a cluster

of vats, larger than those on the marine station. Near the middle of the landing pad, behind one of the rows of huts, a massive pit yawned like an open mouth in the ground: the reclamation area. When it was finished, it would be a maze of tunnels and pipelines and wells that would carry and process the tailings until they were completely biodegraded. And it would all work, Tsia thought, because of one set of chips. One piece of biotechnology for which someone would kill.

Half a kay, she thought soberly, and she would know for sure. Seven mercs, shut off from the node . . . The blackjack who walked among the mercs could not let them reach the stake—the mercs would never live to use the com inside the hub. Time and their footsteps pushed them forward while blackjack simply waited, like cats on a cliff, for the mercs to step under their claws.

She paused at the top of the stony steps and glanced back along the line. Doetzier was still first behind her, then Kurvan just behind him. She waited for the first merc, and as he came abreast of her, he raised his eyebrows in question.

"I have to talk with you," she murmured. He tilted his head to see her better through the steady rain, and she gestured at the rocks as if to give him directions down, but said as quickly as she could, "You're carrying the biochips."

He did not start. He gave no guilty glances or hard looks. It would have been fatuous, she supposed, if he had, but somehow, she expected something other than the blank response of silence.

"Did you hear me?" she demanded urgently. Kurvan moved up into hearing range, and she gave Doetzier an angry look before falling silent. The tall merc said nothing, but started down without her.

Kurvan waited while Doetzier climbed. His lean face looked almost gaunt in the darkness, as if his bones had become more prominent by the hour, and the handsomeness he once projected had retreated in exhaustion. "My stabilizers are shot," he said as Doetzier made it to the halfway mark. "Give me a hand, will you?"

She nodded and extended her grip. He took it and leaned out

to lever himself down to gain a purchase on the next slick boulder. With her feet braced and the wind steady, she felt no unbearable strain. Then his antigrav shut down. His weight and that of his pack came full on her arm. He slipped. His fingers wrenched at her hand. She was yanked off her feet—full-length at the edge. Her legs slipped sideways and back. Heavily, she fell with a brutal thud that smashed her ribs to the rock, and her flexor broke free of her harness. Kurvan's fingers slid from her rain-slick skin. She stared at his face as it fell away in the gloom. His eyes—black eyes—bored into hers; then he twisted away to fall.

"Falling!" she shouted.

Kurvan hit Doetzier like a sack of rock. He knocked the other merc off the stone, and both men tumbled to the bottom in a tangle of blunt shapes. Doetzier hit first, and the thud of his pack across stone was almost as loud as the cracking sound Tsia's flexor made as it struck the rock beside them. A hand flung out like a small white flag; the dark bulk of Kurvan's body crushed it almost instantly.

Tsia was already scrambling down. She leaped, then grabbed a hold; slithered across wet rock, then swung off her hands. Something tawny blurred her vision, and her hands were, for a second, yellow-gold and furred. She shook her head and jumped recklessly to the ground, staggering with her momentum before she found her feet. What stopped her then was the energy surge and instantaneous shaft of pain that hit her biogate like a flood wall. There was an outraged scream, then silence.

For a second only, she froze. She was not aware that she clutched her forearm as if to break it; only vaguely did she hear the shouting from above. Beside her, before he faded into the half-light of dawn, Ruka's eyes registered the figures that clambered down behind. Tsia's own gaze was glued to the two mercs. Kurvan shifted, and as if she broke free of some invisible hold, she lunged forward and yanked him up. Someone cursed. Steel fingers seized her arm from behind.

She wrenched free. "He's not hurt," she snarled. "It's Doetzier."

Still, the steel hand hauled her back. A tawny shape flashed to the side. Her eyes slitted. Her mouth twisted with the snarl she could not contain. The cat responded, and gathered his weight, and Tsia's biogate flashed wide. "No!" she shouted. Her mind seemed to freeze. Ruka flattened out. Nitpicker's eyes flickered, but she did not take her gaze from the merc on the ground.

"He's broken," she shouted at Nitpicker's face. Some part of her brain registered the idiotic words. But the merc did not release her arm, and the pilot's wiry fingers dug steadily into flesh.

"Let go of me," Tsia snarled.

"Shut up, Feather." Her voice was harsh, cutting.

Blue eyes bored into black. There was a warning there. A coldness that radiated out from Nitpicker's biofield like ice forming and freezing the air between them. Tsia shuddered and tried to pull away, but the other woman tightened her grip, and some part of Tsia's brain was amazed at the strength in that slim body.

"Stay." Nitpicker spoke as if giving a command to a dog, and the anger flashed in Tsia's eyes before she felt the message in those fingers. Pressing, tapping on her arm . . . Speaking to her skin.

Her lips clamped shut. The pressure tightened. Words. A message. Wait. Obey. And three words that made her freeze in place and stare at the narrow, lined face. *Gepa'i cha'k. Vaka'kha.* To take from the hunter the hunt. To provoke the hunter to expose himself to the arrow of his enemy.

Nitpicker tightened her grip one more time, then let go and turned to Kurvan. "What happened?" she snapped.

He dabbed gingerly at the scrape that bloodied his cheek. "My antigrav went out, and I slipped before I could get a purchase on the stone. Feather took the full weight on her arm." He gestured toward Doetzier, who sat, propped up, now against a boulder. "I knocked him off when I fell, then landed right on top of him. If it hadn't been for him, I would have broken my neck."

Nitpicker caught Striker's attention. "How is he?"

"His arm is cracked."

The pilot nodded. "Patch it," she ordered.

Bowdie overheard her words. "We can cast it, but that's about it," he said. He did not hide his glance toward Tsia. "We lost the scame in the meadow. And with the medlines down, he can't even block the pain. He'll have to walk to the stake as is."

Nitpicker nodded, and Bowdie turned to help Striker with a medpack. Quickly, they wrapped Doetzier's arm with the thin brown roll of the metaplas cast material. Doetzier cried out once as his arm was shifted and bone ends grated. A sharp, hot smell rose, then subsided. The cast molded itself tightly and shrank. Doetzier hissed this time and paled, and Bowdie gripped his shoulders. A moment later, only a faint lingering scent spoke of the newness of the cast.

Nitpicker's face was emotionless as she turned to Tsia. She said nothing, just looked Tsia up and down, and then turned away. The steady rain washed Tsia's forehead, and she felt the chill like a snake, curling into her skin.

Nitpicker knew.

The sabotage. The death. The accidents. The falls. That look on the pilot's face—Tsia should be afraid. There should be fear eating at her guts as if the guide guild had found her—as if she were betting her biogate against the certainty of the sunrise. There should not be this eagerness swelling up in her stomach. She motioned toward the freepick stake. Her voice was tight. "Half a kay."

The pilot nodded, her expression still cold, and Kurvan gave Tsia a sharp look before turning away to help Doetzier to his feet. Striker repacked the medkit and did not meet Tsia's eyes. Instead, she hefted Doetzier's pack and set it on her shoulders. Doetzier, who had been eased out of it, turned his drawn face to Tsia to give her a long and thoughtful look.

"Half a kay," she repeated quietly. She picked up her flexor from where it lay between two rocks, and turned it over in her hands. She flicked it experimentally, but the weapon did not respond: it was as broken as Doetzier's arm.

Without a word, she tucked it in her harness and turned back to the trail. Bowdie fell in line behind her, Kurvan behind him. Wren, then Doetzier, then the pilot and Striker. It was no coincidence that Doetzier was at the rear. Nitpicker *knew*.

Tsia slogged through the mud-deep grass. No one talked in the rain. One more rock drop. Wren and Nitpicker helped Doetzier down. Another quarter kay. Dawn was upon them, yet the gloom hung on like a leech. The brush thickened as it grew back into the areas cleared by the freepicks; the heavy clouds cut out any early daylight that thought to shine through the gray.

Ahead, like tiny mountains, the rock-gray huts of the freepick stake resolved themselves from darkness. Edges became sharp against the billowing, blowing trees. Windows and doorframes, outlined by the glowing edges of their filter fields, floated in the dawn like massive eyes and mouths, just waking and waiting for breakfast. Day was upon them in a shroud of rain and shadow.

Tsia no longer worried that Ruka might be seen. The brush was so thick that not even a darkeye could pierce it. She did not bother to look for his shape; her gate was as open as she could make it, and he was as much a part of her as the rain that soaked her skin. She hunted now, and the cougar knew it. He could taste her determination through the gate, and his feline mind was eager for the taste of blood and flesh.

When they reached the road that led to the freepick area, Tsia paused to locate the gray-green metaplas stake that marked the freepick boundary. She and Kurvan opened its top to expose the com panel of its beacon, but only its manual links were active. She waited while he triggered the manual com and notified the freepicks that they were on the way in. After a minute, he finished up and closed the marker beacon. Tsia gave him a speculative look as they made their way down the road: he had said nothing about them being on foot.

He shrugged coldly when she asked about it. "I don't give out what doesn't need to be known. Especially to guides."

Her lips tightened. She turned her back on his expression, and let Ruka watch him instead.

When they came to the edge of the tarmac where the road

widened, Tsia paused, and the other mercs gathered in a ragged line. Nitpicker touched her arm. Anything? the woman finned.

Tsia returned a negative pressure.

They waited in silence while Tsia eyed the rain-gray surface. Up close, the tarmac was not completely smooth, as if it was so old that the earth had moved beneath it or it had not been flattened to begin with. The chemical and bacteria vats, when she looked closely, showed cracks at their seams and meld marks on their support legs. On the other side of the tarmac, the hub itself was a dingy gray—a thick, uneven primer color, not a deliberate hue. Even that shade could not hide the fact that, although the freepick stake was new, the pitting and scoring along a quarter of the prefab panels spoke of decades of use. Freepicks never wasted credit on construction details.

Anything on your scanner? she finned on Bowdie's arm.

His fingers pressed back his negative.

She did not move forward. Her skin prickled, as if a hunter crouched close by, but she could see no sign of weapon—or even freepick—waiting there to meet them. On her other side, Nitpicker shifted, and she felt the hard line of the pilot's flexor press against her arm. She could smell the scent of the other woman on the weapon. Unobtrusively, she took it, then subtly she removed the custom wrap on her own hilt and slipped it over the other. Quietly, she passed her broken weapon back to Nitpicker's hands.

She eyed the tarmac again. She could feel the eagerness of someone's pulse. When she went first out on the tarmac, toward the main hub of the stake, her heart was beating quickly, and her breath was short and shallow.

She did not go swiftly or directly across. Instead, she paused and turned and darted a few steps this way, then that. She ignored the massive vats to the right; she gave only a bare glance to the open pit to the left. As if she were an animal, sniffing and testing the clearing, she advanced in hesitant spurts. She breathed shallowly to take in the scents, but it was Ruka's nose that interpreted the odors she sent to him through her gate. The hub—the main complex in which the freepicks worked—with its doorway faint and blue-glowing in the dark, beckoned like a hand, and Ruka knew she would enter. He snarled low in her gate.

Wait, she returned in her mind. *Stay hidden. And wait.*

She did not touch the hut as she edged toward the filter-field door. Scanners were triggered by proximity, but as long as she didn't touch the actual sensors, the bioshield in her blunter would project the scan signals for her heartbeat and body heat as that of a simple biological, not that of a human. She smiled faintly. With Ruka helping to guide her, her actions were animal enough to convince even the most discerning nodie that it was a beast who advanced, not a merc.

She took the flexor from her belt. Keeping it at her side, she tapped the access on the door panel so that her arrival was announced. The door field cleared automatically to transparency, and she could see that, although the door was open, the foyer inside was empty; the three hallways that led out of the entranceway were dim. That was not unusual, she told herself. Even a grounded stake didn't waste power. She spared the halls only a glance before she stepped inside. But she forgot to close down her biogate as she stepped through the door, and the tingling sense of the filter field made Ruka jump in the brush. Tsia jerked with his reaction, then flushed in the warmth of the foyer.

Idiot, she snapped at herself.

She paused inside, and behind her, the door opaqued again. She waited, her fingers loose and relaxed on the weapon, and her eyes and ears alert. But only a single freepick appeared, with a thickset body and a balding pate, and if there was anything but caution in his manner or voice, she could not sense it in him. The danger that made the cougar growl and her skin crawl on her back—it was here and not here, and she could only wait for its action.

She greeted him carefully, and added, "Guild contract BLL-tau-two-six."

"Tau, six-eight, double-XN," he returned. "Contract confirmation?"

She told him the code, and he nodded. For a moment, he studied her as closely as she watched him. She knew what he saw: a short-haired merc with rain-wet hair, who poised on the balls of her feet. A woman with crow's-feet so completely overshadowed by the scars on her cheek that only the deep blue of her eyes was noticed. As for what she saw, he was a freepick—no mistake about that. The smell of mining oils and bacteria was thick on his clothes and his body. The light brown jumpsuit he wore had been through so many scrubs that it was actually thin, while his face was heavy and beginning to slide off in folds of flesh. His skin was coarse with the large pores of a man who spent much of his time with dirt. His hands were thickly scarred, as though they had been cut and scraped so many times they could no longer remember how to make skin, and his fingernails, like Wren's, were so thick that they seemed like plates of cartilage, not nails. She glanced at his face and met his amber eyes steadily. They were clear and sharp, at odds with the deliberate—almost drawling—tempo of his voice.

"Decker got your call-in confirmation from the beacon," he said obliquely, "but the landing pad didn't activate."

"We came overland. Called you manually from marker on the road."

He raised his eyebrows, then nodded toward the outside. "You came through that?"

She followed his gesture, then glanced down at the puddle of rainwater still forming at her feet. She gave him a twisted grin. "Through that."

He looked more sharply at her face, then hair. "Guide."

She raised her eyebrows in a silent question.

He shrugged. "Short hair. No darkeyes, and you stand . . . differently." He made a small gesture over his shoulder. "Grunts are already down in the tubes, working on the tunnels. The rest of us have three bacts—bacteria biologicals, to you—"

"I'm familiar with the term."

He nodded. "—to set up before we can come in and talk. You want to bring your mercs in now?"

There was no surge in her biogate as he mentioned the mercs—no heightened sense of danger in his odor. She nodded. "We'll start contract as soon as you like, but we need to use your scame right away."

He tapped out a message on the com. "Thought you mercs carried scames wherever you went."

She shrugged and motioned with her chin at the panel. "How long has the node been down?"

"Since dawn. Been using manual coms to keep in touch with the grunts." He pointed down the right corridor. "Just turn in there. Puts you in the rec room—it's our main hall. All our med gear is on the left bank of panels, along with our manual coms."

"We'll need a manual map—some kind of overlay—for the layout of this place."

"Not much to see. There's the warren, the storerooms, and the labs for each type of bact."

"Quarters?"

"In the second hut. Mina will show you, once you've checked in with Laz."

"Laz—not you—is supervisor for this stake?" She did not hide her faint surprise.

He eyed her thoughtfully. "I should be flattered—I think. Laz programs our corers. I'm supervisor here."

"Ah. You have a sensor net?"

"Uh-huh. But our nodie won't be able to get it active again until the node comes back up."

"Why not? Manual scans should still be working."

"Had an accident a couple days ago. Fried part of the net and one of our grunt-techs with it. Node maintenance wasn't finished with the repair before it shut down again. So, no scans."

"You have skimmers and tracs?"

"Five tracs. All in the warren." He paused for a second. "You ask a lot of questions for a guide." He watched her carefully, but she merely waited. "Three," he said finally. "Out on M-deck—the maintenance deck, to you."

Her blue eyes glinted. "I'll bring the others in."

"I'll be down in the warren. Call me—Bishop—on two-four if you need anything you can't find. Laz is finishing up right

now. He and Mina will meet you in the rec room in about half
an hour." He made a formal gesture. "You're on-contract as of
now."

"On-contract," Tsia acknowledged.

She recrossed the tarmac warily and rejoined the other
mercs. "Seems clear," she said in a low voice to Nitpicker. The
pilot's eyes glinted at the unspoken implication. "But," she
added, "they had an accident a few days ago. Damaged
the sensor net."

From beside the pilot, Doetzier's eyes narrowed. "Anyone
hurt?"

"One grunt-tech. Dead."

His eyes shuttered, and he seemed to withdraw, but his
biofield flared with energy. Tsia could almost hear him thinking. Puppets, she thought as she looked at the mercs. And the
puppet master was somewhere nearby, arranging his sticks and
strings. She shook herself, then led Wren, Bowdie, and Kurvan
across, while the other three waited behind. With only one
manual scanner to work with, it took Bowdie twenty minutes
to declare the rec room clean.

"No weapons," he said, as he closed his handscanner down
and tucked it back in his harness.

Tsia eyed him blankly for a moment. There was something
in this room, some scent that caught at her attention. Feline?
Marine? It was an odor she ought to recognize, but it was so
faint that it refused to trigger her memory. Bowdie gestured
again toward the door, and she nodded slowly, then went back
for the others.

Each time through the filter field, Ruka cringed, and Tsia
found herself flinching as she never had before. Her skin almost crawled with the tingling field, and she finally realized
that it was the cougar's muscles bunching and twitching that
translated to her as the shivers. It was not until the fifth time
through that the cougar began to get used to the sensation. Tsia
tried to shut out the flinching, but found it almost impossible.
Ruka seemed to insert himself deeper into her mind each time
she opened her gate.

The rec room doubled as a staging area and meeting hall.

There were three tables at one end, and a stack of massive crates at the other. Color bars in the painted designs delineated different sport courts; the grav plates set into both floors and ceilings alternated with the mag plates and bars in snaking diamond patterns. Two doorways led to the outer loading bays; two more led to the warren and labs. The wall behind the tables was a bank of panels, screens, and manual equipment. Three screens were active, the others blank. Doetzier was already seated by the scame. His arm, still cast in the thin sheet of hardened metaplas, glowed under the medical gear's scans as Striker activated it manually.

Tsia, jittery, shrugged away from Wren and paced toward the outer doors. That scent—it was still here, in this room. And it was cat, she realized, not cougar. When Ruka took in the odor through her biogate, he snarled and bristled until she rubbed her own neck to smooth down her hairs. Cat, but not cougar—a local creature? She didn't think so. She tried to concentrate, but exhaustion hit like a fist, and abruptly, she leaned against the wall. Even Striker's face, angular and flat as she moved across to speak with Nitpicker, looked drawn so tight that the skin was stretched like a drum across her cheekbones. Wren's tanned face looked sallow in the light. Where Bowdie's bent legs had seemed to carry the weight of the world, his face now looked as tired.

Wren, standing near her, pulled a pouch from his harness and popped a few nolo seeds in his mouth. "Get rid of the cub yet?" he murmured, spitting a husk sharply into the hisser bin on the wall.

"No."

"Better do it soon. Nitpicker will catch on sooner or later—"

"She already knows." Tsia glanced over at Kurvan and Bowdie where they unpacked the two packs that had survived the hike. She motioned with her chin. "Didn't come out of this with much, did we?"

"Uh-uh."

"But maybe more than we were supposed to?"

Wren chewed thoughtfully on a seed. "Been wondering about that myself."

She opened her mouth to say more, but then remembered the deke in his medkit. She glanced toward the outside doors. "Someone coming."

"That your senses or the cub's?"

"The cub's."

He got to his feet and loosened his flexor in his belt. "At least he's some use."

"Three humans," she murmured. "Two men and a woman."

Wren caught Nitpicker's attention, and the pilot broke off her murmured conversation with Striker. Wren nodded toward the outer wall. "Feather says there are three freepicks coming in," he said softly.

Nitpicker glanced at Tsia. "Are the scanners back up?"

Tsia shook her head. Two more freepicks entered from a side corridor, and the scents in the room shifted subtly. Her nostrils flared.

The pilot's eyes narrowed. "You read it off the cub?"

"Yes," she said deliberately, her voice low enough that Striker could not hear. "And yes, he's still here. Outside near the tarmac." Nitpicker opened her mouth to say something, but Tsia cut her off. "Without him, I'd know nothing of what happens outside—"

Tsia fell silent as the outer doors cracked, throwing light out into the gray rain, and three freepicks entered. The cargo doors had no filter fields, and the rain blew back in a whirl before the heavy slab closed but did not latch. One of the freepicks paused in midstep and reached back to yank it shut. Then the three of them shrugged out of their ponchos and shook off their boots. Air swirled. The foreign cat scent grew sharper, and the other smell—the solventlike thread—grew more distinct. Unconsciously, Tsia moved back a step behind Nitpicker and eyed the freepicks warily.

The tallest of the three was a man so skinny that Tsia could almost feel his nervous tension smothering the other two biofields. He seemed even taller with the cream-colored stripes stretching up the sides of his jumpsuit, and the cream-blond hair on his head. His dark, quick eyes seemed to dart like Wren's from merc to merc.

The woman beside him was average size, with a rounded figure that spoke of both shape and muscle, and a set of lips that should have been full, but were pressed together so tightly that they appeared as a thin line. She and the other freepicks wore the same off-white jumpsuit that the tall man did.

The third man was built like Kurvan. Fairly tall and broad, he had unnaturally white hair, with icy blue eyes and a square jaw. His eyebrows were almost solid across his forehead, and the only thing that saved them from giving him a brutal look was the amount of white in the color that tinged on blue.

The focus in the tall man's biogate fascinated Tsia, and she stared at him for a moment before she realized her muscles had tensed. Was it Ruka, not herself, whose curiosity held her so tightly? She closed the link to the cat until she could feel the cougar only dimly and could hear his snarls like faint wind. Her shoulders twitched. She tried to ignore the sensation. "Stay out of my mind," she muttered. "And let me do my job."

She stared deliberately at the other two freepicks who had entered the room from the other side, through one of the hallway doors. One, a medium-built woman, was black-haired, with dark skin, and eyes the color of amber. The other was a narrow-hipped man with the pale skin of a tunneler and skinny shoulders. His arms, long and stiff, hung from his shoulders like pieces of wood. Like the woman, he smelled of rock and dust even across the room.

The air in the room shifted, and Tsia smelled cat again. She snapped at Ruka through her gate to move away from the door; his scent had clouded the smells in the room, and she could not distinguish the odors. The cougar snarled in return and slunk across the tarmac.

Tsia became still. It was not Ruka whose scent tickled her nose. It was that elusive, foreign scent, the one she had smelled when she first entered the room. The heavy one, that spoke of something new—and the one she had sensed on the marine platform at yesterday's dawn. The feline smell mixed with the faint turpentinic odor of mucus and packing gels, and she cocked her head unconsciously to separate the scents. Was her memory confused by the biogate? The mucus smell seemed to match the scent that Kurvan had had on his hands when they touched on the bridge, but it was not an odor from Risthmus—of that, she was now sure.

The woman with the thin lips greeted Nitpicker. "That's Laz"—she indicated the tall, tense man—"and Decker." She pointed to the man with the whitened hair. She used her chin to point at the freepicks who seated themselves by the door to the warren. "Narbon over there, and Wicht. Wicht is the one with the arms. They're both grunts, but they've got as high a tech rating as the rest of us. They can settle your gear while we talk."

Tsia's lips twitched. If there was one word to describe the lanky man, it was "arms."

"I'm Mina, and—" The freepick's sharp, acerbic voice broke off at the expression on Striker's face. The freepick gave the merc a sharp look. "What is it?"

Striker shrugged, but the closed, shuttered mask that came down over her face did not quite hide her disgust. Nitpicker glanced at the other merc, and Mina demanded, "Do you have a problem I should know about?"

"No," Striker said distinctly.

Nitpicker started to speak, but Mina didn't look at her. "You don't like me, is that it?" she said flatly to Striker.

Nitpicker stepped in front of the other woman. "You don't pay us for our likes and dislikes—"

"No," Mina returned sharply. "We pay you for your skills. It's your job to work here, and defend us if necessary—fight for our stake and die for us if you have to—whether you like us or not. That's your contract. And if you don't do that job one hundred percent to our satisfaction, I'll personally take you before your own guild, sue you for breach of contract, and crush you into dust through your own guild laws."

"That's just like a lifer—to destroy what you can't control." Striker's voice was quiet, but it somehow filled the room and echoed in the sudden silence. "Why bother to communicate to solve a problem when you can crush the differences between us?" She nodded at Mina's expression. "Did you get that attitude from your great-great-grandfather? Or did you develop it on your own?"

For a moment, Mina could only stand speechless.

"Striker," Nitpicker said softly, "go back and help Doetzier."

The freepick's brown eyes narrowed. Nitpicker nodded toward the panels. "Want our nodie to give you a hand?" she asked deliberately as Mina started to speak.

The woman's eyes flashed. She stared at Striker's back. It was Laz who, after a wary look at Mina, responded, "Won't you be busy setting up your gear?"

"We lost most of our gear on the way here," Nitpicker answered flatly. "It'll be a day of two before we get replacements."

Decker shifted, as if he would speak, but Mina nodded shortly. Her voice was still sharp with anger as she cut in, "Laz will get you set up with what we have. I'm the bact-stabber here, and I've got three vats to balance by dusk, so I can't help you till tomorrow."

Wren raised his eyebrows. "Bact-stabber?"

"I make up the bacts—bacteria, to you—and shoot them into the core samples and tailings with a tool that looks like a knife. Laz coined the phrase. It obviously fits me," she said nastily. She turned to Decker. "I'll be in lab three-B. Let Bishop know, will you?" She brushed past the others and stalked to the other side of the room.

Wren watched her stop and speak briefly with the two freepicks at the other doorway. "Mina," he murmured. "Know what that name means?"

Tsia shook her head.

"Earth child."

Tsia stifled a cough. " 'Bact-stabber' fit a lot better."

Decker's lips twitched again, as if he heard them, and Wren turned cold, black-colored eyes to the man. His blunt hands fingered his flexor unobtrusively. Decker didn't seem to notice; his gaze was on Nitpicker. Laz continued to look around the room as if weighing the presence of the mercs against some schedule he held in his mind.

"What can you do right away?" Laz asked. His voice was

curt, his message clear: It would be more trouble to accept help than do without it at all.

Nitpicker was watching Decker, but she answered, "We can begin setting up a scannet, but it won't be active until we get the rest of our gear replaced."

"You were supposed to arrive with all of it ready to go," the man retorted.

She shrugged. "Things come up."

"Things go down," Wren muttered.

Nitpicker shot him a sharp look, but Tsia shuddered at that moment, and both mercs flicked their gazes to her. Outside, Ruka had nosed up to the filter field, and his nose, too close to the field, had been jolted. Tsia rubbed at her own nostrils, then began to pace unconsciously.

"Guides," Decker snorted with disdain.

Laz's gaze sharpened. "We didn't contract for a guide."

Nitpicker gave him a speculative look. "You got one anyway." She shrugged at his look. "Merc guild picks up the tab whenever their skills aren't used."

Laz twisted and eyed Tsia so minutely that she halted in her tracks and turned her head to watch him as steadily as he gazed at her. "Sorry," he said shortly, as he realized he was staring. Then, abruptly, he asked, "Can you call your link to you?"

Tsia's eyes narrowed. "Why do you ask?"

He shrugged. "I always wanted to know that about guides."

She stared at him a few seconds more. The energy of his biofield projected more intensely than Wren's, and it distracted her attention from his words. "Some links," she said finally, "call you to them, not the other way around."

He nodded shortly. Then, as if he had filed that information away to use some other time, he turned back to Nitpicker. "Which of you are the nodies?"

Nitpicker pointed at Kurvan, then indicated Tsia. "He's the nodie. She's a terrain artist, but might be some help anyway."

"All right." He began to walk toward Kurvan, beckoning for Tsia to follow. Obediently, she fell into step and stopped beside Doetzier. There was no sign that he was setting up the system

to program the biochips he carried, and she frowned slightly
and gave his screens a sharp look. He glanced up at her expression, then turned deliberately back to his work. In the
meantime, Laz gestured at the panels. "It's like a jam. Can't
get anything on the node, but I'd swear it isn't down completely."

Tsia nodded absently. "I've had flashes of the node through
my temple links all day."

"Exactly." He glanced at Doetzier and noted that one of the
screens had become inactive once again. "You done with
that?" he asked curtly.

Doetzier opened his mouth to answer, but Laz was already
leaning across and punching in sequences manually. Tsia
watched Doetzier like a cat. She could still feel the points of
light in his biofield. It was like learning to see the color red,
she thought. Once she figured out how to distinguish the tiny
lights from a general biofield, it was as obvious as laze beams
in the dark. Not like that turpentine scent, which she smelled
again. Or the foreign cat smell that clung to this room. She
glanced at Laz, then at the other freepicks. Kurvan's hands,
and the smell of sponge mucus on Decker or Mina or Laz . . .

Something in Tsia's gate sharpened her eyes. Tension
seemed to grow in the room. She fingered her flexor and slid
it unobtrusively from her harness. Laz didn't notice. She cast
a glance at Decker, where he still spoke with Nitpicker. Decker's hands—their muscles were taut even though they hung at
his sides. The cat claws in her head seemed to sharpen. Kurvan . . . Decker . . . The turpentinic scents that matched . . .
Her body balanced itself on the balls of her feet. More
freepicks approached from outside. Her shoulders itched, and
her scalp prickled.

"Kurvan," Doetzier called over his shoulder, a little too
sharply. "Are you finished with the manual link?"

There was no answer, and Doetzier glanced back. He stilled.
Tsia, jumpy as a cat, half whirled before she looked, her flexor
pulled from her harness in a single fluid motion. Instantly, a
laze cut across the sleeve of her arm, burning the air and her
blunter with a crackling, hissing sound. She froze.

Decker had a laze on Nitpicker. The two freepicks—or blackjack—at the inner door had shoved Mina aside, and their laze weapons were trained, one on Bowdie, and the other one on Striker and Doetzier. A second later, three freepicks burst in from the outside. In the sudden silence, the rain dripped from weather cloth in sloppy splats to the floor.

"Zeks," Tsia whispered, unaware that she had spoken.

They motioned for Striker to move away from Doetzier, and the woman slowly complied. They gestured for Bowdie to join Tsia and Doetzier, and with his lips thinly pressed together, the tall, bowlegged merc slowly moved as they directed. His biofield was almost as hot as Kurvan's, and the sparks of his energy felt like tiny stars, as if he was firing himself up to fight.

"Feather, step away." Kurvan's voice was soft. One of his palms was closed; the other was loose, as if it held a weapon they could not see. Doetzier's biofield snapped into a wall so thick that through it she could barely sense his life force. She hesitated. Without glancing back, she stepped forward, as if it were she Kurvan wanted, not Bowdie or Doetzier.

Kurvan smiled. It was not a nice expression, and Tsia shivered. A chill seemed to emanate from his body. His left palm opened, and in it was a shape she recognized: a breaker. Its slight curvature was dotted around the edges with tiny bumps, and she raised her eyes to his face.

"Ever seen something like this, Feather? No?"

Cat claws sharpened themselves on her scalp. Her fingers clenched like a paw over her flexor, and her hand slid into her custom grip. Kurvan's breaker followed her movement. She stilled.

"This," he said, indicating the disk in his palm, "is a distance-focused breaker. The three-oh-nine—this model here—is effective on people, biologicals, even certain types of equipment up to eight meters away." He shrugged his right hand, and a short, collapsible laze slid down his sleeve into his hand. He snapped it out so that both halves clicked together. Its point began warming up the instant its power bar connected with its projector. "And this"—he gestured with the laser gun—"is not a laze like you carry, or a dirtside parlas like Bowdie's, but a zek parlas—a blackjack weapon. You might not have seen one before. I don't expect you've been skyside"—he smiled unpleasantly—"and they aren't licensed for landside use. That's because they don't distinguish between humans and biologicals. I'm telling you this so that you understand that this little toy"—he hefted it in his palm—"will burn you no matter what heartbeat your bioshield projects."

Tsia watched him while the shivers grew in her muscles. Part fear, part eagerness, they set her heart to a fast, hard rhythm against her ribs. She barely understood, in some back part of her mind, that she was taking that pulse from Ruka. "You want the biochips," she forced herself to say. Behind her, she felt, more than heard, Doetzier and Bowdie shift.

"Of course." He gestured with the laze. "Now, move away from the others."

"You can laze them if you want," Tsia said flatly. "It's all the same to me. As for the chips, they're not here, but off-site. And without the node to locate their IDs, your scans will never read them."

Bowdie clenched his fists. "I should have killed you, Feather, when I had the chance—"

From the side, Nitpicker cursed and glared at the guide. "Goddammit, Bowdie, shut her up!"

"Quiet," Decker snarled.

Kurvan eyed Nitpicker, then Tsia with disdain. "Pathetically predictable. You," he said to Tsia, "have never touched a chip in your life. Decker told me an hour ago by beacon that the chips were being carried by someone in this group, and I've watched you, Tsia-guide. The chips haven't once been in your hands."

He took a half step forward, and her heart beat harder against her ribs. She wondered that he didn't hear it—it was deafening her with its loudness, and the closer the laze came, the harder it seemed to pound. Two of the other freepicks—no, blackjack, she corrected with narrowed eyes—moved up to stand on either side. Laz edged away from the points of their weapons. His long-fingered hands twitched nervously. One of the zeks jerked his laze up, and Laz, without being touched, crumpled awkwardly and soundlessly to the floor, where he wrapped his arms around his body and tried to huddle into a ball.

Doetzier did not glance down. "Feather's telling the truth," he said calmly. "Couldn't you tell—when you broke my arm—that I no longer had the chips?"

Mina stared from one merc to the other. "Why did he break yo—"

"Shut up," snapped one of the zeks. Mina subsided, but her eyes flashed, and Tsia could almost feel the glints of fury that darkened her gaze.

Kurvan eyed Tsia. "So he gave them to you, and you hid them off-site."

The cat feet clawed at her brain, and her shrug was almost a writhe. "I took them while you, Wren, and Striker checked out the hub room. The chips are out beyond the edge of the tarmac."

"I see. And I'm now supposed to negotiate with you to find out where they are?"

She shrugged again. "It's up to you. They're shielded. If you haven't found them by now, you'll never find them on your own."

He regarded her for a moment, then smiled at Bowdie and Doetzier. "It seems," he said softly, "I have no further use for you." He indicated Tsia with a tiny motion of his laze. "Step away please." Slowly, she obeyed. He raised the laze and pointed the blue-glowing end at the two mercs behind her. Then he fired.

Bowdie and Striker and Doetizer flung themselves to the side; Tsia threw herself in front of Doetzier. The beam missed them all. For an instant, it clung to the panel behind her. The sizzle burned only air. Nitpicker had lunged, then cried out as Decker's particle laze, with its greener, hotter beam, caught her across the shoulder. Wren got only a half step. He froze with the point of another blue-tipped laze aimed right at his face.

Tsia rolled to a half crouch, and Doetzier got slowly to his feet. Bowdie was half kneeling and half standing under the point of another laze. The room, with its frozen figures and overbright tableau, was like a frame from an old flick. Ten blackjack, six mercs, two freepicks . . . Only their tension moved. Only eyes flicked from side to side.

Mina seemed to start as if from a dream. A low cry broke from her throat, and she scambled to her feet to run from the room. She took two steps before the butt of a flexor struck her cheek and threw her back against the wall. Crouching like an animal, one hand to her face and the other clenched at her side, she stared up at the zeks. After a moment, the man reached down and hauled her by the arm. He shoved her toward the other mercs.

"Weapons on the floor," Kurvan directed. "You know the drill."

Slowly, flexors dropped. The short hilts of rasers followed. A parlas from Bowdie's harness, its greenish barrel distinct among the flexors, lay beneath Nitpicker's image-guided dart gun. Kurvan watched the weapons drop with satisfaction. He eyed Mina for a moment, then met Striker's black gaze with a challenge in the depths of his own. "Should give you some satisfaction," he murmured, "to watch a lifer die."

"Descendant of a lifer," Striker corrected harshly.

"Does it matter?" Kurvan prodded deliberately. "It didn't seem to on the trail, when you were lecturing so thoroughly on the evils of the gangs."

Striker eyed him like a cat. "Everything matters," she returned. Her voice was soft with threat. "Everything is important. That's what the lifers forgot. And that's what I now live for."

"Or die for?" He smiled nastily. "Move." He gestured curtly. "That way."

Nitpicker got another blow to her temple; Wren got one to his kidneys. The scent of burning fabric clung to the air and choked in Tsia's nose. Cat scent, sponge scent . . . Kurvan and Decker matched. Memories triggered: the odors were from offworld. *When the Ixia team up with blackjack. . .* The feline snarling that surged through her biogate almost deafened her ears.

"That one," Kurvan pointed at Doetzier. "That one and those two." He indicated Wren and Bowdie and Striker. "Scan them. Not her—" He shook his head as one of them grabbed Tsia's arm. "She's the guide; she won't have them—her tech rating is too low."

Decker gestured at Nitpicker. "What about the pilot?"

"Too high a profile."

A cat crawled close in Tsia's gate, and a heavier, larger feline seemed to press in on her mind. She glanced instinctively toward the outer doors, then forced her eyes forward. One door was shut tight against the storm, where the first three miners had come in; but the other was cracked—unlatched. The line of sodden gray that edged along the doorframe was broken for an instant. A tawny shape flicked past. Tsia did not look again. She opened her gate as wide as she could, and the creeping paws that curled around her mind became a double set of feet. Ruka's—all four of them—large and wide on the ground, soggy with the water; and the others—different, bigger, and only two, with off-white claws tucked into alien wrists and elbow joints. Tsia blinked. Her mind's eye blurred. Her hands clenched like claws. No one but Nitpicker noticed.

"The case," Kurvan said calmly to Doetzier. "Bring it out."

Doetzier did not move. Nor did the others. No one spoke. Nitpicker seemed to tense. The snarl that grew in Tsia's throat became audible. One of the zeks jerked his flexor to slam her in the ribs, but her balance was poised, and her muscles taut with the reflexes of the cougar. There was a single blur of motion. The flexor slammed in. Her hand caught the spiked point and yanked it to the side as her foot snapped through his knee. The cracking sound was completely drowned by the shriek that broke from the man's throat. Tsia was already leaping away.

Nitpicker threw herself toward one blackjack; Wren dove at another. Bowdie and Striker split as a laze burned the air between them. Blue-white beams seared cloth and flesh, but if there were screams, Tsia didn't hear them. She pounced on a zek as his laze pierced her blunter. The heat of the beam, broken up by the stealth cloth, blistered her side as it passed under her arm, but her sweat had already beaded. She didn't even gasp.

On the other side of the group, Doetzier jumped behind a zek as a beam burned across the floor in a sparking arc. The blackjack woman screamed; the beam caught her across the inner thigh and hip. Kurvan, cursing, tackled Doetzier over the other zek who fell in the way. Like frenzied beasts, the three crashed to the floor in the middle of the weapons pile. Kurvan lost his grip on the breaker. The disk, the flexors, the rasers—everything went spinning across the floor.

A blackjack grabbed Tsia, and she screamed. The sound was inhuman. For an instant, the man froze. She jerked free and backhanded him as hard as she could. Her other hand hooked a vicious punch back across his temple. His foot came down on a flexor; he staggered back. She grabbed his laze before it fell. The beam flashed up in her grip; his hand lunged forward to retake it and was burned across the wrist in a smoking, fat-popping line of blackened flesh.

Tsia lunged back to her feet. And into the arms of a zek whose mouth spewed harsh, foul air and whose eyes were as wild and bestial as hers. Like a sack of rags, she was flung to the ground in a perfect rolling hiplock. The laze flew out of her grip, but she clenched her hands instinctively as she tumbled. The blackjack, caught by his collar, came down in a flip, his shoulders hitting the floor with a smack, and his head tucked to keep from cracking back.

There was no sound in her ears. There was no snarling in her throat. Her mind was suddenly, coldly, silent with the sense of her hands like paws, tearing at the man who drove his fist into her ribs, her gut, her hip—whatever he could reach. She rolled, her hands up in front of her face. Her elbows smashed his jaw. A flexor cut across her calf, searing through her boot, and she yowled as the heat caught her flesh for the barest instant. Her knee wrenched, and instinctively she twisted with it until she jammed it in his groin. His eyes widened. She did not wait for the rest of his reaction. Instead, her hands stabbed viciously into his gut with stiffened fingers. She left him curled and retching on the floor as she scrambled back to her feet.

A surge of energy hit her biogate, and someone cried out horribly. The breaker, she recognized. She glared like a cornered cat. Her eyes could not distinguish bodies; only movement in the room. Her tongue did not taste sweat, but the scent of burning flesh. Someone jerked her back by the collar, and she twisted and ducked right into the hot beam of a laze. The beam missed and flashed on her hip, and in a fraction of a second burned away the weather cloth as if it were silk. She gasped. White fire burst in her mind as the air crisped next to her skin.

The laze flashed again. Instinctively, like the tensing of nerves before a cat actually leaps, she saw the movement in her gate. She lunged before she thought; her hands struck down in a long curve. Something hard slapped her palms. Bones—like brittle glass. Skin—hot and sweating. She jerked; they snapped. The laze flew out and darkened as it inactivated with the loss of the blackjack's grip.

Tsia scrambled for the flexor that lay on the floor. It was hers—Nitpicker's; the colors of the custom hilt seemed to sear themselves into her eyes. Behind her, a woman lunged for the round, flat disk of the breaker. The breaker found the blackjack's hand. The jack twisted as she fell. The disk came up. Tsia flung herself back toward the door. Her shoulder hit and flung it open; her flexor flew out into the rain. But the edge of the sonic blast tingled across her outflung arm, missing by a breath.

Decker, from the side, heard the door and whipped around. The hot point of his laze flashed. A burning blow staggered Tsia so that she crumpled back into the rain. Her eyes widened. He fired again, and instinctively the sweat welled up from her pores. The beam of light hit and seared through her blunter, coming out the other side, but missing flesh as she twisted. Decker ran forward. Smoke clouded her face. Her throat membranes closed as if she danced in a firepit. The beam hit again, but this time it exploded through her body like a shock wave. She could not cry out. Her shoulders, then her head hit the ground like rags. The force of the blast threw her clear of the door and left it slowly swinging shut so that her body lay like a broken doll, while the rain beat against her face, and her blunter smoldered and burned.

19

Decker ran toward her, shoving through the door, then saw the red edge of fire that glowed in the wide hole in her jacket. In the gray gloom, the flame charred her shirt to blackness and curled across her skin. He cast a single glance at her face. Her neck was twisted on the tarmac. Her eyes were open to the morning rain. He turned his back on her body. He never saw the tawny shadow that clung to the side of the hub.

"You, and you, over there," he snapped at Wren and Bowdie. Another blackjack picked up the flexor that Wren had kicked away. Wren slipped a supporting arm around Bowdie's torso, but the woman named Narbon yanked him away by the arm, shoving him hard across the room. Both mercs' eyes were cold with lethal intent.

Kurvan cursed as he saw Tsia's body in the doorway that Decker held open. "Goddammit!" He gestured sharply. Decker shrugged and stepped back inside, his hand keeping the door from shutting.

Doetzier eyed the blackjack without expression. The cast on his arm was blackened in two spots from a laze that had fired right against it. His left cheek was darkening with a bruise, and the swelling had already half closed his left eye. Bowdie was shoved into place behind him, supported by Nitpicker on one side. The man's left hand pressed against his ribs where blood seeped through his fingers. The pilot was in no better shape:

her face was pinched with pain, but her eyes burned as they followed Kurvan's movements.

Wren merely watched with that cold, speculative gaze as the pile of weapons on the far table grew. On the other side of Laz, Mina was breathing harshly—trying to keep herself from screaming—while Striker, in front of her, lay on the floor, raised up on one elbow with her left leg clutched in one hand. Thirty seconds—perhaps more—passed with no noise but Mina's breathing and a murmured discussion between Kurvan and Decker. Then the sound of feet marched in one of the corridors, and Bishop, the heavyset freepick, was shoved into the room in front of another blackjack. Bishop glanced at Laz, then Mina. He took in Doetzier's arm and Bowdie's bloody fingers. He eyed the body that lay outside in the rain, then turned to face Kurvan with a tightened jaw and set expression in his eyes. "The scannet this morning," he said slowly. "And Hanson two days ago—her death was not an accident."

"No," Decker said from the side. "And neither is this."

One of the blackjacks hit Bishop in the kidney, then the gut with the butt of her flexor. With strangled cry, the man went to his knees. They dragged him over and dumped him beside Laz.

Decker motioned sharply at Nitpicker and Bowdie, and the two mercs separated slowly. "No finning," he snapped. "Lace your fingers together and place your hands on your heads. All of you," he snarled as Bowdie raised only one hand.

Slowly, his face whitening as his muscles stretched across his abdomen, Bowdie complied. He hissed only once at the pain. The skin across his cheeks was stretched so tight that the bumps on his nose were white.

Narbon glanced toward Kurvan, who nodded. The woman motioned sharply at the four mercs who stood together. "Scan them," she ordered her zeks.

The tiny hum of the handscanners filled the silence thickly. A moment passed, then another, and then the scantech testing Doetzier looked up. "Got them," he said shortly. "Here. In the harness. Probably in the power strip."

Narbon almost smiled. She motioned for them to strip the

drab harness from Doetzier, and they did so roughly. Doetzier did not resist. The scanners began to trigger their gear off, but she stopped them before Kurvan could. "Do them all," she said flatly. "I want them all clear."

She moved up and took Doetzier's harness, tossing it to Kurvan. Before Kurvan had unsealed more than two seams, the other scantech stopped and turned around. "Wait a minute."

"What?" Narbon said sharply.

"Got another one," he said. "Looks live to me."

Kurvan's eyes narrowed and he looked at the first scantech. "You said the biochips were in the harness," he said flatly. The other man shrugged. "They scanned out."

The second tech looked back at his readings. "I've got another set on the scans," he insisted. He jerked an e-wrap from Bowdie's age-splotched harness and tossed it to Narbon. Warily, the woman unwrapped the package. The thin, small square unfolded and was dropped to the floor. What was left was a thin, gold-toned case.

Nitpicker looked at Doetzier, then Bowdie. Both men stayed silent, but their muscles were tense, and Bowdie's haunted eyes flickered as if he were watching a grave open and stretch out to swallow his body. Kurvan gave them both a long look, then looked down at the power strip taken from Doetzier. He slit the long strip open with the edge of his fingernail. Inside, like a bar of gold in a web of weather cloth, another flat case was visible. He eased the case out of the packing web and opened it carefully. Inside the box, the row of tiny chips lay quietly like eggs. He looked up slowly.

Narbon opened the case in her hand; inside was a second set. She held them out for him to see.

"Two sets." His eyes flicked from Doetzier to Bowdie and back. "Which one is real?"

One of the scantechs examined the two cases. "These are real," he said of the ones that came from Bowdie. "They scan out clear."

"Verify," Kurvan said shortly.

The other man took a reading, then nodded. "I agree." He handed the case to Kurvan.

The blackjack eyed the slim gold case. The smile that grew across his cheeks was almost dreamlike. He closed the case and rubbed it between his palms. Then he slid it into the pocket of his blunter. He ran his fingers on the other flat box and watched Doetzier with an almost absent expression. "And these?"

"Decoys," Narbon said slowly, reading the handscanner over the man's shoulder. "Good ones. Worth fifty, maybe sixty thousand credits on their own."

"Decoys," Kurvan repeated. "To draw us out. And the real ones to slip into the stake while we were then distracted." He eyed Doetzier's flat expression. "You didn't know about the real ones either, did you? You were as much in the dark as I."

Doetzier did not bother to answer.

"Two sets of biochips, and we lose just one jack." Kurvan closed the box and tucked it into his other pocket. He surveyed the silent group, counting the freepicks. "Is this all of them outside the tunnels?" he asked the woman beside him.

"As far as we know." Narbon jerked her head to indicate the outside. "Four of the grunts made a run for it. We got them back, and J'Avatzan is out hunting for anyone we missed." She nodded at his expression. "A bioshield can fool a scanner, but not that one's nose."

"And the ones in the tunnels?"

"Cut off behind a rockfall and locked out of the node by their links. Even after we take the jam off the node, it'll take them a week to dig out."

He nodded.

"Kill them now?" Narbon asked in a low voice. "We've got the chips. We can set the full jam on the node anytime. And with the whole net down, it will be three or four hours before anyone checks on this stake, and by then, you'll be a light-jump away."

"No," he returned, still studying the mercs. "Their IDs are flagged in the node banks the moment they die. It's easier to hide a traceline for a ghost than the ID of a corpse. And if one of them is a Shield, he'll be linked differently than the rest of them—connected somehow to his backup. It'll take me a while to figure out how they're doing it—how to block it or work around it."

"So keep them alive till we leave."

He nodded. "Till then, yes."

Nitpicker's black-colored eyes burned with his words. Her jaw was white, and her weight was still poised on the balls of her feet without seeming to be there at all. Kurvan smiled at her like a shark. "You're clever," he said softly. "And dangerous." He motioned almost imperceptibly with his chin. A zek stepped forward. His long arms swung the butt of his flexor in a single, chopping motion. The pilot crumpled to the floor.

"Take a hint," Kurvan told the others. He walked away with Narbon.

The sickening thud echoed into Tsia's brain with the drumming of the rain. Her biogate was thick with the sense of the cats, and she could not focus through her eyes. She tried to think, but her brain whirled with Kurvan's soft words and the snarls that bounced from one side of her skull to the other. Her throat moved convulsively. She felt the sweat soak her skin beneath her shirt and realized that there was fire heating the flesh over her ribs.

Fear cut through the din of snarls, and she moved her head a fraction. A wave of relief flooded her with an almost nausea-like response. One finger, then another twitched. She had seen the laze, the flash of light. Then her chest had exploded with fire. She moved her arm, slowly—a shift, an edging motion of mere millimeters. She didn't flinch from the flames that circled the hole in her blunter. Her mind was still not focused, and images whirled with the tiny crackling that burned on her blunter. Fire . . . Memories flooded over her thoughts as the pain began to recede. She saw her first view of the firepit. Glistening bodies, swaying in the orange light. And her mother's hair, auburn and glinting as if it, too, were made of flames . . .

Her body automatically sweated to form a vapor barrier against the lick of fire. Like a drop of water in a hot pan, her sweat did not evaporate, but beaded and hissed beneath the flames. She could feel its stickiness washed with the cleansing rain. Her mind saw not the circle of fire on her chest, but the heat like waves of color . . . The world blurred. She blinked. Ruka's hair brushed across her chin. Smoke scent filled her mouth, and she realized that she was smelling herself through the cougar's nose, not her own. *Ruka*, she whispered through her gate. It was the voice of blackjack that answered.

". . . me to stay behind?" Narbon's low voice floated out into the rain. The woman was somewhere near the doorway, out of Tsia's sight. "Use the hisser on them once you've got away?"

"God, no," Kurvan returned sharply, his voice equally low. "Each deke has a chemical signature. It could be traced back to the seller, and then tracked forward to us."

"How long do you want to wait before the node logs their deaths?"

"J'Avatzan wants at least one hour; I prefer to have two or three . . ."

The cougar growled. Tsia tried to blink. Even with the light, she could barely see. The narrow yellow rectangle of the partly open door was surrounded by drab, gray morning. The chill that came through from the tarmac made her feel as if she lay on ice. Her nerves tingled: it was neither weariness nor pain.

She smelled cat.

Ruka bristled. The cat scent, alien and dangerous, was strong and close. Ruka snarled, and Tsia felt her hair, wet as it was, prickle and rise on her neck. She reached through her gate, but she couldn't connect with the foreign mind, except to send a mental snarl. Whatever feline crept on the edge of her senses, it was not one with whom she could speak.

Ruka backed away, and Tsia made a tiny sound. There was a sharpening in her gate—as if a hunter saw its prey. She froze. She closed herself down, stilled her thoughts, quieted her breathing. She was nothing, she thought. She was the downed branch that lay on the tarmac. She was the shrub that stretched its roots toward the hub. Her heartbeat was insignificant. Her mind was primitive and thin . . .

She waited.

Rain dripped into her ears. Sound widened and dulled with the water blocking the canals, but she did not move.

Finally, like a reaver that tentatively peeks from its dike, she tested the feel of her gate. The scent of cat was still strong, but no longer as sharp as a blade, and Ruka had stopped growling. Had the threat subsided? Or was it merely waiting, like a patient adder, for her to give herself away?

The wind softened as she waited, and Narbon's voice floated again to her ears. ". . . keep them? We've got no stasis tubes, and I can't spend my time watching them. I've got to clear our traces from the scannet and get rid of all the weapons."

"There's got to be a secure storeroom or an empty chemical vat."

"All the vats are full, and the storerooms have control pads—there's no guarantee that they couldn't jury-rig a fix to the node from there." The woman paused. "There is the reclamation pit. It's twenty meters deep, and the walls are muddy, rough, and overhung like a dreambar drunk. Take out the pumps and pull up the lift—you couldn't buy a better prison."

"Pumps?" Kurvan questioned.

"Between the rain and the seeps we haven't yet plugged, the water flows into the pit pretty fast. What about the guide?"

"Use the hisser on her now, or leave her till you do the others. One ID dot—I can hide that in an accident log for a while. The rest of them—will they all fit in the pit?"

"With room for a few more if we find them."

"Good. By the time the pit fills enough to float them, we'll be done in here. And if they drown as we're leaving, they'll just save us the effort . . ."

The words burned in Tsia's nerves. She tried to keep from twitching, but the returning awareness was like a fire that seared her flesh from the inside out, not at all like the gentle heat of her disintegrating blunter. Her fingers, then her forearms, then her shoulders began to shiver.

Help me, she sent to the cub. *Pull me from the light.*

Words—images, she sent. Teeth in her blunter, pulling. Fangs caught in cloth and dragging her body like prey. Something tested her shoulder, then the sharp canines bit down. She felt the pull of the fabric, the sudden exposure of her midriff to the rain. Rough ground scraped beneath her. Like chalk on stone, her skin grated as Ruka dragged her on the tarmac. Inch by inch, through a puddle that, in spite of her sweat, chilled her even more; her waist, then her thighs, then her knees moved away from the doorway.

The fire in her jacket was drowned out by rain, so that only wet smoke and sweat was left to sting in Tsia's nose. She could feel her chest now, and the heartbeat against her ribs. Her muscles tingled and shuddered as if thousands of tiny waves of nerve signals washed back and forth.

". . . they're smart, and they'll be desperate." Narbon's uneasiness floated more faintly on the air. "What if they link back into the node through their temple links before we jam it completely? They could have manual coms—and Ayara only knows what the Shield has on him."

"Once you're done searching him and everyone else, they'd better have nothing but their blunters. As for using the node, it would take a genius to get through my webs," Kurvan replied. "I locked them out individually. There's no way they can image the node before or after it's jammed. The only thing that concerns me is the water rising enough so that they could climb or swim out of the pit . . ."

Tsia shifted, and bit her lip at the needles that shot up her arm. She forced herself to shove against the ground. Her shoulders moved a handspan before her arms trembled and collapsed. Ruka growled and pawed at her side. Her jacket smelled like ashes; the stealth cloth, seared in a wide hole, exposed her burned-through shirt and sweat-flushed skin.

". . . use an r-con to lock their nervous system in place? We've got that remote-con unit we used on Interference. Could set it for a broadband projection. That would affect all of them through their temple links. None of them would be able to move their heads to blink, let alone swim or climb."

"And an r-con is as good as a guard," Kurvan returned thoughtfully. "Not even an Ixia can fight a field on high with more than one or two muscles at a time. And humans can't do anything in an r-con field without a shunt . . ."

It was easier this time, to force her arm to her chest. As if the blood began to circulate again, her fingers shuddered. Her eyes began to focus while wind blew the rain into her ears. Ruka crouched with his own ears flat, and his growling kept time to the thoughts that began to churn again in her head. Kurvan and Narbon—they were close enough for Ruka to hear. Could they see through the crack in the door that Tsia's body had moved? A stab of fear triggered her legs to gather and roll her to her side. She pushed herself to her knees, shuddered, and fell limply forward.

". . . how long to adjust the r-con to widebrand broadcast?"

"Ten minutes. There's something else. As the water rises, they'll get pretty chilled. That one, and that one there, might go into shock. And with the weight of their boots and harnesses . . ."

"So they bob a bit," he returned coldly. "Don't worry. They're tough; they won't drown that easily. We'll have plenty of time to clear the stake. Just make sure you do the scannets first." Like troughs of numbness with waves of pain, Kurvan's hushed voice washed over her. "And start clearing the logs immediately . . ."

Tsia pushed herself back up on her arms. A massive hammer of pain pounded her chest, and her muscles seemed to spasm . . . The groan that tried to force its way out between her clenched teeth was a low keening sound. She was sore as if she'd been hit by a skimmer at full speed. She fingered the char-crinkled edges of the hole in her blunter. Her bioshield was gone; the pocket where it had been now was nonexistent. Decker's laze—it had hit her bioshield, she realized; not her flesh at all. It was the bioshield disk that had taken the full brunt of the particle beam. And when the shield had fried, it had spiked and jolted her nerves. Her flesh was neither burned nor split; her muscles were just stunned.

She dragged herself another meter toward the corner of the hut. Then her shoulders wobbled and she dropped back to the tarmac. She stopped, her head hung between her arms. Spatters of rain splashed up from the puddles into her wincing eyes. She shook her head slowly like a cat. Eyes gleaming, Ruka got to his feet and paced away. Tsia staggered up, half-bent, to her feet, wobbled back down to her knees, and forced herself up again. She took two steps after the cat. The skimmers, she thought. She had to stop blackjack from using the ships. And she had to contact the node.

She made it several meters before she fell again. This time, some part of her brain noted almost proudly that she did not hit the tarmac so hard. She was up again almost before her knees registered the shock. The cougar looked back. Tsia motioned him on. If the blackjack weapons could harm a biological, they could kill him as easily as her.

Go now, she told him through her gate. She built and projected an image of shrub brush and the game trails in the leaves. *You must leave. And get as far away as you can.* She built another image, of a mother cat and her cubs. *Please—go back to the coast. Now!*

There was a sound behind her, and she froze. It was that other cat—that elusive scent rising through her gate, not her nose. Abruptly, she shut herself off from her gate, then realized that the visual shadow on the other side of the tarmac was real—that the creature that moved near the shrub brush she had just indicated to Ruka was large and hungry to her blurred eyes. The focus of its interest seeped through her clamped-down biogate. A hunter, intent, and without her flexor Tsia was helpless as a choicer before the lifer boards. The cat-thing hesitated as it came abreast of her, but its head was turned to the forest. She closed herself into a pocket of thought. With a hiss, it moved slowly into the brush.

Tsia waited scant seconds. Then, silently, she ran the other way until she stumbled around the corner of the sprawling hub. The skimmer pad—what side was it on? She cursed as she tripped over a cracked seam in the deck; then the scent of the skimmers hit her through the biogate.

"Ruka," she breathed. She looked back. The tawny shape of the cat was invisible, but she could feel him already slinking back across the landing pad, ignoring her order to flee. She hesitated. There were no shouts behind her, but something seemed to sharpen in her gate. Abruptly, she accepted his help.

In an instant, the metaplas skimmer scents were immediate and clear. Quickly, she turned to her right, eased around a line of vats and past the storage huts. The wide space that opened out was clear of everything but the three sleek shapes. Tsia broke into a run.

A prickling of the hairs along her neck . . . A widening of her eyes . . . The catspeak swelled in her head. She snarled in return. The sharpness subsided, but remained like an eye in a window, peering into her mind, listening to the growls she projected through her gate.

She ran faster as the feeling in her feet returned. She almost barreled into the first skimmer before she slowed down enough to feel for the maintenance hatch. There—along the sides. Her nails scrabbled along the smooth sail slats. The line—where was it? Her nose was sharp, but her cat-fed eyes, blurred through the gate, could not distinguish details. Frantically, she ran her hands over the ship. She could feel its skin, pocked with the tiny marks of age, but the seams of the sail slots disguised the seams of the hatch.

Hurry, Ruka snarled.

The hunter was close. She could *feel* it. And the humans behind that hunter . . . She had no time to finish the thought. Her nails finally caught in the finger slots of the panel; she jerked the hatch off and reached recklessly inside. She yanked the first thing that came to hand, and a heavy coil snaked out, dripping a thin and viscous, brown-black fluid. She ripped the cable free and stabbed her hands back in, only to tear her flesh on the sharp edges of the honeycomb board in which the datacubes were set.

The sudden pain sharpened her mind, and she stopped, staring at the distance to the forest. It was a hundred yards across the deck to the edge of the wind-whipped woods. How much could she carry from here to there? And how much time was there before that feline hunter found her or blackjack searched her out? She glanced down at Ruka, who stayed crouched beneath the landing leg, then back at the trees. Ruka had dragged her on the deck; would he do the same with the tubing?

At her feet, he pawed at the coil.

Yes! The exultation rose in her throat like a scream.

He took it distastefully in his teeth.

To the forest, Tsia sent urgently, unable to hide her joy.

He was gone, the end of the coil dragging on the ground to his side, then between his legs like a heavy snake. Her blurred vision of the ship disappeared. Yanking, pounding . . . A section of the data honeycomb cracked, and a dozen slots broke, spilling the cubes out at her feet. She wrenched at a sensor box and it came free; she threw it as far as she could toward the brush. Another beside it, she yanked out, ignoring the danger codes on its side.

She felt the presence of another cat—a small feline this time. A watercat watching curiously from a hollow in its fallen tree, its nose filled with forest smells: wet leaves, mud, shapers, and deer . . . *Help me,* she urged through the gate. *Hide the box that smells like this—* She projected the scent that clung to the metaplas cover. The watercat hesitated. Tsia caught its pause and projected, as strongly as she could, an image that no creature, animal or not, could mistake: A vast expanse of ground that burned. The smell of rot and death. The weakness that strikes and collapses the limbs . . . *Avoid this,* she sent. *Help me—*

The catspeak seemed to snarl louder. The watercat slunk out of its hollow. It could smell the box faintly compared to Ruka—its nose was not as sensitive. It edged around the shaper den and took a moment to find the case, half-buried in the mud. Then it mouthed the awkward shape, dropped it, and took it up once again. A moment later, its feet padded soundlessly through the forest as it stole the sensor case away. It would come back for the other, Tsia knew. The projection had caught it strongly. And Ruka . . .

She dropped to her knees and scrabbled on the tarmac to gather up the cubes. How many had she torn out? How many had she missed? She left blood on the rough surface and did not care; the rain would dilute it soon. When Ruka appeared again at her side, she held the cubes in her cupped hands and tucked them inside his gums, along the edges of his mouth. He snarled at the sensation.

"I know it hurts," she pleaded, "but hold them in your mouth. Spit them out in the forest, as far as you can get . ."

His jaws stretched and his lips curled with irritation. The rasp of his tongue caught on the edges of her torn fingers.

Hurry, she told him in her mind. *Go!*

In a single movement, he whirled and leaped away. She stared after him and felt the distance disappear beneath his feet. Exultation filled her again, and her lips stretched into a feral grin. It was working— He was doing it for her— She felt the whip of leaves, the brush of grasses along his shoulders as he shifted through the brush at speed. Felt the sharp edges of the octagonal shapes that bit into his gums—

There was a vibration along the tarmac—a sound that traveled through metaplas before it did the air. Quickly, she eased the panel shut. Her sight was clear again without the cat. She opened her biogate to feel Ruka's feet, and the sense of that hunter swept in . . . Close, it searched for her with a menacing intent. Puzzled, it paused, as if it expected feline thoughts and found something else instead.

Her eyes darting from one side of the tarmac to the other, Tsia ran, half-crouched, to the second ship on the deck. The feeling was back in her arms and legs, and her muscles were stronger, but tension made her shake so much that she couldn't grip the slots of the hatches. She cursed and pried at the bays. When one finally came open, she tore at the cabling inside. Ruka slunk back across the tarmac like a piece of solid wind. He took the gear this time without snarling, and loped away. A watercat appeared warily, edging up, then snatching a sensor box Tsia slid across the deck toward his forefeet. Two minutes, and another watercat to help, and she clicked shut the bay and tried to catch her breath.

Daya, why was it so hard to breathe? She opened herself to the cats and let the fierceness of her joy almost choke her. That they did this for her—that they understood . . . She called Ruka to return. There was only one ship left to strip, and it would take two minutes—no more.

She slid along the second ship till she felt the slight outward taper of one of the aft vents. She could almost smell the hunter now in her mind. And there was something else in the wind, too—a scent almost as familiar as her own sweat smell. A scent that spoke of packing crates and flowers . . . Her nostrils flared; her tongue tasted the storm on her lips. She darted across the deck to the third skimmer—the transport—and halted abruptly as she reached the side. It was larger than the other skimmers, and the maintenance bays were farther overhead. How— She hesitated, glanced back toward the other ships, and judged the distance up to the bays. She prepared herself to jump. Then the tarmac lights came on.

Instinctively, Tsia ducked below the transport hull. Her eyes flinched and slitted against the brightness. Half-crouched, she dodged around the landing leg, seeking some kind of shadow, and skidded to a halt as her eyes registered the point of blue-purple-white light that held itself on her chest. The woman who held the laze was as stonelike for an instant as Tsia.

Dark brown hair, green eyes. Even in the yellow light of the landing pad, Tsia could see the woman's coloring against her space-tanned skin. Slender as Tsia, but shorter by an inch, the woman was dressed in the same cream-and-brown freepick jumpsuit as the other blackjacks. She stared at Tsia with cold, shocked eyes.

Tsia could not move. "Shjams," she breathed.

The other woman's eyes were almost blank.

"Shjams," Tsia repeated.

The green eyes seemed suddenly haunted. "Tsia?"

Tsia's eyes blurred, and she blinked to clear them. The brown hair she stared at was thinner and shorter, but the same color as she had last seen it, six years ago. But the green eyes, once so filled with sharp thoughts and laughter, were now shuttered and shallow. The two women stared at each other. The lights cast them both in sharp relief. The rain that caught in Tsia's hair dripped down the scars along her cheek; the rain that struck Shjams clung like tears to her hair.

"You—" Tsia still had not moved. "Here."

"Here."

Light glistened off the water on their clothes, their hair, their faces. In Tsia's mind, the cat feet crawled like worms, boring through her thoughts and making her shiver with the feeling that this moment was not, somehow, real. The silence was so thick it seemed to push away the rain. Shjams cleared her throat. "So," she said uncertainly.

"So," Tsia repeated.

"So, how are you?"

Tsia stared at her for a long moment. "Goddammit," she breathed finally. "It's been six years since you've seen me, and all you can say is how am I?"

Shjams did not change expression, but Tsia felt suddenly that she was looking at a mask.

"What are you doing here?" she asked slowly.

Shjams's voice was strained. "Me?"

"You. Shjams. My sister, who should be up at a docking hammer, not down at a freepick stake—"

"You're the one who shouldn't be here," the other woman said harshly.

Tsia stared at her. She took a half step forward, but the point of the laze did not waver. "Shjams, put the laze away."

"No."

"*I'm* not blackjack. I'm with the mercs—" Her voice cut off abruptly: Shjams did not look surprised. "You know that."

"Yes."

"You're one of them."

"Yes."

Tsia's face paled so that her skin looked almost like her scars. She reached back unconsciously to steady herself on the ship. "You came for the biochips." It was not a question. "You helped them get the biochips."

"Yes."

Tsia stared at Shjams. Her sister's green eyes, shuttered and shallow with some kind of inner mask, stared back. Tsia tried to sense Shjams's biofield, but it was as if her person had been cut up in strips or shredded. There was only a dark center, thick and pulsing with some rhythm that was not Shjams . . . A blackness that ate at her heart so that she, herself, became hollow as an old grudge.

"The laze—put it down," she whispered.

"Please . . ." Shjams's voice was not steady, and there was an anguish in her eyes that rippled like a shock wave through Tsia's biogate. But the hand on the laze did not waver. "Please," she breathed. "Don't force me to use it."

The shadows grew closer in Tsia's gate. She took another half step forward. The point of the laze was blue-white, with purple tints, and seemed to fill her sight with a burning, fiery light. Her gaze rose to the face of the other woman. "You would laze me. Me: Tsia. Your sister."

Rain spattered the ground and ran against their feet. "Yes."

"Goddammit—"

"I will do it, Tsia."

Tsia felt as if some edge of her world had crumbled. Her lips curled, and her hands clenched at her sides. All of a sudden, anger flared up in her guts and burned in the acids of her stomach. It blinded her eyes. In her mind she saw her brothers' faces, closed against the hurt, as they realized that Shjams would not return their coms, would not accept their visits, would not return to see them. Her mother's face, where lines seemed to have etched and age seemed to have settled overnight the day Shjams disappeared . . . Her father, who somehow seemed to shrink and draw in on himself while he threw himself into the training of new guides. And her grandmother, whose blue eyes faded more with every year Shjams had been gone . . .

"Six years," Tsia said slowly. "Six years, and you finally did come back."

Shjams cleared her throat uneasily. "You didn't use to be so concerned with time."

"You call more than half a decade a little bit of time? Daya, Shjams, it's been six years with no word from you at all. Six years of wondering how you were. What you did. If you were sick or unhappy or just off finding yourself, as you claimed. Wondering if we could possibly help. You finally did come back to Risthmus. But not for your family." Her voice grew sharper with every word until it seemed to strike out like claws. "No," she almost snarled. "Six years, and you don't bother to seek your family at all. You just come for a set of biochips. You come back, not as the daughter of the guides

Bayzon and Ellyn; not as the woman who worked her own way through the certification boards; not as a full inspector from the only working docking hammer in orbit around this world. You come as a criminal. As a zek. As a thief."

Shjams took a half step back.

Tsia followed her. "Forget me—your sister. Forget your family. Just look at what you're doing. Do you know what blackjack will do with those chips? Do you understand what can happen—to this world? To any other world in human space?"

"They won't be used against our worlds."

"Who told you that?" Tsia demanded. "And how could you possibly believe such a thing even if you heard it? The Shjams I knew wouldn't fall for such a lie. How could you have changed so much—"

"It's you who have changed, not I."

Tsia threw her head back and snarled, and Shjams froze. For a moment, neither one moved. "I have changed," Tsia said in a startlingly quiet voice. "I've begun to know myself again. But you—you're like a ball of water, spinning without a center."

"You don't know what I am—"

"I can *feel* you," Tsia snarled. "I can feel your intent like a knife already cutting my throat."

"Then go," Shjams almost shrieked. "Go. Run. Get away from here. I won't laze you. Just go . . ."

Slowly, then more strongly, Tsia shook her head. "Who turned you into this?" she asked, almost gently. "Who is using you?"

"No one. No one—"

"It is a friend? A lover who has this control over you?"

"No. Yes, but he's— No— No one uses me."

"Is it the one you ran away with?"

"I did not run away."

"Yes, you did," Tsia retorted flatly. "You know that's the truth."

"He's stronger than you," Shjams said, almost desperately. "His truth is stronger—"

"He has no truth if he's making you live on lies. And he's using you like a slave as a weapon against your own world."

"No, it's not that way at all—"

"Anyone who would kill to take this technology wouldn't care who it was used against."

"You're wrong!"

"Who was it that told you the chips would not be used against this world or any other? *Was* it him?" She stared at the flicker of emotion that crossed Shjams's face. "That's who it is, isn't it? This lover who somehow latched on to you and separated you from everything that used to be important to you. He's the one who told you that lie and all the others on which you have been living."

"It doesn't matter who told me—"

"You're trapped, is that it? You're afraid of his strength? You're caught through him with the zeks and you don't know how to get out?"

"I could have done this on my own."

"You have—*had*—too much respect for life."

"I still do!"

"Not since you took up with this blackjack."

Shjams's voice was low. "You have no right to judge him."

Tsia just looked at her. "Blood gives me that right. Blood gives me every right to look and weigh and judge—and condemn to the hottest, searing hell the zek who uses you to your own death."

"You haven't even met him."

"I don't need to. I see him in your eyes."

"He loves me for myself. He would never use me—"

"You're an inspector, Shjams—or you were. You are the only reason blackjack can get this cargo through customs. Don't tell me this man hasn't asked you to slip the chips through customs."

"It's not like that!"

"You aren't going to get the chips through customs?"

The tension in Shjams's lips turned them almost white. Tsia half stretched out her hand. Her biogate surged. Ruka growled as if she reached out to pet a shaper, and she froze. The heat of the laze point sizzled in the rain and the faint smoke made her nostrils flare. She stared at Shjams as if she had never seen her.

"You are stealing biochips that could spell the end of you, of me, of your entire family. Of an entire world. And you blind yourself with a lie so that you don't have to see your actions in the light. As if, by ignoring them, you can sanction what you do."

Shjams's voice was low. "You don't know what I do."

"Do I not? Kipling said it best: 'When your Daemon is in charge, do not try to think consciously. Drift, wait, and obey.' That's you, Shjams. Lost in the words of blackjack. Lost because you can't find yourself, and anything is better than facing your demons alone—even a greater demon who uses you till you're nothing, and then sucks the marrow from the bones of your self."

Shjams shook her head slowly. A man rounded the corner of the far hut behind her and broke into a jog as he saw the two women. Shjams did not seem to notice. "You can't judge me," she said quietly. "And you can't judge him till you know him. Till you meet him in person."

"Through you, have I not met him already?"

Shjams flushed slowly. The image of Kurvan's lean, handsome face flashed through Tsia's mind, and she took a disbelieving step forward.

"Daya," she breathed. "Is he here—now? At this freepick stake?"

Shjams did not answer.

Kurvan. His visage blinded Tsia to her sister. Kurvan. Who had smiled at her to make her drop him. Kurvan, who had engineered her mistakes. Kurvan, who had made it seem as if she tried to drown Wren. Who had used her like a dog to keep himself safe. Her voice, when she spoke, was almost drowned out by the rain. "I've met him already, haven't I?"

Decker, behind Shjams, was only fifty meters away. Her sister set her jaw. "They're coming."

"I can *see* him—"

"You understand what has to happen now?"

"I'm your sister, for god's sake!"

Tsia took another half step forward. She had forgotten the laze. Shjams did not hesitate. The white-purple light fired into the ground. Tsia jerked back like a cat, one arm up in front of her face. The blast of heat and gas made her choke, and automatically the smoke diaphragm in her throat closed off. Her back rammed into the landing leg. The smoke snakes blew away in the wind while the rain beat the rest of its tendrils down. Tsia stared at her sister.

"I don't know you like this," she whispered.

"You never knew me."

"We're family. Even if you're caught in a . . . a situation—"

"The only situation I'm in," Shjams hissed, "is this one between you and me."

Tsia half raised her hand, but Shjams stepped back again. Decker increased his pace.

"Don't move any more," Shjams said harshly. "I won't give a damn if you die at my hands."

"His name—" Tsia's whisper broke, and Shjams's eyes seemed suddenly haunted. "Is it Kurvan who has done this to you? Kurvan, who has stripped you of your heart? Of your self?"

Shjams did not look over her shoulder at Decker as the man approached more warily. Her flat green eyes bored into Tsia's. She seemed to search for something, and Tsia could not move from her gaze. Something flickered deep in the green, and Tsia's gate gaped so wide that her mind reeled. It was like looking at a dog that had been hit too many times. Like feeling the fist strike again and again. The catspeak snarled. Tsia's lips curled more. Her own memories rose up. All the pain and longing—all the humiliation Tsia had suffered till she won her own freedom . . . Ten years of work and yearning and death that she had tasted with the mercs. A decade of fighting to regain herself—it shone out of Tsia's dark blue eyes like emotion too long trapped within a pressurized tube. And the flinch of an animal shone out of Shjams's.

When Decker stepped forward and grabbed Tsia's shoulders, jerking her to her knees, she did not resist. She just stared at

the other woman and tried to project to her the memories that
flashed in her head: Shjams and Tsia on a storm-roughened
slough, racing skeeters across the water. Slamming into the
waves and flying off their crests till they hit the next swell that
washed in. Two girls huddled together in a cave, trading ghost
stories as they tried to scare each other, until neither one could
stand it, and they both raced back to the sunshine. Tsia standing in front of Shjams as the younger girl was picked on, and
biting out the words in her defense . . . Two young women, lying in the grass and staring up at the stars while they spoke of
dreams and goals . . .

Slowly, as if her mouth was full of distaste, Shjams spat to
the side. Tsia stared for a moment, then, abruptly, closed her
gate. Her face grew still; her eyes grew shuttered. Her jaw was
tight as her fists. Decker looked from one to the other. He
smelled like cat. So did Shjams. Tsia's nostrils flared, and
she cursed the gate that overwhelmed her senses so that she
couldn't even smell her sister over the scent of felines in her
mind.

Decker stepped away from Tsia so he could point his laze at
her from a safer distance. "Where did you find her?" he said
to Shjams.

The woman jerked her chin. "Right here."

"She get into any of the ships?"

"No."

Decker looked Tsia over and noted the burn hole he had
placed in the blunter. "She give you any trouble?"

"No."

Decker raised his white eyebrows. "How did you do it?"

She said slowly, "For a moment, in the shadows, she
thought I was her sister."

The zek raised his eyebrows. The two women looked similar
only in the set of their expressions. Where Shjams had
shoulder-length hair that curled even in the rain and wind,
Tsia's hair was straight and short. Where Shjams had a clear,
natural-olive complexion, Tsia's skin, even tanned as it had become, was still much lighter in shade, and the claw marks that
had scarred her face twisted her expression into a feral mask so

that even their noses could not be compared. Shjams was bustier; Tsia was taller. Shjams had green eyes; Tsia had blue. Decker looked from one to the other. " 'Always the shadow that reflects yourself,' " he quoted.

The woman shrugged.

Decker glanced at the still-open hatch of the skimmer. "You finish up here. I'll take her back to the hub."

"You know she's a guide."

Decker said coldly, "Her gate will be of no use here. She's going in the reclamation pit with the others. In less than an hour, there will be plenty of water in the pit, but there's no open passage to anything nearby—nothing from which a marine animal can come."

Shjams, staring still at Tsia, frowned. "What does that have to do with her?"

"She's linked to some kind of eel or fish. Kurvan confirmed it on the hike."

His words hung in the air. Tsia held her breath while time spun out in a long, thin web like an ancient ghost from the node. There was no change in Shjams's expression as the woman turned away. A sound escaped Tsia's throat, even through her tightly clamped lips. Decker dug his fingers into her shoulder and hauled her up. He shoved her in front of him, then followed her across the tarmac. Tsia, her mind numb as ice and her thoughts as sharp as crystal, did not once look back.

Shjams stared after her, then triggered the hatch and climbed up into the ship. Blindly, she went forward and sank down in the pilot's chair. The soft molded itself to her hips and shoulders, and she cursed its calm complacency.

"She thought I was her sister."

Shjams stared at the blank set of flight screens as if they were a wall. She didn't feel the chill air that circulated from the open hatch. She didn't notice the rain that swept into the cabin from the door. There was a harshness in the air, as if someone breathed with difficulty, and it took her a moment to realize it was her own throat, so tight against the tears, that choked off the breath from her lungs.

"I was," she whispered to herself. "I was."

20

Tsia rolled back against the wet rock. Above, a rough circle of gray light was filled with raindrops that seemed to fall as slowly as snowflakes. The edges of the reclamation pit, outlined with the silver light, glistened from the groundwater. Falling rain splattered her neck and face. The water at her feet was already ankle-deep from the seeps that flooded through the cracked rock walls, and since the gray light didn't reach all the way to the bottom of the pit, and the sallow pit lighting was faint as a lamp in a warehouse, it looked as if she stood in an ebony pool.

From beside her, Doetzier spoke quietly. "Did you get to a manual com?" His voice was so low that it barely reached Tsia's ears over the sound of the running, dripping water.

"No," she returned, her voice equally low. They stood close together with the zeks overhead, at the top of the dank hole. Like chickens waiting for the knife, they stood and stared up at the gray sky circle. Five mercs, three freepicks . . . Nitpicker being lowered as they watched. Nine people waiting to die. And that hunter who crept on the edge of her mind still tested her gate with each breath.

She looked around the pit with distant eyes. Absently, she scratched the skin graft on her thigh. Around her, the cored-out walls were rough with sharp, circular cuts. Four meters—that was all the width there was. Four meters; twenty minutes, and the water already ankle-deep.

For a moment, she watched Nitpicker's limp body brought down the lift by the zek with the long arms. The blackjack and his victim dropped into the darker layer where neither sky nor pit lighting reached, then back into the dirty, yellow-lit area at the bottom.

"How far did you get?" Doetzier breathed the question without moving his lips, and Tsia dragged her attention back to his words.

"The skimmers—"

Wren and the thickset Bishop caught Nitpicker as the zek tossed her off his shoulder. Gently, they lowered her limp body to a bed of rock that stood knee-high above the growing puddle. Laz, his tall frame huddled on a rock, watched them work without moving. While Wren checked for Nitpicker's pulse, the zek rose immediately back toward the rim. He had not brought down a weapon. Blackjack wouldn't have hesitated to sacrifice him if they thought he'd be used against them. The ankle-deep pool reflected his rising shape as a twisted, dancing body.

Tsia looked at Doetzier as his own water-image split and shook and put itself back together. The skin was tight around his eyes, and she could feel in his biofield the control he exerted over his pain. The side of his face was egg-shaped, and the lump from the flexor red-blue with dead blood. His left eye was still half-shut from the swelling; his lip was split and fat. His shoulders were bent as if he were tired and in pain, but his gaze was alert and seemed to snap with the energy that filled his biofield. His hands, hidden in shadow, drummed against his trousers as if he waited, not for death, but something . . . else.

Tsia almost glared at him. His very stance seemed to challenge her to feel less old and weary. He poised like a runner at the mark, but she felt every one of her forty-eight years as a weight on her shoulders, dragging down on her arms. Forty-eight years, she thought. Half a century that somehow had never given her the words or way in which to touch her sister. She waited for the familiar wash of bitterness, but it didn't come. Only a tang, as if she bit her lip and tasted blood.

She did not think about the biochips. She did not consider

Kurvan. The cold that radiated from the stone made her shiver, and she drew her burned blunter more closely around her exhausted body, then hunched against the rain and shoved her hands in her pockets. The sharp edges of the safety cubes pressed against her fingers, and she glanced at Nitpicker. She ought to give them back to the pilot now, she thought with irony. If blackjack had its way, she'd have no chance to return the datacubes later.

Daya, she had no energy left to think. She should be planning, thinking of how to escape, but she could not seem to focus. Her sister's name was like a cry that echoed and split the thoughts in her mind. Even above the background hum of the cats or over the snarling of the cougar, or around the splashing, dripping sounds of the rainwater washing in, her sister's name was a sharp knife in her skull. Shjams . . .

Doetzier's voice was still low. "Did you get inside to the coms?"

Tsia tried to focus. "No."

"Zyas, Feather." His voice was sharper. "Did you do anything at all?"

Daya, it was hard to form the words. "I yanked everything I could from the maintenance bays," she managed finally. Somehow, it seemed like weeks had passed, not simply twenty-eight hours. And still it rained, as if the sky shed the tears that Tsia could not. She glanced at Bowdie. Poetic justice, she thought with gallows humor. It rained so that she could drown her sorrows with the very breath in her lungs. A fitting image—that she drowned in the tears of the world she tried to save.

"From what bays did you pull the gear?"

She could still see Shjams standing there, smelling of cat and packing crates; of the perfume she had used when they were young . . .

"Which bays?" he repeated urgently.

She dragged her thoughts back to the present. "The aft bays just behind the wing slots."

"How much damage did you do? What did you pull out?"

"I don't know," she returned sharply. She closed her eyes

and took a breath and lowered her voice again. "I'm a guide, not a shiptech," she whispered finally. "I just grabbed everything in reach—sensor boxes, power strips, datacubes. I cracked a few honeycombs and tore out a length of pressure tubing."

"And they didn't see the mess?"

"I closed the bays before they got there. Threw the gear in the forest."

Doetzier swore quietly under his breath. "Blackjack will be able to scan out that gear inside ten minutes."

"They'll find nothing before they lift."

He shook his head almost imperceptibly. "Every sensor box has a repair call sign built in. You can trigger its location through the scannet here at the hub. Datacubes too—they're no exception."

"Grounded scannets have a limited range."

"They're not as limited as your throwing arm."

"You don't understand," she said tiredly. "They will not find the gear."

He actually looked at her. "You got it outside the scan range?"

She nodded almost imperceptibly.

A ghost of a smile crossed his lips. "Trust a guide to hide the path beneath your feet," he quoted. "If they can't lift off . . ." He seemed to straighten. "Did you get all three ships?"

"No—only two. They caught me at the transport."

"Sleem take them, that's the one they'll fly out on, too . . ." He thought for a moment. "If the transport was out of commission, we'd have a good chance of keeping the zeks contained long enough to get help—or to recover the chips before they lift off," he added, more to himself than to her.

"Zyas, Doetzier, don't you ever give up?"

"Not while there's breath in my family line."

"At least you could tell me what that is," she whispered sourly back. "Your family name, I mean—so I can die with my curiosity sated."

He gave her a wry grin. "Death isn't reason enough to give up the power of a name."

Tsia could not smile in response. She shoved herself away from the wall and paced the small pit like a tiger, shouldering past the other mercs as if they were not there. In an hour, she and Doetzier would be fighting to stay afloat in an r-con field, not scheming to get back the chips. One hour, maybe two, and the zeks would, if the mercs survived that long, kill them all like rats in a bucket. Her hands itched to climb up the slick sides of the pit, but her mind could see no way out. If she could image the node, she could lower the lift by command as soon as blackjack left. But in an r-con field, no one would be able to move to use a lift even if it was lowered . . .

The water swirled above her ankles. Wren glanced at the water level, then up at Tsia, while he held Nitpicker's head as gently as a child's. He grinned coldly, but there was fury behind his expression. "Well, Feather, at least you were right about the rains."

She stared at him for a moment, then turned back to the stone with stiff fingers. One hour, her mind repeated. She ran her hands over the slick rock wall, ignoring the other mercs. The mud ground like sand on her fingers as she tested the protrusions. Too small, too slick to climb . . . One hour. Maybe two. That ghost line she had in the node—the old trace—could she make it active?

Her feet slipped on the rough, hidden rock and mud. She did not care. Like fingers reaching up, the brown-black water splashed along her calves. Like stones dropped into a well, the rain hit the reflection-torn surface of the growing lake. Shjams. Blackjack. The biochips . . .

Bowdie, one hand still pressed to his side, watched her as she stopped against the rock beside Striker. The water splashed off a protrusion over her head and splattered her eyebrows with droplets. Striker had pulled the hood of her blunter up so that the water ran off the fabric in tiny, constant runnels. Tsia turned her head to meet the other woman's eyes, and Striker shifted, bit her lip, and hissed out her breath. The burn on her leg had cauterized itself as it was made; there was no blood, but the stench of the woman's seared flesh was thick in Tsia's nose. Striker's face, taut and pale, seemed hollow around the blackness of her eyes. She had not been allowed a skin graft.

"All right?" Tsia asked in a low voice.

"Long as I'm breathing," Striker returned shortly.

Mina looked at Striker. "You took that burn for me," she said, her acerbic voice forced and halting.

Striker glanced at her but didn't answer.

"He would have killed me, and you stopped him."

"It's my job," the merc returned shortly.

Mina's eyes flashed. "That's right," she agreed. Her voice tightened with anger. "But there's some part of you that agrees with me, or you couldn't have taken that laze."

Striker laughed. Bishop murmured, "Mina, back off."

She turned on him roughly, but Striker cut in, "I get paid, Mina, so you can have the beliefs you want—no matter how I disagree with them. This burn"—she gestured at her leg—"is just a reminder of how far some people will go to take control over others."

The freepick stared at her for a moment, then turned away. But the shivering that hit her shoulders didn't hide the shake of her anger. Bishop touched her shoulder, and she shook him off abruptly. He glanced at Striker, then moved back to the wall as a shadow moved to the top of the pit.

Decker came halfway down on the lift. In his hands he held a small, red-black box. He used the extension bars of the foot and hand pipes to shift his body close to the wall. Once there, he placed the box on a ledge two meters over Wren's head.

The mercs, watching from the bottom of the pit, became very still. Tsia eyed the box without speaking. The chill that had settled in her bones was offset only by the fire that began to burn in her gut. She knew the shape of that box. She knew the touch of its burning field on her nerves. Knew the searing pain that would strike with every muscle motion—from her lungs expanding, to the blink of her eyes and the convulsive flare of her nostrils. She saw that box and felt her eyes shutter and her expression go blank, and her mind withdrew, deep inside herself, behind the walls of will and survival, where nothing and no one could touch her. She did not move, except to lean herself with her shoulder against the wall so that her weight was not balanced just on her feet. And then, slowly and steadily, as if she began to meditate, she began to breathe.

Decker moved back up the lift, and Mina got to her feet. She stared after the zek and demanded, "What is that? What did you leave?"

Bowdie snapped at her, "Move back against the wall."

She ignored him and shaded her face with her hand. Decker's figure disappeared in a silhouette at the rim of the pit. The lift rose up after him until the thread of its shadow vanished.

"What is that thing?" she shouted.

Tsia felt her lips move. "It's an r-con," she said almost absently. And then the field turned on, and fire swept through her body.

21

Muscles froze instinctively like rock. Lungs held their breath in shock. The eyelids, caught open, did not dare blink as the field from the r-con expanded into the pit. Tsia felt the burn grip her nerves, from the skin that held the roots of her hair to the toes that pressed for balance inside her boots. Her temple link became a whip of electrical pulses that flayed her nervous system. The movement of every muscle burned. The rise and fall of her chest with her breath was a bath in fire that scorched her ribs and lungs. The instinctive clench of her jaw was a punch from a fist of acid.

No one screamed. No one cried out. Each larynx was caught in that sudden, searing pain. This was not like a wash of heat from a firepit, nor the point pain of a laze. This was a ubiquitous burning that struck every cell in their bodies. The pulse that pushed the skin out in their throats—it was a drum of torture. The pumping of their hearts—it was a crushing pain. And still the rain fell and the water seeped in, and the pit pool rose toward their knees.

Tsia hid within her mind from the burning of her body. She knew this pain. Her biogate was shut down tight—the single scream from Ruka had made her jerk it closed. She could not draw strength from him, or any other cat.

Don't move, her brain screamed. Don't shift an inch.

Turn your head, she told herself. Move your feet, or die.

Slowly, carefully, deliberately, she forced her eyes to shift to the left. Her optic nerves shrieked in response. She ignored them, though her body tried to sob. Blindly, she looked toward the r-con. With the sallow pit lights rippling over the gritty, inky water, the red-black box gleamed like a demon's face on the rain-black stone of the walls. Oval shadows danced with their reflections. Pale faces flickered black, then flashed yellow-white as the water shook and rippled at the mercs' feet. Mina, caught standing away from the wall with one hand raised, started to lose her balance, and a hoarse cry ripped itself from her throat. She fell, jerked her arms instinctively, and the cry became a scream. Her body, rigid as a board, struck the side of the pit. Her shoulders took her weight against the rock wall as her head barely missed striking stone. Like a ladder, her body leaned in silence while the cords on her neck and jaw stood out, and she did not dare relax.

On the other side of the pit, Tsia did not take her eyes from the box. Her knowledge of pain did not diminish the shocking burn in her muscles, nor did it protect her mind from the flashback that swept out of her memories. Nerve whips, chains, and r-cons . . . She had felt them all. And reality was worse again than memory had let her believe. She blinked and stifled the scream in her throat. She swallowed deliberately and whimpered. The convulsive movement made her mind tear as if her own thoughts were now made of claws. She forced herself to blink again. She knew what she had to do.

Nitpicker's body was a handspan from the surface of the rising pool. Laz, the only one near the pilot, was still folded up in his long-legged crouch. The other mercs were all standing. Even Striker had gotten to her feet when she saw the r-con brought down. Striker was the only one who had braced her hand against the wall; the others leaned on their shoulders.

"Laz . . ." Tsia's voice was a withered hoarseness. The fire from the r-con field seared away the sound before she even finished it. She blanked her mind and forced her tongue to move again. "Laz . . ." This time, she projected the sound with her guts, and the shock of the nerve burn in her torso cut her off.

"Get—her face—away—from—the—water."

Each word a shriek of torture on her lips and tongue. Each sound a searing flash of pain that licked her jaw and settled in her chest. Doetzier forced his eyes to turn toward Tsia, and he could not stifle the sound that tore from his own lips at the tiny movement.

Tsia did not look at him. She had moved her foot, and then her hand. The water pressed her thin trousers against her leg so that the chill reached her skin like ice. She ignored it like the burn that lanced up her legs and lower back from the movement she dared to force. Her foot, an inch. And then one more ... Deliberately, she turned her head and let the waves of pain wash through her.

"Wren," she croaked. She could not see for a moment. The red-black face of the r-con seemed to have burned its colors into her mind, and waves of light and darkness drowned her thoughts. A minute passed, then five before her eyesight cleared. When it did, she could see Wren's face tight with horror. His jaw was white, his eyes blind. His brutal hands hung limply at his side. Against the muddy wall, his back was hunched in some inner nightmare. And the mindless fear that radiated from his body was palpable in the pit. She did not try to open her biogate to sense his biofield. The flashbacks that tore through his mind froze his thoughts even more than the r-con that locked his body in place.

A shadow appeared in the water, and Tsia felt more than saw the presence of the woman overhead. The zek looked down, nodded to herself, then moved away.

Below, Mina's breathing was shallow; Striker's was tight and controlled. Tsia forced her head to turn again in an infinitesimally slow motion. The pain rubbed up in her mind. This time, she did not black out. She was beginning to remember now. The way to fight the r-con. The pain, she said, did not belong to her. Her mind was separate; her body could scream all it wanted, but it had nothing to do with her. She moved a step toward the r-con, this time inches all at once, and her ears heard someone gasp.

"Laz," she said again, and this time her voice was stronger. "Get—her face—above—the water."

She could feel him staring. She could feel his effort like a push in the air.

"I—can't—" His voice ended in a horrible, grating, cutoff cry.

"You can," she returned. She took another step. The water washed at her knees. "She'll—drown if you—don't. Look at me," she said harshly. The sounds broke from her lips, but she did not recognize her voice. It was raw and shattered, like an edge of glass torn by a metal file. Her words were almost lost in the spattering of the water streamers that fell from the rim of the pit, but her voice went on, chewing, grating at his consciousness.

"You can—do this. One muscle set at a time. Reach down—Lift her head."

He tried to move, and his arm jerked. "I—can't!" he screamed.

"You have the kind of—focus it requires. I can—feel it in your field." Her words went on, but her eyes saw only the r-con. "The fire—is nothing," she said through gritted teeth. "The burn belongs to someone else . . ."

Her foot stubbed on a rock, and her legs tightened suddenly into a flame. For a moment, while the water insidiously crept higher, she could do nothing but stand and wait. If she screamed out, her ears did not know it, though there was some kind of keening there. Carefully, hideously slow, she lifted her foot above the cut rock and onto the tiny submerged ledge.

The pale shadows of the mercs in the corners of her sight were not real against the black walls. Her world narrowed. Focused. Became a single goal: the red-black demon who hung on the rough rock wall. The past, which had taught her to fight such pain, would carry her right to her death.

Someone was sobbing with every breath, but with the claws of flame that tore at her chest, she couldn't tell who it was. She was closer now. That was the only important thing. Closer now to the r-con. Two meters away, two meters above. She could not reach it. The slick walls—the water and mud . . . She couldn't climb even if she could close her hands on the rock.

She couldn't swing her harness fast enough to knock the box off the ledge, but she knew what she had to do . . .

"Daya forgive me," she cried out.

She opened her biogate.

Ruka howled in her mind. The biogate pulsed with pain. All around her, like waves of wind that curled and pressed at her face, the snarling of the cats grew to a crushing din. Even that foreign scent seemed frozen by her pain.

Something sucked out of her mind like a vacuum as the cats tried to close themselves off, but Ruka's link held the gate open. She tried to tighten the gate to a narrow channel, but the pain of her body was in the way. She could tell herself lies, she could pretend she didn't feel the burn, but she could not ignore every one of the billions of synapses that snapped and frayed in the searing field of the r-con.

Help me, she pleaded.

The catspeak surged and hissed.

Help me . . .

Her mind screamed, and something seemed to respond. A wave of snarling washed in. Her body faded; her thoughts crystallized. It was as if her pain were caught and absorbed by a thousand sponges that each took a flame from her body. No one feline mind took the brunt of that fire, as all had done that searing second before. And a tide of catspeak spat and hissed as they swept closer to her body.

A tawny head appeared at the rim of the pit.

The box . . .

An image of the red-black demon . . . A rock batted from above . . . She built the pictures and projected them as if Ruka would understand. The cub disappeared. She could feel him now, moving back to the woods and digging in the mud. He grasped a stick in his mouth and began to drag it back. Another cat shape slipped across the tarmac, carrying a broken clump of bone. And another, from the other side, slinking between the huts.

Here, she directed. The side of the rim from which they would have to bat their objects down into the pit. They couldn't just shove them over the lip: the overhang protected the box.

Another step. Another fire that swept from toe to torso. Another step, and she had to move between Wren and Bishop. Wren's gaze, covered by the darkeyes, could not hide his blind horror as he relived his time in the r-con, but Bishop stared at her as if she herself were the demon.

Ebony water swirled thigh-deep, but Tsia could not see the pool through which she waded in that eternal, slow-motion fire. She could not see the tendons that stood out from her neck like boards. The eyes that seemed slitted and sparking. The fingers curled like a cougar's claws, and the teeth that gleamed in the rain. There was only one thing in her pain-blinded sight: a red-black box on the wall.

"Laz—" She forced the word out between her teeth.

"I—have—her," he returned. His voice was little more than a rasped scream.

The relief she felt at his words was no wash of respite to her body. The fire that burned with every heartbeat ate away at her throat. She cried out through the gate, and the cats overhead seemed to surge like a pack toward the pit. Rain patterns changed. Something hit the rock wall and dropped to splash at her feet; and Tsia, her lips as rigid as her breath, felt the ripples wash against her legs. Her muscles tightened along her arm and shoulder, and she screamed in the flash of pain. Above, a watercat batted a stick under the overhang. It hit Tsia's shoulders before falling into the water, but this time, she didn't jerk. Ruka swatted a bone. The bone came closer. Another stick came closer still. The last stick hit the corner of the box and knocked it to the lip of its ledge.

Tsia moved until she stood against the wall. Slowly, infinitesimally slowly, she stretched out her arms to the pit wall. Another stick fell against her face and neck, then splashed down to the floor. The next one hit her face and lodged between her shoulder and the rock.

Waist-high in the water, she waited and breathed. Something would knock the box off. A stick, a rain-soaked bone . . . She didn't care. Just that it would fall to her arms if she waited. It was the watercat that finally did it—knocked the r-con down. Grating in a tiny sound, it fell and hit her outstretched arms and stopped, tilted like the stick, between her arm and the stone.

Her mind clouded with fire, Tsia stared at it without moving. She dared not shift her arm. If she dropped the box, she would have to bend and search the pool underwater, then bring it up again to turn it off. And without an enbee, she could never hold her breath long enough to move to find the box. But she had it. Here, in her arms. And she stared at it blankly.

Overhead, the watercats faded away until only Ruka was left to pace the rim and cast his shadow below. His eyes gleamed as he glared down into the pit; his fur glistened with rain. And his muscles tensed hers with his pacing, Tsia screamed at him to stop. He hissed, then crouched at the rim. Like a vulture, his head hung over.

Pain lessened with her lack of motion, until what was a searing flame became a simple fire. She regulated her breathing, and tried to calm her heart. Water pressed against her hip. She started to shift her right arm, to move it toward the left, but Ruka hissed from overhead. Pulling herself further into her mind, she stretched her biogate.

Behind her, there was another presence. Wren and Bishop to the sides—it was not them. Someone else moved behind her. A biofield that felt wary and eager, as if coldness turned to heat and fear, anticipation. A biofield she knew with a different flavor. It took her a moment, between the licks of flame, to realize that it was something missing, not changed, that made the field feel strange. She did not turn her head, but in the corner of her eye, a hand appeared that moved so slowly, it crawled like the growth of mold toward her sleeve.

Doetzier.

She could feel the strain in his muscles. Her ears registered sound. Her eyes were still locked on the r-con. As the water rose insidiously, constantly toward her waistline, her body began to sway with the currents in the pit. The box scraped against the wall. She tried to push herself forward so that she leaned against the rock. The fire exploded in her head. She could not even gasp.

Doetzier kept creeping forward. The water continued to rise. The lights in the pit disappeared into the murky pool. Someone must have moved again, because she could hear the strangled scream. Had it been an hour since she started across the pit? Had the fire burned that long in her nerves? She stared at the box and felt her eyes blur until she saw it like a tiny devil, crouching on her arm. Red and black, with winking eyes, now that its controls were visible. Her body shifted again, then trembled, and she realized that the cold had finally invaded. Each shiver sent a shaft of fire along her legs and back, then radiated it down her arms.

The creeping hand was at her elbow, and she could not feel relief. The fingers slid along her arm, as if they took strength or balance from her body. The weathered hand looked gray against the drab shades of her blunter. The wrinkles in the cloth forced Doetzier to lift his hand three times. But he touched the box—that red-black demon—and crept toward the winking lights.

Slow, oh, god, so slowly, as if she burned by millimeters. His fingers did not close around the edges, and she almost snarled at him to take it from her arms. She shivered, violently this time, and the scream she let with the motion out rang in her own ears like the squeal of metal on metal. Her eyes went blind. And then the lock of the r-con on their bodies disappeared, and her muscles, pressing so hard against the rocks to hold the box in place, smashed forward. Her cheek struck stone. Her legs gave way. She slid down into the water.

22

⚜

Chill fluid filled her nose and eyes as she struggled back to the surface. Her ears were deaf for a moment with the water that clogged their canals. Her whole body trembled. The fire was still in her muscles, like a sunburn that fades only slowly, and she worked her jaw for a moment before any sounds came out.

Doetzier still stood near the wall, but he leaned against it now, the r-con still in his hands. Bishop grasped Tsia by her armpits and tried to drag her to her feet, but she shook him off. She tried to take a step, but fell against the bigger man. He caught her and searched her face. "Dear god," he whispered, "what are you made of?"

Her lips moved, but, like Doetzier, she could not yet speak. Her hands reached up to the lapels of Bishop's jumpsuit for support. The odor of oil and dirt in his clothes still cut through her nose, and her lips bared back from her teeth. The freepick shuddered. She tilted her head against his chest to stare up at the edge of the pit. Ruka's eyes no longer peered over the rim. The cats were gone from her gate, and she could feel only Ruka now, retreated to the forest, and that hunter presence near him.

She glanced around. Wren's eyes were still haunted with flashbacks, but he was breathing harshly to control his fear. Nitpicker leaned heavily on Laz. Mina, who stood on the other side of the pit, stared at Tsia like Bishop, while Bowdie moved toward Doetzier and studied the box in his hands. Striker watched in silence, her face an expressionless mask. Doetzier's tortured gaze met Tsia's.

Bishop stared down at Tsia, then across at Doetzier. "I had heard," he said hoarsely, "that there were those—one in every ten thousand—who could withstand the effects of an r-con. Are you one of them?"

"I have a small field warp inside my heels, pelvic bones, and sternum." Doetzier's voice cracked, and it was a moment before he could continue. "It's shielded—can't be detected with normal scans. The warp shunted part of the effects away from my body."

"I should work salvage more often," said Bowdie, "to get some gear like that."

"And you?" Bishop asked, looking down at Tsia's pain-blanched face. "You had a warp, too?"

"No." She pushed herself upright from his support. "But one learns."

"You can't do that your first time in the field."

"No," she agreed shortly.

He stared at her. "How much time have you spent in r-cons?"

She closed her eyes, her arms sculling in the water to keep her balance. "Three months. Solid."

"Dear god," he repeated. He stepped back from her as if she were somehow inhuman.

"Someone coming," she said flatly.

Doetzier turned his head. It was a slow movement, as if he had somehow aged in that hour—or the burn still touched his muscles. He looked at Bowdie, then Laz. "Can you—get the r-con back up there?"

Bowdie nodded. "Give me your foot," he directed Laz. The freepick, his own muscles trembling, took the r-con in shaking hands and looked up the wall to the ledge.

"Don't drop it," Doetzier snapped.

Laz tightened his grip on the box. He stepped up in Bow-die's linked hands, using his own to balance himself against the rock. His tall, gangly form unfolded so that he looked like a spider climbing out of water. When he set the box back on the ledge, Bowdie almost dropped him back in the well. As quickly as their burning muscles could move them, Tsia and Doetzier waded—half swam—away from Bishop and back to the other side of the pit. Nitpicker eased herself down in the water, and Laz took her head in his hands.

Overhead, a face appeared like a shadow against the gray sky. It remained there for only a moment, then disappeared. Tsia could feel the satisfaction in the woman's biofield. She could smell the zek's sense of urgency as the woman walked quickly back to the hut. Tsia's voice was still hoarse as she murmured, "She's gone."

Nitpicker cast Tsia a look. She struggled to put her legs beneath her and stand up on her own. Her face paled, and one hand went to the back of her head. "You said"—her voice was little more than a croak of her own—"you could image the node. What about the lift? Can you drop it down?"

Tsia shrugged, winced, and closed her eyes for a moment as the burn surged, then faded in her muscles. That was something else that took time to remember—the long-term effects of the r-con. "I have a single ghost line active. Nothing on a regular trace."

"How is that possible?" Laz demanded in a low voice. "The node is completely down."

"No," she returned flatly. "Kurvan wanted you to think that. He locked each trace individually. Us"—she gestured at the mercs—"he blocked through our merc IDs. You, he locked out through your freepick codes. Narbon or Decker probably fed him the information to do it."

Mina snapped, and Tsia heard the tremble in her voice. "How do you know that?"

"Because I heard him explain it."

"And the ghost line you have open?" That was from Doetzier.

She shrugged slowly. "An old line. Kurvan overlooked it."

He regarded her for a moment in silence, and she could almost hear his thoughts churning inside his skull. But Mina was looking at Tsia with a frown. "If your ID dot is locked, how could any ghost be viable?"

"Later," Striker said sharply. "Let her work first—to save your life," she said with irony. "Then you can ask her questions."

Mina gave Tsia a strange look, but subsided. Beside her, Laz's energy was tight, and that focus he had used to keep the pilot's head out of the water distracted Tsia until she shut it out. It had gotten easier, she realized, to shut off the biofields. Ruka's voice was so constant now in her head—like a smell to which one became inured—that all she had to do was focus on his snarl. Or try to touch one of the other cats—that watercat still watching, or that hunter on the edge of her gate.

Slowly, she tuned out everything. Then, as the water began to chill her chest, she imaged along the old ghost line. It was still thin, but the false man still moved in Ciordan. It took a minute to catch up the full sense of the web in which he was woven. She formed and sent a command along the web, and the node responded with a surge of biochemical energy. She felt the old ID dot go active. In an instant, warnings triggered across the node. She ignored them. If the guide guild was notified that she was alive, there was little she could do about it. She could either use the web to get out of the pit, or drown with the mercs in the water.

"The rocks and sticks that knocked the r-con off the wall," Laz started. "If you can call your link to help you with that . . ."

"The lift is locked through the node," Nitpicker interrupted. "No amount of pushing from any animal will extend it over and down to us."

"What about linking our harnesses?" Striker suggested. Her voice was tight as she controlled the pain from the burn in her leg.

"There's nothing over which to hook them."

Mina said nothing, but she trembled enough that the water shivered around her. Bishop stroked her arm. She shoved him off. "I'm not scared," she snapped in a low voice. "I'm angry."

Bishop let her go. "All right."

Tsia ignored them. Imaging along a ghost line was like running her fingers along a single strand of an old spider's web. Extraneous images fell away like dust. There was almost no stickiness to the images she was able to find.

"Thin?" Doetzier murmured.

She barely nodded. "This web is so starved for depth that if it turned sideways, I'd lose it altogether."

She created an imaged pathway for the ghost man to walk along. Created a task he had to do that required him to link to the node. Then she walked her mind along the link until she reached the main traces. It took ten minutes to image her way to the merc node lines. Another minute to set up the codes. Thin? she snorted in her mind. She worked so fast that the ghost man's web was as bare of image as a winter tree is of leaves.

Did he wear a certain type of clothes? She didn't care. Did he stand in a certain room to image the codes to the mersat? She didn't bother to define it. Only one thing filled her mind: the link she created to hold her to him, and to pass her on the node. And then the codes clicked in, and the ghost man set a trace from the node to the freepick stake. A second later, the lift pipes extended over the rim of the pit.

"It's coming," Mina cried out. "You're doing it."

"Keep quiet," Striker snapped.

Nitpicker eyed the lift, then glanced at Tsia, who still wore the frown on her face. "Clear?"

"Can't tell."

Laz reached up as if to help the lift down, heedless of the self-guiding sensors in the legs. Wren caught his skinny arm and stopped him from pulling himself up before it came to a rest. "Not yet," Wren said sharply.

"We've got to get out of here—"

Wren's massive hands yanked him away so that he fell awkwardly in the pool. "Not yet," he repeated. "Feather?"

She shook her head. "Nothing human but us."

"Van'ei?" he asked the pilot.

She glanced at Doetzier. "You got anything you want to say?"

He shook his head, but his eyes were on Tsia. She caught his gaze and narrowed her eyes into slits. Nitpicker pulled herself through the water. "Striker, you and Bowdie head for the main hub. Take the freepicks with you. They can get you inside, show you where the gear is. Get the weapons—anything you can find—then meet us near the landing pad." She closed her eyes and thought out the configuration of the huts. "Third hut, closest to the pad; SE doorway."

Bowdie and Striker nodded. Tsia was first up the lift, and the water ran off her like a fountain for the first four meters she rose. The moment her head was even with the rim of the pit, she stopped the controls, looked from side to side with both eyes and gate, then moved up to leap to the deck in a cat-like crouch. Below her, Wren, then Nitpicker rose. Bowdie was next, and his bowed legs made dark curves around the center pipe of the lift, while his long feet stuck out like flat-bottom boats.

One by one, as silent as the hissing rain, they moved to the lip of the pit. They crouched on the rim till they were all up top. Then Bowdie, Striker, and the three freepicks sprinted for the hub. Bowdie and Laz shortened their stride for the others to keep up. Striker, limping and paling with every step, forced herself to run. Wren and the rest took off for the landing pad.

They had gotten twenty meters when Tsia veered off.

"Where are you going?" Nitpicker snapped.

"My flexor—" She could see the blued hilt lying in a shadow against the wall of the main hut. It had been flung away when she had fallen earlier, and she had not seen it before when she ran.

"Doetzier, go with her."

Tsia had not waited for him. She felt the man's agreement almost before Nitpicker finished speaking. In her head, Ruka's snarl was one of approval at the mental sense of the weapon, and Tsia wondered if the cub somehow thought that the flexor translated as a sort of human claw. Silently running, her feet like cat paws on the tarmac, she made straight for it, stooped without stopping to pick it up, and sprinted back to the group. Doetzier ran easily beside her. His biofield still had that wary,

watching feel, but Tsia understood it now. Anyone who trans-
ported biochips must be on edge half his life.

Doetzier sprinted beside Tsia. His longer legs forced her to
take one and a half steps to his every one. "Can you feel the
chips?" he asked as they rounded the edge of the hut and
caught sight of Nitpicker and Wren.

"No." She slid the flexor into her harness straps.

"Stretch your gate."

Tsia stumbled as her foot came down on a ragged tarmac
seam, regained her balance, and snarled. "I'm doing the best I
can."

"If you can't feel for the chips, try to feel for Kurvan—"

"I *am*—"

A minute later, they caught up near the third hut along the
landing pad, where they lined up along the wall, careful not to
touch the sides with their bodies or clothes. There was a solid
door, not a filter door, around the corner. Tsia, then Wren,
moved to it. Tsia pulled the flexor from her harness and flicked
it into a narrow, spikelike sword. They went in quickly, but the
maintenance hut was empty of humans. Two small corers, flexible piping, shelves of thrust modulators and regulators and
pumps . . .

"Clear," Tsia murmured.

Wren gestured, and Doetzier and Nitpicker slunk in. They
closed the door and moved to the windows. From there, they
had a clear view of the skimmers on the far side of the tarmac.
A single figure moved beneath the largest ship, loading gear
into a bay.

"Decker?" Nitpicker murmured.

Tsia nodded. Her hand rose unconsciously to the burned-
through hole in her blunter. She could not mistake the movement of the man who had fired that laze.

"So Kurvan and the others—at least ten, maybe twelve—are
somewhere in the hub." Nitpicker's voice was thoughtful.
"What about the chips?"

"I can't tell from here."

"Can you handle Decker?"

Tsia's eyes glinted.

"We want him alive," Doetzier said sharply.

She cast him a cold look. "I wouldn't have it otherwise."

Nitpicker chewed her lip. "Can you link us through your ghost line to the node?"

"I don't know . . . It's thin." It would take almost nothing to break it now. A thread of bare action without the trappings of the sensor net to complete it and make it real . . . That was a traceline that anyone could look at and log as unreal. Once flagged as a ghost line, it was useless except on a dreamer channel.

"Try it. It could be twenty minutes before Bowdie and Striker get back to us, and we can't move without weapons. Wren, help me scrounge something up out of this place. I want that transport grounded." She glanced at Tsia soberly. Then she reached across and touched her first two fingers, first to her own sternum, then to Tsia's. *"Kai-al nyeka,"* she said in a low voice, using the old tongue of the mercs: firedancer; one who fights with grace.

Tsia looked up into Nitpicker's black irises. The pressure of those fingers was light, but it seemed to press inside her chest and touch her heartbeat.

"You've given me *derori ka'eo*—the freedom victory. And—" Nitpicker took a breath. *"Ma'ke ka'eo*—the death victory." Slowly, deliberately, she said, *"Je paka'ka chi."*

Tsia stared deep into her eyes. She stretched her biogate and felt the steady coolness of Nitpicker's field. Slowly, she inclined her head. For an instant, the two fields seemed to merge, then split through her biogate, and Nitpicker moved away.

Doetzier glanced at Tsia's face. "That was hard for her," he murmured.

Tsia stared after the other woman. "I know it."

He studied the landing pad carefully, watching the rain sheet across and the rivers run off in gray stretches. "How did you know?" he asked quietly.

She looked at him. "About the biochips?"

He nodded.

"My biogate. They stood out oddly from your field."

He nodded again, slowly.

"Didn't you know they would?" she asked.

"I didn't think you had the resolution to distinguish them."

"I distinguished them right away; I just didn't recognize them for what they were. Without the biocodes etched in, they were open. They felt like bacteria in your body. Floating. I felt Bowdie's chips the same way, though much more faintly."

"Jewel-like speckles in a black background?"

She looked at him in surprise.

"I've worked with other guides before you."

"Nitpicker says a guide can feel a bacterium at thirty paces. Why didn't you think I would? Was it what I said back on the platform about my resolution?"

Doetzier looked at her for a moment. His words were soft. "Your past is not that of a normal guide, is it, Feather-*nyeka*?"

There was something in his tone of voice . . . Tsia's guts tightened, and her eyes narrowed unconsciously. "What do you mean, Doetzier?"

"There are things you should understand about your gate that you don't; and there are other things you've taught yourself that the guide guild has never known. Your past is different from that of other guides."

She watched him like a songbird does an encroaching snake, unaware that her lips were curled back from her teeth. An image rose in her head: the memory of a body whose throat was torn by Tsia's hands. White hair and violet eyes, blank and staring in flaccid horror. Her past. Her crime.

Doetzier watched the expressions haunt her eyes. He said softly, "What would you do to be free of the past?"

"Free?" Of the fear? she echoed unconsciously.

"You've been running for years—for a decade, Tsia-*nyeka*. Didn't you realize that, in your flight from what you feared, you became that which you most hated?"

She stared at him, unable to guess what he meant.

"A *victim*." He answered for her.

"You don't know that, Doetzier. You don't know what I am."

"I know you, Feather-guide. As well as I know my own sister."

Her throat tightened at the term, but her eyes glinted. "Then tell me *my* name, if you know it."

For an instant, something like compassion flickered in his gaze. But his words were like bullets of ice. "You are the rogue gate, Tsia Matsallen. The illegal guide of the Ciordani guild."

She stared at him as if she stared at a corpse, long-dead, that rose up to touch her face. Her throat seemed to close; her breath cut off. The chill began in the bones of her toes and neck at the same time.

"Daughter of the guides Bayzon Matsallen and Ellyn Jadietz," he went on. "Granddaughter of the guide and First Dropper Caitriona. Descendant of the Sirian guide Nordon Kadya. Of Niamh, of Jacob, of Ciaran—"

"Enough." Wren's voice stilled them both as he stepped between Tsia and the other man.

Tsia did not move. Her eyes, like those of Ruka's, stared at Doetzier as if she waited for his words to burn through her chest like a laze. "You're the Shield." Her voice was barely a whisper.

"Yes."

"Here for me?"

"No."

"For the biochips?"

He nodded.

"So you're customs, too."

"Yes." His voice was flat, but his eyes watched her closely, as if he were judging her responses to his words. "I know about your sister."

She was silent for a moment. "And now you know about me. My gate. The cats." A wall inside her seemed to break. Its bricks were fear, and its mortar anticipation. He knew her past; he knew about her murder. And the mercs, who had protected her, could no longer do that. The scent of the man was harsh in her nose. Wren's hand flashed out to steady her.

Nitpicker's voice cut across Doetzier's expression. "Her link," the woman said quietly, as she moved back into the doorway, "is clear and fully licensed."

Doetzier did not bother to look at the pilot; his gaze was locked on Tsia. "Her link," he said, "was stolen from the art guild. She killed an artist to take it." His eyes flicked to Wren's cold face. "You're not surprised."

Wren shrugged.

"You knew?"

"It didn't matter to me." His statement, quiet as it was, was almost a challenge to the Shield.

"And you?" Doetzier turned to Nitpicker.

"Why should I care for her past?" the pilot returned coldly. "She's been true to her guild. To my guild. I owe her *derori ka'eo. Ma'ke ka'eo.*" The debt of honor between friends. She met his eyes steadily. "As do you," she added softly.

His eyes narrowed. "I acknowledge no such debt."

Tsia's eyes glinted. "Then what is it now that you want?"

"What is it that you need?" he returned softly.

"Are we bargaining now for something?" Inside her head, the cat feet crawled. "You want me to say that I need my biogate?" Her voice almost shook with the quietness of the fury that seemed to swamp her. "You could order a wipe through the node in an instant, and when you were done destroying my gate and erasing my self, I wouldn't even know I'd been a guide."

"There's always something left," he said softly. "Even after a thorough wipe. Have you looked in Striker's eyes? Do you want to be the same? Wondering where you came from? What crime had stripped away your person? Questioning with every reaction you had whether it was an old, unsurfaced habit or some new, conscious desire that pushed your emotions and thoughts? How often do you think she asks herself if she's descended from the lifers herself? One image from me to the node, and you would be just like that. But worse than a ghost; worse than a wipe—you'd be a naught forever."

Tsia's jaw tightened. "If you have the authority, then you also have the authority to negotiate a link."

For a moment, he did not answer. "A clear link," he said slowly. "Protected status. What would you give in return?"

Tsia's lips thinned. "No giving here, Doetzier." Her voice

was almost a snarl. "No half bargains or promises with me. A contract, legal and verified—that's what I want from you."

"On what terms?"

"I get the biochips back. You give me a link."

"Those biochips represent a threat to your world, not just to yourself or your gate."

"A link," she repeated softly. "That's my price."

"Not your sister?"

Tsia's throat tightened. "I don't think my sister really exists." Her voice was so low, he almost didn't hear it. "She's gone from me. Giving up myself for her would not bring her back. It would only let her run further and destroy me with her running. I want a link, Doetzier."

"You're a guide," he returned flatly. "You can't bargain for a link. It's not in your nature to allow anyone—even your sister—to destroy your world through the use of the biochips."

She grinned, but the expression stretched her lips like a snarl. "The zeks are your responsibility, and your workload is nothing to me. I want contract, Doetzier."

"I want the biochips back."

"In exchange for a protected link."

"If you testify at the trial for the blackjacks we take in," he shot back.

She hesitated.

"Afraid to take a chance?"

"On what?"

"On yourself," he said deliberately. "Or have you lived so long within your fear that you've forgotten what it's like to be free?"

Her lips thinned and curled back from her teeth. "Maybe," she returned. "Perhaps it is only fear which moves me."

"No." His voice was flat and he studied her for a long moment. "Fear lies on you like a blanket, but it isn't a fear for yourself that you feel. It's the fear of what you'll find in your sister when you face her over the chips. It's the fear that you'll someday look in the mirror and see your sister's victim eyes staring back at you." He paused. "She'll have to stand trial," he added softly. "Like all the other blackjack."

Tsia forced her lips to move. "And me?"

"You were a rogue gate before, Tsia-*nyeka*, and you're a rogue gate now. But I see no evil in you. The guilt you carry has never been justified away. You know what you did, and you know why you did it." He paused, and his eyes flickered with something akin to compassion. "And I might have done it myself."

She stared at him, her hands still clenched. "A link, Doetzier."

Slowly, he nodded. "It is done."

23

Like a waterfall that tumbled through her brain, the words came, over and over: . . . a legitimate link a legitimate link . . . Her guts were still tight, clenched like a fist. Her lips were still pressed together, as if she had to hold in the exultant snarl that threatened to burst free of her throat.

Doetzier moved up to the window and eyed the landing pad carefully. "Have you gotten through on the node to link us back up?"

"No." She shook her head. "And my ghost line is still so thin that it could break at any moment. I did locate our ID dots—up skyside, in our skimmer. To the node, we don't appear to have left orbit at all. Scannet never registered our landing, let alone our crash. Kurvan did as tight a job as any three nodies put together: our ID dots are so buried in his webs that even if I had twenty hours instead of twenty minutes, I doubt that I'd get through."

She could feel Ruka to her right, distant and gliding through the forest as he approached the ship from the south. The landing pad, still gray and rippling with the water that ran across its surface, looked like a long lake, on which a silver cricket sat. The three huts on the one side and the two huts on the other were like guardians of a gate. The main hut—the hub—was behind the structure where Tsia and the other mercs waited. Decker left the ship and walked toward one of the far huts, disappearing inside. A moment later, the last ghost line in Tsia's head went blank.

"The jam on the node," she murmured to Doetzier. "It just went on full. I lost my ghost line."

He shrugged. "If we can't use it, neither can they. We're all on manual coms."

"But if they jammed it, they're getting ready to lift."

"I know. We can't wait any longer to move on the transport."

Tsia glanced toward Nitpicker. "Van'ei," she called softly.

"I heard," the pilot responded. "Wren, help me with this stuff."

Wren took some gear from her hands and distributed it in the pockets of his blunter. The pilot pulled at her blunter, wincing at the burn on her shoulder. With a muttered curse, she moved to the doorway. "Where's Decker?"

"Middle hut," Tsia returned. "Far side of the complex. Just went in."

"Anyone with him?"

"No one." She did not say that it was not her own eyes and ears which told her that, but Ruka's senses instead.

Nitpicker nodded. "Tsia, you have the flexor: keep Decker off our backs and in case he's got a com, make sure he doesn't see us. Wren, Doetzier, you're with me. Once we're done at the ship, we'll head for the main hub."

"You don't think the chips are in the ship?" Tsia asked.

"Kurvan wouldn't allow them out of his sight," the pilot returned shortly. "Nor would he put them on board before he himself is ready to go. If he's not at the ship, he'll be at the hub, and we can catch him there before he leaves."

Tsia nodded and eyed the hut where Decker had disappeared. Her mind snarled through her gate, and Ruka's ready answer was quick. When she stepped out in the shelter of the eaves, the other mercs stepped out with her. Doetzier touched her arm, and she looked at him with glinting eyes. He pressed something cold and flat into her hand. She looked down at his bioshield, then up again with a frown.

He nodded. "Yours is fried."

"But you—without this . . ."

"I'm aware of the risks."

She nodded shortly, then tucked it in her lower blunter pocket. With the hole as big as her hand burned all the way through in the center, the jacket closed only at the bottom and hung open across her chest. The shield should have been placed over her heart cavity, but the pouches there were crisped. She touched the shield again and glanced at Doetzier. His biofield was still wary, but there was something else there now. A confidence. An eagerness that verged on certainty.

"I will get them back," she said quietly.

"I believe you." He started to turn away.

"Doetzier—" she began.

He half turned back. He regarded her for a moment as if he was watching her from a distance. "My name," he said softly, "is Ghoboza. Fleming Leshe Ghobhoza Mikhail Avyani Jantzanu Doetzier."

Tsia stared at him for a moment. Then she nodded slowly and turned away to feel for Decker's presence.

Decker was still far enough away that she could not sense him herself, but Ruka's ears listened to his cursing inside the freepick hut. Warily, she eyed the deck. Then, slowly, lithely, she ran. She no longer felt her bruises; she paid no attention to exhaustion. Golden eyes gleamed from the forest, and something else— black eyes? colored slits in the gloom?—gleamed from inside her mind. She tried to reach the strange cat in her gate, to feel its energy through her biolink, but that other feline was cold and irritated and foreign to her mind.

She picked up speed till she sprinted. She could hear the others behind her, skidding through the puddles in her steps. When they reached the transport ship, all four automatically dropped into the shadows of the landing legs. For a moment, Tsia poised on the balls of her feet, listening through her gate. Ahead, still in the hut . . . She motioned an all-clear, and the mercs opened two of the maintenance bays.

She stayed at the nose of the skimmer, one hand on the craft and the other out to the rain, her eyes on the freepick hut. Decker—still ahead. Still unaware of her presence.

Behind her, the other mercs worked quickly. One minute passed. Then two. The door from the hut opened. Decker had his hood up and his head down in the rain, and Tsia hissed at the mercs to warn them. Silently, they closed the bays and pressed themselves to the ship. Tsia began to run toward the zek, sprinting silently as a cat. She could feel him now—his energy, cold as Wren's, but careless. Ruka's nostrils flared, and she tasted that other cat in her gate. Human scent and packing crates. And something else . . .

She drew her flexor as she veered toward the gap between huts, rather than running straight at him. Decker, upwind with his head bowed, did not see her until she came almost even with his feet. Then he caught sight of her in the corner of his eye. Startled, he let out a cry, then jumped into a run after her. He drew his laze, and the hot point of the beam sparked in the air. He did not try to fire; he was still too far away, but Tsia could hear the rain sputtering as it struck the tip of the weapon and exploded in tiny, white-sizzling balls.

She dodged the corner of the last hut in the line, and her nostrils flared. Shaper scent—and upwind. Ruka crouched in the forest before her, and the cougar's scent mixed with mud and the sharp musk of the other beasts. Shapers . . . Neurotoxins and blood-breakers and the speed at which they worked . . . Tsia skidded to a stop and whirled to face the blackjack.

"Don't move." Decker halted before her. His voice, breathless from his sudden sprint, was harsh even in the wind. She started to shift subtly backward, but a beam from his laze sizzled toward her legs, only to bend into the tarmac at her feet. She jerked back, and he fired again, the beam cutting across her arm. The blunter sizzled, but the beam bent away like a curveball. She backed away another step. The forest spattered her with heavy water drops, and Decker followed her with menace.

"The bioshield," he hissed. "Take it out. Toss it here."

Tsia's lips curled up from her teeth, and she bared them in a silent snarl. Ruka's golden eyes followed Decker's movements as if it were the cougar who hunted the zek, not Tsia. *No,* she sent to the cub. *He's mine. Stay back.*

"The shield," he repeated. "Give it here, and I'll let you live."

She grinned, but the expression showed the fanged promise of a cat, not the humor of a human. "As long as I have the shield," she said, backing away another step, "your laze is worth less than its energy pack." She flicked her wrist so that the flexor snapped into a long thin, tapering point. She could feel Ruka behind her, slinking to the side. Decker had eyes for no one but her, and he could not see, with the wind-motion of the brush, the tawny movement of cougar.

"You think that shield will save you? You think you can hide in the woods?" He snapped his own flexor out of his belt.

Tsia stepped to the left and pressed back until her shoulders and hips felt the bending, wind-whipped brush. She could smell the water on the leaves. Her nostrils were clogged with the odors of mud, the broken twigs, the sharp musk scent of the shapers . . . Decker watched her slip between the shrubs; he moved like a snake to follow. Tsia had opened her gate, and her mind was clouded with the sounds from Ruka's ears and the scent of the shapers to her left. A tentacled hunger seemed to creep into her mind; the sense of danger grew. Then Decker closed in a rush.

Their flexors met with jarring force. Tsia's weapon snapped into a hook; Decker's whipped wickedly back. At the same time, the beam from his laze curled before her face and burned the air she breathed. She staggered instinctively, and he flashed forward to strike at her chest. The wind caught his clothes and whipped them in grotesque shapes; she flicked her flexor into a thin blade and stabbed at the core of his energy.

Her blade passed between his arm and side. He overreached and drove his blade across her shoulder, then tried to hook it back. Instantly, she slammed her elbow in his gut and snapped her weapon to a curved blade, but the blackjack jerked his own hilt down. Something smashed into her collarbone. She gasped at the brutal blow. Something tawny flashed in her eyes. Decker cried out. Tsia leaped toward the musk scent.

Ruka—she screamed in her gate. *Stay away!*

The cougar did not listen. His claws raked the blackjack's

back, and one paw reached around to Decker's face and hooked into the man's nose, jerking back his head as if the zek were an elk. With a harsh scream, Decker flipped the beam of his laze over his shoulder. There was a flash of light, the bitter burn of hair and flesh.

Pain seared Tsia's mind through the gate. A burning, crushing fire flared along nerves that she reflected. She could not see through the flood of catspeak and claws inside her skull, and only Ruka's yowl echoed in her ears. There was something in her hand—the blackjack's arm, his flesh squeezed between her fingers. His flexor was gone; his laze beamed across her chest and curved away like a string before a fan. She leaned down as if in a dream, and Decker's face twisted in slow motion. She grabbed soft, fatty, tentacled flesh and yanked it up as if tearing a plant from the soil. Decker's laze was an infinite line of light, flaring out in a long, slow circle, moving toward her chest. Her own arm moved like honey, while the shaper's scent crawled into her nose like lice. Something whipped in lethargic curves around the palm of her hand. The tentacles touched and began to close. Venom glands compressed. The blue-white laze arced in a languid line that her eyes seemed to follow blindly. She felt, more than saw, the shaper's fangs open; the fluid sac scents were sharp in her nose. The toxins were an acrid odor, the saliva a yellow-white. Long teeth seemed to grow in size. Her arm released in a lingering snap. Venomous fangs bit down. On Decker's chin. And the scream that, muffled by the fleshy body, was torn from his throat with his breath hung in the air for what seemed like an hour while Tsia continued, in that eternally slow-motion leap, to jump the shaper's den with the rest of her awkward momentum.

The chameleon clung to Decker's face for seconds before dropping back into the brush. The laze fell to the mud, where its point sizzled and popped. Decker clutched at his chin and stared at Tsia, but his jaw was already tingling, and his lips were going numb. He staggered back, then turned and ran toward the huts.

Tsia did not follow. Her mind was filled with Ruka's pain,

and she screamed at the cougar through her gate. *Stand still. Let me find you!*

She twisted in the brush, searching for the cat with both her mind and her eyes. She couldn't see him, but she felt him close by, and she staggered in his direction. When she found him, she fell to her knees and took his paw in her hand. He jerked instinctively back. She snapped at him through her gate, and with a snarl, he allowed her to hold it. "Ah, Daya . . ." She searched her harness for her medkit before cursing as she remembered she'd lost it before.

Come, she told him. *We'll find something at the huts.*

He yowled, a low, hair-raising sound, and she could only send him a blanket of will to smother it through the gate. Then, painfully, with both of them limping, they eased out to the edge of the forest.

Tsia's mind, half-blinded by Ruka, was locked in a single thought: the biochips—where were they? She eased across the edge of the tarmac like the cat who slunk beside her. Their nostrils wrinkling, their shoulders hunched, they crept to the nearest hut and slipped inside. Tsia's hands shook as she broke open the medkit on the wall and tore it apart to find the salves and skin patches. Manually, she loaded feline biocodes—old codes from old memories—into the medscanner. It took time—minutes—for the scanner to shift the chemical structure of the salve; it took three times as long to shift the molecular build of the graft. And then it took her will to convince Ruka to let her dissolve his fur from around the burn and clean the area for treatment.

She tried to feel for a sense of time, but couldn't seem to focus. Not until the salve began to dull the cub's pain did her mind begin to clear.

She didn't bother to clean up the medkit mess. She just thrust the scattered parts of the kit into a clumsy pile and followed Ruka back out, snapping at him not to worry at the graft that itched and crawled on his flesh. Her hand throbbed with the dulled pain he sent through the gate. But it was half as much as it had been; and in days, if he didn't tear it off first, the graft would fall off by itself. He'd have only a scar to speak of the burn.

The heat in her hand seemed to focus her thoughts as she rounded a hut and caught sight of the landing pad. Points of heat, points of light—so faint in her gate—were they closer now than before?

She could see all three skimmers, silent and waiting, still standing on the deck. There was no movement beneath the largest ship; the mercs, if they had not been caught, must have finished and returned to the hub. Relief tightened her guts like a fist. Her hand trembled against her forehead. The chips were still here—and her sister also. Neither could leave the freepick stake until the Shields arrived. Shjams could not abandon her again. As for the zeks . . .

Her mind began to churn again, but slowly. How many blackjack were at the hub, hidden within the warren? And where could she find her sister among those jacks? Her muscles trembled, and it was not chill, but an exhaustion she could not give in to. Her hands clenched spasmodically on her flexor as she wiped it along her side.

The points of light—she could almost feel them. Closer—they had to be closer than the hub.

How much time had passed? She moved along the huts until she found Decker on the gray-washed tarmac, at the door to one of the storerooms. His outstretched hand, the bent body . . . He lay against the door as if to open it when he lost the use of his hands. She passed him, ignoring his strangled breathing and the swelling of his skin.

She ran across the landing pad. Her eyes were slitted, not from rain, but from Ruka, and she didn't notice the way she clung to one hand as she ran. Behind her, the cougar limped across like a shadow. The pain that blinded him pushed him away, but the biogate pulled like a leash.

Fifteen seconds, and she was at the skimmer hatch. The points of light—her eagerness grew, hot, as if she sucked it through her gate. Three, four more seconds, and the hatch slid open.

And Kurvan turned around.

Tsia froze. The narrowing of Kurvan's eyes, the tightening of his jaw—those were the only reactions that showed the zek's surprise. His smile was slow and beatific. Some part of her brain wondered how wide that smile would be if he knew that Decker lay out on the tarmac with the fang marks of a shaper deep in his face. Her lips moved, but nothing came out.

"I should have known immediately," he said softly. "That you were still alive."

Her hand tightened its grip on the flexor. He eyed her with an almost satisfied expression, and she knew, suddenly, that he wanted to kill her as much as she wanted his death.

"How could you know?" she managed.

Carefully, he moved toward the hatch. "When an ID dot goes inactive, the node lines it carries are placed on hold. But when an ID dot goes dead, the effects ripple out through the node. Ghosts, schedules, contracts . . . Little plans and appointments—they all wink out. It's like a nearly invisible wave that strips you out of the node. I forgot that. I was so sure that you were drowned in the pit that I did not check to see."

He stepped closer, and she could see the pulse beat in his throat. "The skimmer crash—how did you fix it?"

"Mixed signals from the node, plus a small projector that overwhelmed the links of the nav sensors and power couplings. I'd set up the node webs months ago for a crash sequence, but I couldn't install the overload projector until we landed on the platform—projector power supplies only last a few hours."

"And the deke in Wren's medkit—you put it in his pack when you were checking the gear on the platform."

He smiled. A wash of rain swept past. He edged closer.

Tsia felt his focus grow. "The fall on the bridge—you could have died yourself. Why did you risk it?"

"You think you're the only one with antigrav on your harness?"

Her lips tightened. "And Wren's pack—the loss of his antigrav?"

"A remote trigger. Installed at the marine station while you were playing hero to that Landing Pact cub."

"Why?" she almost snarled. "Ayara's Eyes, Kurvan, why bother with accidents at all? Why didn't you wait and kill us here at the stake as you planned to do with those of us who are left?"

"Because brute force always attracts more attention. My job was just to slow down the team. Eliminate as many of you as possible. Get the shooters away with Jandon so we had a better chance of taking over here."

"Jandon could have come back. We could have called him to help us."

"His ship would have fried its own controls the first time he tried to land." He shifted closer again. "You just don't get it, do you? We've had our people in place for months, working as grunts in the tubes, hiding gear in rock pockets where the freepicks would never look. For the last two weeks, our buyer has been sitting up at the hammers, waiting for a signal that we had the chips and were ready to move out of this system."

"The Ixia . . ."

He nodded.

"But if you were only to slow us down . . . Daya," she breathed. "You didn't know about the chips at all, did you? You couldn't have—not if you still went after Doetzier."

He glanced behind her, but Ruka did not growl, and she could not tear her eyes from Kurvan's face. "We knew about the dummy chips. We knew the Shields were setting up a sting." He shrugged at her expression. "We've got credit and other . . . incentives to encourage people to help us. But we didn't know about the real chips till dawn."

"Dawn . . ."

He watched her closely as he said, "I received a coded message from Decker on the beacon this morning—you didn't even notice. He'd heard from our mother ship. One of our contacts had finally traced a set of webs he'd been working on for weeks. And what he found was a programmer with a high tech rating, assigned to the same team that I was supposed to slow down."

"Bowdie . . ."

"His contract with you was only a ghost. He was to stay

only a day—not six weeks—till the chips were set with their codes. The chips were here—with him the whole time. Under my nose like my chin." He shrugged. "I wouldn't have bothered trying to kill anyone had I known that someone was already carrying the real chips. I would have waited, as you say, till we reached the stake and I had backup to take you out. As it was, my job was to thin down the team so we could replace some of you with more of us. Make the job go smoother when the real chips came in."

"And Tucker?"

Kurvan's hand moved casually to the butt of his laze. "He was careless. I locked the lift and let the wind and the bloom do my work for me. If he was the Shield, better for me to have him out of the way. If he was one of you, he was just one less merc to work on."

The pulse pounded in her bruised throat. "I should have known right from the start that it was you."

He smiled again, slowly. "How so?"

"You said, on the platform, that I'd be better at the canyon scans than you. You wanted me off this team. And then you said that you weren't half as good at trees and other biologicals as I. I'm a guide, Kurvan, but you've been working biological traces for over twenty years—twice as long as I. It was a stupid thing to say."

"And now your knowledge is too late to make any difference."

Slowly, as if he were an animal and she was trying not to provoke him, she backed away and unhooked the straps of her flexor.

The blackjack noted the brown and green handle and smiled a slow expression. "That's no good," he said softly. "It's broken. Its biochips are fried."

She tightened her grip on its hilt. "How do you know?"

He followed like a snake. "Because I'm the one who broke it. When I fell on Doetzier. Remember? I broke it like I snapped his arm. And do you know? I'm going to enjoy crushing you the same way I broke your sister."

Her jaw tightened. "I'm stronger than she was."

"I don't doubt it. She was easy. Soft. Like butter in a frying pan."

"She was a person," she snapped.

"She was a victim, not a human being. She had no self-worth at all."

He was pushing her deliberately, but her anger iced her heartbeat as if her blood had not the energy to compare to what she felt. "Self-worth can be built or destroyed—"

"You think *I* am her destroyer? She put herself in my power." He stepped forward again, and Tsia could feel the confidence in his field. "Oh, I made a few suggestions," he said. "Took an interest in her career, told her how smart she was. Showered her for a year with what she thought of as love. But in the end, I merely took her for what she had to give."

"Daya," she breathed. "And you admit it."

"Why not?"

She stared at him.

He nodded as if surprised at her reaction. "I am conscious of what I do, Feather-guide. Your sister—she's useful to me, so I use her."

"But you're destroying her. If you loved her—"

"Love?" Kurvan snorted. "Love is a set of actions that gives one power over another. Just because I bind her or crush her the same time as I use her—that does not negate her skills. A blackjack like me can work for a decade just to get a single hook into a customs inspector. Here, I have a dozen hooks in her mind. I've strung her up like a puppet, and she can do nothing but obey."

"And when you've torn all the value out of her?"

He shrugged. "Then I get another victim to replace her pathetic life. There's always been more power in destruction than creation. It's fast. It's profitable. And it's far more exciting than living within some pathetic set of morals. It's *power*, Tsia-guide. It's control. And it's mine."

"You're wrong, Kurvan. There is power in destruction only as long as you're actively annihilating your goal. When you stop acting—stop destroying—you have nothing left. But when you create, there's always something left over, something to re-

flect your work, whether or not you stop. That's the true power
of life."

Kurvan drew his flexor in a long, slow motion. "There
speaks the idealist." He flicked the bar into a diamond-shaped
blade and tested its edge on his thumb. He shrugged, but he
was now at the edge of the hatch. "Blame me for your sister
if you dare. She chose to be a willing victim."

"And I choose to be none at all."

She flicked her wrist, and her flexor spun out like a lance.
The instant of shock on Kurvan's face did not keep him from
moving. The lance caught in his blunter, not his chest, and he
twisted into a dive as he brought up the point of his laze. Instantly, Tsia snapped her flex blade into a hook and jerked hard.
Kurvan was yanked forward, down onto his knees. He fell
through the hatch like a diver. But the point of his laze flared
out in an arc, and Tsia ducked like a flash from the light.

She changed her grip, and the flexor became a thin bar,
snapping itself out of his jacket. He threw himself to the side.
The laze flashed across her chest, bending as it encountered the
shield's projection, and Kurvan cursed. He threw the laze
away. Viciously, Tsia stabbed forward. But she had forgotten
that her boots were not cat feet. She slipped.

Steel fingers grabbed her by the jacket; thick hands twisted
the blunter collar tightly around her throat. With a single motion, Kurvan jerked her off her feet and flung her brutally in a
short, sharp arc against the ship. Her shoulders hit with shocking force. Her head cracked to one side of the landing leg.
Stunned, she lay without moving.

The pain of the fall seeped out of her bones. She tried to
move her arm, and Ruka snarled violently in her gate. A tawny
shadow flashed. Kurvan staggered. Then he screamed and fell
in a tangle of flailing limbs. The clawing, silent demon on his
back tore at his flesh like hate.

He screamed again. Tsia pushed herself to her hands and
knees. Her mind was blind with pain and fury, and her fingers
clawed at the tarmac as Ruka's paws tore flesh. Like a ragged
work whistle that does not stop for breath, Kurvan's screams

went on and on until Tsia realized that it was no longer his voice that broke her ears, but his rasping, dying breath.

The rain washed away his whimpers till his body was silent and still. Tsia's mind was still blurred by the pain that burned in the cougar's paw, and she could only crouch and stare at the huddled form on the ground. Finally, the rain blasted her in the face and forced her eyes to see. There was a keening sound in her ears, and the whimpering from her throat clogged her hearing in a duet of pain. Ruka's paw—burning still with nerves raw from the laze . . .

Silently, the cougar crawled from beneath the ship and huddled beside the landing leg. The bursts of pain that shot through Tsia's left hand with his motion made her clench her other fist. She snarled in her own silence, trapped between her mind and his while he licked the blood on his paws. Rain, mud, bile, blood; ash and flesh and fire . . . The rhythm of the odors was a morbid song, and Tsia gagged. She tried to hear the cleansing sounds of the rain that hit the tarmac. There was no life field in his body. No sense of stirring—of energy held in check. She felt nothing—nothing at all. Her breath began to speed up, and her heart pounded slowly and painfully in her chest. She felt nothing. Nothing but those points of light— some brighter, some dim—and somewhere close nearby.

She stared down at the blackjack. Breathing harshly, she forced herself to look, and did not flinch at the bloodied water that ran in thin runnels past his body. She looked up at Ruka. Their eyes met. Her head tilted, and she felt the rain, cold against her skin. The shivers that shook her now were neither chill nor exhaustion, but emptiness. There was nothing left of Kurvan. His body was just inanimate flesh. His blood no more than a running stain on the stone. Her eyes could register his shape, and it meant nothing to her mind.

He's stronger than you. Shjams's voice echoed in her head.

Tsia stared at Kurvan's body with lips pressed so tightly together that the muscles of her face were taut. "He's a user," she said harshly. "Nothing more." And as she watched his blood wash away to the soil with the rain, she realized his death gave back to the earth part of what he had taken: Blood. Life.

Fury rose in her guts. Her stomach tightened. "No final gesture," she whispered violently. "No absolution for the things that you have done."

Deliberately, she ducked and crawled to Kurvan's body. With trembling hands, she rolled him over. She searched him, yanking open his blunter, groping in his pockets, ignoring the slashes and tears in his clothes, the blood and open muscle tissue she had to touch. And there, inside the lower pocket of the blunter, she found one of the small, flat cases.

She opened it and stared at the biochips within. Then she sat back on her heels and looked up at the underside of the skimmer.

There were two more things she had to do.

She jammed the flat case into her lower blunter pocket, opposite Doetzier's bioshield. Then, clumsily, she turned Kurvan again. His boots hooked together so that his legs twisted, and she could only get him halfway over, but it was enough. She stripped his laze away. Violently, she threw it across the deck, then jerked a thin, black tube from his harness.

Deliberately, she flicked the tube to its active position and let the acrid scent of the deke reach her nose. For a moment, she held it like a flexor. Then she pressed the hisser's trigger. Like a twisted spirit in the rain, the spray shot out and settled on Kurvan's body. Like a fire, the smoke curled away. His clothes seemed to disintegrate; his flesh blackened and shriveled. And his face dissolved so that, for an instant, only his bones spoke of his presence before they too pocked and powdered and washed away with the rain.

She triggered the hisser off. For a moment, she just stood there. Then she backed away until her spine struck the side of the skimmer. Blindly, her hands wiped at the rain on her face. White hands in the water ... Tucker's hands in the sea ... And here, the black stain of them on the tarmac, washing away in the rain. The choked noise that came from her throat was harsh and animal, and the wind did not soften the sound.

The rain still slanted across the tarmac, and the flat streams of gray washed the landing pad like a delta. Thin cataracts fell from the skimmer's sides; thick clouds still rushed overhead. Tsia tilted her head back so that the rain beat on her face. It was clean of the scent of the hisser; bare of the odor of Kurvan's blood. She filled her lungs with wet air, then slid the tube on her harness.

Ruka growled. The scent of the hunter cut across the snarled paths of her mind. She crouched down and touched the cougar on his face, and opened her gate wide so that she could take the pain from his paw. The burn swept in and engulfed her, but she did not flinch away. She took it in like the touch of the r-con and pushed her mind beyond it.

Then she turned and moved to the hatch of the skimmer and levered herself inside. Ruka did not jump after her, but waited under the ship in the shadow of the landing leg while she paced the cabin above. With her arms outstretched, she looked like a sleepwalker in the ship. As if that physical motion somehow increased the sensitivity of her biogate, she let her hands trace the walls and cubbyholes.

The pilot's area . . . The main or aft cabin . . . The storage boxes in back? She could feel them close—those other energy points—like stars in a moonless night. But where? Her fingers thrust clothing and blunters aside and tore open panels, only to thrust them closed again. Urgency grew with every second so that she whirled in the cabin and ran toward the rear. What shielding would be thick enough to conceal those points of light? Kurvan had said that, with the right scan equipment, it would be easy to find the chips. Fifty thousand credits and Daya knew how much work in those bait chips, but Doetzier had simply had them sealed within his harness.

Tsia halted. She turned back to the clothing. Six sets of weather cloth; six pairs of boots. Four blunters, fully equipped with bioshields in their pockets. Three e-suits—one that could not belong to a human. Scanners and coms and hand units for freepick tasks . . . And four harnesses. She grabbed the straps and tore the seals apart. E-wraps, slimchims, medkits, enbees . . . Nothing like that second flattened case. But the points of light were almost under her fingers. She could feel them as close as her own feet. There was no pulse in their presence, but each point was like a tiny piece of fire that touched her through her gate.

Hurry, Ruka snarled. He projected the scent of humans strongly through the gate.

I am, she snapped in return. She knew they would find her. There was no space on the landing pad that wasn't filled with human scent. She threw the harnesses aside and stood for a moment with her arms clenched around herself. The hard flatness of Doetzier's bioshield pressed against her bicep. Slowly, she became motionless. Why not? she thought, staring at the pile of clothes. What better place to hide a set of biochips than in the one thing that could not be burned?

It took only a moment to check her theory out. It took a moment more to open up her flexor and disable its controls, then those of the three scanners she had found. She called Ruka to the hatch and explained what she wanted. And then explained it again. Ruka didn't like it. She didn't blame him. She would not have liked it herself. But in the end, he agreed. And two minutes later, the cougar dropped from the skimmer with a heavy limp and slunk away in the rain.

24

༄ འ

Tsia was halfway out the hatch when her thigh pocket
brushed against her hand. The sharp edges of the safety cubes
within scraped against her wrist, and she froze. She had forgotten about the cubes. Dormant without a honeycomb, they had
not triggered the scans of the blackjack who had checked her
before, at the pit. She still had them, but if they searched
her again, coming out of the skimmer, with datacubes in her
pockets . . .

She opened her gate and felt the presence of other beings.
The hunter—it was coming, and even at its distance, it was
sharp and clear in her gate. The dull shadows of two humans
grew—much closer to the ship. She looked wildly around. She
had to get rid of the cubes. If they found the safeties on her
person, they'd search the ship for damage. If they found
Nitpicker's sabotage, they'd try the other ships too, and find
the broken honeycombs. And missing sensor boxes and torn-
out tubing . . .

There were access panels all over the ship, and Tsia did not
bother to climb all the way back in. Instead, she hung on the
lip of the hatch and jerked open the nearest bay. It was a configuration bay, and inside were amber, white, and blue honeycombs. All of them had empty slots. White-controls; those
would activate the moment the ship was powered up. Blue—
those were sensors, and the zeks would use those as they
lifted. But amber . . . The yellow shade denoted weapons.

Blackjack would not need those until they reached the skyside quarantine fields and had to run from the Shields.

Quickly, Tsia dropped the safeties in the slots. A second later, she snapped the panel shut. She almost lost her balance, and in her grab for a hold, caught her fingers in one of the harnesses, which came out of the hatch with her as she landed heavily on the deck.

The beam of the laze, which missed her arm, seared the harness in her hands and froze her like a breath in an ice storm. For a moment, nothing moved—not air, not rain, not time. Then, slowly, she turned around. Wicht had his laze pointed at her. Something burst in her head, and she snarled and leaped. The beam of light bent away between her arm and her side. Like a gravdiver, she tackled the zek and threw him to the ground. His head cracked back on the tarmac. In an instant, Tsia leaped to her feet. But she didn't run. She stood as still as if dead. It was not the tip of the second laze jammed into her gut that stopped her. It was not the sense of foreboding that swamped her like a lake. It was not the eager hunger that seemed to grow in her gate, as if that distant foreign scent was locked on her like a breaker.

It was Shjams.

Rain ran down the woman's face in pale, smooth runnels. Wind tore long strands from the braids of hair she now wore around her head. Like snakes or tiny whips, the loose hairs danced and dripped in a darting, moving frame. Tsia could not see beyond the shapes to the expression on her face. It was not until the woman spoke that she realized she sensed no emotion through her gate because there was none there to feel. Shjams's green, flat eyes were hard and still as stone.

Neither woman spoke. The cold seemed to crawl down Tsia's skin with every drop of rain. Ruka began to slink back toward the skimmer, and his musk, carried through the rain, mixed with the perfume of Shjams. Unseen, a mere shadow flickered through the rain . . . The cougar's paws were silent. The two scents of her sister warred in Tsia's nose. Her body, taut with muscles still poised to run, held its position on the pad. Ruka reached the ship behind her, and his hair began to bristle. Tsia quieted him harshly through the gate and dropped the melted harness to the ground.

Shjams stepped forward and stripped the flexor from Tsia's side. Tsia did not resist her. Shjams flicked her wrist, but the flexor did not respond, and she cursed and threw it away. The blued bar skittered under the ship.

Tsia's hand clutched her pocket. "I won't let you take them offplanet."

"It's not something you can prevent. Give them here."

"No."

"Goddammit, Tsia—"

"No, Shjams. Not this way."

"Then like this—" Like a flash, the woman struck Tsia across her head with the butt of her laze. Tsia tried to ride it, but it cracked on her cheekbone and she staggered, then fell slowly to her knees, one hand on the tarmac before her. Her eyes swam. She barely felt Shjams's hands searching her pocket.

Tsia pressed a fist against her cheekbone. She tasted blood on her lips. When her eyes cleared, she looked up. Shjams had the small, flat case in her hand. "Shjams—"

The woman moved away, examining the chips within. She made an inarticulate sound, then looked up to stare at Tsia with suddenly haunted eyes. "You idiot," she breathed. "You yaza-brained merc. These aren't the real chips. These are already programmed—the dummies—the bait chips the Shield was carrying." She snapped the case shut and didn't notice that she was clutching it so hard that her fingernails were slowly turning white. Her face set. "You've given up your life," she said, "not for me and not for your world, but for nothing more than bait."

Unsteadily, Tsia got to her feet. Her lips were curled against the pain, and her jaw was so tight that her teeth ached.

"Why did you come back?" the other woman whispered. "You got away. Why didn't you keep going?"

Tsia felt dizzy, and she took advantage of her unbalance to move forward awkwardly. Shjams took a step back. The point of the zek weapon glowed. Tsia looked up at her, and first one, then another drop of blood fell away from her chin, between her fingers, in a long, slanting arc to the ground. "I could not leave the chips," she returned flatly. "And I could not let you go."

Shjams stared at her for a moment. "You know what I have to do now."

Slowly Tsia nodded. Her eyes did not leave Shjams's face. Shjams stared at her. "I tell you I will kill you."

"You killed me six years ago when you cut yourself from my heart. You can hardly do worse than that now."

"I killed you? You're breathing. Your heart is beating."

"If that were all there was to life," Tsia said quietly, "then I'd leave you to blackjack as you wished. You're dead, Shjams. You've killed yourself, and torn your family with you. Please," she said softly, "come back to us."

"Don't move." Shjams's voice was harsh. Tsia ignored her and took a step forward. The laze flared like a bolt of lightning. The beam shot toward Tsia's heart and bent away as it hit the field of her shielding. The other woman cursed beneath her breath.

"I wonder," Tsia said quietly, watching her with a sad, remote expression, "if you would have fired as quickly, if you had not known I wore a bioshield in my blunter."

Shjams stepped forward and shoved the hot tip of the laser against Tsia's arm. Tsia refused to flinch. Beads of sweat formed on her neck and washed away in the rain.

"Shields only work at a distance," Shjams breathed. "Do you really want me to do this?"

"Is it something you need to do?"

They stared at each other, whipped by the rain, while the pointed tip melted through Tsia's blunter, then her shirt. It touched her skin, and Shjams knew the moment it did; the tightening of Tsia's eyes and the suddenly white cords of tendon were clearly visible in the gray-yellow light. Almost against her own volition, she withdrew the point a fraction. She gave a low laugh.

"All this time," Shjams said bitterly. "All these years, and you and I stand here like zombies. I tell you I have to kill you,

and still you say nothing. No questions. Not a curse. No pleading or pathetic rationale. You haven't changed, Tsia. You'd
never beg to save your life. You just challenge me to take it."

Absently, as if she did not notice the point of the laze that
still smoldered against her blunter, Tsia brushed the rain from
her brows. Her voice, when she answered, was quiet, but her
words hit Shjams like a slap. "I lived," she said softly, "for the
day I could see you again. If you wish to destroy that kind of
love, and me with it—the way you destroyed the ties from you
to your family—that is your choice. I accept it."

Shjams's eyes narrowed. "You? Accepting certain death?"

"I worked and schemed to find you. Our brothers did the
same. Our parents, our cousins, your friends . . . You killed a
part of all of us when you tore yourself from our lives." The
anger flared up inside her, and she clenched her fists, ignoring
the burn from Ruka's paw, which seeped to backwash through
her gate. "You can rip yourself away from us, but there is
nothing in this world—or any other—that can tear the ties
which keep us held to you."

"There is one thing." Shjams reached into Tsia's blunter
and yanked out Doetzier's flat bronze disk from her pocket.
She turned it over in her hands, then threw it away to the
side. The disk hit and skittered along the landing pad like a
plate. She stepped back and pointed the laze again at Tsia's
chest. "It's called death."

Tsia's dark eyes bored into Shjams's. She felt as if a stranger
looked back. Even Shjams's energy was different than it had
been before. She could feel it through her biogate, even though
she traced nothing through the node. "You don't know me anymore," Shjams said flatly—almost politely. "Remember that."

Behind Tsia, Ruka slunk through the rain like a shadow.
Closer . . . Now under the ship . . . Now meters away from her
feet . . . And from behind Shjams, from the corner of a freepick hut, a long, lean figure appeared. Tsia could feel it in her
gate. A cat that was not a cat. An intelligence that cut through
her gate like a laze. It was blackjack, but not a pirate; it was
something else—something more. And its energy was not human. Ruka's hair bristled. The chill spread down Tsia's neck.

"I had a dream," she whispered. "I saw you looking in the mirror."

"I don't want to hear it."

"Your hands pulled at the sides of your face—pulled back at your skin so that it stretched to your temples, your cheeks. Your face became a mask. The mask a caricature—"

"Shut up." Shjams shoved her against the ship.

Tsia's shoulders hit the side of the skimmer, but she didn't take her eyes from her sister's face. "I heard the voice of your god," she went on. "Your demon." Her voice was steady, as if the wind did not tear at its sound. "But the voice was yourself, and all you had to do was stop talking and listen to the silence to find yourself again."

"Damn you. I—"

"You don't want to see love," Tsia cut in, "when you can hide forever in fear. It's easier, you think, to wallow in that, and to make someone else responsible for your life. You're like a lifer who hides behind the preaching of your leader, sucking up to the power you build in his wake. You don't have to justify what you do; he does that for you. You don't have to take responsibility; you just blame your acts on him."

Her lips curled, and the feline figure moved closer. Tsia opened her senses and felt a frigid tang. Nitpicker's voice echoed in her head: Something foreign . . . Something alien . . . And Wren: Be interesting to see the two of you react . . . She forced her eyes back to Shjams. "Look what you're doing in your fear—to yourself. To your family."

Shjams tightened her grip on the laze. "Sometimes, you just find yourself drawn further and further into something until you're smothered by its power."

"Its or his?" Tsia bit out. "Kurvan is not your demon, Shjams. Your demon is your fear."

"You had your own demons, once. I thought you at least would understand."

"I do." Tsia's voice was quiet. She could feel the beast in her gate: intent as the cub on a rat. Its eyes seemed like pools of fractured gold. Its head swayed like a cat. "I was a . . . victim once, like you. But I refused to remain that way. And now

I'm fighting to regain my life. What are you doing with yours?"

"I'm trying to survive."

"For god's sake, Shjams, you're simply killing yourself."

Shjams's face tightened. She raised the laze a fraction. "Myself or you?"

"Go ahead," Tsia said softly. The foreign energy that swept through her gate sharpened like a knife. The seared hole in the blunter was like a target waiting for the beam. Her guts, tight as her fists, coiled further. She forced her gaze to Shjams's. "What harm will there be in the cessation of pain? What possible further torture is death that I haven't already felt since you left? Do you know what I have lived through? You can't do more than bless me with that laze."

"You have no idea what you're saying."

"And you don't know what you do," Tsia returned harshly. "You rejected the ones who love you to become the ultimate victim: someone else's toy. And now you betray not only yourself, but your family with what you do." Her eyes flickered toward the figure that moved closer through the rain. "Or is it more than that now? Do you betray your world?"

"You don't understand what I do, what I am."

"You think not? I know you. I understand you like myself. Something happened to you, Shjams. It shows in every flinch of your body, in the haunted look in your eyes. No, we could never have taken away your demons, but we could have helped you face them. Helped you build yourself back to a strength that could stand alone."

Shjams cursed and started to turn away, then whipped back, the laze sighting in on Tsia's heart. "I didn't want to face them. I don't want to now. Don't you understand that?" Her chest heaved with the effort of breathing, and her face was stretched taut in a mask. "I don't care whether I live," she whispered harshly, "but I don't seem to be able to die."

Tsia did not move. She stared at Shjams as if she could somehow insert herself in the other woman's mind. "But it's more than blackjack now, isn't it? It's gone beyond this planet."

"Damn you, Tsia—"

Tsia couldn't help glancing toward her broken flexor on the deck. "Give me back the bait chips," she said softly, forcing the tension out of her voice. "Even they have a high value. If we return them, we can make a deal with the Shields for you. And if you still love this world and your family—if you still love yourself—get me the real chips," she said deliberately, "from wherever they are in the ship."

The furred figure hissed behind her, and Shjams stiffened.

"A chance, Shjams," she breathed. "I'm giving you a chance. Just *show* me you want to stay—"

Deliberately, Shjams fired the laze. Tsia's sight seemed to burn. She froze with a strangled breath.

The beam hit the tarmac at her feet, not her chest, and the wet landing pad sizzled and popped. Water and crisped earth spattered onto her boots. The smoke scent rose and clogged her nose so that her throat tightened in reflex.

Tsia forced herself to stay still. The tawny figure behind Shjams turned his face toward the woman. His flattened nostrils flared. He looked at Tsia then, and white fangs gleamed in his spadelike face. He had brows of darker, coarser fur, and his eyes were mere slits of color. His voice touched Tsia's skin with a timbre that shivered all the way to the bones of her heels.

"Human," the alien said softly, "yet not human." Retractable claws flared along his wrists and knuckles. "Feline," he breathed, "yet not a cat. What are you?"

Shjams did not take her eyes from her sister. Slowly, as if mesmerized by his presence, Tsia tilted her head to regard the alien through narrowed eyes. He rolled his own head back as slowly, and she realized she swayed in the instinctive pattern of a cougar who was threatened. She stilled the motion and licked her lips to taste the musk on the rain. The cat scent from the platform . . . The odor on Kurvan and Decker . . . Wren's grin when he hinted about the Ixia specs . . . She had been blinded by her biogate. Blinded to the realization that the Ixia were here, on Risthmus, not orbiting above. And if she had understood what she felt before, Doetzier could have called in his

Shields; and Shjams would not now be standing before her with a laze aimed right at her heart.

The alien hissed. Water drops formed on his fur. He moved forward till they were half a meter apart.

Tsia didn't flinch. "Cousin—"

The Ixia shifted, and she watched a claw extend and retract from his elbow with the movement. "Come closer," he breathed. "Let me touch you."

She stretched her lips, and it wasn't a grin, and the Ixia's eyes riveted on that movement. "Come closer to me," she returned in a low voice.

"Tsia," Shjams warned.

The alien laughed. The sound was a mockery of humor, and Tsia could not control the shudder that shook her. The focus— the intent. The wariness—the hunger. The poise and the wide-open senses . . . Her hands clenched unconsciously into curled claws; her jaw swung back into a menacing, side-to-side movement.

Ruka, crouched beneath the ship, began to keen in a haunting, rising yowl. The alien's slits of eyes flicked to the cougar. "Look you, at the three of us," he said. "So alike, and yet dissimilar. So much the same at heart. Yet in some subtle way, you smell like this one here." He inclined his head almost imperceptibly at Shjams.

Tsia forced her words out. "We share the blood of family."

"Ah. But we"—he gestured at Ruka, himself, and her— "share our very souls."

His voice was a low, snarling hiss, but Tsia no longer shivered at the tone. It had insinuated itself through her ears to her mind till it sounded as natural to her as Ruka's voice. She glanced at her sister, and the Ixia stretched out a hand with his wrist and knuckle claws protracted. They stroked across Tsia's cheek, following the scars that ran from temple line to jaw. Unconsciously, she rubbed her face on his hand. She felt his fur along her nose, then her cheeks and chin before she froze with the realization of what she did. With a whuff of breath, the alien leaned down to press his forehead against her face. She jerked back. The slitted eyes narrowed. "I see in you myself," he hissed. He gestured at Shjams without taking his eyes from the guide. "What is her name?" he asked her sister.

"Tsia," Shjams whispered.

The alien's lips parted, and he seemed to smile. "Lan-Lu," he said with that strangely mesmerizing tone. "I am called Lan-Lu Orahn J'Avatzan."

Tsia took a step away from the skimmer, and the alien put his clawed hand upon her chest.

"No. You stay, I think. And that one too," he added, indicating the cougar.

The touch of his fur against her skin made her want to writhe. She licked her lips again, and the alien's eyes flickered with the movement. She reached up and touched his hand. The knuckle claws seemed to stick farther out. Gently, deliberately, she slid her fingers around his and pushed his paw away. "Let Ruka go," she said quietly.

Golden pools of light gleamed in the drowning rain. "Why?"

"Because he isn't part of this. Because he doesn't understand your presence, and his mind is filled with pain from your actions. He belongs with this world, not with you."

"And you, Tsia-human?"

She refused to shiver at the tone. "My mind is clear," she said softly. "Kill me if you must."

"No," Lan-Lu said slowly. "I think . . . not."

Not . . . yet. The words hung between them in the biogate. Tsia felt like a rat caught against a wall. There were other shadows in her gate. Her expression must have tightened. Shjams took Tsia's arm in a hard grip. For a moment, the alien regarded Tsia in silence. She could not read his face, but in her gate, she felt the false acquiescence that hid behind his eyes. The slits of color gleamed like yellow light in the grayness of the landing pad. From the side, a group of blackjack sprinted raggedly around the corner. Beams of light flashed from their weapons. The alien's head snapped around.

Too late, Shjams felt Tsia's tension. Tsia slid like water from her grasp. The alien lunged after her, but Tsia was already running across the deck. Shjams's laze fired like an animal that had its own control, and Ruka, from under the ship, leaped like a grav dancer in zero gee. His paws caught Shjams on the shoulder, and her beam jerked into the side of the ship. Instantly, a long, curving line of black bored along its hull. Shjams screamed a curse. She jerked the laze back around, but the alien stopped her. Ruka streaked away.

Tsia staggered with her own speed. *Go, Ruka,* she snarled. *Take yourself to Van'ei.* The image she sent of Nitpicker's body smell was clear, and the cougar disappeared between two of the squat structures. One of the zeks cursed her fleeing figure, and fired blindly in her direction. The beam sizzled harmlessly away.

She sprinted, then turned and shook her fist at the ship. "I will never give you up," she shouted. "Not in this life. Not in my death."

The wind lifted her voice and struck her sister like a fist. Shjams fired again, but the beams flashed uselessly short. The alien leaped aboard. Shjams followed. Like reavers disappearing down their dike holes, the sprinting zeks dove through the hatch of the transport. Inside, the power packs of the ship fired up even before the hatch was cleared. The sail slats shifted along the skimmer's skin so that it rippled with movement.

On the ground, the mercs spread out across the landing pad like a smooth flood of darkness. Bowdie had a manual com in one hand, his parlas in the other. Striker was far in the rear, her limping run stubborn and steady. Doetzier ran to one side of Nitpicker with his long legs pounding in unconsciously perfect three-to-four sync to the pilot's stride. Doetzier shouted something at Wren who shook his head. The Shield, then Nitpicker caught up with Tsia. The pilot skidded to a stop, and stood for a moment to catch her breath, her eyes locked on that silver form. She did not try to fire; her fibergun was useless against the side of the ship.

The skimmer rose without a sound, but the hatch did not close, and Shjams stood in the doorway staring down at the guide. Tsia struck the air, leaving her hand outstretched, her fingers white with the tension of her reach.

Shjams screamed soundlessly into the rain, and Tsia seemed to feel it through her gate. She cried out and fell to her knees.

The skimmer shuddered in the air. The skin rippled again as the sail slats adjusted. The whine of the motors rose higher.

Nitpicker shaded her eyes, then pulled Tsia by her sleeve. "We have to go. Now."

"I can't—"

"Now!" Nitpicker snarled.

Tsia fought her grip. "They're gone. I couldn't stop them, and you didn't ground the transport—"

"We did. Come on!" she yelled at the other mercs. "Away from the deck. Hurry. Their parbeams—"

Tsia refused to move, her eyes still on the transport. "They can't use them."

Doetzier whipped around. "What do you mean?"

Her gaze finally turned to him. "Those safety cubes from our ship—I had some of them in my pocket. I slipped them into the configuration honeycomb for their weapons."

Nitpicker's own hand tightened on Tsia's arm. "You did what?"

"I put them in the weapons slots. If they try to fire, the weapons honeycomb will activate. The safeties will trigger and take over, and the ship will head straight up—skyside orbit, where they'll stay till you send someone to get them." Her voice slowed at Doetzier's expression. "They might have disabled their own safeties, but it would take them hours to figure out where mine were activating from. And until then, they'll be stuck skyside, waiting for a pickup."

"My god . . ." Nitpicker stared at the ship that whined into its full flight status.

"What do you mean? What have I done?"

Doetzier cursed under his breath. "Dammit, Feather, we wanted them to stand trial."

"I know that. The safeties won't kill them—they'll merely set the ship in orbit."

"No—no they won't."

Wren pulled at Nitpicker's sleeve. "They're coming around. We've got to go. If they loose a parbeam cannon on this landing pad, we'll be flash-fried like oil on the sun."

"Wait!" Tsia clutched Doetzier's arms. "What did you mean, they won't stand trial?"

"We sabotaged the life support," Nitpicker snapped. "They can't go skyside. They won't have cabin pressure. They won't have air. They won't have enough temperature to keep from turning to instant ice. They won't even be able to regulate the pressure flows for their internal systems. If they go up, they'll blow apart like thin glass."

Tsia stared at her in horror.

"It's done! It's done. You can't change it. Now move!"

Wren thrust her toward the far side of the landing pad. The other mercs were already running. Away from the huts; away from the freepick structures. Toward the gray-green forest, where the trees danced like demons in the wind, and the shadows looked like shrouds.

Like a slow-moving hand, the skimmer turned in the air. A rounded snout protruded from its nose. Seeking, it turned and tilted till it pointed along the landing pad, following the steps of the mercs. Tsia could almost feel Shjams's hand on the conn. And when it fired, the crack of the beam was like thunder. The air seemed to split. The metaplas surface of the landing pad melted instantly into a soft, black, bubbling pool. Fire leaped up. The metaplas burned. Acrid smoke warred with rain. As if the beam lifted their feet, Striker, then Bowdie dove into the trees. Doetzier was a second behind.

The parbeam flashed out again. The forest crackled, bursting into a column of brown-black smoke. Nitpicker and Wren dove away into the brush. Tsia took a running step, and half turned to look back. The third blast caught her like that, on the edge of the tarmac, between the fire in the air and the flash of the forest, in a rush of heat and ash.

Her body flew through leaves and twigs, then crashed like a log through the shrubs. Her arms were crossed over her head, and they were the only thing that protected her from smashing her face against the boulder on which she finally landed. She lay for an instant, stunned, her body one massive scream, with the air blasted out of her lungs. She didn't feel the bruised ribs. She didn't notice the blood that ran down her arm and dripped from her hand like syrup. There was only the growing heat that clogged her nose with breathlessness. The fire—she could feel it, growing and sucking her air. Her throat tightened; her smoke membranes closed.

Slowly, as if in a dream, she pulled herself to her feet. The world was a turning image, and her ears did not seem to hear the shout that came from away to her left.

The skimmer still shuddered over the landing pad—she could feel its subsonic whine in her bones. But it was beginning to rise even as she staggered away from the fire that had followed her to the trees. She stepped in flame and barely noticed. The creeping blaze was slow and it sputtered in the rain. Like a zombie, she stumbled back toward the landing pad. She didn't have to call the sweat to her skin. It ran down her face and neck, soaking her body further and burning into her blood. She fell to her knees and nearly choked on the branch that cut across her neck. She snarled like the cats who fled the crisping forest, but she crawled on to the landing pad.

She fell on the smooth, hard edge, and stared blindly up at the sky. The catspeak that snarled in her head made her roll over finally and stagger to her feet. To her knees. To her feet again. A furred shoulder shoved its way under her hand. Her fingers clenched. Ruka hissed.

Above, the skimmer faded in the sky, its sonic hum rising in her bones. She could not control the shivers that shook her. She could not open her gate wider past Ruka, past the cats, to feel a thread of her sister. There was no echo in her gate of Shjams's presence; no final touch through the node.

"It's the way of family, is it not?" Nitpicker's voice was quiet as a grave beside her, and somehow cut through her deafness like a metal scream that shatters a silent night. Nitpicker did not look at Tsia's face; her shuttered eyes were glued to the sky. "When she tried to kill you," she said softly, "she destroyed herself instead."

Tsia stared at the sky. She felt nothing. It was as if her disbelief had warred with her grief until all that was left was a void in which she could no longer think. Her breath seemed to catch in her lungs and freeze so that her chill spread from the inside out.

When the spark came, it was tiny. It flashed in the clouds like a pinpoint strike of lightning. Tiny, and growing orange-red against the gray, rushing sky, the spark became a flame. The flame became a fire. And a tiny sun fell from the sky.

Like Lucifer, whose wings burned as he plummeted, the skimmer twisted and turned, falling to the east. A meteor, whose heart was human, and whose skin as alien as the stars . . . A comet that struck the plain on the other side of the forest like a spear that sinks into mud. A fall of char and ash like snow. Red rain. Ash rain. A black cataract above the gray, flooded Plain of Tears.

Epilogue

Tsia sank to her knees. Not in my death, she had shouted to Shjams. But it was her sister who had died. And now there was nothing but gray storm winds clouding the sky. Nothing but gray-washed tarmac, and streaks of black slagged metaplas where the landing pad had been. And nothing in her heart but a numbness, which spread like shock through her limbs. She pressed her hands to her chest. She could barely breathe for the weight of her own body. The burn in Ruka's paw—it seared her thoughts. Her throat, with its swollen ring of bruises, felt like a collar that tightened and choked off her air. She cried out inarticulately, and it was Striker, not Wren, who touched her. She clung to the woman's arm for a moment, lost in the smoke, while the forest burned in the rain.

Doetzier stared to the east, where the sparks fell in a silent, burning rainbow. "Gone. All of it—gone."

Bowdie followed his gaze. "At least the chips burned with the ship," he said flatly. "No one will be able to use them."

"Billions of credit destroyed," Doetzier said to himself, as if he did not hear the other man. "Thousands of man-hours in tracking blackjack from Denes to Interference to Risthmus. And it's wasted. Just like that. Not a shred of evidence. Not a single zek to stand trial. Not a single hard link to the Ixia. An operation eight years in the making, and all of it for nothing. No biochips. No blackjack."

Tsia opened her eyes and stared at his face. His cheeks were

329

taut, and the hollows under his eyes seemed suddenly pronounced. His biofield was steady now, without the sparks of light, and his expression flatter than she had seen before, as if exhaustion had somehow stolen the definition from his features. She tried to speak, then looked away. Her voice was hoarse with the snarl of Ruka's mind.

Over her shoulder, two silver shapes dropped out of the sky and seemed to hang for a moment over the tarmac. A third ship appeared in the east, over the Plain of Tears. The subsonic hum of the Shield ships vibrated in Tsia's bones. Ruka hissed from the forest, and she called him to her. The mercs parted. Bowdie's eyes looked from Tsia to the cub, then back to Tsia's taut face. Before them, the skimmers began to settle down on the flight deck.

Doetzier cursed again. Tsia followed the ships with her eyes. "There is one zek," she said. "Decker."

Watching his backup ships arrive, Doetzier turned his head. He eyed her for a moment. "Alive?" he demanded, his voice suddenly sharp.

"Was. On the other side of the landing pad. He needs a scame if you want him to live long enough to testify. He had a shaper stuck to his face."

He glanced sharply at her face. "And Kurvan?"

Her face was blank of expression, but her eyes burned like fire in the rain. Her fingers dug into Ruka's fur.

"Dead," he answered for her. "What did you use?" he said, his voice suddenly harsh. "Your bare hands or your flexor?"

"Cougar took him out. Not me."

Doetzier stared at her for a moment. She could smell his disbelief. One of the skimmer hatches opened. Shields began to drop out and sprint across the tarmac in twos, and a large group ran toward the mercs. "And the alien?" Doetzier said. "The Ixia at the ship? Why didn't you stop it from going aboard?"

"Flexor didn't work anymore."

Nitpicker looked at her suddenly. "A flexor only breaks if its biochips are fried," she said slowly. "It was your weapon, not mine which didn't work, and we traded before we reached the stake—you had mine on the tarmac."

Bowdie shook his head. "I saw her give the biochip case back to the blackjack on the landing pad. Her weapon didn't work—they threw her flexor away. I didn't mistake that."

Tsia looked at him for a moment, then turned and gently lifted Ruka's lips away from the cougar's fangs. She ran her finger along his gums, scooping out the small objects. Ruka hissed and shook his head as she let his gums slide back down. In her open palms, the tiny objects glistened with saliva and rain. The biochips.

Bowdie leaned forward. "I'll be damned . . ."

Striker looked at her with wondering eyes. "You swapped them out with the dummies—"

"It was the bait chips which were burned with the ship." Wren touched her on the shoulder, his narrow face stretched in a faint grin as he ignored the hiss of the cat.

"No." Tsia let Ruka slink away to crouch at the edge of the tarmac where the smoke still curled like genies from the hot ground. "The dummies," she said slowly, "are in my flexor. Like Bowdie said, Shjams threw that away on the landing pad. You should find it somewhere near Decker's body."

Doetzier said softly. "Then these . . . these really are the biochips?"

"Yes."

"But the bait biochips . . . If you swapped the biochips in your flexor"—he guessed—"for the dummies I carried in my case, what did you put in that case to give back to blackjack?"

"The biochips from the emergency scanners they had in their skimmer's cabin."

He stared at the chips in her hand as if he could not quite believe she held them. "You actually did it," he said slowly. "You got them back—even the bait chips." He touched the ragged hole in her blunter and fingered the laze-fried edges. He glanced at her skin, unmarked by scars where the bioshield had taken the brunt of the breaker, and the laze had crisped only cloth. "And not a scratch," he murmured. "Not a single burn on you to boot."

She stared at him. Numbness crawled over her heart. The ash trail of the ship in the sky seemed scored into her mind. The fire that drizzled out in the forest seemed to cry out with human screams. Over and over, her memory triggered the hisser tube to stain the landing pad with the blackness of Kurvan's skin. Again and again, Shjams's shoulders flinched against being touched when Tsia tried to reach her . . . Shjams in the hatch, firing down with her laze. The flat, hard eyes, without expression—blank, as if the person inside had been somehow sucked away.

Tsia looked down at the hole over her heart, where the blunter was burned away. "Yes," she said slowly. She looked up, toward the Plain of Tears. "I was . . . lucky."

He held out his hand, but she closed her fist over the chips.

Tsia let the wet smoke from the forest curl into her lungs. Ruka growled, and she looked down at the cougar with eyes that burned. "A link, Doetzier. That was our contract."

He eyed her speculatively. "I know you, Tsia-*nyeka*, and what you want—an open node link will change nothing for you. You're a rogue gate. That's your heart—your self. No matter what kind of link you have with the node, you'll always be hunted by the guild, and you'll always be running from demons." He motioned toward the eight Shields who ran toward the group of mercs. He touched her closed fist lightly. "The guide guild knows you exist again. The mercs can no longer protect you. Come back with me. To the Shields. An open link is only one of the things we can offer."

She clenched her hands into fists so that the biochips cut into her skin. She did not see the trickle of blood that squeezed out onto the tarmac. "I feel the wind against my skin, Doetzier. I taste blood on my lips. I burn with eagerness in muscles that bunch and stretch in my legs." She opened her hands, exposing the chips, then curled them again so that her knuckles were white with tautness. Her mind snarled at the cub, and the growl in Ruka's throat made her throw her head back and scream like a cougar.

Bowdie jerked; Striker shivered. Doetzier shook his head.

"You're nothing but your fear, Tsia-guide. No open link will change that."

Nitpicker glanced at Tsia's rigid neck. "That isn't fear, Doetzier," she answered flatly. "That is Feather's answer."

Tsia stared at them, her head shaking as she cleared her sight of the blurred vision from Ruka. "You don't know me, Doetzier. You never did." She got to her feet. "An open link. We have a contract."

Slowly, studying her with his cold, blackened eyes, he motioned to Bowdie. The other merc pulled out the manual com and handed it over to the Shield. A moment, maybe two, and Doetzier snapped it off. "The node is still jammed from the Ixia ship in orbit, but your ID is set in the traces. When we clear the jam, your link will be shifted. You're clear. And free."

"Free . . ." Her eyes were blank for a moment. Free to take contract with whomever she wanted, wherever she wanted on Risthmus . . . Free to work outside the guide guild—even away from the mercs. Her fist pressed to her, and her knuckles brushed the hole in the jacket where her sister had burned it through. Tiny flames licked her thoughts with the image of Shjams. She stared down at her fist. Then dropped the chips in Doetzier's palm as if they burned her skin.

The running Shields stopped short of the group and pointed their weapons with sharp motions at the mercs. One figure separated herself from the other Shields and strode forward to meet Doetzier. The man, still watching Tsia, did not turn at first. Then, from the edge of the slagged deck, Ruka snarled. Doetzier's eyes flickered. Tsia stepped back from his reach.

The trees no longer bowed, but just whipped and thrust their branches at each other, so that waves of half-burned needles sprayed out across the deck. The fire was almost out, and only smoke curled up now, not flame. In the sky, the clouds lightened and lowered themselves so that they hugged the hills, while the rain filled the air with sharp rhythm. Gray light seeped into the trees from the hidden sun. Gray shadows beckoned in the forest. Striker's eyes met Tsia's, and the expressionless depth of the woman's gaze burned into her mind.

Tsia's voice was low and quiet. "It is a dawn as black as night," she said. "And it tastes like ash on my tongue."

She turned and walked away toward the forest, where the smoke curled up at her feet. Beside her, a shadow flickered. A glint of gray light caught on tawny fur; a flash reflected in golden eyes. Rain slashed across the brush. Then the wind seemed to lift her feet so that she stalked, then ran in sprinting leaps before she was swallowed by leaves.

Author's Note
ಲೊ⊚ಲ

Wolves, wolf-dog hybrids, and exotic and wild cats might seem like romantic pets. The sleekness of the musculature, the mystique and excitement of keeping a wild animal as a companion . . . For many owners, wild and exotic animals symbolize freedom and wilderness. For other owners, wild animals from wolves to bobcats to snakes provide a status symbol— something that makes the owner interesting. Many owners claim they are helping keep an animal species from becoming extinct, that they care adequately for their pet's needs, and they love wild creatures.

However, most predator and wild or exotic animals need to range over wide areas. They need to be socialized with their own species. They need to know how to survive, hunt, breed, and raise their young in their own habitat. And each species' needs are different. A solitary wolf, without the companionship of other wolves with whom it forms sophisticated relationships, can become neurotic and unpredictable. A cougar, however, stakes out its own territory and, unless it is mating or is a female raising its young, lives and hunts as a solitary predator. Both wolves and cougars can range fifty to four hundred square miles over the course of a year. Keeping a wolf or cougar as a pet is like raising a child in a closet.

Wild animals are not easily domesticated. Even when raised from birth by humans, these animals are dramatically different from domestic animals. Wild animals are dangerous and unpredictable, even though they might appear calm or trained, or seem too cute to grow dangerous with age. Wolves and exotic cats make charming, playful pups and kittens, but the adult creatures are still predators. For example, lion kittens are cute, ticklish animals that like to be handled (all kittens are). They mouth things with tiny, kitten teeth. But adult cats become solitary, territorial, and possessive predators. Some will rebel against authority, including that of the handlers they have known since birth. They can show unexpected aggression. Virtually all wild and exotic cats, including ocelots, margay, serval, cougar, and bobcat, can turn vicious as they age.

Monkeys and other nonhuman primates also develop frustrating behavior as they age. Monkeys keep themselves clean and give each other much-needed, day-to-day social interaction and reassurance by grooming each other. A monkey kept by itself can become filthy and depressed, and can begin mutilating itself (pulling out its hair and so on). When a monkey grows up, it climbs on everything, vocalizes loudly, bites, scratches, exhibits sexual behavior toward you and your guests, and, like a wolf, marks everything in its territory with urine. It is almost impossible to housebreak or control a monkey.

Many people think they can train wolves in the same manner that they train dogs. They cannot. Even if well cared for, wolves do not act as dogs do. Wolves howl. They chew through almost anything, including tables, couches, walls, and fences. They excavate ten-foot pits in your backyard. They mark everything with urine and cannot be housetrained. (Domestic canid breeds that still have a bit of wolf in them can also have these traits.) Punishing a wolf for tearing up your recliner or urinating on the living room wall is punishing the animal for instinctive and natural behavior.

Wolf-dog hybrids have different needs from both wolves and dogs, although they are closer in behavior and needs to wolves than dogs. These hybrids are often misunderstood, missocialized, and mistreated until they become vicious or unpredictable fear-biters. Dissatisfied or frustrated owners cannot simply give their hybrids to new owners; it is almost impossible for a wolf-dog to transfer its attachment to another person. When abandoned or released into the wild by owners, hybrids may also help dilute wolf and coyote strains, creating more hybrids caught between the two disparate worlds of domestic dogs and wild canids. For wolf-dog hybrids, the signs of neurosis and aggression that arise from being isolated, mistreated, or misunderstood most often result in the wolf-dogs being euthanized.

Zoos cannot usually accept exotic or wild animals that have been kept as pets. In general, pet animals are not socialized and do not breed well or coexist with other members of their own species. Because such pets do not learn the social skills to reproduce, they are unable to contribute to the preservation of their species. They seem to be miserable in the company of their own kind, yet have become too dangerous to remain with their human owners. Especially with wolves and wolf-dog hybrids, the claim that many owners make about their pets being one-person animals usually means that those animals have been dangerously unsocialized.

Zoo workers may wish they could rescue every mistreated animal from every inappropriate owner, but the zoos simply do not have the resources to take in pets. Zoos and wildlife rehabilitation centers receive thousands of requests each year to accept animals that can no longer be handled or afforded by owners. State agencies confiscate hundreds more that are abandoned, mistreated, or malnourished.

The dietary requirements of exotic or wild animals are very different from those of domesticated pets. For example, exotic and wild cats require almost twice as much protein as canids and cannot convert carotene to Vitamin A—an essential nutrient in a felid's diet. A single adult cougar requires two to three pounds of prepared meat each day, plus vitamins and bones. A cougar improperly fed on a diet of chicken or turkey parts or red muscle meat can develop rickets and blindness.

The veterinary bills for exotic and wild animals are outrageously expensive—if an owner can find a vet who knows enough about exotic animals to treat the pet. And it is difficult to take out additional insurance in order to keep such an animal as a pet. Standard homeowner's policies do not cover damages or injuries caused by wild or exotic animals. Some insurance companies will drop clients who keep wild animals as pets.

Wild and exotic animals do not damage property or cause injuries because they are inherently vicious. What humans call property damage is to the animal natural territorial behavior, play, den-making or child-rearing behavior. Traumatic injuries (including amputations and death) to humans most often occur because the animal is protecting its food, territory, or young; because it does not know its own strength compared to humans; or because it is being mistreated. A high proportion of wild- and exotic-animal attacks are directed at human children.

Although traumatic injuries are common, humans are also at risk from the diseases and organisms that undomesticated or exotic animals can carry. Rabies is just one threat in the list of over 150 infectious diseases and conditions that can be transmitted between animals and humans. These diseases and conditions include intestinal parasites, *Psittacosis* (a species of *chlamydaia*), cat-scratch fever, measles, and tuberculosis. Hepatitis A (infectious hepatitis), which humans can catch through contact with minute particles in the air (aerosol transmission) or with blood (bites, scratches, etc.), has been found in its subclinical state in over ninety percent of wild chimps, and chimps are infectious for up to sixty days at a time. The *Herpes virus simiae*, which has a seventy percent or greater mortality rate in humans, can be contracted from macaques. Pen-breeding only increases an animal's risk of disease.

Taking an exotic or wild animal from its natural habitat does not help keep the species from becoming extinct. All wolf species and all feline species (except for the domestic cat) are listed by national or international legislation as either threatened, endangered, or protected. All nonhuman primates are in danger of extinction; and federal law prohibits the importation of nonhuman primates to be kept as pets. In some states, such as Arizona, it is illegal to own almost any kind of wild animal. The U.S. Fish and Wildlife Service advises that you conserve and protect endangered species. Do not buy wild or exotic animals as pets.

If you would like to become involved with endangered species or other wildlife, consider supporting a wolf, exotic cat, whale, or other wild animal in its own habitat or in a reputable zoo. You can contact your local reputable zoo, conservation organization, or state department of fish and wildlife for information about supporting exotic or wild animals. National and local conservation groups can also give you an opportunity to help sponsor an acre of rain forest, wetlands, temperate forest, or other parcel of land.

There are many legitimate organizations that will use your money to establish preserves in which endangered species can live in their natural habitat. The internationally recognized Nature Conservancy is such an organization. For information about programs sponsored by The Nature Conservancy, please write to:

The Nature Conservancy
1815 N. Lynn Street
Arlington, Virginia 22209

Special thanks to Janice Hixson, Dr. Jill Mellen, Ph.D., Dr. Mitch Finnegan, D.V.M., Metro Washington Park Zoo; Karen Fishler, The Nature Conservancy; Harley Shaw, General Wildlife Services; Dr. Mary-Beth Nichols, D.V.M.; Brooks Fahy, Cascade Wildlife Rescue; and the many others who provided information, sources, and references for this project.

DEL REY ONLINE!

The Del Rey Internet Newsletter...

A monthly electronic publication, posted on the Internet, GEnie, CompuServe, BIX, various BBSs, and the Panix gopher (gopher.panix.com). It features hype-free descriptions of books that are new in the stores, a list of our upcoming books, special announcements, a signing/reading/convention-attendance schedule for Del Rey authors, "In Depth" essays in which professionals in the field (authors, artists, designers, sales people, etc.) talk about their jobs in science fiction, a question-and-answer section, behind-the-scenes looks at sf publishing, and more!

Online editorial presence: Many of the Del Rey editors are online, on the Internet, GEnie, CompuServe, America Online, and Delphi. There is a Del Rey topic on GEnie and a Del Rey folder on America Online.

Our official e-mail address for Del Rey Books is delrey@randomhouse.com

Internet information source!

A lot of Del Rey material is available to the Internet on a gopher server: all back issues and the current issue of the Del Rey Internet Newsletter, a description of the DRIN and summaries of all the issues' contents, sample chapters of upcoming or current books (readable or downloadable for free), submission requirements, mail-order information, and much more. We will be adding more items of all sorts (mostly new DRINs and sample chapters) regularly. The address of the gopher is gopher.panix.com

Why? We at Del Rey realize that the networks are the medium of the future. That's where you'll find us promoting our books, socializing with others in the sf field, and—most importantly—making contact and sharing information with sf readers.

For more information, e-mail delrey@randomhouse.com